Until Stones Become Lighter Than Water

Until Stones Become Lighter Than Water

ANTÓNIO LOBO ANTUNES

TRANSLATED FROM THE PORTUGUESE BY JEFF LOVE

YALE UNIVERSITY PRESS ■ NEW HAVEN & LONDON

A MARGELLOS
WORLD REPUBLIC OF LETTERS BOOK

The Margellos World Republic of Letters is dedicated to making literary works from around the globe available in English through translation. It brings to the English-speaking world the work of leading poets, novelists, essayists, philosophers, and playwrights from Europe, Latin America, Africa, Asia, and the Middle East to stimulate international discourse and creative exchange.

Funded by the Direção-Geral do Livro, dos Arquivos e das Bibliotecas (DGLAB) / Portugal.

 REPÚBLICA PORTUGUESA

CULTURA
DIREÇÃO-GERAL DO LIVRO, DOS ARQUIVOS E
DAS BIBLIOTECAS

Yale University Press books may be purchased in quantity for educational, business, or promotional use. For information, please e-mail sales.press@yale.edu (U.S. office) or sales@yaleup.co.uk (U.K. office).

Set in Electra and Nobel types by Tseng Information Systems, Inc.
Printed in the United States of America.

Library of Congress Control Number: 2018967400
ISBN 978-0-300-22662-1 (hardcover : alk. paper)

A catalogue record for this book is available from the British Library.

This paper meets the requirements of ANSI/NISO Z39.48-1992 (Permanence of Paper).

10 9 8 7 6 5 4 3 2 1

Zé Luis. Zé Jorge. Forever alive.
My comrades

For Gloria
—J.L.

CONTENTS

TRANSLATOR'S ACKNOWLEDGMENTS

Above all, I would like to thank António Lobo Antunes for his help with my many questions about the text of the novel. I would also like to thank Jeffrey Marder and Gloria Love for reading and commenting on substantial parts of early drafts of the translation as well as Ioram Melcer for a memorable conversation about the peculiarities of Lobo Antunes's Portuguese. And finally, I would like to thank Jon and Nancy Love for their general assistance and encouragement, as well as the many capable translators of Lobo Antunes's work into English who have preceded me and from whom I have learned a great deal.

> We are who we were.
> *Motto of CART 3313, António Lobo*
> *Antunes's artillery company*

Africa, in particular Angola, has played a crucial role in the sprawling fictional world created by António Lobo Antunes, from his first major literary success, *The Asshole of Judas*, to the book you have before you, published in Portuguese in October 2017. Angola is a site of both wondrous natural beauty and all-too-human terror, both a region with its own engrossing cultural distinctiveness and a broader stage of conflict between European expansionism and its unfortunate victims, denigrated, enslaved, and forced to accept the norms of a supposedly superior culture. This region of immense contrasts and struggle provides extraordinary material for the *theatrum mundi* of Lobo Antunes's bold prose, at once violent and tender, contravening and exploiting the grammar of the novel and the Portuguese language. Here is indeed a world to discover, as one of Lobo Antunes's critics has remarked, a world like no other in contemporary fiction.

Lobo Antunes's interest in Africa has a biographical element. The writer spent twenty-seven long months in the Portuguese army in Africa; he experienced some of the most bitter moments of the protracted colonial war that ended soon after the revolution in Portugal of April 25, 1974, which overthrew the harsh dictatorship established by António de Oliveira Salazar in 1928. The war in Angola began in the aftermath of the revolt of cotton farmers in Baixa do Cassange in January 1961 and involved approximately eight hundred thousand Portuguese troops over a thirteen-year period and three Portuguese colonies in Africa: Angola, Guinea-Bissau, and Mozambique. Given that the population of Portugal at that time was only a little over eight million people, this expenditure of manpower can only astonish us. Still more astonishing is that the war, even to this day, remains a difficult and largely underresearched subject in Portugal. Lobo Antunes is one of the few major authors to write extensively and openly of the war; *Until Stones Become Lighter Than Water*, though much more than what is typically called a war novel, is perhaps his most frank depiction of the casual brutality that characterized the Portuguese wars in Africa, and, indeed, characterizes war in general.

Biographical Sketch

Lobo Antunes comes from one of the best-known families in Portugal. Born in Lisbon in September 1942 as the eldest son of a prominent neurologist, Lobo Antunes was from early on interested only in becoming a writer. This abiding interest did nothing to comfort his parents, who, reasonably enough, directed the young man to a more stable career: medicine. Lobo Antunes thus studied medicine and spent two years as an intern in London in the late 1960s. Called up for service, he spent six months training in Mafra before shipping out to Angola in January 1971 as medic with the rank of second lieutenant for an artillery battalion. He returned to Lisbon only in March 1973. With a specialization in psychiatry, Lobo Antunes strained to make ends meet in the turbulent Portugal of the mid- and late 1970s, working full-time as a psychiatrist in the Miguel Bombarda Hospital and writing when he could. He published his first novel, *Elephant's Memory*, in 1979 but became famous in Portugal almost overnight later that year with the publication of *The Asshole of Judas*. He continued to work as a psychiatrist until 1985, when he was in a position to devote all his time to writing. He has produced a large body of work from 1979 on, comprising twenty-eight novels and five volumes of short works referred to as crónicas. His talent was quickly recognized by international critics, and Lobo Antunes has won a remarkable number of literary prizes; his work has been lionized by celebrated critics like Harold Bloom, Marcel Reich-Ranicki, and George Steiner, and he counts among his admirers a constellation of important contemporary writers from J. M. Coetzee and Javier Marías to Mario Vargas Llosa.

Lobo Antunes's novels are difficult to classify, and this seems quite appropriate for a writer who claims, not without irony, that he does not write novels. While this claim may seem purely ironic at first blush, there is indeed something to Lobo Antunes's insistence when one considers the immense network of linkages that emerge in the course of reading his creative output as an integral whole. For Lobo Antunes's novels form part of a single large work, an equally ambitious *Comédie humaine*, that needs to be read as a whole if one is to come to anything like a sober assessment of Lobo Antunes's artistic achievement.

African Context

Since you have only this one volume before you, let me familiarize you with the African context of Lobo Antunes's fictional world. I will first give a thumbnail sketch of the war in Angola, followed by a brief discussion of the novel. I will conclude with a few comments about the distinctive and innovative prose style of Lobo Antunes, as well as my attempt to convey some of its more characteristic features in this translation.

As I noted, the colonial war in Angola began as a response to the Baixa do Cassange revolt in 1961 and ended in 1974 with the general withdrawal of Portuguese forces from Africa. In length and result, the war in Angola bears more than a little resemblance to the Vietnam War, with a similarly contested result. Depending on one's political convictions, the war in Angola was either a grotesque and unmitigated failure or a failure that could have been transformed into a Portuguese victory, or at least an honorable peace, in different circumstances with more vigorous political and military leadership.

The war, however, was merely the last act in a long, complicated, and often brutal occupation. The Portuguese made incursions into Africa—in particular, into what became Angola, Guinea-Bissau, and Mozambique—from the mid-sixteenth century onward during the period of radical Portuguese expansion that created the first global empire. While Portuguese adventurers sought to open up new venues of trade in gold and spices, they also initiated an enduring slave trade between Africa and Brazil. By the end of the nineteenth century, Portugal was an established colonial presence in Angola, Guinea-Bissau, and Mozambique, with widespread exploitation of the local peoples engendering a terrible legacy.

This presence was not challenged until after the end of World War II. The challenge came from local independence movements that sought, as elsewhere in Africa, to be freed from the harsh conditions of colonial rule. And like other European colonial powers—the French in Algeria, the English in Kenya and Northern Rhodesia—Portugal resisted all attempts at decolonialization, and this refusal to accede to the emancipatory hopes of its colonial subjects ended up leading to the violence that finally exploded into war in 1961.

The Portuguese troops who fought this war were the product of Salazar's long dictatorship, the so-called *Estado Novo*, the new state, that imposed conditions at home that were not appreciably milder for many Portuguese citizens than those in the colonies. Hence many of the soldiers who fought in Africa came from a kind of European poverty that existed in neither England nor France, at least not to the same extent. They were also closely watched over by the dreaded PIDE (Polícia Internacional e de Defesa do Estado) or political police, which perpetrated atrocities during the war, as the novel shows us. Relations between the Portuguese army and the PIDE were always fraught, and with good reason, since the task of the PIDE in Africa was to ensure the obedience of the army to the prerogatives of the political leadership.

Until Stones Become Lighter Than Water

The novel itself appears initially to be a reflection on the war based on a not wholly unusual incident. Portuguese soldiers routinely raided villages and, as Lobo Antunes himself has noted, these raids were often exceptionally brutal, with whole communities being wiped out, animals and all. From time to time soldiers took orphaned children rather than killing them, though often those children were killed later if they did not manage to escape. Yet some did return to Portugal with the soldiers who had taken care of them. Here we have the bare bones of the plot: a soldier, having assisted in the raid of a village, an everyday event, takes a child and brings him back to Portugal. There the child participates in the central action of the novel, the pig killing. The practice of killing pigs almost as a rite is one deeply rooted in Portuguese culture. The fact that the black child kills his adoptive Portuguese father at that moment is both high melodrama and the fulfillment of prophecy, insofar as many of the Portuguese father's comrades cautioned him about the possibility of bloody revenge.

This revenge plot seems to have a fated, tragic element, which is hardly surprising in a novel so governed from its very beginning by a sense of ineluctable destiny, if not indeed a certain fatalism. Yet as in many other instances in Lobo Antunes's work, the tragic element is accompanied by elements of parody that puncture what appear to be the aggrandizing qualities of the tragic. For if the tragic is nothing if not solemn, emphasizing the dreadful stakes of human life, the comic elements in Lobo Antunes's work are prisms through which the great seriousness of the tragic, its focus on suffering and brutality, is ridiculed. While generalizations are precarious, especially when applied to a fictional output that creates slippery ambiguity wherever possible, it seems to me that one of the striking aspects of *Until Stones Become Lighter Than Water*, as of much of Lobo Antunes's work, is its pervasive respect for suffering coupled with sardonic mockery, recalling Aristophanes, of the sheer stupidity of our limited existence. Thus the pig killing seems to be a metaphor of tragic intensity, and it is, but it is also a darkly comic metaphor insofar as there is nothing dignified, elegant, or heroic about the pig. The highest "value" of the pig is survival, a value that is hardly heroic, hardly dignified, but rather evidence of the ugliest reality of our lives, the unbridled impetus to self-preservation, an impetus that turns every soldier into an animal seeking nothing so much as his own survival.

The dodges and deceptions of this impetus intertwine throughout the novel, its main characters seeking to create narratives that insulate themselves from the horror of mortality as well as the loss and suffering that accompany it. When Lobo Antunes claims, as he is wont to do, that stories are the least important aspect of his works, we may interpret his apparently unconventional claim as pointing to another dimension of his work, a more engrossing one, namely, its open portrayal of a fundamental struggle with narratives themselves, with the promise of salvation or justice that so many basic narratives reflect. Without going into the details of the novel, suffice it to say that a series of narratives wind through it on the background of the pig killing. Each of these narratives attempts to justify or protect those who believe in them from a seemingly more bitter truth, and there is no more bitter truth than the fact of suffering and death, the brutal humiliation that nature imposes on us, in the words of Fyodor Dostoevsky's underground man.

Lobo Antunes's Language and This Translation

This pervasive sense of struggle is reflected in the unique language Lobo Antunes has created over his long career. It is no exaggeration to assert that Lobo Antunes has transformed literature written in Portuguese, and his distinctive style has attracted many imitators in both Portuguese and other languages. I would like to address some significant aspects of Lobo Antunes's style and to explain as well how I have attempted to translate them into English, often with a literalness that may appear jarring to the English ear.

The struggle with time itself is paramount. Lobo Antunes radically attenuates the complicated verbal system of Portuguese by favoring infinitival structures over finite tensed ones. Lobo Antunes's use of the personal infinitive in Portuguese allows him to create a "presencing" effect—much of the novel seems to take place as a performance initiated by the reading process itself. Like other English translators of Lobo Antunes's work, I have tried to capture this effect by using the English gerund, the -ing form. "Pigeons flying," "soldiers shooting," "the man walking"—these are all translations of the Portuguese personal infinitive that imply a static quality as if the activity itself continues uninterrupted by or indifferent to temporal sequence.

This "presencing" effect is also evident in Lobo Antunes's pronounced tendency to omit the verb "to be" in the present tense. An example, chosen at random:

> the engines of the unimogs deafened me, the soldiers, three or four, put the animals on a trailer and their legs so thin, it seemed to me people hidden in the jungle seeing that a trembling in the leaves different from the wind, the doctor drew an oval with a pen going around the white stain of an X-ray

Another example:

> the impression that a fox up there, next to the cemetery, the impression that a genet, I asked the sergeant that he take care of my son while me in Luanda, no one knew of us in Portugal, no one speaks of war, one pretends that it's forgotten or it's really forgotten, me on the street of bars filled with mulatto women and men at the counter, only elbows, as clumsy as me, with the noses in their glasses like donkeys, tied up to wagons, in front of the baskets, with their snouts in the middle of the hay staring at the people while they were eating, a woman disappeared into the cigarette smoke and emerged from the smoke, next to me, with another ring

While this effect creates an awkward English, it is equally unusual in Portuguese, and I have preserved it throughout. On the one hand, the effect gives the impression of a certain timelessness, as if no tense were required in reference to the relevant circumstances and objects. On the other hand, it has another intriguing consequence, consonant with the tendency of Lobo Antunes's style to efface temporal linkages, in that the verb "to be" as copula is suppressed. Rather than explicitly joining objects or subjects with objects, the suppression of the verb "to be" as a copula enhances the dislocation of temporal order by putting in question the basic integrating function of the verb "to be." This integrative function matches subjects with predicates and defines relationships; to omit it in a way that calls attention to that omission creates a prose that we may call paratactic because it refuses to succumb to traditional modes of temporal and syntactical subordination. This is a promiscuous prose that can be linked up in many different ways with other segments within the novel. This is a prose that lends itself to multiple connections, both affirming and threatening each particular connection because so many others offer themselves at any given time; this is thus a prose of a somewhat hidden simultaneity.

The upshot of these techniques is thus clearly to put in question the temporal subordination and logical connection that are crucial to the construction of any narrative. Rather than supplying a story that fits more or less exactly the famed Aristotelian plot structure of beginning, middle, and end reflecting the temporal coordinates of past, present, and future, Lobo Antunes emphasizes the fact that all takes place now, that we live now, that this now is the only venue of what we call past and future, and that these temporal coordinates are in fact created by us as ways of orientation that disorient us in the sense that they turn us away from the essential importance of the present. If, for that matter, the present has long been considered indescribable, the ever elusive "now," Lobo Antunes restores to this "now" a remarkable richness attained by putting in question temporal segmentation itself. Moreover, this refusal to obey the Aristotelian "unities" also undermines another central element of Aristotelian emplotment, that all parts of a narrative prove in the end to fit together with the others in a single, definite purposive manner such that there is no narrative gesture that is not necessary to the conclusion of the narrative.

Hence another distinctive feature of Lobo Antunes's style: the constant shifts in time and location. While it can be argued that these shifts are a kind of montage or collage effect that is similar to techniques deployed in film, the intricate interplay of verbs and persons in Lobo Antunes's work goes far beyond simple montage insofar as he attempts to suppress *any* overriding temporal order along with other ways of creating an authoritative syntax. In other words, by suppressing temporal order, even the most basic sequential order that we often assume, erroneously, to be time in its "raw state," as well as the copulative function of the verb "to be" and other modes of syntactic integration, Lobo Antunes creates a text that challenges the most basic modes of assembling narratives.

Returning to my earlier point, I think it is instructive to look at these techniques as creating a remarkably ambiguous and polysemous text that both relies on and subverts the basic constructive principles of narrative. In a complicated sense, Lobo Antunes puts narrative in question not simply as a kind of lie (since other constructions are possible), but as a specifically salvific lie, as a means by which we seek an impossible salvation or, at the very least, as I have suggested already, shelter from a both expansive and damning present.

Here as elsewhere in Lobo Antunes's work there is both a striking appreciation for the lies we tell ourselves and a harsh rebuke of them, both dour tragic respect and vibrant comic insouciance, admiration for order and repetition coupled with an equal loathing of both, a struggle, in other words, that remains unresolved and, perhaps, unresolvable.

Jeff Love

Until Stones Become Lighter Than Water

My mother was their first cousin, meaning the first cousin of the father, not of the black son who was never his son though he treated him as a son and the black treated him as his father, the cousin of my mother brought him back from the war in Angola, five or six years old, I was still not born, I appeared afterward and remember my stepfather answering, when I asked him about his cousin's reason for having returned with a child perhaps happier there in the backcountry where he found him, that almost all the soldiers came back with mementos, a mask, a wooden doll, an ear in a bottle of alcohol, a boy, one arm less, silences in the middle of conversations where they wandered far away remaining over there, and the idea came to me that in the distance shots and screams were almost heard, my stepfather did not end up in Africa because of his clubfoot but neighbors here from the village did and were different from him, evasive, abrupt, almost all strange that he heard plenty of complaints from the women, these men sitting on a stone in the middle of the garden looking for who knows what or listening to the leaves of trees I didn't know, one instead of fending off the dog with a boot cut its head off with a hoe

—Leave me

and he stood next to the animal's corpse not looking at it, smoking, when the cigarette finished I had the impression that he lingered a while smoking his fingers, his niece left his lunch nearby without him touching the pan, it was the relatives, at night, who secretly took care of his land and the guy at home drinking or in a silent rage against I don't know what enemy, some ended up in the well or strung up from a beam of the chicken coop swaying slowly, one foot with a shoe, the other without, and the chickens pecking the shoe with brisk movements, I'm the one who looks after the tomb of my mother's cousin in the little cemetery next to the first hill of the mountain since she passed away, with so many pine trees whispering slowly, the slope above and birds and bushes in the sun, so gentle, so calm, that one comes to envy the dead, and there they are both, the white father and his black son, beyond two or three other relatives so much older that I don't know who they could have been

(I hope they also hear the pines and the bushes or, at least, the wind at night, scraping, scraping)

like those reduced to blurry photographs

(when had they lived?)

with broken frames, hanging from a nail, crooked on the walls, old creatures no one pays attention to

(maybe they are what I hear at night complaining about not being able to become earth)

just as no one remembers anymore what happened ten years ago at the time of the pig killing, when the black son murdered his white father with a knife still covered with the animal's blood, not another knife, the same knife and the same knife seemed to me for him another, very old knife, I was going to swear there was a very old knife in his head, the black son screaming at the white father

—Remember what you did, remember what you did?

trying to trap his legs afterward with the rope they trapped the pig with until the men, in a storm of kicks and shoves, pushed him, grabbed him, lay him out on the ground, broke his bones, crushed the nape of his neck with the axe, stabbed his throat, his chest, his mouth, his belly, left him next to his white father under the pig, almost without blood, that groaned until the final drop fell in the bucket and the three remained alone in the cellar while suddenly March was beating the frames of the open window.

1

And this night, like so many times over the last forty-three years, I turned to dream about Africa again, not attacks that began always with the machine gun the soldiers called the seamstress singing along with them next to the landing strip, or rather the hundred meters of cleared land where the tiny airplane was hopping about, not ambushes, not mines, just me alone near the barbed wire thinking about Lisbon, watching the river, the ships, the houses

(roofs and roofs)

from the window of my parents' room, pigeons flying around the church, my mother in the kitchen

—Boy

so that I would open the lid to the jam jar for her

—Be patient, I can't

and the tank for washing clothes in the sunroom, the bucket full of wet shirts, one of her dresses, two dresses, on the wire of the clothesline, the workshop of Mr. Abílio, farther away seagulls and Angola with at least one silent kite high in the air, me awakened

—Where am I?

taking time to grasp that the war also ended here, the war ended, my wife fumbling about on the little bedside table until the alarm clock

—So late?

appeared in her hand, not the girl I courted by letter for twenty-seven months, exactly the one I married and who was not really this one, asking with traces of makeup

—Don't leave me

on sad cheeks unprotected by glasses, soon I'm going to find a piece of cotton with traces of makeup forgotten in the bathroom next to the toothpaste full of dents at the end of the spiral

(I don't remember any toothpaste that we opened with a little spike for the first time, the glass with brushes, yours, mine, and another, half bald, that certainly belonged to you because I throw mine away into the waste-basket, I love to press the chrome tab and see it open with sudden energy)

and that comes out there mummifying, my wife with eyebrows raised, not the mouth, always looking at the clock

—So late

while a platoon was entering our room upon their return from the jungle, indifferent to me, with beards to shave, they exhausted, some dragging their gun butts regardless of me, straightening the fringes

—Careful with the carpet

and disappearing into the room's shack of wood and tin, while the second lieutenant was conversing in a low voice with the captain pointing out something beyond the sanzala* over which five, six vultures were floating, and the mess orderly who died some time ago due to an attack, my mother

(the mess orderly, Hoards, Hoards)[†]

shaking twisted plates of aluminum in the cubicle we called the kitchen, my wife, more intelligent behind the glasses

—Are you taking a bath first or shall I?

and thus every eyelash a leg but the eyes did not run out off the face, escaping one from the other with fear of me, they stared at me gave me the idea that with alarm

—I hate it when you look at me like that

perhaps in her head in a way too brusque because

—Sorry

with the mouth trembling a little bit and what a horror the mouth trembling a little bit, if only I could feel sorry, could smile at you, grab you by the chin, who knows, kiss you on the forehead for example but I'm not capable, I don't know the reason why but I'm not capable, the second lieutenant who came from the jungle stretched out on his bed observing the ceiling without thinking about Lisbon, not the river, not the ships, not the houses, not the roofs, while taking a turn around the church, in a flock, the pigeons changed color, black ones farther away, white over here, they traveled on the pavement between the patios, with hands behind their backs, the crowbar of their necks made them move, tomorrow I'll go to the cellar with my

---

*Small African village consisting of huts.
    [†]The orderly's name is Bichezas, both a nickname and a word for a herd or hoard of animals.

children for the pig killing, since childhood I remember men covered by the screams of the animal's tears and by its blood, I remember wanting to escape and my father forcing me to remain there holding me by the shoulders, disgusted, as I vomited

—I wanted a male and they gave me a Fauntleroy

the Fauntleroy dressed like a woman at night when the gypsies camped in the pine forest, bringing the wagons around, one day they found him with his head crushed by a rock and no one was guilty, the head of the National Police* pushed him with a boot

—It happens

his mother and father behind the coffin, it was August and raining, I recall my mother's umbrella and the other one, larger, with which the sacristan protected the abbot, they were the ones who threw the dirt since Mr. Herculano whose work was to busy himself with the dead did not appear, luckily there were always two graves open waiting for clients so that people would glance at each other furtively

—Are you the one who will be the tenant?

or looking into themselves, fearful

—Will that be me?

at dawn the dead drinking water from the pit, on one occasion while coming into the yard to urinate I found an old man with mud on his face smiling at me, I checked through the door window before lying down once again and no one, the first pig not silent in me even today, my father beginning to cut it up

—You can go, pansy

my mother thinking to console me warming a mug of milk

—Let it go that's life

how many times in Angola after ambushes her voice here inside

—That's life

and it was in fact life, it was life, the thornbush of intestines out in the open was life, the shack where empty coffins were waiting was life, four or five Fauntleroys facedown on the dirt road were life, if only the captain warmed a mug of milk for me repeating the same thing

—Let it go that's life

*The Guarda Nacional Republicana (GNR) is the national police force of Portugal.

with his palm almost in my hair, repenting, departing, the Fauntleroy never spoke with me, he looked at me from a distance with two tongues that licked me in place of eyes, me cleaning his spit off my cheeks with my sleeve, examining the sleeve showing it to my mother afterward

—Wash this for me

and my father approving of me from the dinner table, he didn't move didn't change expression but approving of me as he approved of me in Angola all the pigs I killed and he grew cheerful with the screams, the blood, the guts, he with a checkered cap among the soldiers, leaning on a hoe

—My son

interested by rifles, the bazooka, the radio while he began to hear an evacuation helicopter in the distance that landed close to the trees to escape the insurgents, my wife, in a bath towel with a knot in front to hide her breasts that for a half dozen years have made her ashamed, hesitating as always between two dresses in front of the open armoire, at least in this respect she never changed

—This or that one?

with the suitcase, brought up from the storeroom, on the bed so that she can fold the clothes that we should take because of the weekend in the village and the pig killing, the house of my parents, though I had added a room seeing that we are many, us, my son, my wife, my daughter who never married and was born two years after Angola, resembling my grandmother, silent, serious, she was missing only a knitting stool and bitterness until the water of her bones began to twist her as the soldiers were setting up the security for the helicopter on the tall grass and I think that there was no antipersonnel mine now, no bang, no dusty fog, no

—Second lieutenant, second lieutenant sir

on the ground, no absent leg hurting, eyelets of boots nailed into others, the doctor pulls them out

—Quiet, pansy

whenever we return the nurse who couldn't figure out the tourniquets, who couldn't figure out the bandages

—Calm yourself calm yourself

and me silent

—Calm yourself

me silent, my wife put one of the dresses in front of her body

—How about this one?

after raising the blinds the sun in the room with half the dresser lit up by our photograph and a small rose rotting in a vase on top, a pale petal, fallen, was trembling on a doily, the number of things that I, if I let myself, could say about the roses, perhaps someday who knows, one of my shoes on its side, the other, the right one, much emptier than the one on its side, it might be that by chance I have a right foot larger than the left, who is not asymmetrical, seen from above at first glance it doesn't seem so, me looking at my wife without noticing the dress

—It's great

thinking about roses what a relief, roses, merry-go-rounds, lollipops with the little stick, I had to buy them on the pretext, for example, of wanting to free myself of cigarettes, an excuse that everybody accepts once, of course, they stop encountering the little stick in the ashtray, we put it in the kitchen garbage can

—You're polluting all the way up to my room

my wife, hurt

—You don't lift your nose from your feet and assure me this is great you lost interest in me centuries ago

the blades of the helicopter tousling all of us, the pilot making signals for

—Quick, quick

because of the enemy around us, the tall grass leaning far away vibrating, a wounded man, two wounded men, three, not only two wounded men, mouths moving without sound if only the mouth of my wife moved without sound when she dwells on very long stories that are suddenly interrupted by a suspicious question

—What did I just say?

and if I were the man that my father wanted I would respond

—Nothing of interest

while the helicopter, rising, curved above the treetops, almost close to them, in the direction of the camp ten or fifteen kilometers from here transporting the one I am now far away mixed in with the wounded, one of them insisting

—When my grandfather finds out he'll kill himself when my grandfather finds out he'll kill himself

and the second one praying constantly

—Hail Mary full of grace the Lord is with thee

with white teeth on white lips, the nurse dampening their mouths and the water dripping on their necks, pooling on the tendons, vanishing into the armpits, the nurse

—Hang on

too busy to cry, everybody shaking behind the pilot in blue overalls next to the mechanic, all slipping out and inside themselves asking what air is there to breathe, what is it about my voice that I can't hear it, who is speaking in my throat, who is complaining about the cold, my wife to me, with the suitcase closed

—Do you want to leave soon or do I have time to take a trip to the hairdresser to conceal the roots?

staff in leggings and clogs because a whole day standing hiding your roots is a grind

Salon New Wave

they don't hide your torso, nor the belly, nor the buttocks, nor the folds of skin under the chin that ring just as the back curls, the corporal who was speaking of his grandfather will die, my wife checking herself in the mirror of the entry hall after lighting the silver-plated tulip on the ceiling, arranging the nape of her neck with the cautious cup of her palm, polishing her temples with her little finger, moving back and advancing a centimeter, with glasses disappointed in what remained soft up to the plastic frame and the breath of her pupils dulled the lenses, my daughter, thirty years old, already resembling her mother, the same adjustment in diopters, the same steps filled with hips that don't connect with each other, at once fat and boney, cartilage different from ours, enormous, like those of an ox in a rice paddy, each hoof a different cadence, when I see her walk I always look for an invisible Chinese man behind her with a conical hat striking her with a stick, daughter daughter daughter daughter daughter, until you enter into the house you drag the Chinese man along with you I clearly see him smiling above your shoulder, silent, secretive, kind, the helicopter no longer heard and nevertheless, inside me, the Hail Marys continued just as the hand extended continued

—Don't let me die second lieutenant sir

as the prayers followed and me afraid

—How many mouths do you have?

until I understood that we have various ones talking, talking at the same time, insisting not merely on prayer, on fear

—Don't let me die

and me with an urge to respond to him

—Now I want peace
not inside me, aloud
—Now I want peace
and my mother and my daughter staring at each other, now I want peace, don't complain that I have to go to the village for the pig, since I left my parents' house, excluding my time in Africa, I always went to the village for the pig that would begin to scream, still intact, just as we were hanging it up on the hook after we tied it up, its eyelashes transparent, its hooves fastened, its snout
—Blessed be thee among women
blessed be the fruit of thy womb, Jesus, the commander of the battalion to the priest, selecting a knife and checking its blades
—Not this one not that one they don't know how to sharpen them
while I was tying the animal's ankles together better
—Get out of here, chaplain, the show is not for skirts
and the chaplain backing away from the prisoner in a concealed blessing, this in the shadow of the cellar with buckets of blood below it was necessary to get them moving with a spoon, not of metal, of wood, my mother red stains on her apron, her blouse, her arms, the only woman there, with cotton in her ears, pretending that she didn't hear the prayers but shaking with them, who assures me that the mug of milk she gave me for breakfast was not going to serve afterward to collect my blood, put the tourniquets on me quickly nurse, call the helicopter, take me to Portugal because after this jungle Lisbon, patios, sparrows, churches, the wild ducks in the river, so many blacks selling trinkets, wristwatches, rings, wooden giraffes in what cantina did they buy them, the commander handing me a knife
—Kill him
less difficult to enter than I had imagined and the string of Hail Marys silent, no screams, silent, a tooth over the lower lip, eyes slinking back to their eyelids, so far away, something of a thing in him though he was still breathing and that something of a thing erasing little by little what remained human, I will not kneel, father sir, put your skirt away and get up like a man while my wife and me in the automobile, not the unimog* that we called the donkey of the brush in which she never traveled or saw anyone, the general forbade spouses in Africa, on the way to the village

*Truck used by the Portuguese army in Africa manufactured by Mercedes-Benz.

—Tough guy

he said

—Tough guy

now more abandoned, with so many deserted houses, some old people, some dogs, some small goats, and some hens in the almost always empty streets and only the talking of the elm trees over our heads that used to wake me up, shrunken with fear, in winter, at night, when I was little, asking them

—Don't take me away to the mountain

where my grandmother told me that wolves, kites, of the kind that steal chicks, eat them in a rocky hole and me so light, my God, not to mention the gypsies, grave, solemn, all of stone, crouching around a campfire spitting tobacco and speaking foreign upon arriving at the camp the captain ordered us to call the guide

—Where did you take them bastard?

and the kites from the mountains in Angola, surrounding the sanzala from above as well and there was the cemetery in the first one, the guide

—Captain captain

the hillside before the mountains, trying to wrap everything up in his arms

—Captain

the little café on the square, men in berets, one of them

Mr. Idalécio

with the sleeve of his jacket empty because a scaffold collapsed when he worked construction in Lisbon, they were joined to the shade of a wall he blowing his nose pulling tissues out of his pocket, difficult, interminable, dirty, a goat bleating lost, the school I attended two walls today but the spot to go pee, who can tell me the reason why, almost intact, my wife, who never liked the village, silent, just like the guide silent when the captain

—I asked you where you took them bastard

turning the pistol around and smashing the butt into his face, his camouflage different from ours, almost without color, more torn, a thin elbow exposed, a thin knee exposed, practically no button, a piece of manioc in his pocket, no combat rations, like us, in his pants' pocket, the captain a kick at the guide, two kicks at the guide

—Get up bastard

and stomping on his belly, his chest, his shoulder, lightning in the distance coming closer to them, as always from the east, and no rain while the guide pleading

—Captain captain

doubled over himself, with his hands supplicating

—Captain

with a small collar of beads around his neck that one of my sergeants ripped off with a tug, my cousin, who took care of our family tomb, waved from my parents' door accompanied by her nine- or ten-year-old daughter, I don't know, also brown-haired, also fat, ashamed of us, trying to hide it from herself in the interior of the apron if I cover my eyes and don't see them they don't see me, my cousin pulling her

—Quiet

wearing the usual coat, the usual slippers and the usual bun, her smile resembling that of my father who almost never smiled except when I did the exam for fourth grade he smiled and cried pressing me into his belly, drowning me, and the steel pocket watch hurting my forehead with the lid-clasp, I walked for a week with a scratch in that spot, his pants and jacket unfastened and smelling of the armoire, it's enough for me to see a mothball to remember you and the portrait of my grandparents in a frame of china marigolds, some broken, with my grandfather seated, his tie sideways and one of the points of his collar sticking up and my grandmother behind him with her fingers on his shoulders, both in Sunday dress, both solemn, distressed, in front of a Nordic scene, full of snow and reindeer, not to mention the jug of developer fluid alongside it disrupting the North Pole, I recall her beating a spoon on the tin of corn calling the flock and the chickens jumping around her, my grandfather, a neighbor transforming him into two with a hoe because of a problem of, the captain, of irrigation, the captain to the guide

—You handed them over to the insurgents bastard

and the sky blacker and blacker, lightning closer and closer, a sort of solid night, of slate, above us, breaking into instantaneous flames, the flagpole disappeared in ashes, a tree, another tree, all this for the time being without rain, merely sulfur and magnesium, the earth unstable, the tall grass in panic, the wind knocking over huts, the captain, his knees against the guide, lifting and lowering the butt of his pistol, under thunderclaps, indifferent to them, always yelling

—You handed them over to the insurgents you handed them over to the insurgents

mangling his Adam's apple, his cheeks, his chin, his chest and me quiet on his left leaning toward him, me with my pistol following suit beating,

beating, beating mother, me beating, waking up next to my wife, sweaty, exhausted and though sweaty and exhausted falling asleep again to beat more, me in the village smiling at my cousin and her daughter that had begun to cry, my cousin without understanding

—What happened to you girl?

my cousin

—It even seems that they're hurting you

while I was beating, beating, my wife examining the room

—The armoire is full of dust it's better to leave the clothes in the suitcase

beyond the armoire a bed, a lamp without a shade suspended from the ceiling with a horsefly on the cord, my wife looking at it furtively

—As soon as it begins to fly in somersaults I'm getting out of here at a run

the yard to look after, the garden abandoned, the windows crooked, that almost loose plank on the floor and maybe mice, maybe goats

—I'm getting out at a run

and the crickets will certainly prevent me from sleeping for the whole night, the house wasn't like this just as the village wasn't like this, not such a ruin, so many skeletal dogs, so many abandoned houses, so much wind in the streets, so many echoes of our steps from wall to wall, the apron of my mother on a nail in the kitchen, if I touched her her voice

—We haven't been here for a few years son

my voice from the old days responding

—Where did you go?

her sigh I don't know where

—Sometimes we went over there

and over there to the place where if they were not next to the well not in the olive grove that they inherited from their godmother, almost in the next village, meaning half in the next village and half in ours, a dozen olive trees, all surrounded by a small pumpkin-colored stone wall that no one jumped, I hope that some person collects the olives mixed with birds, the bougainvillea of the Fauntleroy, dry, hollow bells trembling, his door opening into a compartment where cats and shadows, my wife cleaning a chair with what must have been a broom before sitting down

—What is not missing until Sunday

and until Sunday what is not really missing, the finches of the mountains gliding, my father smoking on the kitchen step, at the end of the day, sketching on the ground, armed with a cane, parallel scratches that he erased with

his boot and sketching them again without looking at me, my mother with
her back to us putting pots in the oven and taking I've no idea what off the
shelves, sometimes balanced on a tripod to reach up higher, squeezing her
back with her palm, still with a young girl's neck, still with straight shoulder blades despite the waist, despite the legs, despite the ankles that were
swollen and me missing seeing her run in the tomato plants distrusting me

—You won't catch me

and even if she crossed them rather than going around them I couldn't
catch her from time to time I almost raised her skirt and she got away from
me, turning to laugh at me

—You're so clumsy

and she moved away again until she grabbed me by the waist and raised
me up level to her eyes, not brown as I

—We haven't been here for a few years son

imagined, lighter, green spots and yellow spots that the fencing of the
eyelids turned golden, a mark next to her right nostril, her skin suddenly
without folds, smooth

—You are almost my age

she putting me on the ground

—I had assumed

and forgetting me, she remembered me without cause, abandoned me
without reason and me disappointed for suddenly not existing, without a
place in the family, without a place among them, who are my real relatives,
I belong to who, an index finger messing my hair

—You belong to me silly

and me so content with the

—Silly

I swear, content to belong to her like a sewing box or a necklace that was
from her aunt, locked away because

—You never know

in a dresser drawer, so that if she locked me away with it, despite the darkness inside there and only God and me are familiar with the threats of the
darkness, I swear that I would perhaps like it, I think I would like it, I would
like it, my father winking to me

—You want to make him into a pansy?

my mother without being scandalized

—I do

swinging me from one side to another, with me around her neck challenging my father

—I'd like him even if he were a Fauntleroy

when my mother wasn't around they told me, he'd entertain himself by trying on her clothing, he'd put behind each ear two tears of perfume, he would remain in the mirror and offer himself caresses, the Fauntleroy younger than my father by two or three years, smaller, slimmer of course, if my father had felt like it he could have choked him with only one of his hands, me he never harmed, I was his son

—My boy

me to be more certain, this at fourteen or fifteen years old

—You weren't my father?

and he immediately different, resembling my mother how strange

—You continue to be my boy

when I hurt my foot he picked me up and took me to the opposite end of the village so that the blacksmith who learned about bones in the military, fixed it for me until a crack was heard and nothing hurt anymore, capable of jumping, I swear, I returned at a trot with a pirouette at every twenty steps, cheerful, calling him

—Look at me sir

suffering though happy, it's possible to suffer and be happy at the same time, not to be two and also manage to see myself, how beautiful the vines, how beautiful the poplars, how beautiful everything, I'm not going to die one day, I promise, nor age what absurdity, I'll remain your boy forever even though the apron on the nail in the kitchen assures me

—We haven't been here for a few years son

my voice from before, what word more seductive, before, asking them

—Where did they go my God?

—Their sighs I don't know where

—Sometimes we went over there

and over there in what place tell me, I forbid them to be silent or to leave me, for the sake of your happiness don't be silent, I'm fifty-four years old and you thirty or so and thus I'm the one who commands today, I was a second lieutenant, was in the war, I forbid them to escape from me, I want them in this place for the pig killing and, consequently, interrupt the scratches on the ground and the dinner in the kitchen, give a proper chair to my wife, take that beetle from our room, no crickets outside, no snakes in the garden, the house already clean, the card of the Sacred Heart, in the glass with the cracked frame, on the hooked nail once again, father mother me, father mother me, father mother me I didn't write you much from Angola, forgive me, it wasn't possible to speak and then my handwriting, my laziness, my lack of time, I'm lying, I had hours and hours when I didn't go out into the jungle, a string of afternoons in the bed contemplating the ceiling, with a gun at my bedside and I didn't need to clean it, I commanded the soldiers, returning to lies about the letters I didn't want to worry you, I found them all in the village inside a biscuit tin, almost ripped at the folds, I'm doing great, there are no problems, a kiss to mother and for father an embrace from man to man, of course, we are grown up the two of us, most of all no whining, please, I came back a man from the war, after all, contrary to what some claim, it wasn't really so dangerous, more vacation than anything else, a boat trip and then a safari, animals, etc., almost a stroll, a rest, merely one dead in a truck accident there are accidents everywhere it was just like that, a recruit who got injured from time to time but without big problems, some blacks disciplined period and while I sent these sweet candies to Lisbon the rain a kind of solid slate night, heavier and heavier, lower and lower, above us, no more flashes of lightning, the flashes of lightning moving away in the tall grass, only rain, my cousin pointing me out to the daughter glued to her waist

—Greet this man who is almost your uncle

the daughter hiding her nose in her mother's legs

—I don't want to

and you did well not to want to girl, you did well because me occupied helping the captain to lift himself over the dead guide that he continued to insult

—Bastard

wanting to kill him more

—I want to kill you more

kicking him his uniform in ribbons, his shins, what remained of his canvas boots, his arms without flesh, his head whose features were indistinguishable, one of his feet larger than the other like those I have now, a piece of manioc, that he would never eat, slipping out of his pants along with a scrap of dried fish, already rotten, what those stomachs could withstand gentlemen, blood that the rain dissolved until no blood, no man on the assumption he was ever a man, a shard of damaged cartilage on the assumption it was ever cartilage peeking out of a neck of mud and the captain

—Bastard

emptying into him, bullet after bullet, the gun cartridge up high, yelling for the last time

—You handed them over to the insurgents

almost supported by me, exhausted, limp, vomiting in heaves, vomiting on himself balanced on my shoulder, his knees bamboo shoots, ready to slide under themselves, to slide under me, insisting that the guide

—Greet this man

no, my mother

—We haven't been here for a few years son

no, the captain rising little by little

—Take two of the men and bury him where the landing strip ends

suddenly younger than the daughter of my cousin, more defenseless, weaker, more hidden from himself and from me, the captain now on his knees, now on his haunches, now standing and moving away at random thinking that he was going toward what we called the mess, a shack partially of brick and partially of wood with the twisted table where the five officers we were used to eat and play *sueca** on a table made with planks from barrels, seated in chairs made of planks from barrels as well and a roof of pieces of corrugated tin, put together at random, that vibrated in the wind and even when the smallest leaf fell on them, the mess in such a shack, after eating dinner at five-thirty to take advantage of the daylight since at six, without transition, almost without twilight, suddenly night

(how to write about this in a letter to my parents?)

and we shadows, less than shadows, poor immobile ghosts waiting for the first shot, the first spray of machine-gun fire, the first mortar to fall inside the camp so that we run to the ground not of earth, of sand, screaming orders, checking if the personnel in the shelters are firing back at random and how does one put this monstrosity in a letter father, mother, fear, the wounded, how can one explain this, tell me, how can one insist on this me who had to be silent and continue silent forever despite the psychologist at the hospital, on Wednesdays, along with other marionettes who I did not know,

*Popular Portuguese card game.

former officers as dead as me and the psychologist insisting that we should talk, talk, the psychologist who does not understand and affirms that he does understand, younger than us, grown up already without war, not Africa, not corpses, thinking he is listening to us without listening to the wind, not the rain, not the explosions, not the Hail Marys of the wounded, not the smell of the dying, the psychologist after an hour

—We'll meet next Wednesday gentlemen

to the old men who we almost are now, not to the almost boys we were then, me needing to lie down in the bed of my parents, between them, my mother doesn't allow that and thus me on the way over there on the aircraft landing strip stumbling in the grass, with the two men, each with a gun and a shovel and the remains of the guide, me touching the tall grass with a boot

—Here

a half dozen feet under my heels, for what reason more, a half dozen where perhaps a hyena will sniff him out and take him before Angola eats everything and eats everything immediately as it will eat me, my wife

—What are you thinking about?

with me answering, in this village house where now only we two exist, I'm not thinking about anything, I swear, not thinking about anything, I limit myself to making scratches in the yard with a stick, erasing them and making them again looking at you without recognizing you recognizing you with difficulty, smiling an almost tender smile, I assure you that it's not very hard, my wife surprised with me

—How long it's been since I saw you happy

lying down at my side

—We should come to the village more often it does you good

and me not answering her, nodding yes or rather agreeing without words that the village does me good, because I don't agree accepting that the village does me good, nothing does me as much good as the village, it's true, despite the bastards of these starving dogs, of the half dozen old men, most of them with a beret, looking at me in silence, sheltered by a wall, a solitary goat limping up the path with a bell on its neck that no longer rings while me to the men, making them out poorly, making myself out poorly beyond the aircraft landing strip

—Let's go dig over there quickly I don't have the whole night

under the sky now clear, not of slate, transparent with a vapor of quiet clouds above me, constellations that are not mine aloft, presences I ignore or rather those that circulate around here repeating in silence my name and fireflies, blackberries, the echo of the elm trees, water running I have no idea where adding more silence to the silence, on returning from the aircraft landing strip not one light on in the camp, not a sound, the soldiers disappeared with the shovels in the direction of the canvas tents that we called barracks, I took my time to find a kind of cabin where the officers were sleeping with the bed of the captain separated from ours by mats and the straw bed insisting

—Bastard

insisting

—Bastard

insisting

—Bastard

so that now, as my parents go over there, I began to write them this letter made of scratches on the ground.

2

I said that we were leaving at three and as usual
(does anyone still harbor illusions?)
Her Excellency though taking off the afternoon from work deigned only
to appear at six, eleven minutes past six to be more exact my watch does not
lie, for the price I paid for it that was what was lacking and moreover the
hands with an air so certain that I don't dare challenge them, Her Excellency challenges them who at least has nerve enough, dammit, to give away
and sell
— That Swiss junk of yours that besides cost a ton always running fast
and between three and eleven past six
(I checked my mobile phone and was certain, what is time after all, behold us before a question that would take us far afield)
I was seated, suitcase closed, ready, next to the armchair, the only one we
have and it doesn't fit
(it was chosen by her of course, for whom the problem of time, almost
all problems for that matter except one white hair, that I can't see, ahead)
— Look at this misery
(I don't mind)
with the sofa of three places and the impression left by Her Excellency's
fat neck on one of the pillows, the one where she generally plops down
— For God's sake let me rest now
for the soap opera, her knees folded under her body in her calling as an
articulated meter, if I put her in the circus as a contortionist there would be
no money problems in this house if you can call this a house three narrow
rooms with a neighbor below and a neighbor above not settled in below and
above, here with us, at least the flushing of madam discharging into my head
and the chick of the guy below waking me with screams every night
— Ah Carlos ah Carlos
it seemed that she was working a water pump, like those for a well with a
lever, judging by the number of screws blown out from the bed, Carlos who

I would occasionally meet at the building entrance furtively distributing, while sneaking a glance at the elevator and the stairs, advertising leaflets from his mailbox among the mailboxes around it, equitably, one small sheet in this one, one small sheet in that one, so that we won't be jealous of anyone, his sense of justice moved me to the point of suppressing a

—Ah Carlos Carlos

that already escaped from the lips in my heart, so me pumpkining on the armchair for three hours and eleven minutes interrupting myself from time to time with excursions to the window to take a glance at the street and from Her Excellency, one of the sidewalks in the sun and the second in the shade since all the streets were limping, no sign of the kind that perhaps a lover perhaps a clothing shop, weighing all I prefer lovers because they always give money while clothing shops take it, that's to say they take mine because it's already clear that here the chump pays, always the chump of course, that's what he's useful for and just as between three and six an eternity between the times when I feel like strangling Her Excellency with the dental floss with which she polishes herself at night rummaging around herself, leaning over the sink, her mouth immense, in the direction of the mirror, only canines and gums, no nose no eyes, her tongue sticking out like vibrating snakes, vibrating, my head shifting from one side to the other awaking episodes that I have over there like an elderly man among the thousand broken objects in an antiques store, lifting this one, evaluating that one, disdaining a third, dragging a watch out here in order to study it in the light, hanging my glasses on my forehead so as to see it better given that the problem of myopia of the brain much worse than that of the eyes and then in the crate of soft-drink bottles, clouded by the dust of forgetting, arise in me old scenes, scenes more recent, smells, sounds, vague memories, things I considered lost hidden under things that didn't belong to me, they belonged to strangers and I don't know for what reason one encounters there a dog named Sporting, a gentleman who referred to me as

—Alfredo

me who is not called Alfredo and who knows nothing about Alfredo, hold on a bit, wait, a little bit of clarity has come to me or what I thought clarity and I deceived myself, in fact I know nothing about any Alfredo, I suddenly remembered some distant names, Miúdo Malassa, Miúdo Machai, Martelo Chibango, having come from where my God, I recall a woman who was talking with me

—Kamona*

another woman whose features I can't make out to the woman who spoke with me

—Euá†

both barefoot, with rags on their waists, exposed torsos and filed teeth, I recall a river and creatures next to the river, without noses, without fingers, washing themselves with the stumps of their hands, I recall minuscule hens, men smoking pipes made from gourds, my father dressed in green taking hold of me, protecting me from other guys dressed in green

—They're not going to kill this kid he'll stay with me

in the midst of people lying down, still, bodies without faces that were burning in the midst of straw, farm animals that were burning, goats, groans not

—Ah Carlos ah Carlos

different, with the odor of gasoline where they threw a match, a guy in green to my father

—He'll grow up to take vengeance on you second lieutenant sir

and not hearing this because I began to cry without smelling anything except the stench of gunpowder, the stench of bodies and me in the arm-chair of the living room, I must have fallen asleep for a moment and like always when I fall asleep my soul carrying and bringing out mysteries that afterward I would lose without recalling them, Her Excellency shaking me in the middle of the night

—What is going on with you that you won't let me relax?

unkempt, furious, with one of her shoulders showing given that the strap of her nightshirt, by chance red, slipped down toward her arm improving her movements until her features drowned again in the pillow, very distant from me bubbling up a

—Shitty black

that, as is natural, I didn't hear as I've not heard for years

—They always swore to me that the blacks were much better armed than the whites but at least in your case it's a lie

that's no laughing matter, seriously, grabbing me with two fingers and letting me fall, a lip of disdain sticking out

*Child (in Kimbundu).
†Greeting (in Kimbundu).

—A tiny rag

and a tiny rag in fact, a species of ashamed little worm that I hid in my hand praying in the hope that it would come to life with exercise and it didn't, it shrank, everything shrank in me, pride, my stomach, the capacity to think while the humiliation increased, there never will be a woman in my bed screaming

—Ah Carlos ah Carlos

I never had the nerve to offer, sad about my intimate size, the garbage of advertising to my neighbors, tumama tchituamo,* lelo kundjanhire,† fragments of old dialogues heard I don't know where or rather of course I know, in Africa, I just don't know what they mean and how they got here, men smoking with only one gourd with water that they were passing among themselves, women digging in the earth with a hoe while a guy with a gun having emerged from the stalks of corn was talking to them, the goat in agony as a half dozen dogs were tearing off its skin, I liked to disrobe Her Excellency in the same way nibbling her neck

—Say ah Carlos ah Carlos

she wobbling thankful, happy

—You blacks

pulling my pants off in an eager hurry

—How large

while she was hesitating, bleeding, tripping on the husks, falling pleading

—Now

not smelling like an animal, smelling like perfume

—Tear me

and I tearing her with my nails, elbows, knees, teeth by chance one is missing back there, the doctor

—if it hurts, let me know

and how could I let you know my throat filled with instruments not to mention the light that was blinding me, curious how a chair crucifies a person, the doctor bending with a set of pliers over the armchair in the living room that Her Excellency has no way of getting to

(a lover or a shop, despite the pains of the credit card I still prefer the

---

*Take a seat (in Kimbundu).
†Today I couldn't shit (in Kimbundu).

shop, the whites as it turns out much better armed than the blacks, a little hotel in mind, a stained sheet, an unknown strand of hair on the pillow, a bucket for what I don't know in the corner)

and however strange it may appear while she hasn't arrived yet at this apartment I such an orphan, the doctor, was saying, with pliers drawn

—While your wife comes or doesn't come I'll take out three or four more

as the nurse was sucking my saliva out with a small tube, also with a mask, setting down molar after molar

(I have hundreds)

on the doily on the sideboard, between the china Cupid and the glass jar with a half dozen wilted corollas, of the kind woman like, entombed in gray water who offered them to her I don't see her buying them because too expensive and she has to oblige seducers at extraordinary hours at work, at least with the dentist, for heaven's sake, here with me, she will remain lying down now while my father in camouflage waits for us in the village, I'm sure, next to the wall observing the highway below asking my mother for the time and only a truck on the highway from time to time, bicycles, an old motorbike, my father was worrying

—Was there a problem?

pulling his military cap down on his forehead so that the soldiers stopped looking at his features, simply the rapid movements of his mouth

—This kid don't even dream of killing him he'll stay with me

and I understood him because my other father had gone to the mission school now ruins the tall grass

(and bushes and trees)

crushed slowly, up to a dry small open space in the center of the cloister, or rather a few small cement columns already missing a roof destroyed by a bazooka, shards of vases and an aluminum watering can in the corner, the dentist organizing his junk in a small suitcase staring at the dented watering can near my dinner table

—It doesn't look bad there

while he asked me

—Where did this come from?

without reminding me right away of the cloister, it seemed to me that Her Excellency's key in the door and a clear false alarm, there isn't any middle-aged building that doesn't like little games, false open taps, false flushing in the bedroom, a false light in the sunroom because it's clear no real light, the reflection of a lamp from behind the square where a funeral parlor, a butcher shop and a school of Eastern dance, on one occasion passing by the funeral parlor I saw inside, without her noticing me, an adolescent girl with arms high dancing between coffins and candles, as soon as she noticed me she stuck out her tongue at me I don't know for what reason for me being black or a person, I think for being black, me wanting to ask her

—Have you ever encountered a dead black man?

not in a sanzala, in a casket, with a tie like you people, shoes, hands with white palms and dark on the back, flat noses, that sort of woolen hair

—Don't they disgust you?

they used to disgust Her Excellency or at least I did for sure, she'd close her eyelids when I'd touch her and keep still, months back a Sunday, afterward, she asked me to go to the other edge of the casket

—Would you mind putting on a little aftershave next time?

cleaning, she thought stealthily, her breasts and belly on the sheet and remaining for centuries in the shower, if I pulled the rings of the plastic curtain I would find her soaping herself endlessly opening a tiny irritated edge of her eyelid

—Please get out of here

as if I were a leper from the half-ruined huts on the riverbank, almost without features, almost without feet, who walk, sideways, holding themselves up on stumps, the nurse would ring the bell hanging from a tree trunk, and put pills and scraps of dried fish on the side of the path and they looking at him, invisible, monstrous, hidden behind the roots, advancing by a crawl after he went away fighting among each other, threatening each other, beating each other for the medicine, for the fish, looking at each other with hate as they were eating, from time to time a corpse in the river

—Why aren't you all eating it?

the dentist and his assistant were talking below on the street, every time an automobile came near the assistant a short hop filled with elbows toward the asphalt in search of taxis, they lifted my molars from the top of the dresser as they lifted themselves, no vestiges of soothing aromas over there, no forgotten compress, and now no watering can, the apartment as Her Excellency left it, with two or three women's magazines on the sofa, the habitual stopping point from the shop girl on the way to the wastebasket, open at the top with pictures of actresses, a cigarette filter

(Caricocos, Caricocos)*

flattened with swift movements in the ashtray at the same time that she was observing me with disgust for me and disgust for herself

— How foolish I always was

and the lepers peeking at us from the jungle without the courage to approach, a crocodile in the river, two crocodiles in the river, only their sockets attentive to drifting, poised as trunks just under the water and little birds, white, with open wings and stretched-out feet that sought to settle on their backs and they were walking on the scales pecking at them, if, by chance, I kissed her back Her Excellency immediately dodging

— How tedious

trying to get free from the kiss scrubbing it away with her nails, she got pregnant at one point seven or eight years ago, I accompanied her to the midwife and because I wasn't allowed to enter

— It was certainly going to disgust you to break apart a mulatto

I waited for her at the table next to the window of a little café nearby where she didn't say good-bye to me, not even a

— Ciao

for example, she walked across the street not looking back even once, without a shade of consideration the ingrate, in the direction of a ground floor with a square at the right announcing Nursing Station 24-Hour Care and the C of Care almost cut out by an idiotic penknife, a building that seemed older than the neighbors

(there are houses and people that grow old early)

almost without paint, with a scrap of bullfight poster coming apart and window frames not of aluminum, wood and anemic ink, scratched opaque panes, she rang the doorbell and fortunately it didn't happen to collapse, I thought that she might wave to me before entering and of course she didn't wave, the illusions that I'm still capable of having gentlemen, what fools like me imagine, I didn't learn with age, my father assures me, adding that my mother should make sure that I wasn't listening and as he didn't lower his voice I heard

— Perhaps it's for being black, the poor fellow

though with one of my mother's index fingers vertical over her mouth, the other pointing at me and in that moment the diffuse image of a woman

*A cigarette brand.

also black, lying on the ground with a clot of blood on her forehead, various clots of blood on her breasts, less one ear cut off by one of the soldiers with me small attached to her without crying, if I could, I would cling to Her Excellency without crying because people, because I, how have I to explain this, I continue to like her they understand, I don't know the reason why if there is a reason or if there are necessary reasons but I continue to like her you understand, what a foolish thing life, I continue to like her what a shame, to like her, to like her perhaps because I'm black, because I'm black unfortunately and because my father isn't my father nor is my mother my mother though I think that they are or rather I think that they are and they aren't, if they are what's the reason for me attached to a dead woman stretched out on the hemp and me not clinging to her, perhaps it wasn't a dead woman and me not clinging to her, perhaps I've invented it, perhaps I've dreamed it, perhaps another child, not me, hugging the woman, certainly there is another boy hugging the woman and, behold, the matter is resolved, it's clear that another boy and another woman and consequently the matter definitively resolved, my father and my mother in the village period, now that it is completely certain whoever returns to the issue is a pansy, I'm not returning, I don't want to return, I'm not certain I won't return, probably I'll return, go forward, forget that, order a coffee that burns your tongue and forgets that, because of this conversation I didn't see Her Excellency enter and as I didn't see I can be certain that she waved good-bye, it was the only thing missing that she didn't wave good-bye, of course she waved good-bye and I waved good-bye to her though I don't remember, we have been married for eight years and so what doubt is there that we like each other, if we didn't like each other we would separate and to this day we haven't separated or talked about that, the little café, two clients laughing at the counter with the owner, a soccer team on the wall, the pennant of a club on a nail, already quite faded, already with stains, the door of the bathroom with a yellow metal boy taking a pee in a bucket, joined to him by a stream of metal as well and the boy with his nose down to keep track of the direction of the stream with me monitoring alternatively his concern for it and the nursing station, where Her Excellency took off, in the hope of seeing her shadow in the glass panes, already missing when I wake up and find her in the kitchen in a bathrobe warming up the barley, totally unkempt, without makeup, in a ragged bathrobe and the string holding it on slowly coming undone, some old slippers of mine, with a hole that showed her big toe, too large for her, Her Excellency a bit tired and bitter morning wrinkles or rather in one single word, beautiful, my father to the men in green while Her Excellency squeezed my shoulder

—Watch out, if anyone touches him

and you might not believe it but it was good that she hurt me a little bit, it didn't bother me that she squeezed my shoulder one more time, what silliness, that it didn't bother me, I wanted it just like I wanted that Her Excellency a

—Dear

almost without moving her mouth, between her teeth, only lips and tongue, with eyes suddenly enormous, your body finally concrete and me drawing bison in your grotto of Altamira your, excuse the word and please don't get mad, don't despise me, don't grumble

—What can be expected of a black?

don't exalt yourself with me, little cunt, the same one where the midwife is now introducing I've no clue what to pull out I've no clue what, a piece of me or more than a piece of me

— You pay for everything in this life if it gave you pleasure to do it it's just that you suffer

this in a cubicle in the back with a Sacred Heart, by which bulls are the Christ Children always blond and the grown-up Christs dark is what I'd like to know, who will explain it to me, staining the plaster, Her Excellency after paying, it's clear that the midwife

—I sympathize with this pretty young face but I don't accept checks do you understand life taught me not to trust anyone

Her Excellency with a cloth on top, without a skirt, her heels spread apart caught in some sort of hook, one of the sergeants to a corporal who showed a knife

—Watch what you write and take care of the child our second lieutenant is not joking around

lying in a tight sunroom, not very clean, accompanied by a bucket with a frayed rag, that was missing enamel, for compresses and for I've no idea what, that is, I do know but I don't feel like talking about it, I assure them only that if my father were there he would pull his cap down, my father in the middle of the sanzala with the huts around it disappearing and hens without heads, people without heads or without ears, the whites like ears, I gave one of mine to the midwife in exchange for leaving Her Excellency in peace, my father in the village waiting for me and me pumpkined in the armchair rehashing this that won't leave me, the idea came to me now the breath of the earth, the breath of the manioc, the rotten breath of the woman I was clinging to, the dense odor of the blacks that contrary to the opinion of Her Excellency was dissipating here, clarify for me what I became and who I am today, clarify for me, please, I'm pleading, what am I, my father showing me to the plump creature who opened the door for us, suppressing a drop from her eyelashes with her hand

—I was only expecting you tomorrow

upon coming back from Africa

—Your mother boy

not a black stretched on the ground who wasn't interested in my person, with hoops on one of her ankles, a creature with an apron who was hugging my father

—Finally finally

moving away to observe him better and hugging him again suppressing more tears

—Finally

looking at him again

—You've gone gray

she who had forced smiles suddenly serious

—You aren't sick are you?

malaria, a second bout of malaria, now and again me lying down shivering, requests for water, sweat, a dull glance in my direction, phrases that weren't intelligible and Her Excellency without returning from the building, I hope that nothing had happened, no dog without a head, no hut in flames, I hope that no black to me

—Kamona

while she was falling, the knife of a man in green in her neck, the knife of a man completely in green in her neck who I couldn't distinguish from the others, the death of the pig after tomorrow in the village cellar, my parents waiting for us, especially my father waiting for us in the same disquiet which I wait for Her Excellency with in the living room armchair, which I wait for Her Excellency with in the café in front of the nursing station and she doesn't enter the house nor does she leave the station, perhaps she bought an entire boutique, perhaps she is with a man I don't know where, perhaps some problem with the midwife, a hemorrhage, a perforation, a man in green to another man in green

—Kill her kill her

and she with rings on her ankle on her belly in the space between two huts, with bullet marks on her forehead and her breast, without one of her ears, the ear in a flask that my father accepted, looking at me, he seemed suspended, hesitating, he ended up shrugging his shoulders and he accepted, only a phrase to the man in green that bent down, together with the glint of a knife blade, for something more distant, I didn't understand whether a person, whether a kind of root, I think not a person, a kind of root following a tuft of hemp

—Leave his father in peace

this before setting fire to the huts with the help of gas cans from the unimogs and I'm there to figure out how on earth the gas fumes still make me sick today, I remember myself in my father's lap, to the right of the driver, on the return to what we used to call headquarters, still without thinking, it's logical, what I thought for the first time many years later, this is

—Am I not all the ears that he cut off am I not his trophy?

and so don't look at me, don't hug me, don't smile at me, drop me in a flask of alcohol, show it to a friend, put the flask in a drawer and then leave me in peace among things, old envelopes with my name on the outside, not the one I had, the one they gave me afterward, burned-out light bulbs, a screw, three pens without nibs, I want a dark drawer, a very dark drawer where Her Excellency won't kick me in the behind and will forget me, above all, forget me, please forget me like I forgot my other father not knowing whether he was alive or a root and not knowing at all whether he existed, I'm lying, I know, one of the customers of the café to the manager pointing at my chin in a manner that she thought discreet

—Is it just me or is that black guy near the shop window not crying?

in such a way that the manager and the owner of the café were watching me slyly with a casual air, I on the armchair waiting for Her Excellency to deign to return home and the three now no longer at the counter, over there eating at a table, with a soccer team on the wall in place of the landscape that used to be there and the pennant of some club in place of the portrait of Her Excellency's aunt who lived here before us, who invited us to live with her and the cat when we got married and who left us the apartment when she died, for some time the cat remained that hated me more than its owner, all contempt and claws, with resentful eyes, until its heart also took it away or was it the ant poison which I spiced its bowl with, Her Excellency found it in the morning belly up, still hating me but a fortunate convulsion stopped the denunciations though Her Excellency weeping and with the cat in her arms, suspicious

—It was you wasn't it?

in spite of my being distraught about the animal, a glass of water over a saucer given that the whole world realizes glasses of water are useful for everything including thirst, me innocent, me indignant

—The only thing lacking was for you to accuse me of this

and Her Excellency, what injustice, without believing me, I who would have done the same thing to the old lady had thrombosis unfortunately not preceded me depriving me of the vengeance of contemplating her pedaling with cramps on the raffia carpet barfing loudly and there we have the ex-ample of a show that wouldn't bother me in the slightest, the creature who detested me drooling, stuttering unconnected syllables, transforming the house into a mess of features above an immobile mouth, with dentures, happy, free of the gums, biting the pillow with appetite, sometimes get-ting away despite the efforts of the tongue, desirous of emigrating to meet another owner and other menus, some easy soups, hamburgers that don't require any effort, a tender fish without bones and with no need to lift it out of the depths with the fishing net from the high seas showing it around by thumb and index finger

—He would like to fix an abscess in the gums the twit

the other officers to my father

—Are you really going to stick with the kid?

in the interior of the circular camp with dozens of men in green and barracks and sand, a river plain down below where dispersed lights, around the camp huts inhabited by blacks like me, surprised by me not being with them, fewer and fewer blacks given that they were fleeing into the jungle, not looking at things, through things, thin, with enormous feet that con-tinued downward, a ways beyond them until the center of the world, they were coming to ask for food, holding out rusty tins and the kites soaring above them, the chief in a faded uniform covered with ribbons and metal stars, seated in front of a sewing machine, sewing himself instead of the clothing he didn't have, I thought that Her Excellency was leaving the nursing station, I arose and finally another woman, younger, with a dog on a leash, one of those animals satisfied with itself that lets it go later in the passageway with a proprietary ease instead of marching silently, musing, sniffing out a solution for the squaring of the circle in the trees and the tires, my father in Africa to me

—Boy

most of the time not looking at me and hardly ever touching me, it would not bother me if he touched me

—Boy

so that I knew him better from the back than from the front in the camp without a rifle, without a pistol, so easy to kill with a knife in the neck or in his chest and to abandon him in the grass, still, with eyes closed under the sun, flashes of lightning, rain, if I had a knife, if he gave me a knife, I from here to there and the soldiers

—Kid

without hurting me, the captain to my father

—What do you want the child for?

and my father

—He'll go to Lisbon with me

when I barely understood Portuguese but I remember this

—He'll go to Lisbon with me

or rather his black ear, the memento, the treasure, I'm not even a boy, I'm an ear, who will be the midwife how will the midwife be, Her Excellency will command

—Behave like a woman don't cry

because for her Her Excellency certainly not a lady, just a woman

—It gave you pleasure to do didn't it now put up with it that's your duty

so that Her Excellency, what a relief, did put up with it, completely cut apart and she put up with it, her aunt before going silent forever insulted me with a look

—You

and inside of

—You

I who never hurt her, hate, disdain, what she never called me

—Black

What she never asked me

—Aren't you ashamed of being black?

and personally, to be completely sincere, I don't know if I am, no matter how much Her Excellency disdains me I continue to ignore it perhaps
because blacks are stupid, right? They don't understand, right? Nearer to
animals than to humans, right? Like monkeys, right? We should offer them
some nuts and that's it, right? A banana, right? A coconut, right? All monkeys like coconuts, one reads that in books, me seated again next to the shop
window, waiting, no longer looking at the street or the door on the other
side, a door painted white with a white handle and a light bulb protected by
an iron cage white on top, I bet it's on all night waiting for customers, what
lives, as the café is perhaps open all night waiting for black husbands that
live at the same time in Angola like the female monkey stretched out in the
grass with a shot in her head, shots in her chest and without her right ear, no,
the left, without both ears while my father concentrates on the wall so as to
keep an eye on the highway

—Was there some problem?

in hopes of finding the car, of finding me, of waving to me even knowing
that I don't see him because the miracle of identifying him can happen up
there and my turn to wave at him, my arm sticking out of the car in front
and in back, a black arm it's obvious

—What do you want the child for?

my father with my mother, a slightly fat creature, on the step of the
kitchen, worried too

—Did he just pass by on the asphalt?

and my father saying no under the eucalyptus trees just beyond the camp
looking at the savannah where I didn't appear between two burned women
sending kisses with both hands, my father holding onto the camouflage
tunic of a man in green

—Have you seen my son?

and still I didn't pass by on the highway mother, I am still seated in the
armchair waiting, seated in the café, seated on a log in Africa pushing a
small spider with a twig in the direction of Her Excellency's house or a gecko
that emerged from a stone, with feet eager to run despite appearing immobile, the mineral pupils observing me just as I was observing a drab scrap of
sugar in the bottom of a teacup reminding me of an almost naked old man,
painted in various colors, with a wand of rattles and ribbons in his hand,
jumping around a chief resting on a bench and my mother to my father,
not fat, young, in her kitchen apron, looking at me without approaching me

—This is the boy you brought from Angola?

my mother with a waist, without folds in her forehead, without folds on her face, upright, with light movements and a quotation mark of the sun falling from the skylight of the building where pigeons were passing overhead, with their tiny distinct feet beyond the glass, on her shoulder, this at ten after six on my watch, eleven after six to be more exact it's not wrong for the price I paid it was the only thing lacking and moreover the hands with an air so certain that I don't dare to challenge them, I accept the time they give me and keep quiet, I always accepted the time they gave me and kept quiet, eleven after six and that's that or rather precisely when the door of the nursing station and that of the apartment opened and Her Excellency emerged at the same time into the street and the room, into the pallid street, without makeup, with heavy eyelids and rinsed hair and into the room with new clothes, a hairdo, nails painted red and a ring I didn't recognize, I must recognize it from the hole in the bank account, looking at me like she looked at the suitcase next to me, already set, already closed, with a rapid, indifferent glance, asking

—Do you think we really have to go to the pig killing?

installing herself without haste on the sofa with half her left thigh exposed, moistening her index finger with her tongue

(how good to see her moisten her index finger with her tongue)

to turn the pages better.

3

Neither my son nor my daughter who was born two years after Angola
has arrived yet I think that's natural to a certain degree because the Mercedes and the Berliets* always moved slowly due to the mines that no one
ever knows where they are or when they explode, with two columns of men
parallel to us that we saw only from time to time when there was an opening in the grass and six more patrolling up front, from time to time a river,
from time to time a clearing and abandoned huts, my son got married, my
daughter didn't, always angry, bitter, one talks to her and she doesn't respond, we smile at her and she stays serious, I know nothing about her life,
if I ask her a vague gesture to scatter shadows, I think that I never heard her
say father, never heard her say mother, she practically never visits us or if by
a miracle she visits she stays silent, she doesn't invite us to her house I can't
imagine where it is or if she lives alone, they told me a friend lives with her
and I've no clue whether that's true or a lie, which friend, my wife who also
heard took some time to think, the minesweepers not Berliets, Mercedes because the general warned by message that the Berliets are gold, the platoons
should continue ahead and the reason clear, the Berliets are three thousand
contos,† the men five hundred, six lives for a truck didn't seem expensive to
him, so much noise in the jungle, wind in the leaves, birds, the pig will be
dealt with tomorrow, Hail Mary full of grace, when my grandfather finds out
he'll kill himself, my daughter when small used to flee from her mother into
my arms but she began to grow and stopped looking for me, she locked the
door of her room despite my warnings
— Don't lock yourself in

*Trucks manufactured by Berliet, a French auto manufacturer, were used along
with the unimogs in Angola by the Portuguese army.
†Portuguese currency before the adoption of the Euro in January 1999 was the
escudo. A conto was an unofficial multiple of the escudo, with one conto equal to
one thousand escudos. Three thousand contos would have been the equivalent of
around seventeen thousand dollars.

and my wife silent, at least one afternoon

—No one gets anything from her

so that from then on me silent too, when they operated on my gallbladder though she still lived with us she didn't go to the hospital, I returned home and not even

—Hi

not even

—Is it better?

not even a kiss, locked up inside herself at the table eating in silence, I wanted to ask

—Do you feel good?

But my wife's face of

—Please

held me back, her heart unsure, the doctor to me quietly showing me a test that I didn't understand, traces on a strip of millimeter paper where the red pencil drew circles informing

—Careful

the commander who liked to accompany the young men, the two sitting on small benches with slats when he visited us on the frontier

—Does our second lieutenant understand war?

looking at three dogs that were in turn looking at us just as immobile as us, what we didn't lack for around there were dogs, large, small, all thin of course, with as much hunger as the blacks, the majority of them next to the mess halls for the men on the lookout for scraps, when due to the rains the small plane

(not fly, bird)

that brought food and the mail and didn't land on the small strip up over there, hurling boxes of fresh food that broke apart on the ground and them and us fighting on all fours about meat, cod, little bags of vegetables, potatoes, the claws of the beasts suddenly so big and the teeth so sharp, the animals, almost half of them crippled, suddenly violent, cruel, a comrade shooting at them

—Assholes

with me thinking to myself who in fact were the dogs over there, the animals that didn't give up despite the shots or the people so that me to the commander

—I don't understand commander sir but I'm only a dog

ugly too, crippled, cruel, ready to dig into the ground hoping for roots not of manioc, mine to bring over here my mother, my father, my godmother Lucília, my grandmother whom I pulled by the neck

—Am I still alive, boy?

and she sat down to peel carrots right away in the kitchen her eyeglasses fixed with tape

—Don't distract me now with so much to do

my daughter with the same airs I think, the lowered eyelid, the way of walking, the village more abandoned with each year and the mountain mimosas coming down toward it, someday they will invade the houses, the stockade, the square, they will swallow the cemetery, they will swallow the shade of the dead, my grandmother hurrying away

—Good-bye

missing her son in Germany with a small enamel picture on her neck, not her adult son, the little one, with a jacket and bow, smiling with fear bordering on tears, assuring in Christmas postcards

—Don't worry I'll return one day and stay there

and he didn't visit her when she was dying, a telephone call for my father

—The restaurant won't give me a break I can't

my father calmly understanding

—Yes, of course yes of course

and all of them already dead, poor things, returning or not returning here to the village I'm certain that I hear them in the wind, the pine trees shake and it's them

—Boy

weighing on the branches, my cousin who continues to live in the village and looks after the deceased

—Don't you hear?

when small she played house among the graves, she made up little dinners for the dead with leaves and pits and berries

—Do you want more?

She leaned over to me and with a quiet voice

—The dead are strange they don't respond to people

as a great mystery was slowly taking place in the poplars full of echoes, footsteps, silverware, sounds of dishes, voices while a machine gunner was strangling with both hands a puppy that had tried to flee with a piece of meat and the whites around the eyes of both bulging, which one was strangling the other tell me commander sir which will become a small insignificant pile abandoned on the landing strip and which will leave us without seeing us holding a ripped package, red, dripping

—Does our second lieutenant understand death?

slow drops were asking me if me in Africa or on the wall of the garden of the village my father built on Sundays with an unlit cigarette on his ear, not a full cigarette, just a butt with one of its points burning, the wall from which I was watching, my body there but my nose on the highway, the appearance of my children and we were sitting in a circle of chairs at the hospital when the psychologist came in with his tie hanging randomly

—Pardon the wait

and I was thinking that I would be glad if my daughter got married but I see her alone always, pigeons and sparrows already with the rust of age reflected in the half-open window, still she hasn't told us where she lives, still whenever it interests me the usual response

—Don't worry it's not under the bridge

and I believe that it's not because she doesn't bring a blanket folded under her arm and at least she's reasonably clean, you know, reasonably made up, on one of the last occasions she visited us she had a little silver ring that disappeared after that, I tried

—The ring

and all she did to answer was to lift an eyebrow, her hands of the same kind as mine the poor thing only smaller that's logical, me paws, when she a baby she squeezed with force the finger that I put in her palm, what is the reason you don't squeeze it now and the psychologist to me, with folds on his forehead

—Pardon?

perhaps because the eddies of the mist impeded his hearing, suddenly one, two, three, or four and the dogs fleeing, the chief put the sewing machine on his knees, terrified, so many stains on his uniform the poor fellow and shoeless, his misery speaking

—Lutenan sir

and no pride, no authority, patching up the camouflage of the troops, the socks, a sheet, the worn ribbons of the ridiculous uniform the Portuguese forced on him, so itchy, always with a colonial helmet on his head and two women almost as old as he, the chief who no one obeyed, of course, and who no one bowed to, without rings, without a council of elders, without the people worrying about him, as solitary as us turning toward us in an attitude of prayer

—Muata muata*

respectful, submissive, without blankets or goats and consequently without money, it wasn't in front of him that the witch doctor decapitated roosters with his teeth spitting out the heads onto the ground instead of handing them over to him leaving them next to his swollen ankles together with little stones and shells, the agent of the political police the little plane brought every month mixed up with new soldiers, in addition to the chaplain and letters, hailing him while folding his little finger

—Get over here, oh King of Shit

and the captain silent, the second lieutenants silent, the sergeants silent and the blacks silent, our coffins empty waiting to be put away, mine the third from the left counting from the top down, I raised its lid and thought I saw my father inside with wrists mixed up over his stomach and handcuffed in a rosary like his grandparents before him, like Mr. Barros who lived alone, flung himself in the well and the night before stroked my cheek

—Kid, you're the one who makes me old growing so fast

and in the remaining coffins my comrades who were there with me looking at each other without a word, the chief's sewing machine working in a ramshackle way, motionless kites high up in the sky evaluating chicks and not one of my children on the highway, observing better perhaps the wing of a kite trembling, perhaps they forgot or they buried me in Angola without me believing it nor did I hear gunfire before the casket descended, as always so distracted, the hospital psychologist to me

—What are you thinking about?

and the circle of chairs staring at me in anticipation, a cat on the roof of the house staring at me too with the right paw suspended, the mess officer locked the storage room

—I don't want to see you there

thirty-nine coffins I exaggerate, of course not so many of us are going to die and the second lieutenant a short paratrooper, dry, I never forgot his face afterward, next to the little poorly built bridge over the Cambo river with a leg extended in front and his body behind touching antipersonnel mines

*Chief, chief (in Kimbundu).

with the cautious tip of his boot, the second lieutenant of the paratroops
seated in the place of the psychologist

—Do you remember the Cambo river?

and don't worry my friend how I remember, the crocodile in the sun on
the riverbank that having barely seen us slid without haste into the water
and transformed into a drifting eye without a body, a half dozen white birds,
his platoon, my platoon, your uniforms better, your combat rations better,
your guns better, smaller, lighter, more accurate, tougher discipline, orders
barked out, I saw him lose a leg in a cloud of sand, I saw him so pale in the
tall grass while they wrapped a stump in compresses, the nurse, flustered,
was pulling tourniquets from his pack at the same time as the radio

—Send the chopper send the chopper

was calling the helicopter with shouts, the second lieutenant of the paratroops ordering

—I don't want any crying fits

from the almost transparent cigarette papers of his lips without a groan,
a complaint, not even

—When my grandfather finds out he'll kill himself

nor

—Hail Mary full of grace

only

—I don't want any crying fits

so that the personnel may protect the 'copter, so that a corporal may point
a gun at one of the guides

—You'll pay for him

so that the psychologist from the hospital to me

—What is wrong with my legs, friend?

while I was getting up from the circle of chairs without understanding

—You have two how strange what happened at the Cambo river?

where the crocodiles' eyes remain, I'm sure, drifting and no river in the
village, hoping that it would rain so that buckets might be dipped into the
wells, rising up pulling on ropes and neither my son nor my daughter inside,
only dirty mud, leaves, twigs, I'm not telling you, no, they're not worried
about me and blackbirds mocking me in the loquat trees, what is happening to them that they have so much contempt for me, my cousin distressed

—Do you not feel well?

and what a story is that of me not feeling well, I feel fine, at least I don't want your pity, understand, since you're already taking care of my father's grave don't be concerned that you have to take care of me when my anti-personnel mine comes for me and they end up coming every time don't they, a boom, dust, earth and I disappear my waist upside down, you won't have problems because the quartermaster will explain which coffin it is, and if there is another soldier in my casket he'll move him, over here there are thirty-nine or thirty-eight, I believe thirty-nine, I believe thirty-eight I don't remember well, I went away many years ago and continue to be away now, my cousin whose brother went to Guinea

—You're not getting out of the war are you?

and seeing that you're so clever teach me how you get out of the war, tell me, the only one who gets out was not there like the hospital psychologist, the only one who gets out was the one who didn't go, if they had shown me the door I would have been spotted, one day one of our boys opened a hole in the barbed wire, passed the sanzala and continued on in the direction of the jungle

—I'm going to China

he informed those who grabbed hold of him

—I'm going to China let go of me

and since a message was sent to battalion command, they put him in the small mail plane and they should have left him in a rice field because we didn't turn to look at him up above though something inside me continues to push me in the direction of China and nevertheless if my daughter said

—Father

I would turn, enough for her to say

—Father

so that I would turn and she never said

—Father

up to now she would say

—Sir

and fall silent, what happened between us, what did I do to you, daughter, where did I fail, tell me and I'll stop, point with your finger and I'll rub it off, my wife

—You blame yourself for it all

and that's not true, I'm not guilty of anything, I don't get the problems, seriously, I didn't bring my son from Africa because of his mother or his father

(I didn't bring my son from Africa because of his mother or his father)

and on the highway below no one, I didn't bring my son from Africa because of his mother or his father, I brought him I think because I felt alone, because, how stupid to say, my cousin

— Do you want to see the pig?

younger than me by ten years, when a child she had a lazy eye, her mother made a promise and passed it on to her, I don't want to see the pig now, I can warm to it, only on Sunday when they bring it, suspicious, sniffing, there are people who swear that pigs but let's not go there, there are people who swear that pigs are the same as us but I don't see how, they're tied up with their feet behind, they're tied up with their feet in front, they're hanging from a hook, they give us the knife, we find the artery and it starts without any radio nearby

— Send the chopper send the chopper

no security in the tall grass, it starts and the pig

— Hail Mary full of grace

not really screams, shudders, sighs

— When my grandfather finds out he'll kill himself when my grandfather finds out he'll kill himself

and the one who does not kill himself in the well, who does not kill his neighbor with a hoe, who does not kill his wife because of the priest, mine with that eyebrow I know so well

— What's up with you?

it so happens that I'm trying to expel myself from myself and I can't, I'm in the village and I'm not there, in my brain I walk without pause from one side to the other, I'm not able to stop, look at the crow in the poplars, I don't see the square from here nor the old folks with a cap nor the chief with them holding out empty tins to us

— Muata muata

hoping for scraps and there remain a few cabbages for soup, some potatoes, bones with a little bit of fat, my wife

— Do you want me to sit with you on top of that crate over there?

and I can imagine that I'm the pig, imagine for a moment that I'm the pig, perhaps they'll hang me on the hook but who will bring the knife and do me the favor of stabbing me in the throat, which soldier, resentful of me, my wife on the edge of the crate to give me room, what of the girl I met many years ago and with such a double chin, what of your energy, with the first kiss some months before shipping out you with open eyes, indeed with eyes always open, arranging your blouse

—And now?

with fear of your parents, with fear of yourself, so many centuries ago us not because I don't think about that, because I don't feel like it, because, I don't know, I think you didn't see that sometimes, before, that you really didn't see that sometimes, the tepid arm that still trembles, I swear, still trembles, the wedding ring, the ring of your mother, the little bracelet with a golden heart that I offered to you when our daughter was born, I like you, I don't know if I like you, let's proceed as if I liked you just don't make me talk given that when I talk I'm no longer silent and I don't know if I can stand it, my peculiar eyes, shadows of clouds, the cat that used to sleep with me in my child's bed not in the kitchen, on the battered cushion that it used to bring to my room and I smell the cushion with little stuffing and the sour food, my wife not lying on the ground, not without an ear, sneaking furtive glances at me

—You should think less

and now there we have a great truth, I was supposed to think less, especially since the hospital psychologist counsels me to close my head to the past but since the past hasn't really passed at all, it continues to happen, it hasn't changed, kilometers and kilometers of jungle each day with a weapon, tent sheet, and combat rations, careful to put my feet in the tracks preceding me, including here in the yard of the house in the village concerned to put my feet in the tracks that I left an hour or two before because who knows where the insurgents had left behind an antipersonnel mine or a trip wire, pull on the wire with your shin, the grenade jumps and fireworks at stomach level, the number of guts I've seen like that, after it's about washing them, putting them into a bucket, to clean them, to cook them, eat them and give the leftovers to the blacks that come up to the camp to hold out their tins, why the hell doesn't the hospital psychologist get up off his chair and slip away at a trot into the corridor or vomit right there in front of us, looking at us with humble hate like dogs at the end of the world, why the hell is he not missing a thigh or serving as a target to correct a crooked shot

—Do the triangulation first

my wife softly

—There are times when I feel sorry for you

and she won't leave me perhaps because she's old, because she's headed to sixty-six years old, because that's life, because of what she fertilized her grandiose plans with, for example, to be happy where one saw more ambition and from there her eyes open, distressed

—And now?

and now what horror you have to stay with me you've already seen the problem, a boy nineteen years old still not called by the army seeing that a cousin sergeant and thus with influence, promised

—I'll strike the youngster's name from the lists

and according to him, with his thumb and index finger apart by three millimeters, he didn't strike it just by a hair, your late father always with a checkered blanket over his knees and a tray with a deck of cards for patience that even with a bit of discreet cheating

(one queen, one jack)

he couldn't manage, almost without looking at me over his glasses, so timid

—You're not going to do anything bad to my princess are you?

while my mother-in-law born for miracles was working wonders with her small pension, that capacity of women to multiply more bread and fishes than the Gospel of the priests, and the gratitude she received from the Almighty was esophageal cancer, the mother nervous, only bones, pulling on her daughter's sleeve

—I can't swallow

so that the widowed father, still with a blanket but without a deck of cards, stared at us uncomprehendingly

(also what use is it to understand?)

—Why?

Relenting from staring at us, staring at us again

—Why?

and I don't know for what reason, sir, ask God it's possible he might answer, don't ask me I've nothing to do with that nor do I care in the slightest for celestial strategies, if I did I would win the lottery and buy her a new blanket, longer than that one, so that her slippers aren't seen where the feet peek out, this on a timid second floor which your souls didn't fit on and thus you and your parents barely little souls, equal to those seeds that enter by the window full of the lightest pollen and they float, they float, settle down a moment on the dresser, rise again and leave on a tranquil path, they don't realize they've pressed into our cheek a tear of melancholy so pure that it didn't hurt, your mother, disappeared so many years ago, here in the yard of the village just now

—Don't worry, sir

always as sir until the end, poor girl, always as sir, thankful but of what, gentle, she couldn't swallow and nevertheless found a way to console me that if necessary I'd even devour nails, I devoured the father of my son, I devoured the second lieutenant of the paratroops, devoured all the others, I'm going to devour the hospital psychologist and his circle of unfortunates, don't think even a moment that I won't eat you all, I'll eat you, I already ate two or three, I'll eat the rest after and not a tear of sadness, I swear, dry eyes, ferocious, my wife to me

—I don't like that light on your face

and what light girl if I remain the same only I'm trying to hide that tear so that you don't notice it, don't look at me to find it, don't touch me so that you don't notice my shaking ribs, don't put my sheets over me for as long as I don't destroy everything around me, the chief is missing, a scrap of myself is missing, the one that pleads with you

—Help me to forget

almost with praying hands, so small, so fragile, and falling asleep inside me where only thistles fit, things that sting, poison me, hurt, please call battalion headquarters via the radio

—Send the chopper send the chopper

so that the little seed of the helicopter may carry me above the trees of the jungle a long way from this village of old people, from this cellar, from this knife a few hours from now in the pig and in me at the same time, from this knife that curves in me, from this blood, it seemed to me that my daughter's car a rotten wreck on the highway and a band of pigeons above the trees of the cemetery with me thinking that if I could I would destroy her car and the pigeons too, my childhood more complicated especially with my mother pushing the side of my face into the pillow again

—What ghosts?

my mother

—Close those eyes

and with eyes closed I saw even better, a man with a Tyrolean cap

—I'm your cousin Afonso

a lady in mourning opening and closing the fan

—I don't believe you don't notice me I am Palmira son

and I recalled the fan with printed bullfighters, I didn't recall her, my mother pushing with her finger the only eyelid that I had seen, the other taken from me by the pillow

—What did I tell you?

she told me to shut my eyes but it's impossible now with my daughter about to arrive, my wife set up her bed in the old office where on a small shelf a dictionary survived that mold and humidity had fattened, I felt my daughter pushing the gate in front and contrary to what I thought I didn't get up, my wife got up for both of us

—You won't greet the girl?

and if I had my father's cane within reach I would scratch the ground with parallel lines, would erase them with my shoe and keep scratching until she from the kitchen

—Good afternoon

without appearing in front of me, I swear, not a kiss, not a grimace, not a nod just for show, I knew she was talking but I couldn't make out the words, I understood my wife

—There's no reason to bring any food

my daughter whispering something brief like always, she doesn't care about us and so a familiar conversation repeated year after year, the food a small bag of cakes or two small pies or a half dozen loquats, whatever it was with a check inside and my wife pushing her to accept the money adding bills

—This is what was missing

my daughter pretending to be reluctant held them in her almost empty purse as she generally didn't weigh herself down with luggage, she wore the same clothing for all of Friday, Saturday, and Sunday like me in Angola always in the same camouflage, she with a hairbrush and toothpaste if that much, if she had turned up in Africa holding out a rusty tin from the other side of the camp wire it wouldn't surprise me a bit, had I not thrown in the trash the rags of my soldier's clothing I would have put them on now to come closer to her, on one occasion I saw similar eyes in a prisoner who held us all in contempt, the head of the political police brigade gave her a slap and she defied us, two slaps and she defied us more, a kick and she defied us from the ground, a shot in the leg and she continued to defy us, glaring at us always not from below but from above given that we more than buried, despicable, so that shots and shots from the head of the brigade

—Still not happy?

until he calmed down and I can't affirm that she submissive or defiant with us, unconcerned, distant, the head of the brigade to the prisoner

—You can leave now

and really it wasn't until today disguised as my daughter visiting me in the village, I bet that beyond the cakes, the pies, and the loquats a piece of manioc already old, with the same smell as the roots on the paths or the dried fish outside the bags or the Caricocos after the rain, my daughter who for years did not

—Father

never

—Father

my daughter

—Sir

since the blacks don't

—Mister

never

—Mister

the blacks

—Lutenan sir

and our lutenan without responding drawing parallel scratches without hearing anyone not even the

—Good afternoon

that sat down next to him while she erased the scratches, erased the scratches, undid the scratches very far from here, in the jungle ten thousand kilometers from Lisbon and thirteen thousand from Moscow, according to what some soldier from some company before us painted on a sign at the camp entrance, close to the place where the corn was rustling the entire night whispering my name in a voice I knew but was not able to determine whose it was, of cousin Afonso with the Tyrolean cap, of the lady with the fan, of my father ripping the cane from my hand bent over a toad with me

—Leave the animal in peace child

while the toad, I like the word batrachian, while the batrachian, paddling slowly with arthritic difficulty, was disappearing in the flowerbed stopping every two hops with its double chin swelling, no sign of my son yet, already close to night once the yellow sky above the slope and no kestrel gliding immobile wings leaning toward the left they assure that also brave rabbits, foxes, even genets, and I saw only bushes and stones, little flowers, yellow ones, big flowers, purple ones, in September, one morning a badger on a path looking at me, resembling my daughter who not even

—Hi

for show, ambling around with a child's gait in search of a bone buried somewhere she didn't remember, perhaps in her childhood, perhaps in my arms and me explaining the trees to her until she began to stick out her legs and push me away already not liking me, what did I do to you tell me, why have we not cleared up things between us once and for all and my daughter silent or then

—You did nothing to me you with such a mania

and it's there that she gets to the point, as soon as I direct the word to her the word instantly appears

—You

instantly appears the

—Sir

you don't give me

—Father

like your brother, what am I for you, what is the reason that you hate me and my daughter in a mocking tone, passing her fingers through her hair arranging it, she liked to be ugly or ugliness a way to accuse me

—It's your fault that I'm ugly didn't you know?

my daughter who if she were not the daughter of my wife that she is I'm sure she would not be here with her brother

—If you feel like continuing the conversation continue it alone and I'll return to Lisbon do you think I like being with you?

and you don't like being with me why, I never forced you no matter what, I never annoyed you, I never demanded anything of you, you wanted to drop your studies and you dropped them, you wanted to leave and you left, I never gave you orders, I never reproached you, I never intruded in your life, I always accepted, you'd go out dressed like a scarecrow and me silent, you didn't visit us for two or three months in a row and not a peep from me you noticed already, not a peep, if you feel like greeting me

—Good afternoon

I'll respond instantly

—Good afternoon

if you feel like it don't pay attention to me I'll pretend that I don't see and I don't see you not your clothes just thrown together, your shoes almost like a man's, laces undone, your odor of insomnia because you certainly don't sleep well daughter, what do you think about at night in the hole in which you live and this not to offend you but I bet my privates that you live in a really tiny apartment, really far from Lisbon, you live in a hole between Pakistanis in slippers and Ukrainians who work construction, what company don't you think, not one tap works how wonderful don't you think, how nice to be wretched don't you think, the bitch is that I still worry about you, I give you my word that I'd love not to worry and what can I do, it's more powerful than me, I worry, how good it would be not to worry about you, I sleep badly too, all of Portugal sleeping and both of us awake with our eyes on the ceiling that doesn't exist, we exist in a large empty space, you thinking I don't know what about and me thinking about you, what foolishness on my part don't you think, what stupidity, what a mistake but I can't stop thinking about you, perhaps I love you, look, I must be foolish, must no, I am really foolish, but I love you, I don't believe in what I'm about to say but I love you and that's enough drivel, forget my ramblings, I don't feel anything, it doesn't matter a damn except for the second lieutenant of the paratroops, except for cousin Afonso, except for Moscow thirteen thousand kilometers away, except me still in Africa, and it doesn't matter a damn for me except for you, the only thing that does matter is you, the only thing that will always matter is you and so if you feel like addressing me as

—Sir

address me you change nothing in me, I'll continue to be the same, sweet daughter, your father, your friend, your, your refuge if you want it, as you want it, when you want it, if you really feel like escaping from me and returning to Lisbon return I forgive, I understand, I accept, forget the pig killing and return to Lisbon in your rotten wreck I don't understand how it doesn't collapse on the first hill, return to Lisbon since you remain here.

4

From the apartment to the village one hour and fifteen minutes, one
hour and twenty in a car if there are no annoyances on the way, accidents,
construction, a broken-down truck, police with white caps and a yellow vest
ordering us to park on the shoulder for documents and the alcohol test
—Breathe
leaning over my window glancing, the service also has benefits, not all
is sad in this world, the thighs of Her Excellency improved by a short skirt
and I wanting to expose them my wife in the morning in her ragged dressing gown, hastily thrown together, and still without contact lenses, bumping
into the table, bumping into the stove, creasing her eyebrows one independent of the other while turning on the gas to warm the barley with a match
shivering in her fingers not to mention traces of makeup from the night
before that the cotton forgot and crystallized on her face, me to the police
—Enjoy
and the police no enjoyment at all, only
—You may continue friend
in a tone more of pity than command, hopeful that the first curve might
swallow us up, what a difference in fact between reality and desire, one hour
and fifteen, one hour and twenty give or take a bit, adding to it the time
that Her Excellency took still and me at the door to the main room, with
fifteen kilos of clothing for two days, in a rundown village, weighing down
my left hand making my shoulders asymmetrical and in the right the keys
with the little stuffed bear on the ring, almost life size, while she lifting up
the magazine
—Just a minute I'm finishing an article here
or rather the divorce of a soap opera star or the personal adds or natural
products in a capsule that improve erections by forty percent or the week's
horoscope divided into three parts, health, work, and love as the suitcase,
heavier and heavier, brought the said left shoulder closer to my knees, Her

Excellency got up finally with the jaunty lift of a cork that a stainless steel instrument was pulling until the liberating

—Pop

after abandoning the divorce on the low table in front, with a glass top and a small box desirous of being porcelain on top, accompanied by a photograph of her in Salamanca with two friends, each with a seductive flower in her hair, laughing for me or for the man

(for the man I bet a thousand to one)

whom they asked to take the picture in a language of circus clowns full of instructions, affected gestures and grimaces, the three only banalities and straps, Her Excellency already standing

—Are you sure you turned off the gas?

with eyes on me not liquid, inquisitorial so that to be safe I checked the gas and now the windows, I pulled down the shades including those in the main room and stopped seeing, I saw a cube of darkness with us inside, moving really slowly, feeling about, I hurt my knee on a chest of drawers, slipped on my shoes in a thread of lamplight, tripped on the edge of the carpet victim of the habitual conspiracy of objects that I never imagined hated me so much, vengeful God knows why and the shouts of soldiers around me outside and the smell of diesel fuel in the African village

—Burn burn

at the same time as Her Excellency to me

—Until you've dug all this up you're not going to rest right?

chickens hopping about, one of the cabíris* barking, voices, blows, steps, a motor I don't know where started and stopped and started again

—No one gets away burn, no one gets away

shadows, smoke, a goat that had fallen on its knees getting up, a light suddenly illuminating Her Excellency only with a rag from the Congo around her waist, barefoot, her feet black like mine, another woman coughing, I turned the key to the apartment and she

—You take centuries to do anything, dammit

she went out in front of me of course, a lady, without anyone disappearing, merely an old woman watching us from a squatting position on the neighbor's doormat, despite being on the second floor and there being only three in the building the elevator needs the same centuries as me, coming

*Domesticated dog.

from a mysterious, most distant place, stopping exhausted, groaning on the cables just like a man without hands, with arms together in an attitude of prayer, just as the woman groaned, on her knees as well, who was with me in the African village, just as guys in green

—Burn burn

—No one gets away burn no one gets away

still night, above the flames, the shots, and above night and the intact treetops silence, not a transparent silence, a dull silence, still, without wind or people running, slipping, turning to run and slipping again only elbows and knees, only belly, only hips, only teeth swallowing the earth, only an eye fixed on no one, an eye concentrated on itself, only no eye finally and at the entrance to the building the three steps with pots all over, my father moving away from the flames and the shots with his hand on the back of my neck, neck neck neck

—This one belongs to me, don't you touch him

to Her Excellency who as always confused the button of the lock with the light button though the button on the lock announced Lock and the button on the light Light this is a pair of wall lights with weak lamps because we're not very rich in the neighborhood, Her Excellency as always

—Dammit

pressing on the other button with hate and the door turning three centimeters poor thing in fear of pain, things are so sensitive, baptism medallions, table mats, sheets, shoe horns, children's books, with pity for us

—Don't break your nail let me look at that

and we vanishing in our shoes forgetting about them, I escorted Her Excellency, a step back and to the left, with the little wheels of the suitcase jumping on my ankles, struggling with a tendency to veer left, squeaky, wanting to escape into the gutter with Her Excellency already leaning against the car waiting for me

—Wasn't it you who was in a rush darky?

and me beginning to have doubts about the abortion, she didn't complain about the pain, moving with the same lightness as always and that harmony between shoulder blades and buttocks that aroused me once and now I don't know, I think that it continues to arouse me but I pretend not to notice, sometimes in bed it's difficult, if I touch her, even with the little finger, her arm driving me away

—Can't one get any sleep anymore?

in such a way that I turn out the light and the flames appear, the shots, the cabíris that were barking until they shoved a stick in their throats, a stun grenade explodes in five seconds, perhaps the nursing station not a nursing station, one of these days I'll make a discreet short phone call to the police, a nonauthorized spot where couples meet, who is he don't lie, who is he without asking and Her Excellency answering me

—Wasn't it you who was in a rush darky?

with what seemed to be a black bruise between her neck and her breasts but it could be the shadow of a leaf or she may have scratched herself too much, so many possibilities my God, what confusion life, I put the suitcase in the trunk and a twinge in my back that began to bother me, a type of bent crochet needle shoved into my spine, it only remained for me to be old, my father assures me that I forty years old but I don't know how many I'll be when he pushing away the men in green

—Don't touch him

and one of the men in green

—Think about what you're messing with look sooner or later he'll take revenge on you second lieutenant sir

minuscule hens, minuscule goats, a manioc field, two or three people barefoot, unacquainted with rifles, this at sundown, used to come from time to time looking for, that is, the women took the hens and goats up to the edge of the jungle, what I remember one moment disoriented another clear another clear before falling asleep and disoriented upon waking up, my father at the entrance to my room without turning on the light, if he turned it on so many dismembered people on the ground, so many animals that some kind of crows were pecking

—Aren't you calm, boy?

and I am calm sir wait just a bit I'll close my eyes I promise, I want to lean toward the woman and toward the man without hands without feeling anything and I don't know if I should feel, what happened to them, Her Excellency despising me

—Blacks have no soul

already seated in the car with her exposed thighs, looking ahead without paying attention to me, night coming soon, the trees dressed in a different way, another wind in the branches, lights swelling, bats instead of birds because angular flights, a kind of fan with rabbit ears and a rat's face, upon arriving in the village my mother warming up the dinner again

—No problem no problem

taking the smock off the hook next to the dishcloths, my father's cousin to Her Excellency

—prettier and prettier

my father's cousin to me

—Have you gotten fat?

and my sister hating herself on a rock in the yard, I recall her birth, I don't recall her crying, at no time in her life do I recall her crying, when she began to look at us she hated us too except on one occasion when she was searching for me at work me, the janitor

—There is a woman waiting for you over there who didn't want to say her name

and my sister looking at me without a smile at the entrance to the main room, dressed haphazardly and with a very badly arranged bun, looking up because she couldn't be bothered, small and those fingers so ugly

—I only wanted to see you bye

with I don't know what bursting in her eyes that she held back forcefully and she didn't return to visit me so that I wouldn't figure it out, I hardly ever met up with her and if I happened to ask my father his mouth trembled, he nodded to me not to look at her in the window swallowing words I'm not guessing what they might have been, if he happened to have them on a plate he'd cut them up into pieces with the same languid knife with which he cut off the ears to give them to the men in green, imitating the movements of the chaplain with the communion wafer

—Do this in remembrance of Me

but he didn't die in Africa or he died in Africa, I'm not really sure, he would get up at dawn and stand in the corridor between his room and mine while the house was burning without his having given the command

—Burn burn

swelling in his pajamas, mute, my mother took him by the sleeve

—Move

in order to push him back into his room when he tried to grab me and my father from hut to hut, only stakes remained, in the direction of the pillow, stakes, the final flames that were disappearing into the earth, ashes, dead animals, utensils, a few stubborn feathers, straw strewn about, empty jerry cans, what appeared to be bodies without ears, what appeared to be the corpses of trees and the river of lepers down below with the nurses' bell ringing in the wind for the sick deprived of limbs, noses, mouths, crawling in the mud and we're not seeing from the car because all still in Lisbon, looking at the lights of the ships in the Tagus under the last purple clouds that precede dusk, if only my mother were to speak with me and help me understand her, the impression that, between us, I may be wrong but the impression that between us a dialogue whose phrases we would lose in pronouncing them because the ears that they cut off from us were swallowing and then hiding them inside me so that I can't reach, on the roadway northward an illuminated service station, people's silhouettes, cars, in a few seconds my mother

—Son

with a painted smile on her serious face and still not a smile, guessing what was going to happen and I didn't know whatever it was, I bet that my father waiting for us at the wall of the yard trying to distinguish us from above, raising his hand and suspending it because not our people, a small cattle truck full of calves, a tractor, the almost dead village with so many abandoned houses and so many streets eaten up at random by tall grass that only old people older than age inhabit, with freckles on their wrists and on the bald spot and legs that try to impede movement, Her Excellency to me

—Don't count on me for the coming year

and in fact I won't count on you since in the coming year you've already left me for sure and when leaving a guy in the street waiting for you who will enter our place, without ceremony, if you linger, not a black like me, a white who commands me

—Quiet

not referring to me, evidently, as mister but as you

—Don't get near her

and Her Excellency next to him

—Did you hear?

from time to time a detour on the highway, warehouses, buildings that were barely distinguishable from night or were born bit by bit from it, like sunrooms with drying laundry in gentle good-byes, the soldiers, no longer men in green, soldiers, to my father

—He'll take revenge

who poured out jerry cans on the huts, fired, ran, pulled the bolts and seconds afterward, five seconds afterward, the mud and straw and the grass and the mats and the mortars rising up weightlessly into the air, to the right of the car the Tagus where the antelope came to drink, I have the idea of antelope, of a woman lifting me up from the ground because of a type of log with feet and scales that was crawling slowly over scraps of garbage, on the other bank more lights, factory chimneys dissolving into the dark, a large airplane, with lights on its wings that was coming lower, coming lower, Her Excellency appearing to me as having fallen asleep and thus not concerned with the crocodile approaching us

—Is there much left?

and rain, rain in Angola, not here and despite everything I slowed down because I don't like to drive on wet asphalt, I hope my sister in the village as well and my father dressed as a janitor, leaning toward me

—A lady is waiting for you who did not say who she was

she, five or six years old, asking me to pick her up

—I'm afraid

interrupting herself suddenly to ask

—Why are you black?

and to my mind she continues to be fearful, hiding herself from people, she visits no one, she doesn't speak, she sits alone in a corner, appears and disappears without a sound, it amazes me that she doesn't jump from the window like cats or hide on a high branch of the Judas Tree in the yard observing us thinking that we know nothing of her and don't see her, I didn't answer Her Excellency because two consecutive curves and trees with a strip of lime painted on their trunks were threatening me, a short way from here we leave the river behind and the farms begin, forgotten little towns, bicycles pedaling on the shoulder, last year the gypsies' mule next to a kilometer marker, with each hoof going its own way and its mouth wide open

—Kill kill

I bet covered with flies and ants if I came closer to it, Her Excellency shook her arm and the perfume brushed against me, how much you spend per week on those gold-plated bottles that is how much I spend per week seeing that you haven't worked since the company closed and the miserable unemployment benefits are not supposed to give anything for magazines from the kiosks two streets above ours, always with fine ladies confessing to the owner with the false hair due to a treatment of the ovaries, it's me who pays so you can make yourself desirable to other men with me armed like a fool at the window of the café while you in a brothel disguised as a nursing station because life gets difficult, look at that circle of blacks squatting smoking the same pipe and grilling crickets on a thin stick, I had no idea

why in my memory this is funny, what we stock in the cellar without noticing, crickets, varnished, moving their legs, my father never my name, always

—Son

despite arranging one for me with his surname, upon giving me the card

—You'll have the same name as my father

and me learning Portuguese, it's true the crickets, I don't want to forget
them, and lose the Luchaze language, some words continue

—Mona*

to wander alone, without weight, in a hiding place in my head speaking
to themselves, they invented a date of birth for me, a month, a day

—In my opinion he has a March face

they hesitated between March and end of May

—He resembles March more look at his profile

and March then, March, I was born in March in Lisbon and of my parents, not of blacks, what are blacks without ears good for anyway, stretched
out in the yard, which soldier put them in a bottle of alcohol, no longer
dark, white, only now almost transparent cartilage, the rest was being eaten
by animals, plus the defoliant the T-6s† released on the ploughed fields and
everything around dry, only the hyenas and the birds with curved beaks that
devoured among themselves anything they wanted, the tiny red gasoline
light of the car began to flash and the jaw of Her Excellency leaning into
her chest letting the back of her neck show, smooth, supple, that exited me
suddenly what hadn't happened to me for months with any province of her
body, a little voice in me content

—Hi neck

and my fingers leaving the steering wheel, to linger on the back of her
seat, playing piano on the headrest, sliding down slowly to the collar of her
dress, suspended next to the nape of her neck, moving in the air, guessing
at the tendons and the beginning of the spine and when they were about

—Burn kill burn

to reach them, to squeeze her, burn her, kill her, Her Excellency instantly
awake, sitting up straight

—Don't you dare touch me black

*Child.
†North American T-6 Texan, a light propeller plane.

with me realizing that the little gasoline light not a tiny red point on the dash, enormous, flashing and disappearing, flashing and disappearing, my fingers

—Don't you dare black

again on the steering wheel, submissive, innocent, useless, realizing that only whites can burn, kill, cut off ears and our destiny fits us, to be burned, killed, mutilated, and still for what reason another identity, another land, other parents if I don't leave Africa, remain in Africa, die in Africa raising my stumps up toward the whites

—Chindele*

while I fall gentlemen though I try to get up, while I keep silent though I try to speak, while I die though I try to live, I

—Chindele

and Her Excellency

(beyond the neck such thighs in and outside the short skirt, the harmony between the buttocks and the hips, the well-defined waist, the corollas of her breasts, the stalk of her throat so easy to, the mouth that I would like to push down to my fly while your long nails undo my buttons, your lips, your tongue, your care with your teeth, and shoulders that vibrate, a back that vibrates, the other hand in you and me happy in the car, me with eyes closed and still driving)

—What is that?

and Her Excellency

—Stop right now with your dirtiness black

at the same time as one of the elders is offering me a grilled cricket, extending a vessel with marufo,† responding to me

—Euá

to me who appears and disappears like the tiny red light not of gasoline, of the final remains of the hut, burning, it haunts me, soon the village, soon the house and despite the night my father next to the wall of the yard observing us trying to identify people by the outline of the car, by the exhaust fumes, by the headlights, now that he thinks that he likes me which of my

---

*Term referring to white flour (from corn or manioc or other plants), also used to refer to whites (in Kimbundu).

†Alcoholic beverage made from palm trees.

ears does he prefer for his bottle where it will become, it's a question of months, cartilage, that my sister has to search for in some chest of drawers opening it and then closing it

—I only wanted to see you bye

and vanishing from me, sister, sister, and then the first wagon on the highway appeared announcing

—You're near

with a dog lifting his snout and tail raised sauntering among the wheels, after the wagon two bicycles and my father's voice

—Don't pass them so that you give them space to fall

back when he hadn't yet given up explaining the world to me, now and again calling me at work

—Don't worry that's nothing I feel like wishing you a good day I must be getting old bye-bye

this more or less at the time, ten months ago, a year at most, when my mother began to complain of tightening in her kidneys before that she never complained, she suddenly stopped slapping her hand with force on her back, if we asked she would smile, that is she would pull the corners of her lips up

—A little discomfort without importance it's passed already

and it was clear from the stretched skin on her temples that it wasn't passing, if none of us close she serious, transported back to herself with the care of one who carries a full glass of water on a tray, it would hurt her to go up the stairs, to go down the stairs, to get up, struggling so as not to need support, with eyeglasses breathing quickly, after the appointment in the clinic the doctor called my father away

—A problem in the right kidney the disease has already spread

my mother to my father

—The doctor confided what to you?

my father too quickly

—They are stones

my wife still more rapidly

—It really seemed so

and she never returned to the issue, what for, in the final account only stones, what do stones have, what harm do the stones do, look what story more funny, stones, almost gives me the desire to laugh to say that they are stones, let's not speak anymore about stones, what a relief, it's done, they operated on her in September and my mother full of tubes and cannulas in a completely white room minus the chocolates, which she did not touch, on the bedside table, my father

—They didn't succeed in fishing out all of them you have to continue the treatment that dissolves them

my mother whiter than the room, weak, taking hold of my father's fist with pity for him

—Yes of course

pity for my father, for my sister who had not visited her, for me

—forgive me for making you sad

she looked at the tree beyond the window and that was all or almost all, my father was missing not stroking her palm with his finger and pulling the phrase out of a hat

—Who becomes sad with stones?

my mother in a whisper she thought funny, poor thing

—Sometimes it's the stones that become sad with us

so that they are both at the house in the village waiting for us, my mother for the time being didn't get that thin but she remains white, from time to time a transfusion or saline because some person recognizes that the stones are hard, nor is it necessary to waste spit on the issue, they are hard mother that's true, they are hard, what can we do with their hardness, how do we manage to put up with it and yet my mother in the village waiting for us along with my father, as white as in the room all white less the chocolates that she doesn't touch, on the bedside table, with eyeglasses breathing more and more quickly while my father pretended not to notice and he pretended badly the poor guy, it was clear from the flutter on his forehead, the flutter of his jaw, in his phrases from time to time, poor father, broken, my mother understood too and nonetheless in silence, distant, so distant, distant is unfair and will be unfair, the little gasoline light stopped flashing and became continuous, wide open from fear, Her Excellency finally noticing the light

—What is this?

somewhere between apprehension and fear as if she had discovered one of those stinging insects or a lipstick stain on my collar, me to Her Excellency

—Do you know any gas station around here before the car stops?

and how was she going to know if she never drives, she sits in the passenger seat contributing with her short dress and thighs that are at least among the things she takes care of, to give color to the trip and that's it, how many cars have you been in, don't lie, who did you meet at the midwife's, around us only fields and plane trees in the darkness of the new moon, how many kilometers are left to get there, three, five, seven, eight, an isolated house very far away, no, a warehouse, no, a barn, I'm sure calves over there, dogs barking, perhaps a gypsy encampment, we are swaying on a railroad crossing without a signal with ties missing and where Her Excellency, almost with the top of her head on the roof

—Are you nuts?

She who in general

—Are you nuts or what?

Now only

—Are you nuts?

observing me slyly as if she were afraid of me and the possibility that she was afraid of me was not unpleasant, it was of the sort that at night, in bed, if I ordered her

—Come here

she would come with no fuss, the bad thing was not to have put a tight bridle on her from the beginning a woman left to her own devices sooner or later takes liberties that is their tendency, a tight bridle and muzzle and though the bridle for horses, mules, donkeys, and even the reindeer on Santa Claus paperweights that we turn upside down and return to their standing position and witness spirals after spirals of straw pretending to be snow, though, I used to say, the tight bridle for horses

(let's abbreviate omitting the other animals)

and the muzzle for the dogs I'm certain that they understand where I want to go, the problem is that late now because Her Excellency took the bit in her teeth and there is no one stopping her anymore, I swear, it's that there is no one stopping her anymore and there we have an example of a thing to teach to our sons before it becomes useless knowledge as it is in my sad case, meditate on it, the disgrace of a man whose wife walks all over him, poor fellow, finally, we were driving on the railroad crossing without a signal I think, no, already on the other side of the railroad crossing with a signal and I began

(I have these instincts, I'm black, we don't reflect, we intuit, I got away with it by the skin of my teeth imitating a guy who would assure me that I'm not looking, I'm finding)

to notice the smell of the house in the village beyond the smell of my parents and my sister

(there has to exist some advantage in being black and it's not necessary to expand on this you all see the thing)

this on the side opposite the railroad crossing that didn't recommend Stop Listen Look, I suggest that we proceed all of us with this noble advice in the pocket that will save us from annoyance without end, not only the smells of the house and of my family, that of the cherry tree in the yard, that of the little garden, that, less pleasant, of the closed compartments growing moldy all year long not to speak of the wasps and mummified beetles on the floor that if by chance we walk barefoot get squashed by us in a horrible yellow and sticky vengeance, against the heels of our feet, curious that only upon thinking of the house and my parents a melancholy comes to me a type of flush not to mention the fear that my mother etc. but let's not think about that now, perhaps the heart of Heaven will soften and anyway, dammit, the stones that want to kill her, are going to kill her, are killing her, I don't want more stumps pleading noi ears in bottles nor

—Burn burn

nor

—Kill

not chicken feathers here and there like the gusts of flames, not decapitated cabíris, without paws, not my mother

—Yes of course

smiling, don't be good, don't have pity on us, hate us that we will continue to live, insult us, throw us out

—They disappeared from my sight

cry, try to rip the sheets, refuse food, the car motor stopped working trying to call to itself, exhausted, from the depths of the gasoline it had, me holding her hands

—Mother

or a kind of

—Mother

who was devouring herself, no, I

—This is the only thing missing

when many more things were missing, whistling with two fingers in my mouth for example, throwing peanuts up high and catching them with my tongue, making smoke rings, some inside the others, the car was slowing down, slowing down, I heard somewhere to the left a cow lowing, the plane trees were whispering like the eucalyptuses of Angola before an attack, my mother testing, out of love of elegance, if the false teeth were holding on her gums and the cheeks not concave, straight, the car, swinging the double of a gondola, with Her Excellency more and more nervous

—If you were white, perhaps you'd save me

finally stopping on the shoulder, near the corpse of a cat and Her Excellency in a defeated whisper, frightened by presences as light as the rustling of leaves, insects that entered by the windows in twisted circles, the threat of darkness after I turned off the lights because the battery was not that good

—My God

and besides the car not new, of course, the money doesn't stretch for everything, you wanted clothes, you wanted shoes, you wanted the beauty parlor, you wanted fancy things to cover your shoulders, with my salary, I had to leave your feet uncovered or vice versa money isn't elastic and robbing old ladies in the subway in the meantime, well, that's not my way, a big bird

(an owl?)

almost crashed into the hood hooting, not the squeaks of sparrows, rough threatening sounds, the bushes ferocious, the darkness scowling, what would my mother feel, poor thing, waking up at night thinking

—I'm going to die

my father sleeping next to her and she, so alone, looking at an infinite ravine right next to the mattress and saying to herself

—I'm going to fall I'm going to fall

with the air around her fleeing the lungs, my grandmother rattling out good-bye as she was falling, the house so high up over there which she could not return to, a relative lost centuries ago to a gentleman with a moustache entertaining himself by burnishing a callus

—Isn't it pathetic?

and it was really pathetic, it was so pathetic, Her Excellency and me inside the car, still, perplexed, and I don't know how many kilometers from the village, one, four, nine, you count for us, if my father were there he would rise out of the flames, the explosions, the mutilated bodies, from the depth of horror taking hold of my elbow preventing the men in green from hurting me

—This one is mine

preventing them from throwing me onto the ground, from crushing my ribs, from cutting my ear off, from putting me in a bottle of alcohol with eyes open, crying, a man in green to him pointing me out with a rifle

—Sooner or later the black will take vengeance on you

while the last embers, around us, went out one by one and the last huts ashes, the last hemp plants ashes, the last cabíri groaning, the last goat dead, Her Excellency

—And now?

for the first time in years seeking out my hand, taking me by the hand, taking it in hers, for the first time in years looking at me without rancor, without hate, without any contempt so that I, in the middle of the night, at the same time close and far from the village, close and far from my parents, close and far from the violence and the shouts, so that I for the first time in years and for the first time inside the car inclined the seat back, pulled her dress up, became a unicorn, and announced into her mouth

—Love

chest against chest

—Love

stomach against stomach

—Love

teeth against teeth

—Love

while the large butterflies of May, with terrible antennae, fat, repugnant, were turning around us, while no wind in the grass, willows I think but I may be mistaken, plane trees, mimosas, elm trees, poplar, dammit all, it doesn't matter, Her Excellency and me chest against chest, stomach against stomach, teeth against teeth at the same time that an owl, at the same time as bats in the direction of an apple tree, at the same time that the first lightning flash far away, still on the frontier with Zambia, approached us jumping over the Tagus, at the same time that the kidney stones were getting larger, at the same time that my mother smiled, at the same time that my sister with her finger pointing in my direction

—You

accusing me I don't know of what crime perhaps for having said to her that if our mother wished, teeth against teeth, I would help her to die and she furious with me

—You

because her mother was not dying and mine already dead, only an ear, only stumps instead of hands, only gasoline spilled on top

—Burn burn

Only rags, not stones, only scraps of cloth, not blood, scraps of bones, not meat, when Her Excellency and I finished I ordered her

—Clean yourself up

cleaning myself up too, I adjusted my shirt, adjusted my belt, adjusted my jacket and she adjusted her hair with her fingers without calling me

—Black

silent, Her Excellency silent, Her Excellency where is it that you just appeared, silent and so I went to fetch the suitcase in the trunk, I ordered her

—Let's go my father is waiting

and we started to walk ahead on the highway.

5

Of course my son's lateness worried me a lot more than he knew for my having told him what happened forty-five years ago besides being perhaps the last pig killing his mother attends, the doctor wants to put her into the hospital when we return from the village in order to try out a new treatment on her that can or cannot give results and the most natural is that it won't these things with the kidneys always bring problems, his words, but at least the remorse for not having tried won't remain with us, I spoke about this with my wife at the dinner table without her touching a thing, not the soup, not the fish, I cut half a banana into slices for her, took her fork, put a slice into her mouth and my wife passing it from one cheek to another without chewing while me pretending that I was chewing too

—The doctor spoke about a Japanese medicine that swallows pebbles even more small stones

and she looking at me for a long time in silence, moved by me

—I didn't want to be in your place sorry thanks for pretending

putting her hand on me thinking that wrapped in a smile and me a smile equal to hers, where is it that such sad happiness just appeared funny how there exist a thousand kinds of tears so that next week, whatever the concern, the Japanese medicine beginning its work and she gaining force, animation and color most of all, beginning to get interested in her house again, watching the television news

—What's going on in the world my God

and me just agreeing without looking, what's going on in the world in fact, jealousywarpoverty, a room in the clinic once again where the only thing not white were the chocolates that I bought seeing that they did not permit flowers, not one of us ate them and they went on piling up, chocolate bars, candies, those umbrellas from when we were small with little plastic walking sticks, I understood that my wife pain because eyes closed, not one fold on the face, only the eyes closed and the eyelids different from sleeping eyelids, it was clear that she seeing me without needing to look because at the end of so much time together we don't need looks, even from behind we know just as we know that this house in the village from the weekend forward always empty, I don't believe that my son or my daughter will return here, dust, the insects and the tiles remain departing one by one like my hair leaves me lifted up by the comb of the wind, our bones will always stay growing like those of skeletons in museums and those of mules, note the hips of the house and its shoulders now enormous, the jaws that increase, monstrous, ferocious, the garden where vegetables rot, expanding, the solitude of the tree next to the wall, perhaps a buried person that was blooming slowly growing branches, of course my son's lateness worried me as forty-five years ago the lateness of my brother worried my father, I don't resemble him, I resemble his mother always sitting on a bench, in a long skirt, closing a secret candy in my fist

—Don't say anything boy it's our secret only

and it continues to be our secret only because I said nothing to anyone, so many years after you died I continue in silence, I didn't let it out to my wife you see, we have a secret though I cultivate it alone, I remember his moustache and his left eye

(left eye?)

the dull left eye, not dark not light, a fog

—What do you see, ma'am?

and she inside a black sheet, with a rosary in her hands

—I see you tormenting hens, child

going over the beads in whispered prayers, my father on the wall looking at the highway, always lighting the already lit cigarette with bad matches that broke on the sandpaper, entering and leaving the house with the haste of a cuckoo humility and all, it remained only to sing the hours, my stepmother

—Do you want to make me crazy too?

this forty-five, forty-six years ago, several months before graduating as a second lieutenant and embarking for Angola in a ship full of silence and cries or rather the silence shouts and the shouts silent, who can translate this into ordinary language, me tied to the washbasin in the cabin, new braids, vomiting, if only a candy from my grandmother in the luggage or chickens handy to prod with a cane and they stumbling one over another fleeing me, my father at the wall with two cigarettes lit, three cigarettes lit, ten cigarettes lit, there is whoever works in the circus with a dozen balls in the air, on the dock military marches together with rain, the general on a balcony moving his silent mouth, there were loudspeakers that stole his voice mixing it with the anguish of seagulls, I see on your faces the joy of going to serve the Fatherland and me serving the Fatherland soaking my shirt with tears, my jacket, my tie, a phantom drooling poor fellow who I thought was me, my stepmother to me pointing at my father

—See if you calm him down before he gets an aneurism

and so much rain in the Tagus in January my friends, so much rain in January with me not thinking about my father, thinking about the pig killing, the knife, the bucket of blood, the guys who I didn't know, in pants now stained red, hanging the animal better so that I got closer to my father at the same time as a pair of headlights on the highway below were turning into the country road that led to the village and my father relieved, happy, applying a slap to me that altered the order of the innards

—Your brother will get a scolding for his lateness that will leave him walking sideways

walking triumphantly toward the entrance gate, going through the house to turn on all the lights that were not many, even the burned-out ones, I swear, ordering on the way to my stepmother who was warming the soup

—The soup quick now that guy has deigned to arrive

reaching the door on the street at the same time as a jeep from where two policemen were getting out neither authoritarian nor rapid, bent, slow, who he knew for sure because he knew everybody, so sociable, as popular in the village as in his neighborhood in Lisbon, full of slaps on the back and pinches on the stomach, full of

—Hey asshole

friendly even when he was speaking with the priest

—I'll get you a girlfriend get ready

me who didn't have girlfriends in Africa nor used any, lutenan sir, lutenan sir, black women, as if it could be the voice of my mother who died of diphtheria when I was three years old, I remember a voice

—Are you asleep?

and the smell of stew emanating from a person lying in my bed with me, I remember a spoon that was coming closer, immense, to me and it hit my teeth with a metallic sound

—Open your mouth eat

I imagine a dress moving away, an immense world around me, chairs, tables, high knobs that I couldn't reach and that's it, I don't remember crying

—Mother

and suddenly my stepmother whose spoon didn't hit my teeth because she put sugar in everything though she always smelled of stew but less, my father strange, to the policemen

—Did something happen to my son?

without them answering him, quiet, one short and fat, the second with brown hair and both with their caps in their hands, he couldn't make out their features but it seemed the brown-haired one of those guys with only one eyebrow, this and whose hair does not stop at the top of the nose, if I were one of such a group, I'd get a razor so as not to look like, kill kill, a barn owl or a screech owl, there was a little shaving of the moon on the side of the pine forest and a thousand murmurings of night were audible, made by the grass, crickets, and other little children of the dark not to mention the leaves of course shivering even without the wind and my father in a murmur

—Kill kill

more and more pale

—Did something happen to my son?

the policeman with two eyebrows, short and fat but at least normal, flung his cap toward the seat of the jeep and did not miss what luck

—Did something happen to my son?

so that encouraged by the success with the cap

—I think that it would be better to speak inside

beyond the grass, the crickets, the other things and the leaves, bats but where are there no bats, sometimes we find them dead, with their wings open and rabbit snout, covered with ants, the African ones not black like ours, much bigger, brown, if by chance they bite we'll need the rest of the day to itch ourselves well beyond leaving blemishes, my father to the policeman, now moving his hand back on the way to his forehead in a kind of dizziness

—Did something happen to my son?

and military marches and handkerchiefs that were shouting and rain and people in tears up to the water's edge and dozens of seagulls perched in line on the high rooftops, dozens, hundreds, thousands, millions, millions of seagulls on the high rooftops, more seagulls than army, more seagulls than people, repeating along with the general

— I see on your faces the joy of going to serve the Fatherland

the seagulls around the ship that was getting smaller on the way to the river mouth

— I see on your faces

and the rain getting lighter little by little, when it stopped the joy of serving the Fatherland stopped as well, I was left on the bunk in the cabin where everything was fastened to the wall, bed, bedside table, wardrobe, pity they didn't fasten me to myself and in the window, round like the dreams that I never had in pentagonal form, the rain, me sitting on the bunk twisting my wrists my father coming into the living room with the policemen

— Did something happen to my son?

the three standing between the chest of drawers and the sofa with my stepmother and me looking at them, the one with two eyebrows his thumbs in his belt swallowing, swallowing and the other with one eyebrow scratching his neck until the one with two eyebrows let one of his thumbs loose staring not at my father but at something beyond my father that seemed to interest him, I turned and the wall only with a crack, not even a picture, next to the hole made by a nail, the urge to question what is fascinating in the hole made by a nail even more so without a nail, the thumb no longer on the belt and strangely the thumb opening the mouth

— Friend

with the crease of the cap all around his head, including the forehead, like a tight halo, my stepmother waiting in suspense, with checked slippers already old since from a certain age onward all shoes hurt, more space is needed for deformities of the bones and toes that continue to grow, lumpier, twisted, I'm sure that in the coffins of the cemetery immense feet, wooden, pointed upward tearing the velvet of the lid with yellow nails and finally breaking the lid, who swears that the poplars above the stones were not feet once, full of our calluses and opening the phalanges of the branches, the thumb repeating

— Friend

to my father in the village and to me in the ship and the face of my father suddenly drained of features and color like the face of the second lieutenant of the paratroops finally drained and the features whirling around the immense drain of the mouth, he a child running behind the goats in the north, he spent years in the seminary full of the fear of God, a woman

—Undress

in a small town in the country but which, with a crooked blind paralyzed on the window and the second lieutenant still not a second lieutenant, with the suitcase with which he had fled from the priests, the suitcase that he thought lost and now, imagine, he found himself in Africa again as he tried to smile, he thought

—At the least I'll take the suitcase

but where to my God, the second lieutenant waiting for the helicopter and neither sadness nor fear, only my wife patting his hair

—My child

almost wrapping him as she wrapped him already this afternoon when he came down slowly, without pain, inside himself while the soldiers, leaning, waved good-bye to him, the last thing he was conscious of was what they engraved on the piece of metal he carried around his neck, 78902690RH+, that they had to nail it onto the coffin and he with sadness, gentlemen, so much sadness and due to the fact that he didn't understand because he asked

—Sadness?

but the soldiers who continued to wave didn't respond, one of them with a bazooka put his hand on the shoulder of a comrade, the woman who caressed him an old woman in these parts thirty or forty years old, the second lieutenant of the paratroops twenty-two and trying to understand

—How did this happen how did I meet her?

until giving up understanding whirling inside himself like water from a tap faster faster coming closer to the drain, he thought almost indifferently, somewhat surprised and that was all

—It must be death

and in fact it was death, I'm sorry to agree with you, I swear, that it bothers me to admit but sorry that it precisely was that, the hospital psychologist to me, fixing his tie, with his own death at some point in him, but without mines or explosions, his own death, still minuscule, in his lungs, in his esophagus or in the liver, it doesn't matter, try to touch it, doctor, you walk around here when the doctor has less hope

—That's right

when he has less hope

—Now I'm here I arrived a bit early we have time still

and the psychologist pretending to be distracted, pretending that he didn't hear, his wife curious

—Isn't it death that is here with you?

fortunately not angered, not angered for goodness sake, neither of the two was guilty, that's the way it is, it's not worth protesting, arguing, questioning

—Me?

with hand on my chest, that's the way it is, during the trip to Angola at a certain point another ship and after not one other ship all the way to Luanda, no island, water, your unhappiness water or if you prefer your joy in going to serve the Fatherland, cotton coffee oil the Berliets are gold, the men who patrol and the men, what else could one do, were patrolling, my father toward his thumb

—What?

almost soundless, soundless, a quick pop

—What?

with his body softening on the only sofa that was there and continues to be there (it's a house in the country)

with one of its legs replaced by bricks that my daughter sits on from time to time, leaning frontward, oblivious of us, my father toward his thumb, attentive and inattentive at the same time

—How was it?

looking at the lighter that he took out of his pocket and the policemen, my stepmother and I looking at the lighter as well, funny how the whole world, Australia, Russia, was converging on the lighter, even the dinner table, the Chinese figurines on the console, the second lieutenant of the paratroops returning up here

—Sorry to have returned I promise not to take any of your time but did I not forget to wish you good luck?

the one with the single eyebrow forgiving him

—Go on

the one with two eyebrows to my father

—A tire blew we think I don't know how much they'll give for that pile of scrap metal

my father interested, thinking about the rims

—Are you really sure that it's worth nothing?

because there are garages that buy used parts claiming afterward to their clients that new

—We installed a German oil pump

clients look, they see only wires and cylinders that they don't have a clue about and it's clear that they swallow the hook, if it had been only the, you only, correct, if it had been only the second lieutenant of the paratroops dying it would have been like the other, nobody lives forever, now so many boys cheerfully going to serve the Fatherland frankly my general, man to man don't you think that they exaggerated a bit, the one with the two eyebrows to my father

—If he manages to save a screw that's already not bad friend

and it wasn't good like that but that's how it was, perhaps he could have fixed it up a little here and there to make things clearer, now I think that they understand better my concern for my son's lateness, I brought him from Africa you recall, I picked him out alone the huts were still burning and though my wife when I arrived home with him

—You could've got a kid a bit less black

she took a liking to the little one just as she takes a liking to everything, that's understood, there are mothers, I'm always astonished by the junk she keeps, strings, burned-out light bulbs, the first smile she gave him, I don't recall anymore how it was and she ready to show him unsticking it from an old electricity bill

—It's here

a sincerely common smile, do you want me to give you another smile now, my wife offended with me buried it once again in the envelope, worn out, very faded, between her index and middle finger, a smile so timid

—I've not seen that one again

and no point in arguing they aren't changing their minds, they are complicating things and that's it, if I threw it in the trash, the Carmo and Trindade would fall,* she who is a comfort for the soul sticking up all her feathers

—What happened to my smile?

we with hands on our chests, so innocent

—Me?

---

*The expression may be translated as "all hell would break loose." It refers to the collapse of two churches in Lisbon during the terrible earthquake of 1755.

and the feathers opening and closing drawers, furious

—Who doesn't know what I buy for you

even playing with him under the pile of silver wrappings for chocolates from when we were six years old, smoothed out very well with a fingernail until not even a trace of folding, if by chance a wrapping tore they sealed it very nicely sealed up with a bit of transparent tape, here today in the village it's not my father worrying, it's me, fortunately until now no police jeep turning without haste next to the plane tree that at night does not get dark like the other trees, it stays the same, the only one with a green canopy among the black canopies, raising itself up to itself in a perpetual midday, I recall it so well, I who don't like vegetables very much, in Africa as I remembered, I, I, I, as I remembered in this moment, in the circle of chairs at the hospital with the psychologist, the operations major so small, bald, brown-haired, here with us, in the company, the only time that he left the protection of command headquarters during a great mishap, with defoliant, napalm and the South African pilots, codename cousins, who were not conversing as the psychologist does not converse, he listens to us frightened I hope with fear of airplanes, the cousins who threw us out lazily at five meters above the ground and two days from the target, who isn't afraid, my wife weighing down on my shoulder at midnight

—Ready

despite the kidney stones incessantly consuming her like those horrible teeth, reaching her liver seeing that the doctor, discouraged

(commissioner Blood of the People was advancing backward like the cancer)

—Checking the liver

and her skin different

(the footprints began in the river instead of stopping but the tracks on the edges, the guide showed, deeper than the toe and thus the smart one backward, one of the sergeants to me

—Are we crossing the water?

and we are crossing the fucking water, fool, the faggot's walking behind us and the psychologist without finding a position on the chair, tormenting his jaw, just like my wife didn't find a position in the sheets because a bone in the hip, because a bone in the back, because perhaps I'm an old woman and which bone and which old woman, it was the stones, it's the blood rotting, it's the body that's giving up, it's her weighing down on my shoulder

—I'm here)

the operations major, small, bald, brown-haired, never getting near the
camp, always smoking a short cigarette holder and without blowing smoke,
leaving it like mud jamming his mouth and so much shit in you major, how
about the commissioner Blood of the People next to him or walking backward with a Kalashnikov in the air, how about pebbles in the kidney, not
many, two or three were enough fucker, we brought some women and some
children, taken from the ploughed fields who were waiting for the political
police and the Spanish wife of the brigade leader who liked to apply electric
shocks to them, the funeral of my brother in the village, after the autopsy
in Lisbon, my father and me outside the old building where they cut up the
dead and that didn't have tiles, waiting, my father to me

—If your mother were here

and then silent, me with an urge to ask

—Did you know that João was gay?

without asking of course, my father who heard what I didn't say

—Don't insult the dead

my brother who gave the impression of being a man to take seriously and
finally look, a slob, my stepmother

and my brother a vague gesture trying the food in the pan

—I have time

the same size as me but better looking, thinner, his nails perfect, a ring
with a pearl on the little finger that rolled up in a circle to pick up a glass,
one afternoon, five or six boys at the, one afternoon the operations major,
one of them made up, at the funeral and two women of the same sort as

(my mouth hates what I'm about to say)

my daughter, they all must have worked at the same women's clothing
store, with the owner, an old guy with hair dyed blond who always kissed me
with a strange sort of kindness

—You're not bad looking young man

and my brother calming him down immediately

—Jorge

separating me from the old guy pulling my arm, we always got along well,
we never argued, on one occasion he made a request of me very serious

—Don't be unhappy like me

me with a stupid face looking at him, why unhappy, almost sorry to have
asked our father after you died

—Did you know João was gay?

not to offend him, but to offend you who always protected me, gave me money, sometimes stroked my cheek and me wiping it off with a sleeve backing away, sorry, don't hold it against me but you made me nauseous, a fairy, if you didn't put on eye makeup, if you didn't use creams, if you didn't wear that perfume that repelled and attracted me at the same time, me in panic

—Am I a fairy too?

and it pained me to understand that you understood my question, that you were afraid that I, that you didn't want that I and if I'm wrong correct me, it doesn't offend me if you correct me because I like you brother, I like you a lot, perhaps you've nothing that makes me, the operations major, like you but, alright, I like you, what it pained me to know you inside that box, how the sound of your steps pained me, how the sound of the earth on the lid pained me and the cemetery employees trampling over you afterward, our father put his arm around me but it wasn't his arm that I wanted, it was yours, your arm, brother, pushing me

—Let me stay there in the depths and let's leave there has to be a café nearby

the two of us in the café, you and I in the café, you

—Now that I'm dead we can really talk

and over these years we've talked don't you think, no matter whether people think that we've not talked, how I would have liked to receive your letters in Angola, in the horror of Angola, one afternoon the operations major, I'll try to say this fast, one afternoon I saw the operations major, always with a short cigarette holder and without blowing smoke, leaving the smoke like mud to jam his mouth arrive dragging a pregnant prisoner toward the barracks where the quartermaster was piling up bottles, bags of food, beer, this to the left of the storage house for the caskets, he left the door leaning, leveled the prisoner against the wall, brought an empty crate that, I cannot go faster, that he turned upside down, bent the knee of the prisoner, put her foot on the crate and she silent, submissive, unbuttoned his fly, fumbled around inside, ordered

—Don't talk

and hooked himself to the woman, coughing from tobacco, while me at the entrance, while the corn was rustling with the force of reeds, dry stems, empty cobs, my brother

—What horror

in front of me in Angola, in front of me in the café, a bird singing in the cemetary, my father pulling me

—What horror

or before my father pulling me

—Let's go son

and let's go father, let's go now, take me to the house in the village, call my stepmother and leave me in bed, the operations major still with his cigarette holder in his teeth left the quartermaster's barracks where the woman was looking at the ground, he more brown-haired, redder, fixing his pants, my brother on the edge of the bed asking me

—You're not afraid anymore?

and I wasn't afraid now because he was with me, because he liked me, because I wasn't a fairy father, don't fret because you didn't leave a fairy in the world despite mister Jorge

—Dear

which was, logically, a sign of friendship and who doesn't have friends sir, you have, I have, my brother, what is bad about that, mister Jorge had didn't he, the political police took the prisoner away two or three days later together with the others in a column of special troops that didn't catch mines what a relief, with the paratroops patrolling almost the entire route because the Berliets are gold, three thousand contos is gold, the men who patrol and the men who were patrolling while the machine gunner, in a kind of small tower on the top of the Mercedes, was turning the sight toward the grass to the left and the right, my father died almost twenty years ago asking me

—João?

with me responding to him

—In a minute he'll be here

and my father so happy, the policeman with two eyebrows to him

—There are things that happen when you least expect it

returning to the jeep with his colleague and lowering the angle of the headlights swaying in the differing levels of rain, as they left the son stopped being dead and will arrive in a minute, my father looking for air to breathe just like a blind child feeling its way in the emptiness with spiked lips

—Tell him that I'm waiting for him

and he's definitely remained like that until today inasmuch as he's not just anything, not some remains of cartilage in the earth because this is the end be patient, we will disappear completely, neither the idea of our shadow on the ground will remain, nor will it return because the dogs won't even recognize it given that it ceased to smell and regarding the smell how I liked to select the route through a landscape of smells, me to the operations major

—Don't you feel any remorse for abusing the prisoner?

and the operations major to me without looking at me sucking the muddy smoke from his cigarette holder, quietly

—Go fuck yourself second lieutenant

while I arranged my father closing his eyes with my thumbs and fitting his false teeth into his jaw, he younger right away, with fewer wrinkles on his face, asking me

—That little guy next to the unimogs telling you to go fuck yourself what is he the major?

the hospital psychologist to me, uncomfortable

—This is for veterans who gave you the right to get your father involved here?

and you within reason friend, I'll drive out the family and prevent mister Jorge, always with a white fan in his hand to bat his eyebrows at them

—So pleasant with these poor troops so precious

my wife a grimace from time to time because, we know, the stones hurt, if she would notice me looking she'd wink, from time to time she'd come up to the wall of the yard and spend a little while with me

—You're not cold?

observing the highway without anyone not even a slow jeep moving along and I'm not cold don't you all worry despite the day forty degrees Celsius and frozen nights in the dense fog, the wild dogs who don't know how to kill, galloping near a donkey from the scrubland biting at its ankles, a female fastening onto its neck, another trying the hindquarters, the major always with his back to me swallowing and vomiting his empty cigarette holder

—Tell the second lieutenant to go fuck himself

resembling the pig from the day after tomorrow, with transparent eyelashes, that I visited in the pigpen, indifferent to us, chewing, the nape of the neck fat, rosy head, the whiteness of the skin, narrow legs, my wife

—Don't worry our son is coming

with one of her hips stuck and her dress, how strange, suddenly wide, the hospital psychologist

—Is she sick?

and she is not, I swear, completing her kidney treatment and after a trip to the Salon New Wave and returning from there very attractive, with her hands as they should be and her Sunday clothing you're not going to recognize her, as a girl she was nothing special because modest, if for example one turned to ask her, as if for the first time

—Would you permit me to accompany you?

instantly she becomes twenty years old again, all flushed, full of shame, stumbling over words that didn't come and excuses that she didn't have, wanting to respond

—Yes

and

—No

at the same time, staring at me, ceasing to stare at me, staring at me again, letting out a

—Maybe

of which she soon repented and, as happened to my father, my son without coming, it seemed to me two people on foot on the highway, one of them in front carrying something, putting the thing down to rest and picking it up again, the second slower, with whatever it was not too large in her hand, this after midnight since no one out there anymore, people that is plenty of old pigs going to bed early and not a light in the village, one or another puppy without a cent, one or another owl between two pits in the wall, me walking next to my wife thinking

—What am I talking about now?

thinking

—Will I ask her if she has a boyfriend?

thinking

—If she had a boyfriend she wouldn't let me walk with her

this years before the operations major

—Tell our second lieutenant to go fuck himself

me to my wife

—May I ask your name?

and my wife very distressed, stumbling over herself though she did not take her eyes off the pavement

—Do I respond or not respond?

My wife softly

—I'll tell you after

so softly

—I'll tell you after

as when after our wedding she asked me

—Don't hurt me

with her white nightshirt with lace and bows that her mother got for her

—On the first night put this on

and she clumsy, nervous, trembling with eyes closed because seeing me nude frightened her

—Promise me you won't hurt me

me in underwear and an undershirt, just as frightened as her

—I promise

pulling the sheets up to my jaw, pulling her sheet up to the jaw, taking her lightly by the hand moister than mine that I dried on the bedspread and I felt the rushing of your blood did you know that, though the light was off I saw your breast up and down, as rapidly as a sparrow's heart and the little hole of your belly button, with my index finger inside it, growing smaller and bigger, one of your feet rubbed against me and escaped, me lost in anxiety, so silly,

—What size are your pants?

without hearing

—Thirty-seven and a half thirty-eight

and the big toe very long, the other toes very long, you very long wanting to get dressed, to say good-bye, to escape and me lightly kissing your hair, your forehead, finding a living ear, not in a bottle of alcohol, that protested immediately

—You're tickling me

but it didn't go away, it opened up like a shell under my tongue, that moved around it, fastening itself and whose arm is this around my shoulders, whose other arm is this on my back, whose lips are these on my neck, on my chin, on my mouth, who is spelling my name centimeters from me, almost inside me, inside me, who is guiding me to a slow cave that is moistening me, that pulses, that tightens making me bigger, who uses my voice to whisper

—Love

who became a wave much bigger than me that grows

—Love

lifts me up

—Love

stretches out on the sand

—Love

recedes slowly

—Love

someone behind us, at the kitchen door

—We're here

and an unkempt woman, exhausted, with her shoes in her hand and a black also exhausted following her, carrying a suitcase informing me

—The car ran out of gas we had to come on foot an eternity to get here.

6

I thought I had arrived at the house in the village, with my father waiting for me, and finally a second lieutenant in camouflage much younger
than the one sitting in the armchair of barrel boards at the entrance of the
little shack with a zinc roof, in front of the flagpole, that served as a mess, accompanied by another second lieutenant with a beard to shave and his butt
on an empty case of beer cleaning a G-3,* the second lieutenant in camouflage who brought me from the bush to me

— How many times is it necessary to say that I don't want you in the huts?

pointing to the sanzala next to the barracks from where people were fleeing almost every day, despite the camp's barbed wire, toward Zambia because the real chief, not the puppet chief with the sewing machine who nobody obeyed, was calling them by messages that arrived at night, from the
eucalyptus side, and the army didn't notice, half shivering from malaria and
half sleeping, I thought Her Excellency also with me but I alone, barefoot,
small, with the second lieutenant's shorts that reached my shins and a torn
shirt, without color, missing an epaulet that the sergeant gave to me, on Sunday mornings, the witch doctor, painted and with feathers, would cut the
head off a rooster after the drumming, dancing always, so rapidly that his
feet were not visible, and drink the neck boiling, with blood trickling down
his chest to his skirts and old women, bent over, turning around him, the
second lieutenant suddenly my father, worried about my car

— Did you lock the car?

while my mother

— You must be so tired

and the back of her neck now quite narrow, my mother who at a certain time widened with age, a blouse covering her shoulders, one leg less
limber than the other and my father on the armchair of barrel boards, no,

---

*Assault rifle of German origin used by the Portuguese army.

on my grandfather's little sofa looking at Her Excellency and at me, with eyebrows mixed for a moment and distinct the next, the living room less clean, stains on the towel, the lid of one of the two trunks open, forgotten, and this was not what I knew, it was not here that I stayed, if my mother, though white, danced with the remaining old women, if the witch doctor had offered her a rooster feather, if she rattled to the left and to the right a tin of conch shells the kidney stones would leave her body in order to rattle as well and my mother fat once again, happy, my father now a second lieutenant now almost an old man, the second lieutenant with the edges of his mouth downward

—I don't believe it

and the old man relieved

—And this one?

the doctor shirtless, barefoot, observing, while a nurse cleaned the blood off him, X-rays, analyses

—There is no doubt that the American medicine cured her

and the crickets out there on a tree trunk in the yard that owls frequented, of course I locked the car, sir, tomorrow we'll call the local garage, Her Excellency's feet almost as black as mine, dirtied by asphalt, dust, earth, and she was massaging them hating me for not changing but silent in front of my parents, my sister more standoffish than cats, soon a jump from the window and she'll disappear into the night, what were you thinking about, sister, why are you here with us, what do you expect from life, at times it seems to me that you want to sit on the ground, your jaw over your paws, supremely distant from us, other times I get the idea that an impulse to speak but you never talk, you don't smile, you are uninterested, you look with dull eyelids at Her Excellency, when in a few months our mother will die don't cry, they greet you and you immobile, they hug you and you rigid, they console you

(for what?)

and you don't listen, you're not dressed in mourning, you aren't carrying a handkerchief tight in your hand, you don't raise the sheet that covers the face of the deceased, you don't kiss her either, one single phrase distant

—Ah yes?

and behold you in the churchyard observing the shop windows and traffic lights, if I knew where you lived, if I dreamed up where you work, a notary office, a travel agency, a government office, I don't know, I would wait for you in the corridor

—I only wanted to see you bye

and I would get away immediately moving ahead through the corridor feeling you on my back, there are times when it seems to me something related to me, I don't say friendship anymore, I exaggerate, a point of affection, a point of, what a large word for you, don't get afraid, apology, esteem, it comes to me like that and of course it's not esteem, indeed we are blacks, so close to monkeys, we don't even dream about what this is, we kill roosters with a bite, we eat raw innards, we don't cover our privates, we haven't a clue about emotions, the noncommissioned officers to the second lieutenant, mistrustful of me

—Sooner or later wait for the blow the boy will take vengeance

my mother's soup with reheated flavor, she at the table with us evidently in pain

—It's not a big deal sorry

pushing the discomfort a little bit to the side in order to be able to smile with the expression she lifted up piece by piece by the cheeks and she was trembling, the poor thing, her face barely holding up, my voice in silence, hating myself

—She's going to fall she's going to fall

and the second lieutenant almost with hands extended to try to support her, what are you feeling tell me how is it to die, during the rains a woman and the goats, two or three, with me, a woman still with her ears stuffing me with a piece of reed that she was introducing into my mouth, I have an idea of this like I have an idea of the thunderclaps and the mud, like I have an idea of the wild dogs chasing deer, the tip of a breast, this not very clear, confused, already so old, the god Zumbi* in a niche, hemp strands burned, Her Excellency at midnight

—Don't stop talking

without me distinguishing her from an indignant sheet where ankles were pedaling and from which appeared two fingers that pinched my back, my father to me

—You frightened me with your lateness

and a pair of policemen with caps, one with two eyebrows, and the second only with one though my father much younger, almost the same as the

---

*Spirit of the dead, from the word *nzumbi* (corpse) in Kimbundu and similar to the word *nzambi* (god).

second lieutenant, now here now in a ship that was leaving, leaving as a band marching tunes and many handkerchiefs on the dock, my father

—How I thought about my brother because you didn't arrive either

and here is something new look look, or rather the uncle he didn't mention tumbling down to me from the sky, killed in an accident more or less in the place where my car was or rather a curve that brought bad luck to the family, at the same time that my mother was peeling an apple for Her Excellency and an apple for me

—With only a soup they'll still be really hungry

as if we were holding out to her rusty tins from the other side of the barbed wire, Her Excellency so ugly with hair thrown together, her dress fallen from the stained hanger of her shoulders and her dirty feet, twisted, seeking to gain strength in a bucket of lukewarm water beyond that she was missing one or two teeth in the back whose absence I never noticed, funny that we're made of pieces at random I don't know who puts them together and, by the way, why are they of that form, why not remove the kidney with the stones from my mother and insert another in there, Her Excellency finally extremely plain, me so stupid, what could have charmed me about her, I have the feeling my sister on a bench, satisfied with me, the feeling my mother, who was listening to both of us, raising her voice despite being silent too

—Children

that only my sister and I would understand since Her Excellency busy with the apple and father wrapped up in memories of his brother, with pride in him and, how strange, ashamed of his pride, my father perhaps, I was wagering that for sure, who knows, because ashamed of himself too, so many shadows in people, so many shadows in me and inside the shadows napalm flames, a man with arms spread wide who was growing in the air and falling into ash afterward, as white as a leg bone, the ribs so white and right after black, then the second lieutenant, still not my father, running over me without seeing me

—Kill kill

not manioc fields not corn not hemp, shots from bazookas, machine guns, G-3s, what happened with your brother, second lieutenant sir, what happened to me, my father who spoke so little

—I'm sure that there are times when we'll still talk

me with knees against a woman looking for her breast, me lying against a

woman hiding in her breast, the demobilized gum of Her Excellency growing, the horrible noise of her jaws chewing an apple, chewing me, me finally
finding the woman's breast and no more milk, the second lieutenant, still
not my father, went back and forth running, a helicopter gunship, two helicopter gunships and the gunners talking with the pilots, that is moving their
mouths right above me, blacks falling before reaching the jungle, the goats
taking off and returning because the flames in the tall grass were chasing
them, the tree under which the elders used to smoke disappeared, the captain

—Quick

the captain

—No one is fleeing toward the river no one is fleeing

and after tomorrow the pig, more screams, more blood, the loquat tree
in the yard, the little garden, my mother weighing down on my shoulder

—Fortunately you arrived

in a voice that for weeks already was becoming different, coming from
very deep in her throat, very deep in her body, she, once so energetic, sitting
on a bench existing so much less, with open nostrils swallowing the air and
my father suddenly with fear

—You

looking for her in her voice since I didn't find her in herself, sometimes
half asleep I felt her next to my bed, huge, with her knees against the mattress and her head almost on the ceiling, worried, smelling of what women
smell at night or rather the secret drawer or the mysterious trunk, to check if
I was sleeping, when her footsteps went away me alone, so alone, me

—Mother

without words, only the groans of the neighbor down below whose rheumatism made him cross through his ceiling and our floor and lying down
next to me, he was going down the stairs full of legs and walking sticks moving unsteadily trying to bring together everything under the trunk of his
body, the woman helped him if a foot more rapid or more independent got
away, how hard it must be to command so many shoes, the pendulum of
the living room clock moving with the dignity of the fat over a circle with
Roman numbers that increased its importance like dates on statues, my
father wound it with a key immediately under VI, covered his mouth with
his palm if he or the clock one stroke behind the stomach because of the last
dinner, Her Excellency for once silent, not shouting out orders, not bossing

me around, looking at a piece of apple that was oxidizing on the plate, no longer white, brown, even when sleepy I notice the cracking of the loquat tree in the yard and of the cardboard wings of the owls searching for mice, hedgehogs, my father knocking the chair over and looking around leaning on the wall, my mother to us in a thin voice while she was setting the chair upright

— He's in Angola for a few more minutes and he'll return

and this every year during the pig killing, the rest of the time almost always calm, now and again he would react to a distant door or steps in another apartment asking, indecisive

— Is it them?

my mother continuing her crochet

— It's the neighbor with rheumatism poor fellow

my father not believing her fumbling around himself in search of the weapon that he didn't have anymore, suddenly limber, young, thin, with hair, my mother much older than him, of course, without taking her eyes off the needle

— It's done

and my father, recognizing the crochet, returning little by little no longer in camouflage, dressed like us, getting used to Lisbon, to the house, to himself now, my father ashamed

— Sorry

accepting a glass of water, not a canteen, accepting the porcelain shepherdess on the doily for the dresser, accepting the little chandelier on the ceiling, accepting us, though a part of him counting his fingers, squatting on a brick, at the entrance to the mess hall, my father repeating to us

— Sorry

while in the yard my sister looking at nothing, I wish so much that you could help me, sister, I don't really know with what but you might help me and nonetheless how might you help me if you can't help yourself, do you by chance have a person who, what question stupider, it's obvious you don't have anyone, you're alone, you're nothing more than a tiny straw the water is carrying away, it sticks to another straw for a moment, it gets loose, it continues, Her Excellency too tired to try to humiliate me, to give me orders, denigrate me with her friends, the black, the darky, if he opens his hand, he'll fall from the tree the idiot, here for our benefit the second lieutenant sharpshooter should have left me in Africa letting out screams, smoking

Caricocos, cutting the necks off roosters with a bite on Sunday mornings and drinking their blood, giving information to my brothers with Kalashnikovs, receiving electric shocks from the Spanish woman at the outpost of the political police

— The dunce seems to like it look at his teeth

and soon morning my God, soon we'll go to the garage in town to look for gas, turn off the little red light, kill the pig, and the racket finished forget Her Excellency and leave, she'll stay in the village perhaps they'll kill her next year, they'll hang her by her feet over the pots, figure out where the artery in her neck is, bring the knife near, two, three, or four peasants in rubber aprons with those unlaced boots of the poor, outside blue clarity of the fleeting sort that precedes the morning and the first falcons from the mountains driven by hammers in the air watching over the chickens, the chicks, the first groups of wild ducks toward the lagoon, the first genet, lingering, stretching in the thickets and the old men, one by one, on the way to the square, I remember so little of the jungle, the soldiers when the second lieutenant wasn't there

— When you grow up you'll be an insurgent

looking at the traps in the wire, counting the soldiers, describing the positions of the mortars and the location of the storeroom, the Swede who came to look for fuba* with the others jotting down everything, with the end of a pencil, on a notepad, my mother to Her Excellency and to me

— Can't we take a break for at least a few hours?

and then for the first time since I got out of the car with the suitcase, I don't know how far from here, I was sure that I had a body or rather not really a body, a soft thing and without definite limits resistant to changing place, suspended from me, weighing down on me, that I tried to drive to the room dragging it with both hands across the floor outside while Her Excellency followed me limping with her shoes hooked on her index and middle fingers and one of her heels in pain because an uneven spot in the asphalt twisted it so that, I swear, I almost had pity for you, had pity for you, pity for you seriously, you must be unhappy, I want you to be unhappy and at the same time I don't, I'm a black husband smelling like a black

— Doesn't he smell like a black?

and besides smelling like a black that squashed nose, that thick mouth,

---

*Corn meal (in Kimbundu).

that hair impossible to comb if not with a nail or a shard of glass, that white of the eyes, so much whiter than ours, where the pupils wander, that taste for loud suits, for huge ties, for gold watches, gold rings, gold bracelets, golden wires on their necks, Her Excellency looking at me with disgust

—Darky

and me accepting the

—Darky

me humble, me superfluous, me obedient, the room a cubicle with a narrow mattress on a little metal platform, a tulip of pink glass on the ceiling that was missing a bulb just like his own ceiling and the walls missing paint, the first steps of the pigeons were audible on the roof tiles, the first claws, the first cooing and the first compact knives of wind that precede the morning, on the door window with the half-open shutter some bush with two or three leaves vibrating in the sun and the others still dark, quiet, Her Excellency pointing out the bed to me

—There isn't space for two you'll have to sleep on the carpet

and it's true how annoying, there's no space for me, the carpet a square of raffia once red, that I remember, content to be called a carpet

—The lady is right friend

and who are we to gainsay her opinion about things and so much more correct if to top it off we are born darkies though my father taking me by the arm warning the soldiers

—You're not touching this one who is mine

so that I didn't lie down on the raffia, I squatted in a corner, my knees in my mouth, without opening the suitcase nor taking out my pajamas, without taking off any clothes at all, I took my shoes off only despite being generally obedient they resisted coming off since my feet swollen on the way and my shins the size of my knees, without bones, Her Excellency didn't unbutton her dress, with arms stretched out protesting with the pillow in a grumble that I didn't understand, the noblewoman, she who at her parents' house slept in a sleeping bag in the living room in the company of her sister, her nose almost rubbing the legs of the table, not counting a nephew on the sofa where her mother would sew, I'm not exaggerating I swear, it was like that, on the other side of the Tagus where the swamp reeds spoke with people, the captain to the second lieutenant referring to me

—The best would be to have the doctor look at him in case the kid a sickness from the backwoods of the kind that spread to us

—Another second lieutenant, doubtful

—My captain really believes that dogs pass their problems on to people?

without the captain hearing him busy dictating messages to the radio that made a knot for an antenna on a stick of a hut, this in the morning still because they arrived at the end of the night as Her Excellency and I arrived in the village after climbing up the slope in steps stumbling at random one on another, my mother from in front of the door

—Sweet dreams

with Her Excellency indifferent to her already with closed eyes

—If anything I can swear to you that this is the last killing

she who if it weren't for me would be working with her neighbors at the edge of the bush offering herself to truck drivers, with a large stone in her bag to discourage bad debts or that they would try to pay with a half-naked doll that danced on a nylon string flapping around in the rearview mirror together with a rosary whose cross would swing happy, I confess that there were occasions when I availed myself of those ladies who were mistrustful of me despite the help of the golden wristwatch and the mounting of the ring

—Do you have money black?

they with their faces under their elbows so that I didn't kiss them and therefore our second lieutenant should have left me in Angola, looking at lepers down below, one or another crocodile, the antelope that the cabíris barked at, my mother who even from behind gave evidence of how thin she had become, it's hard to imagine what the stones are capable of

—Any problem son?

and the doctor his nose in the analyses winding up my father's courage

—The regatta isn't over yet we'll see we'll see

with wild dogs that I don't know how nobody saw in the hospital, those snouts, those ears, passing by the reception sniffing around for us, the doctor raising his glasses to his forehead

—We'll see

until my mother vanished behind the screen and then he leaning over us, softly

—With luck perhaps six months

straightening up cheerful over our heads

—That blue jacket looks good on you madam

a rather old jacket as a matter of fact, a bit worn out on the sleeves

(as far as I saw she never took care of herself)

a metal butterfly with open wings on the lapel and my mother next to the screen pretending to be content, freeing, with her fingers at the nape of her neck, the hair taken prisoner by her collar, sighing a

—Thank you

timid, did she hear the doctor did she not hear the doctor but certainly she heard my father's face whose bones were wrinkling each other because fear was squeezing them, squeezing and therefore I threw my mother into the wastebasket and replaced her right away by the one she was when I met her, still young, pretty, and who was there in the dresser where she kept her old treasures, a doll without an arm, a school notebook with copied notes, a dry seahorse in a small bottle, medals, pictures, what remains in the sand of memory when the waters of the past recede though she was missing a little rag bear and the voice from the puppet theater of a single aunt censuring her from above

(everything so large then except for her)

with cruel disdain

—When will you grow?

with the second lieutenant returning to defend her covering her ears

—Don't listen

and how can I not hear, explain to me, if I hear even your distress about me, worse than Africa, worse than war, worse than the second lieutenant of the paratroops when they put him in the evacuation helicopter with an IV that served no purpose at all, taking his leave of all of you

—Good-bye

and now how can I prevent the stones from continuing to grow, the doctor pointing the pen at my father and me, touching the X-ray near the brain

—It's got this far already

my father thinking that if it's got here it's got everywhere and if it's everywhere what can be done, my father to the doctor in the hope that he would deny it

—You think with luck six months right?

the doctor avoiding looking at him, with pity for both, totally occupied with keeping the tests in order in his cardboard file

—This isn't mathematics perhaps there are miracles perhaps there is God

while the helicopter with the second lieutenant of the paratroops rose up disturbing the tall grass, leaning to the left, moving away from us abandoning a

—See you later

that the next rain would drown, my mother looking at the butterfly on the lapel in order not to look at my father and feeling guilty for ceasing to take care of him, so defenseless human beings, so fragile, so incapable of surviving without us

—Shall we go then?

and what will your life be after me, poor thing, beard badly groomed, shoes to polish, one button less on your shirt, I have to leave him dozens of soups already made, a note on the kitchen counter explaining how to light the stove, turn on the water heater, set thirty seconds on the microwave because he forgets gentlemen, where the basket for pills is, open the mailbox every week because the electricity bill, the water bill, and gas already now, the polish next to the shoes, shirts size thirty-nine, remember, in the second drawer, the broom and the mop in the bucket behind the ironing board in the left corner of the sunroom, the telephone numbers for the plumber, the kids, and the dentist on the dresser in the living room, the thermometer on the bedside table along with the keys that we don't know anymore what for mixed with a little sheet of instructions for the washing machine in eight languages, don't read it in Danish, a broken screwdriver, little coins, what will become of you? Get yourself a woman fast, maybe Tita who is a good person, the winter blankets in the trunk right at the entrance because they can't fit in any other place and most of all forget about Angola that perhaps never existed just like the stones didn't exist, we had to invent whatever it was to occupy ourselves wasn't that right and so you invented Africa and I so that you didn't have too many hobbies filled myself with imagination and discovered a cancer, you like the butterfly on the lapel don't you just as you like that I'm all dressed up for you, Her Excellency inside her sleep

—Filipe

just as you like that I'm all dressed up for the doctor, Her Excellency rolling up for herself more of the sheet

—Filipe

as the door window clearer and a woman with gray roots in her hair and after the gray hair blond, with some nails still with traces of red, the thumbnail chewed right down to the root and I don't smell perfume, I smell oil from the stew

—Do you have money black?

I smell the little son, I smell the slime of eels in the Tagus, with eyes enlarged by a little bit of cheap eyeliner that the first tear, emitted with a yawn for example seeing that from thirty on we don't control these trivial things, will take away

—Do you have money black?

and my sister already outside in the yard, perhaps she walked the whole night in the village, she went up to the cemetery, she went up to the chapel, she lingered in the square, it's impossible that you don't know about mother sister, it's impossible that our second lieutenant

—This is mine

didn't tell you, second lieutenant sir

—You

and his wife looking at him from far away

—Sorry

while the stones continued to spread and were gnawing, gnawing, you turn on the oven here, the lighter for the water heater is this button you see, the bottle for cuts says Alcohol but it's Hydrogen Peroxide don't forget, you're certain that you don't want me to put a different label on, so many explanations poor thing, so afraid that me, how will it be to be alone thinking about you, entire afternoons waiting the captain

—We'll leave tomorrow

standing smoking next to me eyes beyond the savannah with a letter from the Metropolis in his hand

—When will this end?

my sister next to the cabbages in the garden smiling silently and not a smile, another expression, always another expression with her, Her Excellency awake looking at me scratching her back with pensive fingers

—What time is it?

I bet with Filipe in mind as well, who the hell is Filipe other than white and it's clear, Filipe white and me a chimpanzee found in a hut, euá, while trying to lift me from the wall which I was squatting against the legs without force they didn't help me or the woman on her stomach who finished at the end of her arms, where the fingers stop, the second lieutenant left the hospital with mother and a band of gypsies waiting in front of the Emergency, the wind moving in the village brought trees from the cemetery, stone slabs, look at the stray dogs of the barracks here and the sergeant who if he didn't have mail would have shot at them, the eddies of dense mist originating I don't know where, Her Excellency without getting up

—So late

now blind now seeing

—I'm really stupid to be here with you what a dump

my mother in the corridor, in the kitchen, with one shoe heavier than the other, I bet that since she didn't see anyone, she held herself up on the furniture, if we found her a grimace pretending to be amused

—I just stopped to think it's age

me with an urge to shake her, angered

—Stop with the silliness of the stones mother

noticing the second lieutenant, barefoot, only in pajama bottoms, half a beard to shave and the razor in his hand, Her Excellency seated on the bed, with her dress from the night before

—I hope that at least we'll continue to have hot water

she who bossed around everybody including grandmother

—Shut up ma'am

and the old lady only slippers and a widow's handkerchief obeyed, I never saw a body so minuscule nor ankles so thin, a daughter with one wandering eye

—Stop quiet you skeleton

cut her fingernails sighing with anger, the house where you lived worse than this one but with the advantage of not smelling like a black

—Open the window you pollute

though the river stank with the breath of the dead like common graves, father despite living in another place with another wife appeared from time to time at lunch hour, ordering his wife

—Quiet

the sounds of falling objects were audible, a chair, a brush and father leaving six minutes after tightening his pants and combing himself with his palms even the van with the broken exhaust, all coughing, cracks and springs in disharmony the one with the others where a colleague from the storehouse, his cap with the company name, was waiting for him and for me to buy the gas and convince the mechanic to help me with the tank and to take a look at the motor, to avoid problems, the car is no longer new, I don't know how many hours on your feet without the moon and on a highway where there exist no streetlamps there is construction, fields and mansions exist and the night crawlers, the danger of wild dogs attacking my shins like they used to attack the antelope, they would hang from the rump, from the neck and the hooves, I recall that, I think I recall, I recall but I don't know if I'm inventing the memory, such diffuse episodes, so vague, for example a woman, a man, a young girl still smaller than me that if she appeared with me perhaps for Her Excellency to assure me that blacks all look alike

—You all look alike

I told this to my sister and my sister as usual impassive, Her Excellency

—They all look alike

while we were walking trying not to stray from the asphalt, suddenly blinded by bright lights that filled us with smoke, a truck of calves that were screaming asking for help and disappearing from us, without any help, on the first curve of plane trees, I hesitate if my mother the woman who held me protecting me from wild dogs or the wife of the second lieutenant with a butterfly on her lapel who referred to me as

—Son

and who answers me, which of the two my mother in fact, me to my sister

—Are you certain that you are my sister?

and my sister raising her eyes from the flowerbed, silent, if you're my sister why don't you look like me seeing that Her Excellency claims that all blacks look alike, if they didn't look alike they were whites and I not white, I'm a marmoset good for getting around among the trees, tell me who is my mother, who is my father, the second lieutenant or the one that was with his wife in Africa and who am I now, all so complicated, so strange, Her Excellency without understanding

—What the hell kind of talk is this?

in search of a bar of soap and a towel in the suitcase pushing away clothes, blouses, underwear, shoes, all extracted from my bank account it's clear, studying herself with rage, inviting me to study her

—Look at the monster you've turned me into this night because of the breakdown in your piece of shit car

a piece of shit car, a piece of shit black, a piece of shit life, please turn your back while I get dressed, don't you dare look and above all I forbid you to repeat what you did on the car seat or in the quartermaster's storage room, I don't know in which, when you obliged me to put my foot on a crate while you looked in your pants, you short, you brown-haired, you bald, with a cigarette of muddy smoke in your cigarette holder and without blowing anything out, leaving it to float in your mouth or rather exactly as the second lieutenant told me, a lot later, in the Lisbon apartment or here, perhaps here in the little garden with lettuce and cucumbers, perhaps in Africa in the manioc field since everything gets confused for me in my memory and the wife of the second lieutenant my mother, the wife of the second lieutenant always next to me when malaria came, bringing me water, measuring my fever, putting her hand in my hair, changing the sheets, giving me milk to drink and the glass, I swear, the glass sweet and soft, the glass resembling, I won't say, the glass suddenly a part of her, the glass that I wanted her breast, it was her breast, capable of protecting me from the wild dogs, the helicopter gunship, the bazookas, the shots, the doctor to the second lieutenant, my father, the second lieutenant

—The regatta isn't over yet we'll see we'll see

the doctor to my father, the second lieutenant, my father after my mother, wife of the second lieutenant, vanished behind the screen

—Perhaps six months with luck

and then straightening up cheerful over our heads

—That blue jacket looks good on you madam

that blue jacket, that cloth from the Congo, that blue jacket as a matter of fact already a bit old, a little bit worn down on the sleeves, with a metal butterfly on the lapel, not gold not silver, metal, with open wings on the lapel and my mother, not the wife of the second lieutenant, next to the screen, freeing with her fingers at the nape of her neck the hair taken prisoner by her collar sighing a

—Thank you

shy and for a moment I thought that my mother only while the stones were leaving her kidney toward her whole body they were eating her from within until only the bones of the liver remained, the bones of the lungs, the bones of the bones, the second lieutenant who brought me took me one afternoon to the mission of the Spanish priests abandoned with what was left of a brick cloister around a dry fountain, cells without doors, a deserted chapel with only one part of the altar and a piece of bucket or watering can above, around the mission acacias with purple flowers up to the graveyard with a half dozen wooden crosses, several signs with a date and name and under the crosses I bet nothing seeing that the land of Angola devours whites quickly, Her Excellency returning to the room inside the towel

—It's cold

and as she spoke with me in an almost normal tone I thought yes, it was cold, a little wind in the vegetables to cope with, the feet of wilted hemp, the manioc forgotten, the motor of the mail plane at some place in the jungle, I slept in the second lieutenant's bed with him and listened to him speak during my sleep like Her Excellency at times

—Mommy

without being able to awaken, I recall the body of a Swede they brought to the camp and an agent of the political police aimed his pistol at him and put a bullet in his belly though dead and though dead his body moving, my mother to the second lieutenant, whispering behind a closed door

—I'm going to die am I not?

and no response because the second lieutenant occupied with emptying the pockets of the Swede, the second lieutenant to my mother, while they were separating papers distracted

—Obviously not

or before the second lieutenant's voice not

—Obviously not

the second lieutenant's voice

—Shut up

more than that, the second lieutenant's voice

—Please shut up

the second lieutenant's voice old now, without camouflage his platoon not with him, the second lieutenant in a circle of hospital chairs not responding to the psychologist, not looking at him, not aware of him at all, reading the Swede's papers after smoothing them out against his leg with the cleaver of his hand, my father to my mother in their room in the house in the village

—Neither of the two of us is going to die you hear?

and to himself afterward trying to convince himself

—Neither of the two of us is going to die

while a flock of crows rose up from the poplars crossing the willows toward the mountain and at the exact moment when the second lieutenant

—Neither of us is going to die

my sister started to shout in the yard.

7

When I returned from Africa any noise frightened me and me on my knees looking for my weapon that I didn't have anymore and thought I still had in order to kill the door latch or the neighbors' loud party, high heels machine guns, bazookas men's footsteps, the sighs of the wounded or the dresser drawers, my wife trying to make sure that I didn't notice her and the result was that I wasn't able to take my eyes off her since the clamor that she didn't make deafened me, the caution of her heels for example gave me the certainty that soon living children were going to be trampled who would shrink with pain, the windows would open in a protest of torn cloth from the Congo over a body, that of my wife, suddenly enormous, preventing me from fleeing seeing that dozens of arms grabbed me whispering

—Quiet

taking me to a hideout in the jungle where a commissioner would sink a pistol into my belly button if by chance she was going shopping pulling a cart with two cross-eyed wheels that jumped on the carpet, the poor things, under a volley from a Kalashnikov, the boss at the same time absent and everywhere, in the living room, in the corridor, in the sunroom, staring at me with sewing glasses at the tip of her nose that called me

—Tuga tuga*

me trying to explain to her without being able to get away

and she seated of course, crushing with her little finger, at the edge of her eyelid, the disappointment of a tear

—Perhaps you don't like me anymore

and, I swear, you're wrong, what silliness this, I like you only Angola won't leave me, where I definitely am, so many wild dogs around the camp, so many kites up high, so many insurgents waiting for me here, I want my grandmother Benilde, I want my godmother, I want that both say to me

*Pejorative term referring to the Portuguese.

—Quick quick

tucking me in but don't turn out the light, above all don't turn out the light and give me the tin locomotive losing color and with a dent I don't know who made, not me, to hold it tight against my heart, I want the mess orderly without splinters in the neck, in the ribs, asking

—Second lieutenant sir

as if I could help you and I can't Hoards, I can't, the helicopter didn't arrive to pick him up

—It's gone second lieutenant sir

while I insisted with the soldiers that they put the stretcher inside and one of them with his hand on my shoulder

—Stay calm it's over

when there were attacks Hoards grabbed hold of a mortar, put it in the vertical position, a shout of fear spread in the camp

—Hoards is at the mortar

and we moved farther away from him than the enemies out there, Hoards always with the portrait of his girlfriend in his pocket

—The Thin One

they put it with him in his coffin and she must have been married to another because Hoards didn't come back, he remains in Angola, ah Hoards, Hoards, trying to hear the mortars, he served us dinner, canned tuna with beans, with stiff white jacket

—Officers

at five-thirty in the afternoon because at six night always, the diesel fuel of the expensive engine, ah Hoards, Hoards, that earth so rich eating you up in an instant, little plates of seeds, English sauce that the captain used to receive, my son at a corner of the table who didn't cry didn't talk, slept next to me in a bed of palm fronds, eating with his hands, returning from Africa the urge to ask my wife get moving, walk around the house, exist, touch me with real fingers, step on my foot, push me, don't leave me alone continuing to accompany me, tomorrow the pig with its feet tied stretched out on the ground, my cousin who takes care of the grave

—How it's going to scream good Lord

and if it were only screams, tears too, me to her

—Did you ever drink animal tears cousin did you ever drink mine?

and she silent staring at me, almost as old as me, pain in her vertebrae like my mother, always a scratched up smock, her husband in Germany letters from time to time

—I'm counting on going there at Christmas

and he didn't come, he sent clothing, a ring, desire that you hadn't gotten fat and that it fit you, how pigs cry, guess, I had to sit down in the square under the acacia with the remaining old people and sticking to its edge contemplating time in silence, not the time out there, the years here inside remembering when I went searching for my father to have dinner together and he came and the cane and the aneurism and the cap that remains on the coat rack in the entrance sir together with a black hat and a forgotten knitted jacket that still smells of tobacco, still smells of you, what I remember better, who knows for what reason, don't get mad, is your nose and the way you would order me

—Give me your arm

because an aneurism in the belly hampers the legs and grinds you down, he wanted to lift his heels and they didn't lift anything, it seems that they are dying before us and are looking forward to sinking into the earth, after seventy we only survive out here with belly up, we go down gradually, we give less trouble, Hoards Hoards, I don't recall the name of the one who took your place, I see joy on your faces etc., fuck off general, my father never took off his vest, never unbuttoned his collar and my mother on the step into the yard waiting, relieved

—Are you really serious?

—What is an aneurism?

Calling me aside with the hand back and forth

and here between us what is an aneurism in fact, something that explodes and dies drowned inside, my daughter-in-law in the kitchen with me when the morning sun pushes the loquat in the yard, with birds and all, almost up to the table with a stone top where we used to eat and a few leaves rubbing against us

—The coffee tin?

not really a question, an angry search as if the coffee tin, an old half-rusted biscuit box and with engraved hunting scenes belonged to her, me, doubtful that it in fact belonged to her, looking around without paying attention to her, already vaguely guilty how strange, my daughter-in-law a way of speaking without question marks that put me on the defense and after, tall, aggressive, with a hardened little eye that didn't smile, judged, so different from my wife always saying sorry and with timid requests to be excused

—Female with high stirrups*

as my father would have said if the aneurism hadn't done its work

—Female with high stirrups

and afterward some curls on the nape of her neck, over her long hair, tempting to any man, even though he might try to resist the curls firmly, with I don't know what quality they have, they softened him, if for example, my wife with us, and despite the stones, it was enough for her to look slyly at me and I understood, luckily the branches of the loquat always hid me a bit but they also gave the impression that my fingers leaves, now in the light now in the shade vibrating like those of prisoners forced to dig the ditch for the head of the political police brigade and squatting down inside waiting for the bullet, the doctor in the circle of chairs at the hospital

—It can't be true

and that's right friend, it can't be true but it happened, no matter what, my daughter-in-law, no matter if I tell her the place, no matter if I tell her the day, two lines of ants, one ascending the other descending, from the kitchen floor to the windowsill through which the loquat entered, beyond the loquat the cemetery, the mountain on which they assured us genets and foxes, my wife still lying down, her eyebrows on the ceiling

—Over here I was thinking about my mother

with the butterfly jacket, from the day the doctor praised it, not in the dresser, on the back of a chair like a trophy so that she could be proud of it from time to time, in certain ways you didn't grow up how good, you remain a little girl, there are times, I swear, when I feel like giving a kiss to your way of looking, to the simplicity of your joy when you managed to blow out the candles on the cake with one breath applauding yourself, happy, and me hugging the girl you were still so proud of yourself, if you don't mind call me love again have patience, call me love again dear, where does the shirt of our first night stop that your

—I was over here thinking about my mother

gave you, I don't like them teaching me about the washing machine or about the water heater or about the place for things, I feel like being happy

---

*Expression used of a woman who is haughty, picky, or "hard to get."

with the way that you deal with these strange complications I who know only how to pull the weights of the cuckoo clock and to be amazed at your way of organizing the world, the head of the brigade to me keeping his pistol in the holster, in the tone of one producing evidence

—The weeds are being pulled out second lieutenant sir

amazed at your way of organizing the world, my daughter-in-law to me

—Your son

and suddenly growing silent shrugging her shoulders and waving not with her head, my son who after three months spent with me, therefore still in Africa, said to me for the first time, suddenly

—Father

he who didn't speak Portuguese said

—Father

sitting on the ground playing with some sticks, all concentration and fingers, I never saw anything as serious as a child playing without noticing me, almost at my feet and very distant since between the sticks and him a secret understanding and despite being able to touch them I don't know where they were, what exists closer is always, that life taught me, the most difficult to ponder, I looked at the room and my wife no longer thinking about her mother, asleep on the bed with the butterfly jacket on and then I understood that she had buttoned it up against death that in her mind threatened her not from within, sitting on the mattress looking at her or in the shape of medicines on the bedside table, a glass of water, a thermometer, these disguises of hers, she thinks a bit, hesitates, decides, puts her hands on our foreheads, and goes away leaving us or rather leaving in our stead what we alive are not while the butterfly gets bigger on the jacket, wet rags that are growing in our temples and wrinkles different from the ones we had appear to make us wiser, more serious, our hands so much hands, a little bit of stagnant pupil on the eyelid, a relief that diminishes in the sheet, my mother touching me on the arm

—What was that?

approaching with difficulty, recovering her face, putting her fingers on my cheek

—Let me sleep

and my daughter at the entrance to the room, her palm on the knob, not pretty, poor thing, not elegant poor thing, with a twisted skirt that didn't match with the blouse where a button came off, giving the impression of being bigger than the others, asking for help in vain, who in this life, tell me, assists the buttons, who is interested in them, my wife, never bothered by time, suddenly troubled

—What time is it?

as if the hours were measured out for her, what did she know for certain about the kidney, she didn't ask the doctor about anything, she restricted herself to agreeing nodding her head, but appeared untroubled, did the tests and the treatments that they told her to, she didn't look at herself in the mirror to measure her misery, she didn't regret her slightly lame right leg, aware of her insomnia because her body too immobile and I'm sure with eyes open thinking about something, imagining something, sensing something, if I touch her she indifferent or then a smile because the darkness changed, that is, the darkness persisted but with her closer to me inside it, almost like thirty years ago, almost like forty years ago and regarding years I don't know for sure how old my daughter is, I have to do the count starting from the time when I came back from Africa but at what time did I come back from Africa if I remain in Angola, wild dogs and wild dogs that pursue the two of us trying to bite our ankles, our knees, trying to jump at our throats, the head of the brigade to me, hurt

—When will it be that the people of this country come to understand that we are taking care of them?

and the hospital psychologist while the head of the brigade aimed the pistol at him and he waved the barrel away with the side of his hand

—I don't believe it

my daughter thirty and many years or so and I'm the one who doesn't believe now, a wrinkle starting at every edge of my mouth, my son, older than her still no wrinkles, he's black and for blacks age comes quickly, instantly, one morning, suddenly the body with no muscles, red eyes, difficulty walking, my daughter-in-law showing me the empty tea cup

—I'd like another

without moving from the bench but with more thighs in the voice, it seemed to me that the pupils suddenly and nonetheless I'm certainly wrong, people are confusing sometimes, I'm seventy-three years old, I'm her father-in-law, I continue to command respect, not even a hint of extravagance, my wife believes in me completely, the only bullshit that happened to me was a stupidity centuries back with a colleague from work after a business meeting with the director in which I sat next to her and then a knee, by chance sharp, under the table, I thought it was involuntary, I moved over a bit and the knee insisted especially while the owner, I don't remember her name or rather I remember, Teresa, drawing diamonds on a pad while the owner was talking and me, not listening to the words, looking at the diamonds and nail polish missing white in fact, on her index finger, as if she were taking notes the white polish wrote down an address rapidly under the diamonds, on the pretext of adjusting the pad she spun it over a little toward me with the tip of her ballpoint pen hitting the address while the knee more active, I read the name of the street, the number, the floor and when I wanted to check better if right or left the ballpoint underlined it before crossing it out, the knee a definitive pressure of having agreed, me a pressure of exactly right, thinking myself uncomfortable because just the night before I had celebrated years of marriage that we commemorated with our small children and a cake with ten candles and after that in our room, door closed, where my wife put on her nightshirt from the first night, so white with lace, that continued to fit her despite being a little less wide, a little worn, in certain spots the lace a little bit yellow not only because for us time passed and I didn't wear pajamas, I covered nudity with a sheet, my palm found your wrist, her head moved from the pillow to my shoulder and her mouth

—Love

softly, in a thin voice, but

—Love

given that she was discreet in everything from the first day, from expansions to sicknesses, even today with the stones and the six months with luck she won't bother anyone, if I ask her about discomfort she always responds

—I feel great

though her circumflex eyebrows over her straight eyebrows that really become noticeable because they cast a vague little shadow over the eyes that become darker, the poor things, whoever doesn't know her buys it, those who know her understand, I was looking for an address with the

—Love

in my ears and the arm pulling my back toward her, a street not very far away but in a confusing and very large neighborhood, climbing, filled with tiny shops doing alterations, a modest laundromat, modest restaurants for workers, a modest establishment for locks and keys, a modest dentist on the ground floor but a pompous sign announcing implantology, two modest butcher shops, almost next to each other, with peeled corpses on hooks

—When will it be that the people of this country come to understand that we are taking care of them?

a modest and melancholy florist and upon seeing red roses, not very fresh ones, in the shop window the

—Love

resuscitated, a

—Love

with nails that hurt me inside without mentioning a burden of remorse that burdened my soul, the street a piece of work because the numbers of the doors instead of one, three, five etc. had one a, one b, one c after the number and therefore I began to think them infinite besides hardly illuminated, boarded-up buildings, missing tiles, twisted gutters and scraps of posters already with various winters waving rags, the door of number eighty-nine open, with an iron hand holding a ball instead of the bell and the light switch broken, a stairway of high steps and metal handrail that shook more than me, dissolving in the darkness to which I added a complaint of

—Fuck

added up to

—Love

increasing the guilt and hindering the climb, the narrow landings, one of them blocked by a baby carriage which it took effort to get free from since it appeared to have hooks that grabbed, held me, demanded that I remain with them, letting me go finally against their will, in a grumbling of springs, I began to discern a skylight on the

—When will it be that the people of this country second lieutenant sir

ceiling, like those with square panes of glass, white with dust and garbage in a diffuse clarity and silhouettes of pigeons here and there, unlike doves they sleep poorly, pigeons, always afraid that the insurgents, always afraid that a cat or an owl or the like will shoot at them, grab hold of their feet, crush their spine, eat them, my wife in her place on the sofa, with a less sunken cushion, embroidering in front of the television without sound that she wasn't watching, to know that there were silhouettes moving around nearby, even if on a screen, consoled her, and the fact that I knew all the junk and all the emotions that lived in that house made me feel even guiltier, by my reckoning I was on the third floor just as my colleague wrote quickly on the pad, this as much as my brain without blood seeing that all the blood in the legs due to the effort to climb and, as a consequence, deprived of red blood cells that oxygenated me I understood, stupid me, confused me, on the third floor no baby carriage, just a plastic garbage bag with a knot on top from where a bottleneck peeked out smelling of orange peels and two doors each one with a doormat, the one on the left with a Welcome half rubbed out, the one on the right with a caravel almost completely rubbed out, with a fat hull and fat sails, tacking in a high tide of hair and which of the two doors that of my colleague my God, besides not remembering the following problem emerged: was the right on the right and the left on the left for whoever climbs the stairs because when going down the right would be called what when climbing up was called the left and the left what when climbing up was called right what seemed nonsense to me or then what right and left they had to see from inside the building, in front toward the direction of the street and from the back toward the doors where the right is at our right and the left at our left, what seemed reasonable to me, if nothing else because it would not lead to changing my life, in relation to the same apartment, from the right to the left and from the left to the right although this solution brought, at least, one additional problem

(I dispense with others equally complex that also came to mind and that I will not enumerate only so as not to tire you)

that consisted in knowing on what side of the landing was the street seeing that the landings capable of various positions and who assures me in good conscience that the streets, just like people, don't alter, for example the widest streets that we knew as infants and revisit as adults suddenly narrow, of course one can always advance the hypothesis that we were the ones making them larger but we in fact did make them larger and how much and how, questions of extreme difficulty and of aleatory response, pregnant with emotional factors and in conseq

—On your faces the joy of going to serve the

uence fallible, me trying to say, a bit presumptuously, there are times when presumption is not harmful and always reinforces a bit, even if a little, the ego that in certain and determinative moments is so necessary, isn't that true, the sad one, with a small dose of affection, attention, care, and while I was sounding the subtle noise of the troubled sands of memory in the hope that the pad of my colleague would emerge, even a little clouded, between a lead soldier without arms, that I lost in the house in the village, and the imperishable nudity of my cousin Yolanda, who later became so fat, doubled over frontward, her back to me, picking out a bra in the dresser drawer and upon turning around in a shout of a woman stabbed

—Get out

installed in my soul the solid certainty that has to this day remained unshakable, that woman constitutes without doubt the only possible salvation for man, but leaving aside my cousin Yolanda whose memory continues to disturb me with her well-proportioned protuberances and recesses that fat, I presume, unf

—Hoards is at the mortar

ortunately, erased, fat, sugar, the difficulty breathing and the round eyes looking at us with fear

—I'm going to die

and in fact cousin it is like that but forget what made a man of me, though a man stunned what really consoles her, consoles us always all of us, in the cemetery or in life and as regards right or left having failed metaphysics I decided to try the two doors each one with its button for the bell with a different color just like times and desires tastes change too, wild dogs with enormous ears, a boyish gait and mouths always open, each one with his long string of drool swaying and tiny cruel pupils, I pushed on the first button, on the left of whoever climbs the steps and not necessarily corresponding to the third floor left for the reasons already deduced and a monstrous chiming of cathedral bells, which cathedral, of an infinite monastery, shook the building from its foundations up to the skylight and poor me with it, subject to a tornado of ferocious ringing, me with the urge to plead for help shouting a

—Love

that dozens of bells immediately drowned out preventing my wife from hearing me, it's possible that I had sensed something vague, a type of disturbance, discomfort, sigh but I'm sure she didn't think about me, she thought about a tightening inside between her stomach and the nape of her neck or about the drafts of air from her soul when the windows inside of us open toward the past like my peephole opens toward cousin Yolanda showing me how the whole world fits into one single woman, Hoards served us dinner, tuna with beans, with a stiff white collar

—Officers

Hoards who the helicopter didn't arrive to pick up with the picture of his girlfriend in his pocket

—The Thin One

between two girlfriends, arm in arm with them, the three smiling half ashamed next to the cedar tree in a garden in the countryside, to whom were the others married and perhaps they had forgotten about you, perhaps they hadn't forgotten, ah Hoards Hoards, no matter how strange it seems, friend, I still remember your laugh you who despite the vertical mortar didn't kill anyone and you were looking at the bodies in a respectful terror crossing yourself three times and kissing your thumb, the first sergeant showing me your bracelet of dull silver, the date with a meaning I didn't grasp engraved inside

—What to do with that?

and we sent it to his family who never thanked us, perhaps the Thin One might value it more but she would not thank us either, for

—I see on your faces the joy of going to serve the Fatherland

for what and afterward what words, and then I'm not an ace at prose, the problem is that the date on the bracelet, that still intrigues me to this day, I don't know what to think of it, if by chance I asked her in the house in the village on the night before the pig killing

—What do you reckon she thinks of it?

I doubt they would respond to me, it was so many years ago wasn't it and there's nothing that's not forgotten, second lieutenant sir, if we didn't forget, you were a second lieutenant in Africa weren't you, you know about this better than me, I'm here to give lessons, sorry, how am I going to make a living, the second bell a distant jingle like a sparrow with only one wing that's giving up on the ground, my daughter-in-law to me, heating water

—Do you feel like more coffee?

or rather a blue flower spitting out angry petals and the mattress of my room a long sigh, you only stones aren't you? almost stones only, your voice saved you, your fingers saved themselves

—Come here

and I was coming, squeeze my hand with force, with more force, don't leave, behind the door of my colleague from work silence, after the silence shoes getting louder and louder, a slit only, her nose in the slit, with the nose a whisper

—Go away fast my husband arrived earlier than expected from Porto

the whisper becoming a voice

—We don't need Bibles, thanks

and the door closed, the doormat with the caravel extinguished, me in the darkness of the landing waiting for the shadow of the pigeons on the skylight up above to help me to go back down, it's not only light, there are shadows that guide us, that of my grandfather for example

—Watch out for the step boy

that of my uncle Jerónimo who the invitation card from Canada took away and offered me an air pressure gun for the thrushes in the village which I never aimed not even at a toad at ten centimeters let alone at a bird, my father to me

—The best is to keep that thing you can still get hurt

well before Angola, of course, well before getting hurt, three pigs in the pigpen, ours the biggest, chewing with transparent eyelashes, from time to time a sigh, from time to time a sob and me looking at it from the wall calculating its weight

—My husband arrived earlier than expected from Porto we don't need Bibles

and when the lock clicked a voice from inside

—Who was it?

my wife

—Love

so many years passed, my son in a bathrobe

—Any coffee left?

Insisting with Hoards

—Any coffee left?

and Hoards looking on the counter, I understand, already on the first step, the colleague from work to her husband who arrived earlier than expected from Porto

—One of those Jehovah's Witnesses that want to explain by force the mystery of Christ to people

and I was going down the stairs, beaten, with remorse for my wife, mad at myself, detesting myself, distressed with those immense steps that confused my legs, afraid of the baby carriage, I no longer recall on what floor, where will it attack me again, the head of the brigade with a saddened gesture

—Is there someone who might misunderstand our work do you know?

suddenly almost human, almost unhappy, almost fragile, almost tender, almost grabbing my shoulder, moments emerge for me in which if I could I would hug everyone, what silliness, Hoards serving my son

—A bit watery don't you think?

as if he a white like us, not a monkey seized in a ploughed field, as if he not an enemy, if I had my G-3, if I had a knife, if I left him in Africa to serve as mascot to the next company instead of taking him back to Portugal, to Lisbon, to my house, instead of giving him my name and considering him my son, the street again long and narrow, the little shops, the buildings, my wife looking at the hours on the clock in the kitchen and returning to the sofa, still not worried about my lateness, still not annoyed by the stones because this was so long ago, I crossed paths with my colleague from work two or three times afterward, two times, one in the corridor and the other next to the bathroom that instead of paper to dry hands flung an electric breath through a chrome spout that didn't dry no matter what and forced me to mop my fingers off with my pants, the colleague who didn't greet me, on the first occasion she began immediately to blow her nose dissolving in the tissue and on the second she stopped short, looking toward the window in search of who knows what in her purse, perhaps for herself

—One of those Jehovah's Witnesses that want to explain by force the mystery of Christ to people

perhaps for herself while I continued to walk on the street passing by a variety store, a funeral parlor, an automobile workshop, a boutique with naked mannequins that reminded me vaguely of cousin Yolanda and me almost a tender smile equivalent to a palm on the cheek of the child I was and she stared at me indignant, already with the fold between her eyebrows that would continue to grow even until today

—Don't you touch me

because my parents had warned me, with severe expressions that frightened me, not to go near strangers not to accept chocolates, from time to time a cross street to the left with me thinking

—I go this way don't I?

since I began to fear that those infinitely repeated numbers in a's, b's, and c's would never end or rather walking for days and days without respite, feeding myself here and there in somber little cafés until the money fled from my wallet, a post office closed of course, a second funeral parlor that covered in sheets the shipwrecks that preceded, I to the head of the brigade

—Perhaps you're right

me, until the money in my wallet fled what did no harm because right afterward not the end of Lisbon, the end of the world or rather a sudden steep slope and looking down, there a lot on the bottom, stars, I wanted to call my mother, wanted to call my grandmother, wanted to sit at the edge of the sidewalk in the hope that an angel, perhaps the psychologist in the circle of chairs at the hospital, would hold me in his arms and take me away presenting me to his wife

—One of my patients traumatized by war

now and again a taxi, one or two trucks, an ambulance with the name written backward, ecnalubma, because rearview mirrors are left-handed and here an idea that would never have occurred to me, what geniuses can do, the head of the brigade holding my collar

—Good that you understand me

puffed up, gray-haired, in a yellow uniform, coming from the helicopter without insignia to interrogate prisoners and afterward kilometers of anxiety a small square far away, like those with a slide, swings, and public tables for the old folks' dominos, there was always one in a wheelchair, there was always one with a beard, there was always one who took cigarette butts from his pocket and smoked inside his tongue, there were always all those without holding their pee, there was always a guy with a gas can over his shoulder watching, and crippled old ladies, and pigeons, and a duck shaking its hips for having lost its lake, my son here in the house in the village tranquilizing Hoards

—Not really Hoards not really

while the Thin One and her friends whispered laughter, looks with contempt for my daughter-in-law of course, tomorrow's pig continued to eat with one of its ears sticking up and the other down, I hurried toward the little square since there exists a little square though full of huts and blacks me safe and there she was in fact, without the Methuselahs of dominos and those injured with two canes but with a palm tree straight up to the sky, ready to clean the dust from the furniture of the angels, upon arriving the bark of the second lieutenant during training, with boots lighter than ours and without a half-full canteen hurting more, without a tent cloth, without Mauser, encouraging the platoon without bronchitis

—March slowly and at ease

and we staggering blindly repeating in a type of cough and secretions and shortness of breath

—Angola

always he

—Is ours

with the corporal instructor shaking our arms

—Answer cadet

insisting with us

—Is ours

in a dying wail from a cave that likewise hardens the steel, likewise forging men, pity that they don't teach us to sigh softly

—When my grandfather finds out he'll kill himself when my grandfather finds out he'll kill himself

that we have to learn at our expense, alone, just as we have to learn alone

—Hail Mary full of grace

just as we have to learn alone

—Kill kill

the immense palm tree high up over there dissolved in the darkness between murmurs and cracks like all palm trees at night at the same time as me, during the training of my platoon, running with lighter boots, without a half-full canteen, without a tent cloth, without Mauser, screaming

—Angola

toward the creatures in agony that answered

—Is ours

my son in the house in the village Hoards

—Thanks Hoards

and Hoards so dignified in his coffin despite his bandaged head and the fly on his right toe cleaning his neck with his legs, the lid of the casket when closing trapped it inside so that you still have a girlfriend boy a lot of good she'll do you, the general on the dock speaking of the joy on our faces without taking off his gloves, when he finished it doubled the joy on our faces and he put it in his pocket, right after the little square of the Methuselahs, with palm tree, three streets on the right, a street in front and two streets on the left, this respecting the direction opposite to that of the hands of the clock, in one of the streets toward the left, at a distance, the river, lights on the other bank, what perhaps was a steamship, me to the recruit I was

—March slowly and at ease

me to me

—March slowly and at ease

in an avenue with an unlit cinema that seemed familiar, next to a hostess bar in front of which a white motorist was opening respectfully the back door of an expensive car, with diplomatic plates, from which emerged, laughing, a pair of blacks much better dressed than me, without stretching out to me rusty tins asking for food, despising me that is not looking at me at all, I never noticed pants so starched, I never saw shoes so polished, I never smelled so much French perfume, I never wanted to have a weapon so much as I did at that time and to sweep them away, looking at their bodies on the ground, jumping at every bullet, I never felt so much like asking for a knife from a corporal to cut off their ears, their hands, the parts they were going to use in an hour or so, my son to me without putting his coffee down

—Father

and Hoards dead because they killed him spinning with his fly under the earth, my daughter-in-law getting up with fear, my son supporting the knuckles of his fingers on the table without recognizing me, recognizing me without recognizing me

—What is going on father?

While a kite was turning in slow circles over the camp, while a flame burned down below, while the witch doctor showed off to the people

—Euá

the decapitated rooster with whose blood he drew on his own body, always dancing, arabesques without end, I see on your faces the joy of going to serve the Fatherland, I see on your faces, on the double march, the joy of going to serve the Fatherland, I see on your faces joy, kill kill, burn burn, of going to serve the Fatherland, the blacks almost at the entrance to the bar without looking at me, my son

—Stop with this father

and what am I stopping with this, you don't see that I can't stop, no matter how I try and, I swear, that I try, I ask you to believe me, no matter how I try I can't stop, the first black returned but the machine-gun fire pushed him against the light and he dropped on the ground shaking, his knees on top of his shadow and afterward stretched out on his stomach

—My shitty gorilla my shitty gorilla

next to the door of the bar, the second tried to grow toward us with his hand up

—Friends

however, the first burst from the gunner threw him against the car, the second kept him on his feet, the third folded him in half by the stomach while he raised an arm

—Muata

and slipped slowly from the hood swaying in a final

—Muata

continuously, when entering the house my wife in her tranquil voice without interrupting the movement of the needle

—It's not late is it?

not noticing the camouflage, not noticing the G-3, not noticing my huge fingers, my voice that hates itself

—What people like to hear at work meetings, my God

and while my son, relieved, went back to his coffee

—He disguised it well, look now

I sat down at my place on the sofa, proposed

—Let's go to bed at least?

And my wife, agreeing, put the embroidery away in a basket

—Love.

8

When I awoke Her Excellency wasn't in the room, she was in the kitchen with my father and the loquat tree drinking coffee because everything enters with the day, leaves, birds, the rust from the water pump, the lung of the mountain almost quiet that though almost quiet fills and empties us, besides Her Excellency and my father I had the idea that the soldier from the mess in Africa whose name I don't remember but who died warming water for them, if he were alone with me, he would sweep the floor and give me scraps from food tins, when I looked at him he vanished while my father asked

—Do you feel like a snack with a sardine second lieutenant sir?

and my father suddenly much younger, slimmed down by I don't know how many days in the jungle, marching slowly but not at ease because of the antipersonnel mines and trip wires hidden in the tall grass, sometimes a gazelle or another animal bumped into one of them and a bang was heard far away that forced my father to move with care on the mosaic in the kitchen where the reflection of the loquat tree dripped beads of light that the least breath of wind shook, Her Excellency with only one of her buttocks on a high bench from where a leg too long for her short dress stuck out and sincerely I would prefer that she covered it, I don't believe that if I at work from nine to one and from two to six that leg spends the whole day in the apartment, as the soldier was dissolving for me

(I have his name on the tongue but it won't come out it won't)

—You got to get moving with the writing child

pointing out to me Her Excellency with the discreet jaw and therefore he also didn't believe that Her Excellency made into a nun in a cheap T2* at the exit from Lisbon in Pakistani sandals with turbans neither above or below, scratching us inside on the head and the soles of the feet, if he had arrived earlier he would have found her and a girlfriend in the living room

*Small apartment, with two rooms.

caressing each other's knees in amusing secrets, their voices two octaves lower, folded like pocketknives on the sofa, staring at me with the sidelong glances of a tailor sizing me up

—So black isn't he?

with disgust, jostling each other in mocking glances and me capable of killing them, I had the impression that my father, worried about me, hesitated between telling me and not telling me about Her Excellency and ended up not saying anything at all chewing on painful certainties and bitter thoughts whereas my mother, behind his back, kept trying to calm me with a difficult little wave of her hand made of her fingertips and a smile that got interrupted halfway concerned to balance a tear on her eyelids saying that I hope I'm not mistaken but I was sure whatever they might want that on days like these it's clear that you'll have difficulties boy, my sister, always opaque, distracted from us or pretending to be distracted from us, motionless in a chair her eyes fixed on nothing, who do you go home to, what do you want, what do you hope for, Her Excellency's leg growing larger as she got up from the bench not as legs get up, as ropes unravel, as five

(they seem always to be more)

red nails flattened out in order from the big to the small toe that continue to make me want to kiss them, asking the second lieutenant in camouflage or in pajamas, in pajamas, the same worn pajamas, always the same, as in Angola, I remember this

—More coffee?

and my father looking at me in silence with the loquat tree out there between us instead of hiding ourselves from each other it brought us closer together, with so many birds now on my shoulder, now on his, sparrows, a blackbird, I wonder if thrushes, there are times, perhaps I don't believe but there really are times when despite the woman without hands who took care of me I almost like you, so much sun in the village and tomorrow's pig eating without any screams in the meantime, only sniffing, I felt the presence of my mother though I didn't see her because a silence thicker in their room than in the rest of the house, not breath, not throat clearing, not an animal that is going to be killed and therefore she'll also not die, no reason to die, madam, you have two hands, two ears, no one is tying your ankles and suspending you from a hook, approaching you with a knife, the doctor to us, with solemn eyes

—Perhaps a little less than six months

lingering to look at us in a kind of shame at the same time as the

—Perhaps a little less than six months

was spreading its bitter stain and my sister suddenly fast, she always so slow, going away slamming the door, her nose in the window of a clothing store outside, a strange attitude for someone who was never interested in clothes, my mother returning from the screen, still fixing up her blue suit for us, intrigued

—You all seem sad

and we, of course, are not sad, what silliness, why on earth do we have to be sad, for your information we are fine with the tests, this, I know, is going slowly because there's no stone that's not hard, look at granite, look at basalt, look at schist, but it's going calmly, the American medications are working miracles, medicine has come on like gangbusters in four, five years at the most hospitals deserted and thousands of nurses unemployed poor things not to mention the funeral parlors losing money the pallbearers asking for handouts in the cafés, my mother in the house in the village while the soldiers were moving on leaving behind decapitated goats, remains of huts that were still burning, ashes that spirals of deep mist dispersed, Her Excellency with half her breast sticking out of her dress found a box with sheets of sugar, held it out to me to open it so that she didn't break her nails or hurt her fingers, with me applying force on it sometimes, my lips pursed, if I was hungry, already five or six years old, I remember the woman without ears I don't know who she was or it didn't interest me to know who pushed one of those empty breasts into my mouth, if by chance I asked my father

—Who was that?

the second lieutenant who brought me answering for both

—I've forgotten already

that was not the truth, he didn't forget, how can he forget unless the whites different from us in the same way as Her Excellency is different from me, if I tried to hug her in the house in the village in front of my father

—Don't get near me monkey

and my father to me

—Son

and my mother to me

—Son

whereas the second lieutenant, seated in a kind of armchair made from barrel boards, was cleaning his gun breech in silence with a little bottle of oil and a rag and continued for hours to clean the Walther without looking at me, drinking a glass that the soldier who was busy with the mess had handed to him so that after the dinner his steps uncertain, he happened to stumble, he happened to fall, he happened to be on all fours on the sand unable to get up, crawling, losing his strength, falling again, dragged by two sergeants

—Second lieutenant sir

up to the barracks where he slept, mumbling unconnected phrases

—I see on your faces the joy of going to serve the Fatherland

or

—On the double march

or

—March slowly and at ease

or

—Hail Mary full of grace

or

—Sons of bitches sons of bitches sons of bitches

varnished with snot and spit, moist with urine, moist with sweat, moist with feces, insisting with the sergeants

—Sons of bitches

and the sergeants laughing still dragging him

—Sure second lieutenant sir sure

holding him up, one of them holding his legs

—Sure

and the second the shoulders

—Sure

with one of his boots, with rubber and canvas, slipping off showing the sock more holes than sock, showing the narrow ankle, showing the red heel and the holes, the ankle and the heel in agreement with the sergeants

—Sure

a distant microphone in the rain because January, because cold, because military marches that the waves drowned

—Sure

and a ship moving off and handkerchiefs and shouts, the handkerchiefs and the shouts

—Sure

with me sucking the empty breast of the woman who I can't guess who she was, I hate the prospect of guessing who she was, I forbid myself to guess who she was, sucking the empty breast of the woman without hands, suck the belly of a goat while she drives out her offspring, suck the belly of a female cabíri, suck Her Excellency who never wanted to get pregnant by me, suck my mother dying in that room over there, surprised by us

—You all seem sad

and we do appear so sad don't we, so sad, or rather me not well, perhaps my father after the sergeants laid him down and turned off his light with all of Africa around him, the trees, the flames, the huts, the impiety of rain on the zinc roof, the night before leaving for the jungle, I who slept on a piece of mattress at his side, noticed him with eyes open in the darkness as I notice my mother now in that room over there, keeping watch on her own body and trying to understand her own death that was invading her bone by bone, muscle by muscle, bowel by bowel, your death already in your features but not in your eyes, I'm sure she brought from Lisbon her nightshirt with lace and a little bow also white in front, almost comical being so old and the second lieutenant still not a second lieutenant next to her, dressed in pajamas, thinking torturing her feet with his feet

—And now?

distressed, indecisive, I caress where, touch where, I'm waiting that she, I turn out the light I don't turn it out, I speak to her I don't speak to her, I look for her I don't look for her, I say to her that I love her or hug her only, it's so difficult to live, so complicated, what would my brother do with other men and the idea of my brother with other men I bet it horrified him, how do they entertain themselves, urge to ask him now in the morning, in the kitchen, with the interminable leg of Her Excellency and with me, while the loquat separates us, while the woman without hands calls me

—Muana*

without looking because the blacks never look, they look in the same direction and that's it, they live alone, they disappear alone, they must be born alone and, as a consequence, I was born alone like them, my sister as usual immobile every year waiting in the yard and what are you waiting for tell me, my sister without words and me understanding her without words

—I really want this family to end

without my understanding why she wished us harm desiring that we end,

*Child (in Kikongo).

she remained in a corner of the cellar with us during the death of the pig, leaning on the wall, looking for I don't know what from us

—What do you expect from us?

and she staring at me without answering me at the same time as the pig was screaming and I sure that my father's cousin, who looked after our dead, with the key to the tomb in the pocket of her apron and what reason to carry it, four or five coffins, each one with a kind of sheet on top, no, six shelves and four coffins and thus two empty shelves, one on each side, that always terrified me, I don't remember tombs in Africa, they left it to the wild dogs to come eat us, Her Excellency covering her eyes with the back of her hand

—What horror

looking at her without seeing her, looking at me without seeing me, looking at both of us and only when looking at both of us seeing us in fact, since I got married I've not been with any other woman except on two or three occasions with the Cape Verdean mulatto always with an umbrella that used to clean the office, she'd arrive when we were leaving, staying there alone, without making a sound, almost nonexistent, mistaken for furniture, smaller than the wastebasket, smaller than the broom, with her head bent toward the ground, sweeping, scrubbing, as the day went on the loquat tree again and us, in the kitchen, without being able to hide from each other, looking at each other like the wild dogs, in a way that frightened us, if by chance I lingered, running around with a file, noticing her even behind me tidying up the desks or struggling on all fours with a stain on the floor, she appeared, she didn't come, she disappeared, she didn't go away, I didn't once hear her, I believe that no one heard her, her voice or her footsteps just like I almost don't recall hearing the woman without hands who tried to fill my mouth with an empty breast, just like I don't recall the sound of the grasses in Africa, still now what I hear is tomorrow's pig eating, eating, the woman and the man who lived with her, squatting on a small bench scraping out one by one with a bit of wood the jiggers in their feet, one afternoon I lingered for a while with some documents, this a little bit before the streetlights went on, when the tipuanas no longer began waiting for the night, or indeed I lingered on purpose with the documents looking for them in the wrong cabinets and sure that Her Excellency in the house talking with her girlfriend, now and again one of them

—How awful

putting her face on the shoulder of her partner

—How awful

breathing on her neck and then the back of her neck straightening up ashamed and returning to the shoulder again

—What a nasty woman

with her palm on a knee that was not hers, with her palm on a thigh, the thigh protesting

—Ah you're making me ticklish

while the pig bent toward the aluminum barrel, after Angola my father as far as I saw didn't drink again, he ate, ate and thus the sergeants not

—Sure, second lieutenant sir

silent, Her Excellency to her partenaire

—Naughty girl

Her Excellency to her partenaire

—Very naughty girl

at the same time as an index finger lightly traced her profile drawing it slowly in the air and the lips landed on a tiny birthmark at the edge of her jaw

—So sweet

the Cape Verdean not a peep, quietly, on all fours in front of the stain like the pig in front of the bucket eating, if I traced her profile drawing it slowly in the air and my lips landing on a tiny birthmark at the edge of her jaw

—So sweet

the Cape Verdean without perfume of course, no makeup, badly combed, poor, in clothing that smelled of sweat, of many people, of stew, of little money, of menstruation, of lye and thus instead of an index finger in front of her profile, instead of lips on a tiny bruise at the edge of her jaw, tie her back legs, hang her up on a hook, grab at random one of the knives and stab her fast, me operations major, me bald, me brown-haired, after putting the prisoner's foot on the crate from the quartermaster's storeroom or the Cape Verdean's foot on a paper basket turned upside down, and now shout, shout, don't keep quiet like my mother who is going to die keeps silent, don't accept like my mother that she's going to die, and she knows she's going to die, accepts it, don't go away remaining like my sister out there in the yard, as distant as possible from us, shout while Her Excellency hides her eyes with the back of her hand

—What horror

and

—What horror
in fact, you're right
—What horror
the absence of perfume and makeup
—What horror
her hair badly combed
—What horror
poverty
—What horror
the smell of sweat, of many people, of stew, of little money, of menstruation, of lye
—What horror
my own smell of black
—What horror
the smell of the woman without hands and of the man on a small bench, but what man would this be, who lived with her, horrible my smell of black that only a black woman understands, only a black woman accepts, only a black woman forgives, only a black woman doesn't notice it while my knife in her body, while my knife entirely in her body, turning around, leaving, entering again ready to explode in a thousand tiny metal fragments, desks, papers, telephones, a calendar two months behind, in May when we're at the end of July, I reckon that July twenty-nine and really thinking I am certain, July twenty-nine, July twenty-nine, July twenty-nine on the wall over there, July twenty-nine note well, write on a piece of paper, keep the paper, don't forget, remember that July twenty-nine, remember always that July twenty-nine, my father to Her Excellency that she moved away from her friend, both on the sofa looking at him thinking
—Perhaps the old guy saw us
if he saw it on their faces and worried that the second lieutenant, that my father had seen them
—What's the old guy going to think?
at the moment the old guy to her
—I'm going with my son to the garage to deal with the problem of the car
in the town five or six kilometers from here, cutting through the fields, maybe three or two, more than three I don't believe child, me to my father
—I've not been a child for a long time sir
and my father insisting, suddenly with the eyes from Angola

—More than three I don't believe son if you get tired I'll put you on my shoulders I promise

because a child despite everything less difficult than a half-full canteen, a Mauser

—What are you aiming at from four hundred meters

he taught me and me despite everything a child less difficult than a half-full canteen, a Mauser that aims at four hundred meters and a tent cloth, this not, of course, on the double march, this slowly and at ease, because of things bring the rake so that a sheepdog won't bark at our legs, Her Excellency toward the dark sugar paste that was left in the bottom of the coffee

—I'm going to change clothes I don't want to scandalize the yokels

sending her friend a disguised kiss that my sister caught in her hand with the rapid gesture she used to hunt butterflies, large flies, her palm would buzz, taking off their wings, the buzzing stopped, me to my sister

—Show me

and only a dead insect its legs shriveled up my sister at my workplace

—I only wanted to see you bye

and you only wanted to see me because if you don't like me, if you aren't interested in me, if you don't talk to me, my sister with her back to me always moving away, without a wave, without anything

—What do you understand of life you're so dumb

me to the Cape Verdean whose clothes were completely unkempt

—Do you think I'm dumb?

she was disappearing on all fours without answering me grabbing a cloth again in order to struggle with the stain, my father and me together once again like before in Angola when he was unable to sleep and brought me in his arms up to the entryway to the barracks, us side by side without noticing the sentinels in the shelters with metal boards, thick planks, and sandbags, my mother to me, leaning over my ear while he suspicious, tense, went sniffing around in the night

—Your father never left Angola

how many times at dinner did she point this out to me with her eyebrows

—Don't you see?

while he suddenly as far away as possible from us remaining over there, he right behind the guide

—Sweep more

the corn dry cardboard leaves crackling along with what was left over of

the station head's house, a hole without window frames in what had been a
window, my sister

—What do you understand of life you're so dumb

and between the village and the town, little farms, gardens, an abandoned storehouse missing slats whose door with a loose lock slammed, a
half dozen very old olive trees already gray, useless, loaded with knotted hair,
I had the idea that a crow but no crows exist here, robins, magpies, if I came
across the Cape Verdean it's clear that I wouldn't talk to her, leaning on the
walls trying not to exist, so poor, one afternoon she came to work with a child
who didn't dare to play in the office, though we marched slowly and at ease
on the way to the town the second lieutenant tired, the canteen half full,
the Mauser and the tent cloth weighed him down, I noticed one of his legs
slower that he steadied up by hitting his thigh

—It doesn't obey as it should this one

the time in Africa already distant second lieutenant sir is it, now baldness, white hairs, us with fat in our muscles, the joints resist, what happened
to you sir, do you want me to call the sergeants to hold you in their arms
making fun of you

—Slug

though the sergeants old too, unable to cut the ears off and chop off the
hands, to set fire to the huts, to decapitate the hens, my mother to me, in a
whisper

—Almost always after dinner your father falls asleep on the sofa

not second lieutenant, sir, your father, I discovered the stripes in a drawer
already faded between unmatched keys, a ceramic knob and a photograph
of a well-groomed man with lush eyelashes, smiling, my mother

—Your uncle who died in an accident on the way to the village

had said that no crow but it seemed to me that a married couple crowed
when getting up from a boxwood, the first houses of the town, the first alleys,
bicycles without anyone leaning against a wall, emigrants' residences with
limestone lions and painted tiles, more streets, a square, the jeep of the National Police, a garage at the end after a café with a patio of two tables and
a faded umbrella with a crooked pole in a cement block asking us for help,
my mother already awake trying to get up, relenting, closing her eyes with
what looked to me to be a tear growing round between two eyelashes that
she dried on the sheet pretending that she believed in the stones, why not
pretend that I believe in them, that I believe the doctor, since he pretends

with us, mother, he pretends better with you, he understood us talking softly on the other side of the screen, understood that we kept silent when we saw her, that our bodies were changing, livelier, happier, not aware that he was aware of us, that we invented a good mood and hope, my father to himself pulling his voice out from the depths

—This summer we

and which summer sir, stop with this, have some sense, don't annoy her more, there will be no summer for her, there will be a summer without her, an empty chair at the table, my sister in the kitchen burning flavorless lunches, Her Excellency in mourning not from grief, what grief, what does my mother matter to her because the black, according to her friend, favors her, the

—It looks lovely on you

it makes you more appetizing, more sensual, more mature

—This summer we

and this summer, understand, her absence only, her shoes in the armoire still, her clothing gathering mold in the drawers, her empty mirror, two or three forgotten hairs that remain on the brush, a vague scent of perfume, not perfume, only the smell that insists on remaining on the pillow, a light indentation of the body on the mattress, me in her place on the sofa so that my father stops imagining that you remain, stops seeing you in his room, in the corridor, in the sunroom

—You can think that I'm foolish but I was certain that your moth

stops talking to you when we go away, after we leave, he covers his face with hundreds of fingers and even so in the spaces between the fingers her smile or her look or her

—Love

with him imagine, her

—Love

what hassle, with him, be patient take that

—Love

also, that nightshirt, those thin straps, that lace so faded, take the slippers from the bedside table and that hook or tweezers or what there is to take a bath with that I saw next to the soap in something metal, turn off all that is you in our life and now in the house, even this ruin here in the village where she stumbles on herself at every step, a crochet needle shining in a scratch on the floor, a handkerchief fallen behind the dresser, the clay plate with scythes suspended from three little hooks on a shovel, the man from the garage after greeting us and the sickness of a son that the polyclinic has no way of understanding, the problem is in the children who don't explain themselves, that whine, point the belly upward and it's done, there's not enough to fill a gas can, the clay plate with scythes suspended from three little hooks on the wall, he put the can on the truck missing the ring finger of his left hand, cut off by the army

—Kill kill

entering suddenly, having come from nothing and disappearing cease-lessly in the village where he lived during the war just as I suppose his mother

(in Angola I still had no mother, I had a person who held out her breast and I ask you please not to change what I think, my mother is here living slendidly, not dying of cancer, inconvenienced only by the stones and the stones are being cured, it's evident that they are being cured, it's clear they are being cured, they are being curcd)

just as I suppose that his mother without ears and with hands cut off, look at the hens whose heads the soldiers pull off, small, thin, still gamboling about, look at so many people fleeing, look at me suspended in waiting, the man from the garage stopped the truck next to my car

—From here to his father's house on foot is a stretch that doesn't end

and the highway so different during the day, without huts, without goats, without cabíris, without the raft to cross the river, without the small birds sit-ting on the crocodiles, without men smoking a mutopa* that looked at me, trees much smaller than those of Angola and that didn't threaten me didn't groan, asphalt instead of dust, lawn grass instead of tall grass, a wispy rain, without echo, almost no smell in the earth, almost no presence of the dead, nor an odor of manioc, nor a reed mat, my father not young not in camou-flage, an old man half poor, in civilian clothes, because you old, I don't want to offend you but you old, if they were to hand you a fieldpiece you'd remain looking at it indecisively without daring to pull the bolt

—How does this work?

the car leaning on the shoulder in sad abandonment, already old, already scratched, from what I don't know who, yesterday or today, stole one of the

*An African water pipe.

tires, only women in the house in the village now, my mother, my sister, Her Excellency changing her clothes in her room, who assures me not accompanied by her girlfriend, who assures me not asking her

—Kiss me more

and slow caresses descending her belly, fingers on her thighs, on her lap, the loquat now entering now leaving by the window, the cabbages to water, the man from the garage to me

—Kiss me more

no, the man from the garage to me scratching his chest

—If there are none of these tires you'll have to order them in the city count on two or three days

and me answering like the troops

—Kill kill

while the man from the garage to my father

—Almost certain it was the gypsies

who are logically always the ones guilty for everything and thus cut the heads off their mules, burn their wagons, cut off the hands of their women, those long hands, those dark braids of hair, those forlorn dogs, with a short step, that follow them, Her Excellency with teeth suddenly enormous on the pillow, tearing up the sheets with her ankles

—Ah my dear

while my father's brother to my father, the little gas gauge light off, the motor more or less, the man from the garage

—We've gotten this far we have to see about the tire now

my father's brother to my father, amused, much more elegant than him, grabbing the back of his neck with his hand

—Where did you get a black son naughty boy?

with me thinking about my mother who at that hour must have been looking in the room without thinking about anything not even tiredness, not even her pain, not even the movements she had difficulty completing, she felt her ankles far away, side by side, unreachable

—Are those mine?

and certain that they didn't belong to anybody, this breath that leaves my mouth and only sometimes is mine, these two fingers of which person evaluating my face stumbling on my bones, discovering the dryness of my skin, surprised with new wrinkles, so deep, I'm not like this, I'm not this, the bell of a sheep in the alley but since flocks don't exist anymore, in the time of my in-laws the village still alive, women with tanks balanced on their heads, my daughter throwing pieces of brick at a lizard without ever hitting it, the son my husband brought from Africa and I didn't have to give birth to him, I received him only, a child that didn't run away from me and didn't seek me out, I saw him there as if stuck in another place, another space like me now, if for example my father

—Girl

perhaps I didn't hear him occupied with looking at the river from the window, my husband calming me down the poor fellow

—You're going to be cured of the stones don't worry

me still capable of smiling at him

—Of course I'm going to be cured

pressing a little on his arm

—I'm fine

and it's true, I'm fine, on the first night we spent together he so distressed, so timid, thinking

—And now?

thinking

—What am I going to do now?

thinking

—How am I going to be now?

so that I had to teach him what I didn't know in the hope that my body perhaps knew and really slowly my body a shell, really slowly my body calling him, receiving him, freeing him of his fear making him my fear, freeing him of the fear of failure making him my defeat, my husband

—Dear

not like a man, like a child calling for help

—Dear

afraid to drown in me

—Dear

and me, not him, whispering to him

—Love

me so far away, me equal to my daughter throwing pieces of brick at a lizard without ever hitting it.

9

And when the supply column didn't arrive due to a bridge that the insurgents dynamited or an attack or the like, it strikes me that this village is more and more deserted, these empty houses almost without tiles piling up inside themselves with grass growing in the spaces between the floorboards and a cat looking at us before scurrying away, without windows or doors, sometimes one slamming no one knows where, here and there despite no wind and me afraid of the dead searching for me around here whispering my name, when the supply column didn't arrive, before we ate the dogs or we ate each other, we requested a pair of unimogs, we put a radio in one of them and a gunner with a machine gun in the second and left the camp in the hope of hunting antelope or water buffalo, not on the dirt roads of course, but off road in the high grass and the engines roaring, you could make out the company barracks as they receded from us in the distance by a diesel moon shadow that was becoming thinner, me on the driver's right and a forlorn bunch shaking on the seat behind me while the unimog leapt over uneven terrain, little hills, hollows, suddenly tiny lit-up eyes but they were small animals or misshapen trees whose leaves shone, good that my father passed away without witnessing the death of the village, he is there in the cemetery in the care of my cousin who always greeted him

—Uncle

when she cleans the tomb though she talks more with my mother of course, I'm certain that though there is one outside and one inside the mahogany there is no lack of topics, me for example

—Is the boy doing well?

my mother if I enter not a peep, from time to time, and that's enough, a bump in the coffin scant remains of bones, what more does she possess now poor thing, bones and a dress that time unbuttoned for sure, no broom remains for her to sweep herself from our memory, squatting on a bench in the yard sewing under the loquat tree, talking to us without raising her glasses, it was the eyes that came out of the glass, much smaller through the lenses, looking at my belly with disgust

—You've gotten fat

because since I flapped my wings and without her vigilant love regulating my life I began a sad and irreversible spiral into misery and decline, my wife can't make the dishes I like in the same way, she doesn't prevent bouts of flu as well with wine soups and it's not only the soups, it's the way we serve them, she or rather the old lady does not understand that the secret is in the way a person makes us eat, my son who was always very sensitive understands, taking him back to his childhood he becomes what we want, my wife always alert

—Love

waving while I, pointing to my mother, identified her with a grimace

—Poor thing

and my mother jumping right out of her glasses

—I bet you like it when the idiot makes faces at me girl

initially I thought the motors of the unimogs scared the animals that come to drink at the riverbank but if we don't get too close they don't get skittish, they watch us slyly, they forget us and everything just as they are not frightened by the crocodiles next to a fallen tree trunk or a family of bad-smelling wild dogs at a trot, with ears as sharp as their snouts, the captain turned on the light of the second unimog evaluating the surroundings, lingering on a lone water buffalo that stared at us, chewing, he ordered

—A burst of G-3 fire

other water buffalo with calves, the bull guiding the group higher up, alert, scratching the ground, my father to my mother

—Leave him in peace

insisting for a moment with her glasses and disappearing hurt, without the lenses your naked face mom, receding losing its features, what's left of your nose, of your mouth, of your eyebrows hanging on your forehead at random, the machine gunner set up the tripod on the seat of the unimog with his loader helping him with the band, at night, I swear, and what long nights in Africa, not the short ones like in the village, enormous, with the silence ready to tear itself apart in a thousand sounds, a deafening silence that prevented us from hearing ourselves though we noticed any weightless branch that fell on the earth, one night, I swear, I discovered a lioness crouching no longer running, yawning in the tall grass and the wild dogs around her without her fleeing them, my father's grave the second in the first row counting from above or rather exactly where the mountain commences, between the tomb and the mountain a wall and right after tall trees at the top of which, from November on, storms are born stumbling downward that collapse in the thunder of pianos whose keys crack in a rain of notes, of strings that break and broken hammers, my mother praying to Saint Barbara the Virgin, with the lost handkerchief in her hand

—My God

lighting a prayer candle, my father looking at the captain in Africa, my wife so young at that time, without any stones, on the twenty-fourth of every month, the one on which we got married, the lace shirt, the body a shell, her arm on my neck and it didn't hurt to have the light turned off because the streetlamp lit up the room a bit, because a tipuana branch almost against the window, because no footsteps no voice from the floor above, no cracks from the furniture, no noise from the pipes, only the echo from each move of yours, only your closed eyelids, only our fear of each other, only my mother looking at me

—Boy

only me trying to convince her

—I swear that I've not gotten fat ma'am

only my blood with so much force in the temples, my desire, my fear, we're not going to die ever right, only you teaching me what I didn't know that I knew, I'm not able, I'm going to be able, I'm not able, I'm able, your knees, your feet, the living miracle of your feet first far and then almost next to my face, and then on my shoulders, and then on my chest, and then next to my face again, and then everything growing and emptying out, growing and emptying out, growing and emptying out, and then

—Hold me

as I'm going to explode, I explode, my mother praying to Saint Barbara the Virgin, that mess my hair and you

—Love

even sleepily

—Love

even with shame

—Love

and your arm on my neck

—Love

while tomorrow's pig is chewing pieces of worm-riddled apple, pieces of old carrots, pieces of slop, peels, bones, scraps, the pig devouring my mother, devouring us, the pig suspended from a hook screaming, the pig

—Love

I swear that the pig

—Love

even if you don't believe the pig

—Love

even if my knife or the knife of my son

—Love

the captain

—The two unimogs next to each other

the machine gun and the G-3s, the jungle, the river, a dozen water buffalo bent over the water there, still, waiting like the pig waiting, the captain standing up in the unimog

—Open fire on my order

and the flashes of water and the enormous trunks and some fruit rotting in the grass and Saint Barbara the Virgin and crocodiles perhaps, collarbone-shaped pieces of root from the lotus flowers, without body, my father to my mother or to the machine-gun loader who was holding the band, identifying my wife and me

—Leave them in peace, the poor things

and suddenly the two unimogs going down on the right, always in first gear and with the lights at maximum, to meet the water buffalo, swinging, twisting themselves, almost falling, straightening up again, removing branches, surrounded by a cloud of insects and we jumping out of our seats, almost falling, slamming our butts against hard things, iron, wood, shooting straight ahead at random and sparks from the barrels, explosions, hisses, the machine gun and the G-3s firing in the direction of the animals, a corporal screaming, almost standing

—Hit them

the water buffalo looking at us without fleeing, lit up by the light, the captain's Uzi shooting too, the second commander

—I don't like this piece of junk made by the Jews if by chance we hit the ground with them even lightly they burst into song right away sons of bitches he about whom they said that teeth marks in the ears of horses that didn't obey him, now and again he took off his boot showing his heel to the doctor

—Look at me only this gout doctor tell me if I didn't deserve to be in the hospital in Luanda no one is winning this war

the captain attached to the bench with his left arm and shooting with the right, dancing like a scarecrow in rags like the jerks in the unimogs my dear parents all is calm here a tranquil life peace and calm it's a real holiday no casualties in sight and there are still some who believe in the propaganda of the communists it's enough for us to shoot a light volley to make the blacks run who are all cowards, the hospital psychologist to us

—Are you all certain that you are not exaggerating the horrors?

and we're not exaggerating sir, I assure you that we're not exaggerating, the only bother is that these holidays are unfortunately so short and go by fast we're together again so my mother can lament that I've gotten fat since my weight is a drama for her not for me in the same way my father's diabetes a disease not just his, misfortune, you've noted, steals from all people, the way you pointed out a shelf in the tomb to my cousin sticks with me

—I want this one

perhaps because of the window through which I could see the mountain and entertain myself with the birds, the trees and the genets that would emerge up there to patrol the chicken coops when in truth this did not entertain because you not more than bones that bubble and that faded dress, death suits you with the rest starting with your eyes since your glasses did not travel with you, for months they lived in the sewing basket with one of the lenses stuck to the frame with glue until I threw them in the garbage, my wife sad for herself you spoke ill of her

—Don't you have pity?

with me answering her

—I'm getting fat in a way that doesn't disturb me

though the collars fit me and the belt buckle is still on the same notch, fortunately she didn't have time to rejoice with your stones, to tell the neighbors, to give out advice and orders, they told me that while I was in Angola she always in mourning not for me, but for herself

—My son

with mine much greater than my son's, the opportunity to lament to the neighbors

—We suffer more than them at least I suffer much more than the boy and so let go of my hand, don't annoy me, go to hell ma'am, the water buffalo first quiet, with heads lowered, after snuggling up to each other, blacks and whites in the clear light of the headlights, the soldiers, outside the unimogs, running toward them and me running too, don't burn the huts, don't take their ears off, don't cut their hands off, stumbling on a ridge, getting up, continuing to run, only the gunner with the machine gun in the unimog, much stronger than the seamstresses of the insurgents, turning the barrel to the right and to the left over our heads, with little red flames in the barrels while all that, the machine and him, was jumping, one of the water buffalo, a female, knelt down staring at us, there were no blacks escaping, there were no huts, one of them slammed itself against the unimog without being able to get up, a sergeant to the driver

—Run it over

I was slow to understand because of the screaming, the wild dogs were looking at us from a distance, hidden in the tall grass, since when has my wife, not, since when we've not and even so a smile but so poor, only a parenthesis on each side of her mouth, pulling the lips upward you can't imagine what it costs but I try, on the other side of the screen, while dressing alone before hearing you conversing softly, full of fear, about cancer, I like the metal butterfly on the blue jacket and all of you not for that, I who hate the death of the pig and keep silent, I who am very afraid of this illness and want so much to believe in the stones, to agree with the doctor

—Of course yes the stones

cheer myself up with the doctor

—Of course yes this will resolve itself

the water buffalo on its knees, the G-3s and the machine gun that didn't stop singing, the loader a second band, the loader a third band, the captain's movements and shouts drowned by the enormous bangs and the flashes in the darkness, my ears unable to listen, my mouth unable to speak, me to my wife still not my wife

—Would you permit me to accompany you?

and she at first as if she didn't hear me, then hearing me, then astonished, then the head lowered, a tad hesitant

—Maybe

a crocodile slowly emerged and quickly disappeared in the river mud, with half of its eye socket submerged and half out of the water, the second lieutenant that commanded the supply column hidden under one of the trucks crying from fear during an ambush, glistening with tears, snot, piss, dust, grabbing the grass of the dirt road and a sergeant kicking him, we don't take any risks at all, I swear, amusing holidays, the sergeant pulling his leg

—You asshole

so as to tie up his ankles, to hang him from the hook, to push the bucket toward the blood, to stick a knife in the neck and hope that little by little he'll stop twisting his body and be silent, me to my wife in the room in the village the one where my parents slept when the house still smelled like a house, people still on the street, the priest on the way to Mass on Sundays, always with a scarf because his throat weak, stumbling over his Latin, pulling out paragraphs from the book, the sergeant to the second lieutenant

—You piece of shit

the hospital psychologist to us

—You piece of shit?

and the captain waving his arms ordering that they cease fire, I helped my wife get up, dress

—I'm fine

her ring not on her ring finger, on the middle finger so it wouldn't fall off, everything slips off the fingers, she managed to walk, to warm up the food, to sit at the table with us, to serve us, when young she was a teacher at the school and thus knew the mountains, the rivers, all the verbs, they transferred the second lieutenant from the ambush to the north, the small mail plane picked him up without anyone saying good-bye to him, holding out his hand to me I put mine behind my back, the second lieutenant

—You don't want to greet me?

not offended, accepting, keeping his useless hand in his pocket in a sort of secrecy

—Perhaps they'll remove my stripes

and I only turned to see him centuries after, a gray man like me accompanied by a girl whose colors didn't match

—My daughter

that's her dress, the shoes, the sweater, an oval patch of vitiligo on her left cheek

—My daughter

not really resembling him, I managed to shake his hand and he moved, grateful, he was losing hair, parting it lower, he worked in insurance, introduced me to the vitiligo

—A comrade from the army

and the daughter's face now alert asking in silence

—You're not going to treat him badly are you?

and I'm not going to treat him badly relax child, that was a long time ago already, who remembers, the sergeant who called him

—You piece of shit

died millennia ago, everyone has forgotten, my wife in the kitchen too but only we two now, it almost seems that we've returned to the beginning doesn't it, when all was recent between us, without offspring, without bitterness, without humidity on our walls, life in our pocket like a new coin, neither of us crying under the truck, so aware of our rings my God

(yours now on the middle finger the poor thing)

that we saw them even without looking at them, so aware of them on the finger, through the window our daughter out there, squatting on a stone next to the wall, I never understood her indifference, her silence, if I asked her

—Where do you live?

Silent, what do you feel for us, I ask myself if when my wife used to go out shopping the shopping cart was not a pretext to visit you, we approached and the water buffalo fled, one remained stretched out sideways, looking at us, the captain's Uzi forced her head to fall and even with the head fallen she was breathing, with a worried calf next to her, dirty with her blood, licking her and bumping her trying to wake her up, an animal without antlers dying too, the barking of the wild dogs was audible at the jungle's edge, the engines of the unimogs deafened me, the soldiers, three or four, put the animals on a trailer and their legs so thin, it seemed to me people hidden in the jungle seeing that a trembling in the leaves different from the wind, the doctor drew an oval with a pen going around the white stain of an X-ray

—I'm not pleased about this here in the lung

speaking to me on a stool like those with a hubcap, give it a little shove with the shoes and it goes up and down turning, there is something in me that still wants to try it out just like, for example, slides and swings continue to tempt me, I never completely lost my innocence, me more interested in the prospect of moving on wheels than in the vitiligo

—Ah yes

and my son, much older than me, full of censuring eyebrows

—Father

knowing that if by chance the doctor were to leave the room, called by a nurse

—Would you mind coming here

because someone ill in intensive care or a question about a colleague or the like, I would crouch on the stool, the X-ray as pretext, for a happy trip on it, dancing toward one side and toward the other pretending to be absorbed in thought, turning toward the window on this side and toward the door on the other

—I don't like the stain on the lung

and the window and the door serious, thinking, my wife

—Can't you sit still?

I suspect with an urge to try out the stool as well, who in this world doesn't feel like whirling around if only a few centimeters, who doesn't keep childhood in his soul, for safety, with the insurgents on all sides, we returned to the camp taking a different route under the moon very much larger than ours in Portugal, surrounded by a halo of vapor, a savannah where animals were hidden, a gazelle leapt out at a gallop and disappeared in a jump, not really a gallop, a leap, two leaps, immobile for some time with its legs extended and its snout upward floating in the tall grass, if only my wife floated in the same way her kidney stones it's logical that they wouldn't reach her, he warned her

—Don't come down, your kidney won't get you

because if we don't come close to what we have here inside illnesses won't manage to get to us, the lights of the camp distant and the small pale lamps of the huts in a circle, certain that the soldiers sleeping supported by each other, if I were an insurgent I'd blow all that up in an instant with a recoilless cannon and run into the sad misery of the sentinels of the Fatherland, wooden partitions, canned food, skeletal dogs, empty beer cases, no rotating bench, nothing useful, my father looking poor fellow

—You live here?

and tomorrow's pig eating pushing away the other pigs, its eyelashes, I've said it already, transparent, a sweater on its back, the teeth so large, when my son and I returned from the town we were arriving at the camp coming up the incline that led to the house the captain's unimog in front with two dead water buffalo and mine following without any water buffalo, shooting a G-3 round into the air, my wife, already dressed, cleaning the kitchen counter in circular movements slower than before because something, or rather a stone that escaped from the kidney, hindering her mobility, her eyes, until landing on us, unprotected, orphaned, the solitude of the ill moves me and frightens me, to what extent do they believe us, to what extent do they know that we lie, to what extent do they understand this macabre theater, this idiotic good mood, this false joy

—Very well very well

and what does that mean

—Very well

now that you're going to die, just a few more weeks, perhaps a few more days, a few more hours and that's it, the advice

—Don't speak

because speaking is tiring isn't it, now that we've got our hands dirty here between us how will it be with me, I don't want to know, don't tell me, the kidney too or some other thing, the throat, the knee, this bother here

—Don't worry if you've lost your appetite that's nothing grave but the doctor, seriously

—We'll do some tests

the doctor I won't say whether pleasant or unpleasant, I'll say that with one more wrinkle perhaps the same wrinkle for all, perhaps he's suffering because of the gallbladder or something

—Until I know the result I can't proceed at all

and a sluggish, soft, farewell handshake, his eyes fixed on me who doesn't understand what they are saying, a sideways glance at my wife, a sideways glance at my son, his mouth at the edge of a phrase and changing his mind, becoming silent, five days until the laboratory completes its tests, but five or six waiting for the diagnosis so that my appetite vanishes with worry, drinking water every morning before weighing myself on the scale so that the numbers that appear in the little square between the feet increase and even so three hundred grams less and three hundred frightening grams, tomorrow instead of a half bottle I'll drink a whole bottle, I won't pee before, I'll hold my poop for afterward, I'll keep the slippers that, though light, always help a little, I won't remove my pajama pants, I'll remain with the razor in my hand that, though light, doesn't float, the captain to the troops pointing at the water buffalo from a chair that Hoards put outside for him

—I want this meat salted

and their eyes open, moist, the smallest with a fly on its iris, everything eats everything in this place, at least we in the village eat the pig only, we bring the rest, including the screams, to Lisbon, my wife shaking her head in sorrow

—What horror

continuing to crochet, there were times, when I felt like dying, the platoon that posted guards outside the camp always returned before daybreak, they began to distinguish the trees and the nursing station when a purple strip on the horizon, the eucalyptus not as black, the barracks where the men were sleeping more defined, the machine gunner who never spoke with anyone, never smiled, on his knees in a piece of canvas lubricating the barrel, the doctor to my father

—If we change your wife's treatment it's possible we'll get the best medical results there are surprises

stretchers with silent creatures, the ill in a small room, with heads in their hands, on long benches, an old woman pulling a pot and a fork from a plastic bag attempting to get a girl next to her to accept a little stew and the girl, with eyelids always closed, pushing away her arm with her elbow

—Leave me

not interested at all in the soldiers that cut apart the game, in camouflage already faded with use, the canvas laces of the boots replaced by string, my wife had to refuse a piece of water buffalo tenderloin just as she had to refuse me if I touched her in the dark

—Look your parents might hear

or rather no

—Love

a tired murmur

—Look your parents might hear

as if my parents, already long dead, up there in the cemetery, with the cypresses and the mountain bush deafening us, not to speak of the weasels, the wild cats, the badgers, the wind, though the dead more attentive than us, always watching us, envious, alert, could understand whatever it was and who knows if my mother to my cousin when she was cleaning the tomb

—Do you think those ones still have time for trivial nonsense?

indignant with me, bringing together a sulk inside her glasses, my daughter looking at us pretending not to care about us, my son's wife on the sofa, without her girlfriend, boring herself with a magazine she took out of her suitcase looking at us without looking at us, thinking about her black husband who smelled like a black

—The black who smells like a black

with contempt, with hatred

—What could have come over me to marry a darky I see how people look at us with more pity for me than for him

my son who in her opinion should be in a village surrounded by barbed wire holding out rusted tins to us in hope of a bit of leftover soup or a piece of dried fish instead of sitting at the table with us, sleeping in our beds, occupying the same space as us, the captain died in an ambush two or three weeks before we turned to the north, the insurgents' seamstress suffocated him with bullets, he fell from the Mercedes with one of his empty eye sockets, the helicopter came to search for him, one of the second lieutenants was promoted, they passed him the stripes and we forgot him, two or three small mail planes still arrived with letters from families, then no letters, then another captain who didn't talk with anyone, always in his office to deal with the sergeant, not one word except for one night

—I don't agree with this war

and we eating in silence, the political police came in a helicopter without markings but a guy in civilian gear, with a pistol and handcuffs on his belt, an inspector or something like that, they invited him to pack his bag, the captain to them

—I don't need a bag

and he left with the guy pushing him

—Do you not understand the example you're giving?

The captain without looking at his face

—I hope so

the pilot a grimace and the fingers forming little horns while the machine took off, sideways as always, disappearing toward the north, what happened to the captain, how many years in the

—Communist communist

camp at S. Nicolau, in forced confinement, in Caxias perhaps, a brigade head

—You're no longer an officer boy we can talk at ease

and two nobodies behind breathing on the back of his neck, my daughter-in-law to me

—Is that really true sir?

and though my daughter out there at the edge of the garden oblivious of us her expression

—Shut up

the wind that came from the mountain brought with it the dead mixed with the mimosas, the oaks, the cedars, my mother-in-law remained living with us after she was widowed, with clothes in her suitcase under the bed because locking it with her key nobody could rob her when we heard her coughing at night my wife

—Forgive

no more

—Love

of course because emotions fade, the

—Forgive

that perhaps means the same thing in a different way though the other way hurts, accompanied by a timid complaint

—We aren't the same are we?

and perhaps you're right, how did this happen, we mustn't be the same, I stay quiet in the bed when you touch me, I hear your mother breathing, I hear the mattress, I hear her bitterness

—You all

and hear her speaking with you or with your sister-in-law who visits her from time to time, whispering so that I don't understand though I understand the tone and the fact that she doesn't like me, for that matter she didn't like me at any time not at the beginning when me but a timid boy, always with a buttoned jacket out of respect for her and with hands outside my pockets also out of respect, my father-in-law who didn't detest me

—Sit

and me with shyness until my legs asleep, I didn't dare touch you if we alone for a moment, I didn't manage to answer your smile much less imagine that I was caressing your hand, I remember a green dress that you had, I remember your legs, I remember your feet that could have been prettier, unfortunately a bit large, not deformed of course, a bit large me who liked delicate feet and yours with a callus on the third toe but I accepted them like that, in the midst of many others I discovered them right away because they deformed your shoe, whoever doesn't pay attention would ignore that, the second commander to me

—Let's promote him to captain in place of the traitor for the next three or four months

and some new stripes that shone, not my second lieutenant's stripes, faded, more and more insurgents arr, the second commander shaking my hand

—We believe in you

iving from Zambia with 120 mm mortars, recoilless cannon, Russian instructors according to the political police, some prisoners, brought the night before, sitting on the ground waiting, trucks that went to look for water in the river returning, two helicopters on the landing strip, the river Cambo after the trees with a raft that crosses it on the riverbank, a python that suffocated trying to swallow a goat, with the feet behind hanging out of the mouth, my daughter-in-law to me

—Didn't you bring anything valuable back from Angola?

and my wife's hand suddenly on mine without me realizing it because so gentle, so

—Would you permit me to accompany you?

thin and me happy, I swear, me happy, me

—Can I talk to you more intimately?

my wife, still not my wife, without answering, eyes lowered, so timid, her hair brown, not black, one thought it black, looking more carefully and brown, a vein barking on her neck, her soles avoiding walking on the lines that separate the blocks of the sidewalk's shoulder what happens to you even today, long footsteps, short footsteps, the concerned question from time to time

—I didn't tread heavily did I?

I who hadn't even noticed if she treaded heavily or not

—Of course not

this even when leaving the doctor, this even yesterday when we were coming to the village, the car at twenty or thirty meters from the door and you slower than usual, supported with my arm's strength, you tired

—I'm not heavy?

and you weren't really heavy because you already didn't weigh much, because the kidney stones had become little by little lighter than water, the remaining second lieutenants when they noticed my brand new stripes

—Captain sir

the first sergeant

—Captain sir

the other sergeants

—Captain sir

the men

—Captain sir

the corn rustling in the camp

—Captain captain

my daughter-in-law charmed

—Mister Captain

and despite everything a strange shiver when seeing the pig eating in the pigpen and suspended suddenly with a kind of tear in its transparent eyelashes.

10

When I said to Her Excellency that we'd probably have to stay alone
for two or three more days in the village after the pig killing until the arrival
of the new tire for the car, she suddenly got up off the bench staring at me
with the hatred with which the troops, when I was small, invaded our village shouting, shooting, setting on fire, killing us, these are not really people,
just forms mouths and eyes screaming, giving orders, insulting, trampling,
throwing offensive grenades at the huts, destroying everything, Her Excellency
—What shit
despite the presence of my father in the kitchen, my mother relaxing
in her room, my sister sitting on a stone in the yard without looking at us,
please speak with me sister, Her Excellency
—Two days in this dump don't even think about it
and my father's features descending a bit, he liked the village that one,
my grandfather took him as a child to hunt partridges, they climbed next to
the wall of the cemetery, and crouched in a thicket of rock roses with the
dog panting its tongue hanging out, Her Excellency
—Don't dream that I'll stay here
while night transformed itself slowly into morning and a first sun, bright
green in the treetops, my grandfather with a cap like my father and a cigarette no longer lit in his mouth
—Almost there
both caps in adult size or rather the one I wore, with a burned strap falling over my ears, hopefully Her Excellency running among the huts giving
orders to the kitchen pans don't kill both of them, a breeze was moving
through the grass next to the earth, a distant daughter-in-law, the pines a
crack from time to time, my father already with second lieutenant's stripes
though child and an old knitted jacket, from his mother, with sleeves
rolled up
—You don't hear it?

and in fact tiny sounds in the boxwood, the rubbing of feathers, gurgling, sighs, all on the edge of silence, all on the edge of nothingness, the head of a partridge between two stems, now to the right, now to the left, mistrustful, alert, my grandfather's fingers taking hold of my father's wrist ordering

—Quiet

and Her Excellency immediately asking him, severe

—Are you talking to me?

in a tone that made the animal disappear, my grandfather bothered by her

—Who's that?

my father who didn't know her yet, he was a child

—No idea

as the barrel of a hunting rifle, not a G-3, began to lengthen without haste from my grandfather's shoulder, a second partridge next to the first one's spot, a flock of wild doves crossing through the village down below, what a pity the time of the storks is already over, everything is floating here, my grandfather's index finger missing a nail due to an accident when a child, not because a soldier had cut it off, neared the trigger taking off the safety, my father wanting to cover his ears, the dog crouching preparing to jump, hips higher than its snout, my father with eyes closed afraid of explosions ordering the troops

—Cease fire cease fire

at the same time as the partridge suddenly disappeared, my mother in the kitchen to Her Excellency

—Two days that's not much time

in a voice that took its time to arrive at words, pronouncing them almost without touching them, I've already seen pianos like it that sang alone, I've already seen children cry without sobs in the syllables, only the eyelids spoke, my sister in the garden approaching, as when little, with a lizard on the wall that vanished into a crack, the dog brought the partridge that was still shaking its wings and my grandfather hung it by the neck from a hook on his belt, I saw his neighbor, a widower without family, hanging like that, his neck twisted, turning next to the cellar ceiling, turning with a hat toothpicks on the band, one shoe turning over the cement floor as well and the second fallen, sideways, like a wounded animal, Her Excellency

—Horrible

with a G-3 in her hand, having forgotten to order the last huts to be set on

fire, having forgotten to sit down in the unimog and get away since the insurgents had not appeared from the river, my grandfather's neighbor to my
grandfather, loosening the cord around his neck a bit

—Who's that?

while my mother answered him

—Our daughter-in-law Mister Barros

with the sideways shoe examining her, so critical

—You could have done yourself up better

because the hair badly dyed blond, because the collar didn't go with the
dress, because she detested the village

—As soon as the pig is dead I'm getting out of here

—Longing for a place without partridges or rock roses or old dogs almost
blind in one eye, drooling around a dead bird, my grandfather to my father

—You in Africa did you have mutts to bring you the dead?

or did they leave them for you in the village, in the midst of ashes, so that
the insects might eat them or the wild dogs or the hyenas, Her Excellency
observing the coffeemaker in the intrigued voice of a young girl that almost
made me like her

—Why is it that the things in the shop windows look better than those
we have at home?

helping the woman without hands to put the manioc on a mat and I remembered the mango trees full of bats and a pregnant goat that someone
moved away with his heel, I don't remember them speaking to me, I remember the distant rain mixed with streets and houses, not one minuscule hen,
not one snake, where am I finally, antelope trotting toward the river, soldiers
on their knees shaking sand off around a mine, my mother changing position, with a grimace, on the bench, my father

—Are you in pain now?

because at times a stone, due to the angle of the body or the like, switch-
ing place and before calming down in a new spot, looking for a comfortable
space, hurting, the doctor to us

—She lost only a half kilo last week the new treatment is perhaps having
an effect

and my father back at the camp doing what he believed, my sister never
asked her anything, she didn't come to the doctor's appointments, she didn't
talk with her, on one occasion my father

—You don't care about your mother?

and my sister silent, sometimes at night I sensed her walking in the garden in the darkness trying not to trample the vegetables, what was her reason for coming to the village to attend the pig killing, she would arrive after us without greeting us, sometimes a nod from her jaw and she vanished, if my father called her

—Daughter

she pretended not to hear or then she became immobile waiting until he gave up

—It's nothing

without the courage to look at her, almost escaping from her, what happened between them in Lisbon or here, when he returned to the village for the animal's death, every year a different animal of course and every year the animal eating, eating, at first the screams used to scare me, I felt like screaming too and wasn't able to just like I wasn't able to scream in Africa while they tore off ears and cut off hands, I wasn't capable either of protecting the woman who introduced her empty breast into my mouth or the man who never looked at me and lived with her, always smoking a mutopa with his friends, that one a shot in the back followed by

—Traitors

with a shot in the back of the neck, my father

—I wasn't a bad person you know that?

and in reality he didn't turn to me, he turned to my mother and my sister, my sister as if she didn't hear or then a

—Don't speak to me anymore shut up

inside her silence, the doctor to my father

—I swear that I feel sorry that I don't believe in miracles

˙Her Excellency afraid

—I don't want what happened to her to happen to me

and my mother looking at my father without words, oblivious of him, without a complicit gesture, without any

—Love

absent, my father's father pointing out Her Excellency with a cigarette

—What did that one say?

my father right away

—Nothing

in the same way that if both were in the African village, in front of the ashes, bloodstains, and decapitated animals he would lie

—I didn't know that

me not happening upon the reason that he had been interested in me and had prevented me from getting hurt, he brought me to Portugal in the hope that my mother might help to make me his son also but now the kidney stones, but now the illness, but now the closeness of death prevented her from doing so, her nightshirt with lace didn't exist anymore or existed in the bottom of a drawer that no one found but her arms distant from her shoulders, but the doctor showing her more white stains in her lungs, in her bones, in her liver, but

—You have to live without me I can't manage

with the phrase replaced by what she imagined a smile without being capable of a smile, my father who didn't like me, used me in the hope that she would like him, my father at the same time he and the pig that he would eat, would eat, the pig that he would kill tomorrow as he killed people and goats in Africa

—Burn burn

as he told me that he watched the political police kill prisoners, as he perhaps helped killing them, as tomorrow he will sink the knife in and listen to the screams, the groans, the slow teardrops, as he will leave my mother alone in the hospital at the moment of death, as Her Excellency fearful of him if she sensed him nearby

—No

as he has to pretend not to hear if my mother is calling, leaving for the cemetery to curse the dead, as it pleases him that Her Excellency despises me

—The black

as when the woman of the cut-off hands who I lived with asked him

—Chindele Chindele

and acted as if he didn't hear her, he looked at me and looked down again, sitting on the back of the woman as if he didn't see me, he lifted the machete that was in the hut where we lived, I recall the smell of hemp, the smell of the earth, the hens only necks squirming on the ground, goats they blinded with wires, an old lady her mouth open without sound, Her Excellency to her girlfriend

—Daughter

while she kissed her shoulder, a T-6 throwing defoliant onto a field, my mother the back of her neck extremely thin washing the dishes from break-

fast in a bucket, me being put in a unimog by my father, almost naked, barefoot, Her Excellency regarding me

—So dirty

preventing me from getting close to her, me dirty, the troops dirty, my
father dirty, dust, engines, blasts, planks that broke, the lepers next to the
river grunting, two or three birds with bare necks waiting, my mother sitting
again, exhausted, drying me in a small cloth, the doctor to her

—The pills have not taken away the pain?

weighing her on a scale satisfied with the result, showing her the graph
that my mother never looked at

—Thirty-six and one half kilos give or take a little the same weight

almost content, almost effusive, almost able to hide the false notes in his
voice, my mother to the schoolteacher

—What about my son Dona Cidália?

together with the youngest students learning the alphabet, it's a day with
wwwwwwwind and I like wwwwwwind, the teacher with a pencil sticking
out of her gray hair

—He has to go

with me, much older than the others, so aware of being black, occupying
a tiny desk, drawing bent letters in a notebook, drawing numbers, the boy's
godmother at my side to Dona Cidália

—He can't change his desk, and I like the wwwwwwind, is he afraid of
the black?

ready to push me with the, it's a day with wwwwwwind, umbrella, while
the godson rolled himself up in her legs hiding his face in her belly, at lunch-
time I would eat alone in a corner with a spoon, incapable of holding the
soup, rolling it up in my fingers, the lunchroom worker mistrustful of me

—It's better to boil the silverware afterward who knows what illnesses
he has

women without filed teeth or breasts sticking out, no men sitting on
the ground smoking in silence, people came at night looking for manioc
and gave instructions next to the corn, the pig for tomorrow in the pigpen
sniffing, sniffing, the pigeons of Cardal Florido circling around the village,
sometimes, with the east wind, one smelled the lake, that is mud, moss or
was it the dead from the cemetery who were speaking with us, Her Excellency to me

—When your parents die this house will be sold

thinking about money as if someone bought it, in a few years only bricks and ghosts here, that of my grandfather hunting partridges, that of the dog buried I don't know where, my mother's stones piled up in the tomb with the phrase

—I'm in no pain at all

breathing from above, with her word

—Love

which we forgot, the doctor saying good-bye to us

—I'm sorry

not in his white coat, like other people, an everyman, if he lived in our building we wouldn't notice him, we used to meet him taking the mail from his box, leaning forward separating papers, a vague greeting and he forgot us, perhaps lingering on me a bit because I was black

—A black

at certain times even the impression that my father

—A black

and all of Africa returning to him, the second lieutenant of the paratroops, the other under the truck crying, the inspector of the political police to my father

—Are you really going to take him?

and my father without words because busy cutting hands off, cutting ears off, leaving me alone though there are moments when a person needs company even that of some black, someone who one might enjoy and try to like, he could take care of himself through me, many years ago my mother not

—Love

no arm for so many years, for so many years they, for so many years me

—Father

knowing that I'm not his son, for so many years my sister stopped being his daughter, one day I'll speak about this, she hates him, it's impossible that she not hate him as he hates himself and due to what happened to my mother not

—Love

my sister at my workplace

—I only wanted to see you bye

and moving away along the corridor, for whom did you come to the vil-

lage every year tell me, to witness the death of which of us, leaning on the
wall at the end looking at us while the pig sobbed calling us, Her Excellency
trying to cover her ears

—Don't touch me leave me don't touch me

while her girlfriend caressed her hand

—Alright alright

kissing her forehead, her eyelids, her mouth

—Alright

older than her, perhaps the same age as my mother, owner of the clothing
store where Her Excellency had worked at times, the girlfriend

—Try on this dress my jewel

with her in the fitting room which a curtain closed, to adjust it better on
the back, the bosom, stretching the fabric highlighting her buttocks, approving of it

—It'll kill

—Arranging her hair, pressing on the horn at the tip of her nose

—Pópó

with a little laugh coming not from the mouth, from the throat, with
closed eyes with her rings trembling

—If you had any idea how you affect me

caressing the back of her neck

—the little girl I didn't have

Her Excellency with closed eyelids trembling too

—You make me ticklish

while her girlfriend was looking for the base of her legs

—Are you ticklish here too?

the pig that was coming tomorrow in a truck, mistrustful, coughing, held
by a cable on its neck, with a bucket of slops in front but without eating, distressed, the second commander in the third Berliet after the minesweeper
jostling elbows with my father pointing out some bushes on the left side of
the path on the way north

—Something is happening there

seated with me on the ground at his feet, with some camouflage shorts
cut by the chief with the sewing machine that reached to my ankles and a
hat of my father's that covered my eyes and a cloud of dust from a mine in it,
screams from monkeys and the squawking of birds crossing branches above
us, soldiers entering the jungle and G-3s and grenades and a machine gun

turning and insults and falls and a Chinese in an orange uniform and a corporal falling, if you had any idea of how you affect me, getting up, falling, and an offensive grenade in three seconds and in five seconds an explosion in the jungle and my father with me content observing the pigsty

—A pig bigger than last year's

that will take longer to bleed, to die and thus more sausages, bigger hams, chops for six months and if my wife no longer alive, and certainly not alive, for six and a half months, someone said, the doctor, I hope

—Pork not a chance a grilled chicken

and a second sergeant screaming at the doctor, Her Excellency to the owner of the store leaning the back of her neck against a rod searching for her girlfriend with her fingers fumbling about, asking her

—More

lie, not asking anything, a bazooka in the jungle, two bazookas in the jungle, broken branches, falls, the mask of a bush falling, a black kneeling on the ground slowly, Her Excellency complaining

—I must be mad

not really a complaint, a little laugh, not really a laugh, sobs, already barefoot, with red nails, with nails always red, ceaselessly scratching the ground, how I like your toes gentlemen, to hold them in my mouth, to suck on them one by one and her hips already in the air, her buttocks in the air, her mouth as distant as possible from me

—Ah mother

my father jumping from the truck bursts upon bursts of fire, my sister

—No

and my father

—Shut up

while the

—No

increased, while the

—No

diminished, while only her elbows pushed him, while something in something quickly, while his palm red, while his face torn, while my mother without hearing, hearing without hearing, while an antelope lifting itself up from the tall grass and disappearing farther ahead, while me silent drawing letters in school, a page of As, a page of Es, while Dona Cidália with glasses over my shoulder

—Very good very good

while me black, so black, while a woman without hands who was looking at me first and afterward stopped seeing me, while the pig, that will only die tomorrow, was eating me, eating, I don't have hands either, I don't have ears, I almost don't have a head, I don't have a head anymore but I continue to see, the second commander with the pistol now because the G-3 jammed, the machine gunner above us, the loader with only one shoulder

—Big sons of bitches big sons of bitches

the witch doctor lying on the truck looking for tourniquets in the nurse's backpack, the owner of the store to Her Excellency

—Ah my treasure

smelling of old meat so strongly, smelling of face powder so strongly, smelling so strongly of the perfume one finds in deserted elevators, belonging to old ladies who had certainly already died, a corporal with an Uzi sweeping the path shooting at the insurgents, shooting at us, a wounded man without a boot limping toward my father

—Second lieutenant sir second lieutenant sir

the operations officer on all fours in the cab of the Mercedes hiding in his hands, the doctor to my father and me

—After the pig killing we'll have to admit her there are always things that can get a bit better

my grandfather's partridge hat in the coatroom of the house in the village still, with a small feather on its band, the dog buried under the loquat tree, for what reason do they always bury dogs under trees, the helicopter gunship emerged suddenly whirling above us, dear parents sometimes we play at war without anyone getting hurt of course they make us white the others black and it all ends in a friendly lunch they sent us here for holidays I swear, my grandmother to my grandfather

—Do you believe this?

and my grandfather silent while the ducks were passing quacking in a type of triangle, with a female in front, toward the lake, my mother in the hospital thankful for the peaches

—They are really starting to look good to me, I swear

and she didn't touch them, I bet she offered them to one of the nurses when we were leaving

—It's a pity that you remain there hurting yourselves

the pain medicine made her sleep from time to time, she woke up with us around the bed

—Have you been here for a long time?

my father rubbing his mouth on her forehead

—We came just now

when we didn't come just now, we came a bit earlier leaning over her wasted body, my sister behind us looking from the window at the buildings, the clouds, the airport in the distance

—The doctor assured me that in a week I'll be on my feet

two patients with her in the hospital room, one who slept the whole time, the other who asked us, a rosary in her fingers

—Don't you think I'm a little bit better?

and not a little bit better not a little bit worse, she was melting into the mattress, now and again she asked her fantasy dentures to become more healthy, younger, with a puffy-cheeked smile, happy, the teeth improve one's mood gentlemen, the soldier was kicking the corpse of a black face-down on the dirt road, with canvas boots like ours to the top of his thin ankles, Her Excellency to me, in a panoramic gesture that included the house, the garden, the cemetery, the mountain, the injured that were collecting the stretchers

—I assure you that I won't stay here for two days while you wait for the tire store

with me inside the Berliet giving orders to the troops, dear parents we moved yesterday on a long walk but without any problems toward Baixa do Cassange still more secure than the East imagine my luck the whole town fancy dozens and dozens of enormous mango trees in a row and cotton plantations all the way to the horizon where we have to stay getting a tan living it up for the rest of our holidays, the patient with the rosary in her fingers, the one who must have been her daughter, because the nose identical, sitting in a chair next to the bed, also with a rosary, who now and again cleaned her face with a corner of cloth, nodding no to us, with resigned eyelashes, when she supposed that the little bit better was not looking, with two widow's rings on the left hand, so simple to die, enough to trip on a wire, a sickness, a shot from a Kalashnikov or from a G-3 and that's it, or not even that, the soldier stretcher-bearer, his guts exposed, holding them out to the company doctor

—Doctor

who didn't dare to take them, so pale, dear parents don't worry it wasn't me it was a kid from Matosinhos or from Póvoa almost always silent almost always serious he didn't get many letters he didn't write any I remember that one day he showed the wire he wore around his neck to a second lieutenant if by chance something happens to me, please do me a favor, tell me sincerely if you don't think I'm a little bit better, of sending this to my father and now two sergeants

—Fuck fuck

collecting the dead, a leg pulled, an arm pulled, what was left over got wrapped up in tent cloth, dear parents duty is so easy they don't protest they don't refuse they don't get bored they accept, the hospital psychologist getting up suddenly from the circle of chairs

—You aren't able to be silent?

and the problem was that we weren't able to be silent just as the guts couldn't stop slipping from his arms, guts like those of the pig tomorrow, living guts, a species of interminable snakes always sliding, feces, blood, membranes, the second commander vomiting, the operations officer hiding under a tent cloth

—Leave me in peace leave me in peace

my mother to him

—Love

trying to help him pulling him inside herself, calming him

—It's all over alright alright

and my father looked like he was crying it seemed, what stupidity crying, without aiming the weapon at anyone, his face hiding in the pillow, and lifting his face

—Sorry

dear parents in less than three months we return I would like so much to miss the house in the village and I don't to miss you and I don't to return to hunt partridges and I'm not capable of hunting of talking to you and I don't talk to you of confessing and I don't confess the one with the guts was called Lorenço da Conceição Mendes and at a certain point he suddenly became silent with what remained of his entrails spread out on the earth everything is put back again into his belly sewn up it doesn't matter with what thread it's forgotten

—Crush the head of that black with the butt of your gun crush crush

the second commander sitting on a root

—It can't be it can't be

but finally my major it could, it could, how funny that the blacks are the same as us inside, the same flesh, the same bowels, the same, I swear, bones, wild dogs over there in the distance lined up watching us, quiet, only moving their ears, the hospital psychologist to the circle of chairs that turned little by little like trucks

—You really aren't able to be silent?

me five, or six, or seven years old, I don't know, Her Excellency despising me

—You

and Dona Cidália content with me

—If you continue to learn like this in no time you'll be white like us

this and the alphabet, numbers, already some words, Clara likes pigeons a lot, how pretty is Antoninho's tricycle, phrases, in the pockets of a black with camouflage different from ours a camera, papers, lines written with a pencil on crumpled pages, an envelope with photographs of the camp, marked with arrows and circles and the place of the storeroom in red, the second commander to the captain

—How did these assholes manage to do this?

the captain

—If we don't get out of here fast they'll return

the ammunition for the bazooka is used up and the machine guns, all is well dear parents all is well they broke down, count the men that we still have capable of charging into the jungle, a half hour ago the fourteenth he said that it had two platoons on the way while the helicopter was coming and going transporting the injured and the dead were waiting some above the others mixing body parts, rags, features, while my mother

—Son

called me from the bed in her room in the village, my great-grandfather's bed, my grandfather's bed before it became my father's bed, where one to the other

—I love you

or none of them to the other

—I love you

or both in silence thinking that

—I love you

and in reality alone like Her Excellency will leave me alone waiting for the man from the garage to repair the wheel when there's no longer anyone from my family in the village except the deceased, who don't belong to anybody's family, in the tomb in the cemetery on the hill of the mountain, in the midst of the smell of rock roses, of the smell of trees, of the pines where the light gets lost, of the darkness full of impossible animals from the night the hospital psychologist tried to remove

—Shut up

without succeeding in removing them because they always return, they remain with us, they don't ever abandon us, my father to my mother who was not listening to him

—Forgive

leaving the yard toward the pig, that we'll kill tomorrow, eating, eating, the pig for whom we still don't exist, we will exist here only in a few hours, incessantly eating not only the slop, not only the peels, not only the scraps that they give him, our remains that they'll give him while the patient in her room asked with a rosary in her hands

—You don't think I'm a little bit better?

dissolved into the mattress, the false teeth in the hope that she'll become healthier, in the hope of living, in the hope that no one would take her from here, far away from us, in the hope of remaining with us forever, in the hope of smiling to us when she didn't smile to us at all, looking at us with shyness, with fear and terror

—Help me

like my father to my mother

—Help me

like me to Her Excellency

—Help me

and how useless to ask

—Help me

if we are alone, if my mother to us

—It's over

disappearing into the gate on the way to the highway down below where no one will see her anymore.

11

I ordered the soldiers to make a bed of palm fronds for the child, that I put in the officers' barracks next to mine between the posters of naked ladies who were smiling always in love with us, but I knew he remained sitting the whole night, immobile, with a piece of manioc held close, looking at me in the dark, impassive as during the attack when we suddenly entered, opening fire, into the village, minutes before morning, on the opposite side of the river, with a helicopter gunship from the South Africans following and the gunner who didn't speak to anyone, not even his comrades, he walked in the camp his hands in his pockets and a type of panama on his head, almost leaning on the pilot, almost with his legs sticking out, choosing his targets one by one, this man, that one and the child without avoiding him, quiet, his hair discolored by the food that he didn't have and the stomach swollen with hunger, his belly button sticking out, standing still between two huts without worrying about the flames, the bleating, the screaming, watching his mother crawling on all fours toward him, shaken by the bullets, without being able to reach him, his father trying to defend himself with a broken homemade rifle, a half-blind old man, the left half of his face longer than the right and huge gums, that reached his ankle, he fell asleep afterward with his palm open, he ended up forgetting him and he must still be there if the hyenas spared him and the wild dogs more interested in tearing apart goats, the child who to this day, already a man, has not stopped staring at me without curiosity or hatred not seeking to understand, my grandfather to my father, holding out to him the tip of the fork above the partridges

—Take care with the buckshot from the shotgun the dentist will return here only in April

the child who to this day, already a man, has not stopped staring at me feeling I don't know what, thinking I don't know about what, without ever touching hugging me blacks don't touch don't hug, my father pulling round buckshot from his tongue with care, clapping when they are respectful

—Euá

not noticing when they are contemptuous, my wife to me in the room, looking at the door she who was always cautious

—Do you think that the little one has gained any friendly affection for us?

and he could have gained some, I don't know, because if he fell ill he held on to the wrist when we leaned over him, so tired in the sheets, so alone, so distant, he seemed fearful that we would leave and the troops would return, so many ears cut off, so many hens stumbling about without heads, so many hands that don't exist, so many starving rats coming up from the river, could it be that the blacks have things similar to ours, could it be for example that they grow cheerful, suffer, sometimes they greeted us in the village around the camp

—Moio*

smiling but is it really a smile my God, is it really a smile, my wife in the beginning if she had a caress for him, she studied her fingers right away to see if stained, the first time that he attempted to kiss her on the forehead she lingered in the mirror to check if the lips the same, they seemed to be the same in fact and nonetheless she wanted to swear that the smell changed, strange, unpleasant, not of a person, of an animal, one afternoon, suddenly, without any reason, the child to her

—Mother

the same way to me

—Father

during a bout of bronchitis, still with a cough, and we looking at each other, embarrassed, perplexed, my mother without ears and hands, me under a beam of the hut still burning, the pilot pointing out to the gunner an almost intact hut in whose entrance a woman was praying on her knees before rising up in a clumsy jump and stretching out on the ground, two or three days afterward returning to the camp we saw the gunner walking alone in the sand, a panama on his head and a beer bottle in his hand, without pay-ing attention to anyone, he got up, he sat down, he got up again looking at the savannah conversing with himself in a language I didn't know, my wife to the child, almost hugging him

—Son

hugging him

*Greeting (in Kimbundu).

—Son

dressed, not in her lace nightshirt, and not

—Love

as to me when we married, helping me to, receiving me in herself, she to the child

—Son

the helicopter gunner stretched out on his bunk in the officers' barracks, with the posters of women smiling all the time, very blond, he arranged the pillow, took his pistol out of its holster, took the safety off, put the tip of the barrel at the point where the throat becomes jaw, said

—Good night, officers

to us and almost all his head on the ceiling, pieces of brain, cartilage, teeth, bones, blood too on the zinc roofing and his chest shrinking and expanding breathing still, the pistol a second shot when it fell to the ground, my wife to me holding onto my shoulder

—Sleep

no

—I love you

of course

—Sleep

because perhaps my features on the ceiling as well, when they cleaned them up tomorrow's pig could eat them, the gunner's boots suddenly so still, so big, his shins skinny, no ring on his finger, one afternoon one of our soldiers started to walk constantly going forward walking all the time, they grabbed him in the savannah with water up to his waist, surrounded by a chorus of frogs

—In a half hour I'll be home leave me

shaking us off, not struggling with us, this, he thought, in a tiny town in the north almost on the border with Spain, stone walls, little chapels, genets, half of a saint in a niche with a small glass jug and a cousin who didn't talk, didn't eat alone, didn't understand orders and slept with his godmother, enormous, obedient, silent, my mother to, it's a day with wwwwwwind and I like wwwwwwwwind, me

—Wouldn't it have been better to leave him in Africa?

the child on the ground, not in a chair, eating with his fingers, I took him to the jungle with me for fear that the soldiers, for fear that I wouldn't find him when I returned

—The boy?

and silence, one of the corporal drivers without looking at anyone at all

—He must have left without our noticing

and of course he didn't leave without their noticing, the officers' barracks empty, we don't want blacks here, they sleep our sleep, they eat our food, they detest us, sooner or later, it's a question of time, he'll avenge his father, he'll avenge his mother, bring the insurgents with him and shoot us one by one, he knows the placement of the mortars, he knows the storeroom, he'll put a grenade in there, my wife no longer

—Love

to me, where does that love go, how time fades everything my God, but to him

—Son

and the people on the street mocking me

—Son

and afterward he's drawing the letters already, already he speaks about wwwwwwwwwind, he's beginning to get fat, to grow, to have opinions, to disobey us, the doctor from the hospital

—Are you afraid of your son?

and I don't know if it was him who put the stones in my wife's kidney and will finish with me later, the commander of the South African helicopters to me if you worry you'll die, if you don't worry you'll die therefore why worry and followed by a sort of smile if they ask me whether I like the child or not I can't answer, I like, I don't like, I like, I don't know why you worry, the gunner

—Good night

and after the whole body jumps on the mattress though only one small part on the ceiling, the rest tranquil, the shins, the boots, the brown-haired skin of his legs while tomorrow's pig continues to eat, why not, if he worries, he dies, if he doesn't worry he dies and therefore why not eat, his eyes red, his eyes so red, the trees curving under the helicopter, full of a wind only from them, sometimes a bazooka wrecked a tree trunk and a woman holding out a baby to us before falling with him, aside from the blasts some noise, an old woman supported by a stick who took time to kneel, that is she knelt slowly and stayed that way until we left the village, murmuring alone not words of course, these grumblings without connection of the blacks because, as the sergeant insisted, they aren't people second lieutenant sir, be convinced by what I say they were never people, suddenly a wild boar crossed through the huts running and the gunner to him

—Good night

also, tomorrow's pig eating and the commander of the South Africans drinking, drinking, not whiskey, not wine, not beer, marufo like the blacks, marufo, marufo,

—Why are you worried?

I never tried it, never wanted to, not one goat, not one cabíri left over, if I could, I would order them to make beds from palm fronds for all, if I could we would all sleep until there was no more Africa and on this the hospital psychologist

—Shut up shut up

the hospital psychologist

—Are you afraid of your son?

I don't know if it was him who put the stones in my wife's kidney and will finish with me later, the commander of the South African helicopters if you worry you'll die, if you don't worry you'll die therefore why worry and followed by a sort of shiver, presuming they ask me if I like or don't like the child I can't answer, if I cut off one of his arms I wonder if he would understand what I feel, I think he would, I think

—Father

and I don't know why but pleased, my wife started to remember her white nightshirt once again, I began to find her on the bed before we lay down, watching her brush her teeth at night, with her already dressed, smiling inside the foam, the blacks scrub their teeth with a little stick, not with a brush, I see on your faces the joy etc. while the rain didn't stop falling in Lisbon, only in Angola I saw the truck with our coffins, my wife next to me in our room, her voice softly

—With the light on I'm ashamed

while with the light off a small sigh

—Love

an arm on my neck, her body still waiting, the captain beating with the butt of his gun the soldier from the mortar platoon who refused to go into the jungle and he on the ground on all fours while my mother

—Don't hurt me

not

—Love

my wife

—Don't hurt me

because at times my knee hurt her leg, because one of my sharp elbows on her shoulder, because I caught her hair, because I stepped on one of her feet, because my fingers with too much force on her skin, because me always afraid to be thrown out, because your circumflex eyebrows over closed eyes, because the posters of the troops' blond women diverted my attention, because the officers' beds shaking, because a soldier dead, not dead, sleeping, who I laid down next to me, because the pig and me eating, eating, because the T-6 with the napalm in Chalala Nengo, because at times, I swear, I didn't mind dying, because I woke up in the middle of the night in Lisbon looking for my weapon, because messages on the path Desert desert and me looking at the papers written in pencil Desert, because the dogs tried to steal our food, they jumped on top of the table and fled with it passing the barbed wire and hiding among the stems of hemp, at the entrance to the huts, that were smoked for the festivals of the dead that the deceased attended with eyes open, seated next to the chief, wrapped in Congo cloth covered by flies and larvae and then the child next to me suddenly

—Father

in the midst of the drums and dances, he

—Father

only, without any singing, almost leaning on me, if I changed place he changed place, if I walked he walked at my side, if I had to go into the jungle I grabbed the neck of some soldier and passed the G-3 in front of his face

—If he's not here when I return you'll pay

even today I don't know for what reason, I felt alone perhaps and it was like being the owner of an animal that though he didn't speak was always better than nothing, my father inherited the dog from my grandfather for hunting, I had to shoot a burst into the back of the black who took the child to stay with him, I hit her chest, I hit my own as the Angolans do, the boy looked at me and that's it, one of my comrades

—The child will infect the barracks

but after a sideways glance he withdrew, gave up, a pig will be stabbed tomorrow and me in a column to Chiúme with Pedro Afamado* in the

*Important revolutionary leader of the ELNA (Exército da Libertação Nacional de Angola).

bushes of masks, the best is to let him eat distancing himself from the other animals showing them his teeth, my wife afraid

—You made such an angry face just now

and me shoving her away with my snout, pushing her with my side, going up to the Mercedes with a sergeant with a G-3 and the corporal who surveyed the jungle for me, struggling against the desire to put my head on my wife's chest, to caress her neck, to say

—Sorry

preventing her from dying pointing the Walther at the doctor

—I don't want any stone inside my wife cure her

so that returning to walk in the neighborhood after dinner, in August, lingering in front of the shop windows already turned off while night, while still not night, while only we two, while your feet were walking inside me as well in a secret lightness while I explained to you in silence

—I never told you but I

while I whispered

—I think I was luc

while I tried hard to whisper to you

—Love

I was never able, imagine what bullshit, to whisper

—Love

explained like this it seems idiotic, sorry, but I

—Love

myself, I swear to you that

—Love

myself, don't make fun of me but those sappy women's words in my mouth

—Love

to be able to say them before arriving at thirty-eight, this is at the door to my house, thirty-two, thirty-two A and it didn't come out, me wringing out the

—Love

and the

—Love

nothing, the mouth refusing, the tongue caught, the grocer's shop and the travel agency closed, the building in scaffolding where a distant cousin of my mother lived and a dog always with a muzzle, unhappy because unable to bark what could be seen in his eyes, only some indignant sighs, there wasn't a tree where he didn't leave a half dozen soulless drops, I went there one or two times blinds down, sad as could be, busy conserving mysterious sorrows, those hidden out of shame or modesty, the cousin from time to time a long sigh and thus in my opinion remote melancholies, deaths, mourning, debts to the butcher, humiliations, who doesn't suffer in this life raise a finger and let it be known, stepmother for all right on, my mother's cousin a wrinkle of eternal conformity that we, at the risk of being unhappy, get used to, what a medicine, if one sees things well all is less an evil than dying, for me two buildings are left in order to declare

—Love

and hopefully I'll succeed, there are creatures for whom one doesn't make much effort and for others, like me, a mess, I was never expansive, I always concealed my hurts, one morning, coming from the supply column, even the chaplain jumped with a mine, he remained for a long while on all fours in the sand looking for his glasses, fortunately, not one shot from the jungle, it must have been an old device, forgotten, that blew a tire without bothering us much and only after discovering him did he complain about his left ankle, the nurse bandaged it up and the chaplain said the Mass almost without limping, just a bit awkward, with one of his eyes much bigger than the other because one of his lenses got bent, the soldier that the doctor instructed to extract teeth put them straight enough with pliers, at least it wasn't necessary to sink a knee into his chest or to keep an abscess in a compress, a mulatto passed by us on a bicycle, whistling and I made good use of a ride from the whistle for a

—Love

whispered, discreet, my wife who didn't understand

—Did you say something?

and me silent of course, there are words better left unrepeated, they took their boots off, and between a

—Love

pale and nothing silence is always better because we can always hide inside what we are feeling like, my wife still not the stones at that time, a bit fatter then because with age lightness gets lost, the footsteps deeper, the waist disappeared and then with the birth of my daughter, is it what the pig would suspect about tomorrow, the sleep shirt didn't hold up on the seams unless she didn't breathe, even with all the air out, one could make out a little bit of the exposed stomach, if I met her now I wouldn't ask her permission to accompany her despite the stripe in my hair lower and a sample of double chin, don't lie that I'm the same, I'm not, it's enough to look at my belt two holes wider, I'm coming closer to death through subtleties like this, spots on the backs of my hands, pleats in my eyelids, a tooth that lost its shine, the absence of a handrail on the stairs that we didn't notice earlier, the weight of the shoes swelling and thus climbing up two steps at a time impossible, only one God knows, from the third on we started to count them, from the sixth or seventh on the pretext I don't know if I forgot the keys in the house so as to search my pockets and give time to the heart to slow down a bit, weaker on the temples, less hurried in the stomach because with the years the poor thing is going down, gets entangled in his guts, remains beating down below, there must have existed suspenders that lifted up the soul, there must have been a slow march and at ease that gave hope to life, I see on your faces the joy of staying one or two months more, at home, in slippers, alert to the miseries of the organism, no more elbow around me, no kiss in the ear, the enormous nose hairs in the mirror that get bigger and the little scissors that can't get them, how to jump from a helicopter, how to invade the village of huts, how to get across a river and perhaps shots, perhaps grenades, perhaps insurgents on the bank waiting, perhaps crocodiles sliding on their own into the water, perhaps lepers in the sun on the sand, also without hands also without ears, balancing on their own stumps throwing us bits of earth or getting away from us, my wife, pregnant with my daughter, walking without any elegance on swollen calves and sleeping in the corners, hair thrown together, without dye, with an old bathrobe that leaves one cold I don't know where and the memory of the posters of the women of Angola it seems with pity for me, she plops down on the sofa looking at the wall, settled over the mess of her feet until a hairy thing, a daughter that I don't feel like touching, stuck in an alcove squealing the whole night like bats in Angola from mango tree to mango tree, the T-6s came from the north to bombard the people in the villages with napalm and the clothing burning, the features, the gestures, a pilot didn't want to get out of the machine after landing

   — The dead will kill me friends

   they brought him down while he insisted

   — They are going to kill me

   my daughter so ugly, so ugly even today, from childhood on she's avoided me and nonetheless every year present for the pig killing, my mother

—What's going on with your father?

and silence, it's clear she escaping to the cemetery or the mountain without fear of the genets, the wild boars, the dogs without owners hunting hens from the bush, in winter they would prowl around the hencoops because in the morning footprints in the frost, the mule of my father's cousin on a slope, only bones, almost without any teeth in its large jaws, there were occasions when its trotting could be heard outside, second lieutenants shaken with malaria vomiting on the ground that rotten sweat of the sick, the doctor giving an injection in the infirmary to the pilot who screamed

—I'm going to burn up I'm going to burn up

like the blacks were burning up, the cabíris were burning up, an old man rolling on the ground was burning up, my daughter to my son

—Is it this year that you'll finally kill our father who killed your father with a bush knife?

and it wasn't, the pig always, animal blood, not mine, in the bucket, animal screams, not mine, in agony, blind animal eyes, also not mine, in the cellar and my daughter, of course, angry with her brother who wasn't her brother

—You're not his son when are you going to understand that you're not his son when are you going to understand that he killed your parents?

suddenly much larger, furious, punching him in the chest

—He killed your parents

and my son silent thinking, my son

—He killed my parents?

remembering the hands cut off, the ears cut off, the man who lived with his mother lying on the ground, half on a manioc mat and half on the grass while I grabbed the child's shoulders warning the soldiers

—Don't touch him

not for love of him, to secure my authority

—Don't touch him

for selfishness, for the desire that you'll recall forever what I did and not seek vengeance ever, you'll accept, that's war isn't it, we had orders didn't we, the chaplain

—My God

my cousin surprised

—You still remember all that?

and how many times at night I continue to wake up with the insurgents' machine gun on the landing strip and then a mortar, then a second mortar, my daughter-in-law to my son, shaking him in the bed

—What racket is that that won't let me sleep?

bullets that were vibrating wires over our heads, the hospital psychologist in the circle of chairs surprised with us

—I don't feel anything

despite one of my comrades to him shaking his vest

—Get down

a second comrade also on his knees, a third, a fat guy, with an almost new suit, crawling on the landing strip, a telephone ringing in the corridor that no one answered, asking for help from whom, calling for whom, the telephone pleading

—Don't leave me alone

like me to my wife, without words but knowing that she heard me

—Don't leave me alone

and my father though dead so long ago next to my bed indignant with me

—You seem a boy what cowardice is that?

because me curved over myself even feeling my urine in the sheets, almost crying, almost the

—Don't kill me

not in uniform, in pajamas, with a teddy bear playing with a ball already a bit threadbare on the chest, the remaining troops in pajamas as well, each with his bear and his ball, uncombed, barefoot, with plastic pistols and toy machine guns that forced them to imitate gunshots with their mouths or pretend to cut the ears off each other with plastic daggers, one of them began to whine because he was missing a leg

—When my grandfather finds out he'll kill himself when my grandfather finds out he'll kill himself

despite his grandfather calming him down

—Don't worry your leg will grow again

the ceiling light buzzed like a helicopter up above, circling around the dresser tops, the doctor from the hospital worried

—Stop with this before someone gets hurt

and from time to time, someone with his face to the floor announcing

—I'm dead

with closed eyes and hands crossed on his chest, my father's cousin who looked after the tomb

—So many dead today

with a fox looking at her at the edge of the mountain and the first mimosas waiting for March, the operations officer aiming at a girl in braids while searching for cigarettes in his pocket

—Lock the prisoner in the storeroom the war is barely over here in a half hour I'll go over there

putting her foot on the crate, lifting up her dress, touching what none of us saw the

—Quiet

looking for herself with legs apart, my son's wife to the owner of the store, curious

—What does that fool want?

the mountain falcons suspended over us watching the hencoops, balanced in the wind, there was a stuffed one at the pharmacy, above the cough syrups, that smelled of moldy blanket, with claws on a piece of varnished branch, the corporal with the bazooka before firing

—Is there anyone behind us?

and the old house of the station head with the insurgents inside falling slowly, I saw one of them on his knees, a colleague on all fours, already blind, advancing toward us, one push, two pushes, and his chest on the ground, my wife to me

—Are you going to fall off the sofa?

because my body slipping sideways along the pillow without my noticing, my son grabbing hold of me

—Hold on

it seemed to me that after the conversation with his sister he less close to me, looking at the pig that didn't stop eating in a different way, almost as if he hated it who at times seemed to me to take pity on the animal just as much as a black has pity on anything, looking for the best artery in the neck for the knife, that would bleed the most, that would kill with greater suffering, my son bent toward the animal looking at me, thinking, looking at me again, if we were now in the barracks, he would forget me, he walked in the huts with the remaining blacks, he didn't speak with me and my daughter looking at me too, in the garden if me in the house, in the house if me in the garden, calling her she didn't answer, she waited for me to get up in order to sit down at the table, she didn't drink coffee with us in the kitchen in the morning, she drifted between the gate and the wall, if my wife

—You don't speak to your father?

silent, not even at birth, if I recall, did she cry, I remember her saying at a time when I got worked up with her

—You should have died in Africa

and who assures you that I didn't die little one, who assures you that I'm alive, my father at times

—Are you certain you returned from there?

so that me probably not here, in a coffin from the cemetery with all those stones around it, those slabs, those crosses, those tombs, me far away, me alone, for how many centuries my wife not

—Love

for how many centuries my wife silent or answering

—I'm fine

she not looking at me at all if I asked her how she felt, an

—I'm fine

oblivious, the doctor to me

— It's natural that people when they feel uncomfortable become more difficult

because feeling bad, because the pain, because, isn't it true, the proximity of death or what they think death, I wonder for that matter how they imagine death, as to me a sort of void but who can conceive of a void where we are not, probably when we die no more than being quiet, with polished shoes, listening to poplars in their cracking of armoires, the birds happy with the caterpillars of the deceased, my wife who due to the advancing disease is beginning to listen to what isn't there

—You don't notice the rain?

when no rain in the village, only the pig to eat, there are moments when I wonder if it wouldn't be better to give up these trips, except my cousin already here I don't have anyone other than the remains of the dog under the loquat tree and a voice explaining to me softly

—Don't speak to me now you'll scare the partridges

while the dog's nose began to tremble, the tail vibrated, the teeth were bared, the back undulating and with the first sun green the first partridge, that is the eyes, the beak, the tail feathers, the crest toward the right and toward the left touching the morning, the shotgun rising slowly while my father

—Don't move

me who was not breathing, on all fours on the earth, listening to a tiny sob, another sob, a wing flap, the bushes waving, my father supported by his knees, the trigger hitting the cartridge, the dog galloping out from the grass, he hitting me in the back

—I think I got it

as my son had to aim at my neck with my daughter inciting him

—Put the knife in deeper put the knife in deeper

with my wife

—Love

helping her hold onto me while grabbing the back of my neck, while grabbing my wrists, while forcing me to be part of her, my wife

—Love

preventing me from escaping, from shaking her, from getting away from her while something in her voice turned into screams, while my legs, bound with rope, could not run, while the helicopter gunship, closer and closer, was suspended over me and the South African sniper was searching for my forehead, took a shot, two shots, and moved off, at an angle, as I was falling, toward the barbed wire of the camp.

12

My father kept coming every year to the house in the village to kill the pig in memory of his father just as his father did during his childhood in memory of his grandfather and as long as I can remember he brought us with him always and forced us to witness distressed as could be, chewing sobs, the animal's agony, hanging from an iron fishhook, with a basin for the blood where my mother was moving a wooden spoon the stray dogs were looking at the door, if someone dared to enter my father, with a rubber apron on, would send him off stamping his foot on the ground, the village small, without a spot on any map, a half dozen narrow streets, the small cemetery on the mountain slope, old women with firewood on their heads, birds very high up, very far away, and me hating all this, that is the people and the place, if my father spoke to me I didn't respond, with my mother's look still free of illness, only the palm, from time to time puzzled, evaluating her back and forgetting it, reprimanding me in silence, she never got my attention in any other way, I don't remember ever hearing my name from her, I was born five or six years after my father came back from Angola and for so long I didn't hear about Africa, now and again a friend from the army ate with us but never a word about the war, practically not a word about anything, my father cut the meat for his colleague who had a crippled arm, for a few moments something resembling a helicopter propeller appeared turning over the building before moving off and the ceiling lamp was swinging a bit, some Hoards, I don't know who it was, would emerge suddenly to lift the wine bottle with a towel and he served us both while the crippled arm, missing a finger, in fact the ring finger with the ring put on the middle finger, vibrated, the crippled arm not really an appendage, a bump hidden in the sleeve and which, out of politeness, one avoided looking at, if by chance an ambulance siren on the avenue the bump got larger, if no siren we almost forgot about it, everything had happened too long ago to be important still and nonetheless for my father and his friend, how strange, though neither spoke it didn't stop happening, the mine in the Berliet, the officer without one of his shoulders, shots from time to time, the radio that couldn't get hold of the company

—Chopper urgent chopper urgent

with knees on the ground on the telephone and on the other side hisses and a confused request

—Repeat repeat

or it seemed like

—Repeat repeat

the guide who didn't die taking his shoes off to flee faster without any sniper aiming at him, an insurgent in the grass, looking at them, whom a pistol blinded, my mother went out to the kitchen with the tureen, brought the fruit basket and in uniform number two, coming from I don't know where, some Hoards again, my father sighing

—He came in handy that one

cutting an apple for his colleague and an apple for my father, this at the same time in our living room and in the ruin of the old station head's residence that served as a mess, full of geckos in the vine and holes in the floor, where the Katangese officers, squatting and a red cloth around their necks, looked with wire hooks for the mice that they roasted for eating on the entrance step, when my father's friend said good-bye to us the radio continued to try to get hold of the company moving the antenna from one tree to another while the captain became infuriated

—And now?

without believing that they might notice us in the house in the village next to the cemetery and the mountain where the mimosas bubble up, so as to kill the pig that here for a month only ate, ate, without Hoards paying any attention, my parents, my brother, and my sister-in-law in the living room and me alone in the garden without speaking with anyone not looking at anyone, next to the loquat tree where they buried the dog years ago, I recall being in my mother's arms surrounded by a fever that barked jumping around me, I recall the kites and being afraid of the murky brightness of the moon in the window when they left me alone in my room and voices following down the corridor a different tonality softly asking

—Are we going to bring her with us?

intermingled with that of my sister-in-law

—Is there no one other than you living here

except for the gypsies that passed on the highway, filled with dark shadows and rattles and a half dozen old men on the wall of the square, every time I come to the village besides the hope that my brother will kill my father with the knife for the pig nothing else interests me, I never said where I live, if I live alone, where I work, if I work, if I have friends, what for, my father and other second lieutenants spread the soldiers out through the jungle in the hope of spotting the insurgents if they returned, the radio only messages from other battalions, the South Africans whispering in their language, when they didn't want us to understand them they used it in front of the Portuguese, I used my silent mouth and they don't understand me at all, I don't greet people in the elevator or on the landings, of course they recognize my face but I keep pretending that I'm visiting or the like, I think that I don't like anyone, what sort of creatures could I like and what's the point of liking, what gets done with liking, what is to be gained by liking, the radio announced that two platoons were on their way, except for my family's tomb, that my cousin looks after, she covers the deceased with a tablecloth, puts little jars with wallflowers on top, cleans off the leaves of the poplars with a broom, almost only strangers in the cemetery, older that those from the war in Africa buried I don't know where those ones, Hoards always helpful, with a cloth to dry the dishes on his shoulder and the bride, the Thin One, married to a goldsmith

—Do you want me to get them for you young lady?

me without looking at him, of course, what difference does it make for me, when the last ones disappeared I was still not born, two platoons, various casualties, they had to leave them in the jungle, lifting them up on their shoulders only if they stayed back and afterward the corpses weigh more than one expects, a ring on the finger or watch on the wrist are enough to make it so we can't hold them up, when a minesweeper driver asked my father to keep the wire on his neck I don't know how our second lieutenant, even slipping it into his pocket, managed to hold it up, similarly I can't understand how my mother still endures the kidneys, I see her here from the garden making lunch with movements so halting, so slow, despite the wide blouse I could count her ribs, if we continuing like this for a little I'll be, now here is the advantage, the only one in the family, not close to my parents, not close to my brother, not close to the village, in this cheap building on the outskirts of Lisbon from where a tiny corner of the river is visible, seagulls, factories, warehouses, don't stop eating pig, don't stop, eat one by one my mother's stones as well, perhaps I'll still manage to set fire to my family and the house in the village pouring the gas can out onto the armoire, onto the trunk, onto the sheets, onto the furniture, onto the quantity of useless garbage that there is over here and in me right now, you've barely finished the last line of this book you get a match so that nothing will be left of us, of what remained written and you forget us, my sister-in-law to her girlfriend, thanking her for a ring

—So dear

extending her hand out against her breast, in the mirror, so as to see it better, the first time that she dined in our house my mother put out a table-cloth embroidered by my grandmother and the service, with floral patterns, kept in a sideboard and on which we'd never eaten, I think it was the first time that I realized that my brother black just like I realized that the people on the street looked at him if he went to pick me up at school because I still didn't know the way, when we rented this house the landlord, when he saw him, hesitated thinking about the other renters, one afternoon while coming down the stairs the lady from the second floor to a friend

—Aren't you picking up the monkey smell?

and my brother pretending that he didn't hear, he asked me almost afraid afterward

—Do I smell like monkey to you?

every time he left the room he returned to open the door and leaned inside to breathe in, it smelled like the mountain, the village as well, not him, my mother started to smell like the medicine after getting sick, my father smelled like sleep when he nodded off following dinner, on certain mornings the window of their room open and two pillows from the bed not side by side, creased one on top of the other in a corner of the mattress in the same form as a bit of exposed sheet, on my mother's side, as if it had been pulled, my mother blushed when she understood what I was looking at, straightening it out quickly with her palms, after she got sick the bed always perfect and the pillows round, the only difference was that my father, now and again, arrived later, with what seemed to be another perfume over-powering his and my mother's face, when he kissed her forehead, longer for an instant, she continued to sew in silence, attesting to a quick movement of her fingers that were holding the needle and then all following as before, my father feeling guilty inside the newspaper, neither Africa nor Angola was ever spoken of, he and my brother in silence but if a louder noise, a door, a drawer or the like, the pages shaking, my sister-in-law to us, nervous

—Has there ever been peace here?

the house in the village much smaller now than when I was a child, my grandfather's shroud of cigarette paper still in the ashtray, two caps in the coatroom, my father's and his, waiting for a partridge dawn, there are moments when I hear them sleeping in the thickets that sleep of the birds consisting of unsettled sighs, agitated feet, sobs, round eyes that they heard, the doctor to my mother

—With this new medicine I assure you that your stones will become lighter than water

and the desk came, the screen came, the white stains on the X-ray that the red pencil circled, a portrait, on the desk, of a lady with a child in her arms, neither of them surrounded by a red circle and that the doctor thus did not see, if it had occurred to me to ask him

—How was Africa father?

the newspaper still bigger, with a shoe beating on the floor, distant as could be, he must have had dogs that instead of partridges grabbed us by the kidney stones, my brother answering for both

—Almost nothing remained in my memory

an old man with a sewing machine, a painted man dancing drinking the neck of a hen, old women clapping

—Euá

a pipe in his mouth, minuscule dogs in the sun, grass burning, rivers, my father to me

—How you have grown child

and I hadn't grown that much, I'm thirteen now, my breasts starting to grow, I return alone from school, I got a friend called Elisa whose thighs my uncle touches at times recommending to her secretly

—Don't tell your parents anything

while she is thinking

—What's to tell if it's just this?

a finger at the fork of her body and the others alert in the corridor, in the kitchen, her father distrustful, in a thicker voice

—If Aurélio arrives, let me know right away

he who wouldn't leave the younger sister of his wife alone always grabbing her skirt

—When will you stop trying to get away from me girl?

and in fact the younger sister of his wife getting away slower and slower
slapping his hands

—Always bold the rascal

in a type of abuse that changed into laughter, my brother to me in a slow
voice that doesn't belong to us, coming from far away, with which we nar-
rate dreams

—There was a woman facedown in the hut without speaking to me if
there wasn't enough manioc she gave me her breast

a woman facedown, without speaking to him, whom the cabíris were
sniffing tearing her clothing and the creature trying to fend them off with
a pestle, one of the cabíris, groaning with hunger, bit one of her legs, a second lieutenant grabbed him by the waist and lifted him into the air while
my brother pushed him away, a scrap of wood burning, the corn burned
up, a single Kalashnikov still shooting, it wasn't clear from where, against
the troops, behind the corn perhaps or next to a ploughed field and that a
grenade silenced, the wind from the thick mist was audible, the stalks were
audible, the G-3s were audible but in the distance, the loquat of the house
in the village was audible its leaves drying up, everything dies here as well
except the pig eating, a little goat shaking its head in panic calling a dead
female, a hen throwing itself, fluttering, against the clay of a hut, my sister-
in-law hidden in her sleeves

—I can't stand this

my grandfather in a murmur to the dog

—Quiet

before the partridges noticed, my mother getting up from the sofa on her
way to her room with the stones, still, I swear, heavier than water, hindering her walking, not cancer, it's clear, one thinks right away about cancer, it
doesn't make the thing less, stones only and as to cancers today's Medicine
is no longer what it was and in many cases I swear, if not always, one manages, my brother to me

—Almost nothing remains of Angola other than explosions and rain and
blacks running

a child sitting on the ground who was crying, a black from Zambia, hidden in the bushes, trying to tear papers and put them in his mouth and the Flechas* got him, my brother

—Nothing is left over from Angola perhaps the image of my father giving orders

there are no photographs from that time, my father burned them in the yard, squatting, stirring the ashes with a small stick and burying them afterward, in one of them my brother in his arms, both curled up in each other, getting blacker, until they were transformed into a spiral that floated for a while and vanished over the wall, there goes their past, there goes the war, there goes my young father, thin, with a black still thinner in his arms, only bones above and below the round belly, my sister-in-law freeing herself from him with an elbow in front of his face

—Don't touch me

fearful of the illnesses that he certainly had, of his dirtiness, the lice, her girlfriend, in an expensive dress, trying to protect her

—Where did this black child emerge from?

while Hoards, with a not very clean apron over his camouflage, was helping my mother in the kitchen after leaving the mortar aside, that everyone was afraid of, at the door of the yard, with an open box of grenades, that they didn't aim at anyone if not at him, the pig, on the road above, continued to eat, if he felt like it, he'd eat me, the Thin One with her two friends, outside in the garden whispering, my father's cousin in the cemetery waxing the coffins of the tomb with melted wax and a bottle and replacing the flowers from the small jar, there were my grandfather, my grandmother, my father's brother, a cousin no one knew about just like no one knew the reason he was there with all the others, who was, perhaps a mistake, a guy belonging to the family next door answering some other casket

—I'm finishing something I'm going in a second

my mother surprised

—So many people here in the house is it because I'm going to die?

so many here in the house, so many red circles on the white stains, so many lepers limping between the yard and the highway, eating roots, moving on all fours, sleeping on the ground under some palm leaves, conversing in shouts and then the pig with eyes on me interrupting its eating, throw-

*African troops trained by the Portuguese.

ing it pears, bananas, pieces of bone, scraps until my father's knife in its neck, until my brother and don't worry you're not dying, mother, because the stones are getting less and less heavy, less dense, to be frank even lighter than water, the doctor at first incredulous, after verifying better, after that calling his colleagues

— Have you already seen this?

his colleagues

— It can't be

trying more X-rays and then agreeing with him, exactly these words

— We have to agree with you

while my mother's arm around my father's neck and she pulling him toward her

— Love

she who for so many years silent again

— Love

she young, timid, in her lace nightshirt, wearing some old sandals if in the middle of the night I started to cry in my room, awakened by my father's desperate pleading

— Don't let me slip out don't let me slip out

while the bed protested, poor thing, in a groan of wood, this in Lisbon, in the dark, with the horn of an ambulance in the distance, always with people, coming from the nearby café, guffaws in the street, and footsteps, and whistles, and a can being kicked, my mother

— What's wrong daughter?

with the sleeve odor from my father's pajamas still on her back and on the stones, lighter than water, separated from each other, here and there, my mother smelling at the same time like a woman and my, don't stop eating pig, please don't stop eating, my mother smelling at the same time like a woman and a man, how strange, like a man's skin, men's perfume, that odor of theirs a little like an animal and a little like beer so different from ours, the smell of timidity and fear of when they approach, the dread of no longer being when losing themselves in us, desire to call us

— Mother

and at times they call in fact, even when they insult us there's always a

— Mother

hidden, even when they beat us always a

— Mother

who pleads stay with me, hold me in your arms, wrap me inside you again, my mother

—What's wrong daughter?

Sitting on the bed

—What's wrong daughter?

almost crying as well, cry with me ma'am, because we don't cry both of us, because we don't feel alone both of us, because we don't stay with each other always, me to the doctor not asking, affirming

—My mother won't die

and nonetheless, to be frank, it doesn't matter to me whether she exists or doesn't exist, I don't feel her absence at all, I don't like you at all, I swear, not you, not your husband, not the idiotic black who is here with us always worried about me, always smiling at me

—Sis

always looking for me

—Where is she?

while the stones slowly turn around us, the doctor to my father, opening his arms without understanding

—Look she's improved

the finger sententious, while my mother was getting dressed

—If she lasts a month or two we're lucky

and one less person to bother me with her presence, her questions, her worry

—Daughter

her fear that I'll die of hunger out there

—You work doing what?

offering me money secretly, offering me food, an electric space heater for winter

—Are you certain that you're not cold?

Just like the black God bless her

—Have you been eating well?

because in her opinion me thin, me weak, with a strange skin tone, me always in the yard without worrying about anyone, getting wet if it rained and it didn't rain getting too much sun on my head and whoever gets too much sun on the head will be number one for congestion, leave me in peace for once, don't look for me, forget me, with a rented room so that they don't notice me and up to now they haven't, my father to the soldiers

—Let's return to the camp

drinking water from the leaves, eating roots and grasses, a wild boar decomposed in a trap that the blacks forgot while the pig cabbage and beans and potatoes with my father evaluating its neck and the path of the knife like his father before him, the grandfather before his father and thus all of them present, all of them, at dawn, accompanied by the dog, immobile, waiting for partridges that began to wake up on a mountain ridge, when I was small my brother walking with me on his shoulders in the village and me hitting his head with closed fists

—Fast fast

while he was running under me each time breathing with greater difficulty, each time more tired, stumbling on a beam, straightening up, stumbling again, me pulling his hair

—To the house black

and my brother

—Thank you ma'am

with a sigh, poor fellow, me encouraging him

—The wall is visible already

when the wall was visible already

—The loquat is already visible

when the loquat was already visible

—The garden is already visible the house is already visible

when the garden and the house were already visible, my father, in a vest, digging up I don't know what, my mother, with the apron slipping onto her hips, hanging clothing outside and me, what an idiot, a tear or rather almost a tear, let's not exaggerate let's not become sentimental now only because I remembered this, me on a small sofa in the place where I live looking at the window without seeing the window, not the supermarket on the other side of the street, not the car garage, not the beginning of the night and farther away, behind all this, still a sun without color and already moon, the bright lights of the town in the distance, the halo of Lisbon far away, my mother closing all the windows and turning on the lamp in the living room that when flickering makes the curtains and the furniture older and sadder, the ceiling yellowed from tobacco smoke, a nail on the wall, without anything hanging, rusting the limestone, my brother put me down on the floor

—The race is over

and he massaged his shoulder blades for a while, in fact black, a black, my grandfather whom I never saw, died centuries before since all people who have died become ancient instantly, it's enough to look at their clothes in photographs, it's enough to hear their voices always so strange, so sharp, with an out-of-tune piano playing, behind them, to someone whom I had also never seen

—A black grandson me you say?

puffing up his chest indignant and on the way a glance at my father

—Did you see what you went and found for me?

and with the windows and doors closed, frankly, I didn't see where the cat that lives here entered unless a broken tile or the like, as a child I spent whole summers hunting mysteries in the garden, geckos, ladybugs, pieces of mica, now I come for the three days of the killing merely hopeful that the woman, dead facedown in Africa, will take vengeance against my father, the pine trees in the dark and from childhood on the same bat screaming my name, my mother turned on the light for me and not even a shadow with us

—What bat?

just stones lighter than water floating suspended, my mother's doctor to his colleagues, showing them X-ray after X-ray

—And this one?

my sister-in-law to my brother, softly

—I can't stand this anymore

me to my sister-in-law

—You're right who can stand this anymore?

imagining not the pig, my father eating bent over his plate ignoring us, my mother distressed

—What's wrong with you?

and my father leaning over the table oblivious of us, chewing always

—I can't stop

my father who since the war couldn't stop, the psychologist in the circle of chairs at the hospital

—Aren't you able to be quiet even for a moment?

and sorry friend but I'm not able to be quiet, too many people without hands, too many ears in bottles, too many helicopters, too many wounded, too many huts burning, too many dead, the operations officer checking out the female prisoners, the second lieutenant crying under the Mercedes holding out to us his own shit

—Help me

at the same time that he tried to ignore us, my father kicked him toward the dirt road and he

—For the love of God don't kill me for the love of God don't kill me

this chapter, that should have been mine to write, my sister stole it from me, Her Excellency grabbing me by the arm

—Get the suitcase and let's get out of here

looking with disgust at the old furniture, the dining table, the chairs, the ceramic ballerina in a sort of forgiveness that softened my mother, or rather a sudden childlike smile that forced me to smile in turn with the idiotic desire, I don't know why, to hug her, that is more than just hugging her, to hold her in my arms and remain like that for a long time feeling her heart on my neck, rapid, tense, she since the stones always so serious, with a furrow on her forehead that she didn't have before and made her look older still

—A neighbor gave me the ballerina who was called Arminda when I turned six

changing its position a little, now turning it to the right, now turning it to the left, now bringing it a cautious millimeter closer to the edge of the bookcase and stepping back to observe the effect

—So pretty

in a voice older than her voice now, much rounder, much happier, much more closely resembling her, my mother to me softly,

—She's called Constança

in a whisper that I understood right away as belonging only to the two of us, her parents never knew, her schoolmates never knew, a great aunt to whom she made confidences never knew, my father didn't know, of course, as we men don't know anything important if for nothing else because in their minds we understand nothing, my mother repeating

—Constança

touching her with the end of her finger on the base of her neck which meant various things at the same time, some difficult to explain in words and that men don't understand either while puppets, I swear, understand, look at the cardboard angels for example, look at the clay saints and like the blacks, whatever one may say, a bit closer to puppets than us, and therefore more capable of figuring things out and it wasn't only the stones, now lighter than water, it was what I felt for her, don't cut her ears off, don't cut her hands off, give me your empty breast, hide me in your rags from the Congo, don't stop looking at me, even if you don't see me don't stop looking at me, walk with me among the goats, the cabíris, the collapsed huts, the soldiers who pour gasoline on the manioc mats, the hemp leaves that they forgot to smoke crushed on the ground, we used to cut the tips off the bullets or dig a cross in them so as to break more bones, so that the liver or the lungs in pieces, so that a whole fist could fit into the exit wound, the chief still murmuring something, his Angolar* still crawling on all fours before giving up, Her Excellency to me

—We'll get a truck from Lisbon and come for the car afterward

not angry at me, not with contempt, asking me, the sensation that if I wanted I could touch her, pull her into our room, undress her, spread her legs with urgent elbows, and order her

—Quiet

in the certainty that Her Excellency's arm, like my mother with my father, around my neck and don't stop eating pig, don't stop eating, keep getting fatter, certainty that Her Excellency, also with a ruffled nightshirt, helping me

—Love

making me bigger

—Love

guiding me

—Love

repeating with my mother's voice

—She's called Constança

the only phrase that I needed in order to feel her with me for the first time, I swear, no mockery, no contempt, no hatred, my father leaving the second lieutenant behind

—A coward

moving me away from him, asking the doctor while a leper chased another there down below, not talking to him, not calling him, grunting

—Still some hope?

watching the screen with a jumping lip, my father in panic too

—Still some hope?

under the Mercedes refusing that they pull

—Still some hope?

always grabbing me by the shoulder when showing me to the soldiers

*Another language of Angola.

—Don't touch him

showing me to the pig

—Don't touch him

showing me to Her Excellency

—Don't touch him

despite the door to the room closed, an old cubicle for storage halfway in the corridor with a rocking chair of torn straw, a sewing machine needing another needle, a bald broom incapable of sweeping, the bed from when I was small and in which the two of us used to sleep here in the house in the village, uncomfortable, shrunken, with half of the body suspended from the void, the loquat tree knocking against the window, a wagon now and again or a bark or a bird pecking the vegetables, me hugged by Her Excellency

—Euá

closer and closer to Her Excellency

—Euá

as closer and closer to the woman with hands cut off who slowly leaned over me without touching me, almost without touching me, touching me, speaking with me in a language I didn't understand while she pulled me toward herself, not standing, not seated, held out to me

—Euá

or not at all

—Euá

silent, held out to me with an impassive face and despite impassive

—Euá

her knees, her elbows, her lap, her naked belly button, her naked thighs, her feet rubbing against mine

—Euá

and something in me almost exploding, exploding and me calm, in peace, me so to speak, if I dare say, happy, me almost

—Love

imagine it, I'm certain that me almost

—Love

while the pig's mouth, suddenly immense, was devouring both of us.

13

At Christmastime the supply column brought four women stuck between the crates of the last Mercedes, not very young, not very attractive, not
very clean of course, with soldiers' caps on their heads and in camouflage
clothes too large for them, looking fearfully at the tall grass and the trees
on both sides of the dirt road, my grandfather to my father softly, without
raising his weapon, passing a slow finger between the ears of the dog
—Those are not partridges that's a hedgehog watching the burrow
already with the first beetles, the first butterflies, that sort of difference in
the back of the neck that precedes the heat, soldiers from both sides inside
the jungle and from time to time crushed branches, protesting reeds two
or three soldiers in front sweeping for mines, a bumpy tin on the ground, a
rainy sky in the west still very far away, after the first curve the slope that led
to the camp where wasps were swarming over a pool of stagnant water, my
daughter on a stone in the yard without speaking to me or looking at me,
when little I used to sit her on my knees going up and down
—Little horsey little horsey
and she laughing with pleasure, with fear and with the pleasure of fear,
she content, with her hair to one side and then the other and a missing baby
tooth next to her incisor, not one wrinkle my God, still not one wrinkle, her
skin so smooth, dimples on her elbows, dimples on her cheeks
—More
her tiny toes, round, brown eyes, not really brown, green specks and now
unfortunately glasses, her mouth serious, closed, with a parenthesis on each
side, what happened to you, what happened to me, the column entered the
camp truck after truck, with the blacks from the huts observing at a distance
and the soldiers jumping down from the cab, the G-3s a stronger sound than
the Kalashnikovs, every time I put my daughter on my knees she messed up
my hair
—Run
and me holding onto her ankles afraid to trip in the garden and fall, a

scorpion appeared on a stone and raised its tail at once, the troops were looking at the women from a distance while the quartermaster helped put up, hammering them, the wood planks for two canvas tents with dry mattresses missing straw inside, in the column a mail bag without a single letter for me, my wife used to write me once a week, ashamed of her handwriting

—It's so ugly

where she told me about whatever would fill the paper with me thinking about her body, if you still remember me, the women who the captain came to observe, with a second lieutenant behind, three dark-skinned and one almost albino, thin as a rail

—Not as bad as last year come on at least none of them is black

they undressed in the tents while a sergeant was giving out tickets to the soldiers

—Five minutes to speed up the service they have to leave later today

and my grandfather annoyed because not one partridge, the dog stood up, turned over itself and lay down again, her snout resting on one of our shoes, waiting, you could feel her breathing between impatience and sleep, a tick was noticeable on her right ear despite my mother taking a rag from time to time to scrub it with oil, she had to leave her outside for a night because the smell

—Little horsey little horsey

infected everything, even the laundry basket, my grandfather coughing

—Dammit the animal

because the stench bothered his lungs, the soldiers formed a line in front of the tents with a ticket numbered in pencil in their hands

—When five minutes are over you'll come right here naked you'll dress yourself out here and that's it

I wonder if my daughter remembers my knees, perhaps yes, perhaps no, almost certainly she has forgotten them, now from time to time they hurt in winter, I am walking very well and one of my legs is missing, it's disappearing from the tibia down and then it returns still weaker, trembling, my son worried

—What's that?

my daughter indifferent, the same will happen to you don't worry, wait a few years and you'll see, unfortunately I'll not be here feeling myself avenged when you move forward limping because you daughter must become old too, you'll have a stronger correction in your lenses in order to thread the needle asking

—Where are the scissors?

and they in the palm of your hand, you talking with a little ball of spit on each side of your mouth and us though we don't want to looking at the little balls that flatten and grow with a fascinated repugnance, I haven't seen the pig yet today but surely he's continuing to eat, the idiot, without remembering death, in Africa when leaving for an operation not even a small scrap of dental sponge would fit onto my gums since my guts were so tight, perhaps my grandfather's partridge did not appear because it felt the same way, it was enough that a leaf shook for a G-3 to be pointed at it, nervous, the corporal behind me

—Little horsey little horsey

calming me

—No one sets up ambushes one hundred meters from the headquarters second lieutenant sir and me with an urge to squeeze the idiot's neck

—Shut up

a fool who they hit in the lungs later, showing me his red palm, intrigued

—I feel nothing is it blood?

and of course it's blood, cretin, a little bit more on the left would have hit you in the heart and you would have croaked, just because of that silliness about the one hundred meters it wouldn't have bothered me to see you in a coffin, including offering me the chance to order the salvos when, it seemed to me that my daughter a glance at me but it quickly went elsewhere, they could put you down on the earth, the officers returning to Lisbon in wooden jackets, the enlisted men are buried over there, a cadet will be sent to the home to give the news and deliver some money, promising

—When they have room in a ship they'll bring him

and they remained next to the landing strip fattening worms, there is hardly any place here for the living, all piled up blocking the streets, how much more for the dead, the sergeant who oversaw the visits to the women shaking a tent that was rocking back and forth

—One minute and I'll kick you out of there dummy

with a nurse placing a drop, despite everything hell she's my daughter, why on earth doesn't she care a whit about me, of antivenereal cream on the finger of each one

—Scrub yourself well you fool if you don't want it cut off and you'll live the rest of your life squatting to take a piss

a line of grunts with their middle finger in the air to contemplate the shiny yellow drop while my son squatting in the yard with a small hoe and watering can, a soldier who was always offering the rest of his plate to the stray dogs in the camp scraping the aluminum with a knife, to the partner in front of him in line

—I'm certain that I won't be able to

checking, disappointed, in his pants

—It would really seem so

the women in camouflage were visible through a slit in the canvas, the three dark-skinned ones and the white one, almost albino, nude on the mattress cleaning themselves during the pauses with a torn piece of towel, if my wife were there certainly with the lace shirt and not with her eyes on the ceiling like these, closed, the soldier who certainly wasn't going to be able to one who if, my grandfather's first partridge finally because the dog raised her ears with nose held out, my daughter when I asked her

—Why don't you speak to me?

slamming the gate of the yard and vanishing into the village, some of the soldiers who left the tent fixed up their uniforms and tried to get back in the line again

—Little horsey little horsey

or they negotiated about who would drive the next minesweeper in exchange for a ticket in the line, at a certain point it seemed to me that I saw my father in the midst of them, forgotten by the partridges, with the dog sniffing the tents without understanding, my grandmother to my grandfather, mistrustful

—You didn't hit one partridge?

and me without understanding since my grandfather deceased a long time before the war, I remember him in the house in the village without being able to speak, choking with the soup spoons that my grandmother held out to him and one eye sticking out more than the other, yelling for help in silence, where she wishes that he stayed during the night I sensed him in the dark, with a blanket in his lap, melting in the big chair looking at me, from time to time his throat

—You

of that I'm certain, his throat a

—You

confused who agitated the dog and let me look inside with the same intensity and the same kind of fury, angry with the blanket, angry with his destiny, angry with my father killing the pig for him because you no longer give any orders sir, none at all, he lies down when we lay him down, he rises when we raise him, he spends the afternoon in the garden since they put him there, he doesn't decide, doesn't solve, he obeys, his pocket watch on father's vest, the dog hunting partridges with him, I can't as his wife obeying his son, not herself, my cousin to me

—Don't you think that he seems angry?

the supply column left during the night with the four women stuck between the crates of the last Mercedes, little horsey, little horsey, waving good-bye with the trees now enormous, the tall grass as high as possible and the immense night birds around the headlights, for an instant it seemed to me that aside from the four women my son's wife along with the owner of the store that improved her hairstyle, they disappeared on the curve before the bridge where the black women were working the open fields, the white station head lived with two of them and some mulatto children oblivious of us, sitting on the ground eating worms, if we tried to speak with them, they vanished into the hut where they all slept, the station head a second corporal already old, fat, to whom the quartermaster, referring to him casually

—Take it

handed over as alms a packet of overdue rice or insect-ridden spaghetti, perhaps he hadn't been the station head, he turned up there before the war, from a small poor plantation, and was staying because they asked nothing of him, the mulatto children probably not his, of soldiers from companies prior to ours, with the dates on clay tablets one above the others joined to the flagpole, me with my daughter on my knees up and down

—Little horsey little horsey

holding onto her wrists and she laughing with pleasure, with fear and the pleasure of fear, with her hair to one side and then the other and a missing baby tooth while now all the teeth my God, the whole body, all of her, not resembling her mother or me, a stranger, while I thought for what in hell she called me

—Love

seeing that she didn't look like any of us despite my wife

—There are times her facial expressions are just like

and then a boom

—Yours

when the mine blew up under the first vehicle in the supply column, right after the curve, and after that the offensive grenades, and after that the Kalashnikovs, and after that the bazookas, and after that at least two machine guns, and after that the G-3s, and after that the psychologist in the circle of chairs at the hospital

—How horrible

with the trunk of a plane tree close to the open window behind him and a nurse on the patio laughing to the other nurse, and after that a cat on the roof, and after that two cats on the roof, and after that pigeons fleeing the cats, and after that me

—Little horsey little horsey

and after that my daughter kicking me with her ankles

—More

and after that a sign on a tree trunk that announced Lisbon 10,000 km, Moscow 13,000, and after that us running toward the column, and after that the soldier who dumped the leftovers from his plate scraping the aluminum with a knife announcing to his partner in front of him in the line

—I'm certain that I won't be able to

falling, and after that us, the second lieutenants, trying to join the platoons, and after that a driver alone in the unimog passing us all, and after that the unimog falling sideways in a ditch and the driver quiet, half inside half outside it, and after that me, forgotten by little horsey, little horsey, running also at random shooting bursts toward the tall grass, and after that the pig not eating slop, eating us, and after that two women in camouflage under gas cans that were burning, a dark-skinned one and the white now missing a thigh, and after that the supply corporal vomiting, and after that the psychologist in the circle of chairs at the hospital with his eyes closed, and after that an insurgent trying to escape protecting his body with his elbows, and after that a soldier squatting on the ground, his mouth open to us and his two palms in blood from his chest, already without eyes, already without lips, meaning they were there but not there, and after that the body of a second insurgent jumping under the bullets, and after that the captain shouting out orders that no one obeyed, and after that no pig eating, and after that my daughter emerging out of a shortcut from the town, and after that the girlfriend of my daughter-in-law caressing my daughter-in-law

—Doll

and after that my little son hanging from me completely, and after that the third woman in camouflage facedown on the ground, with her hair out of the cap and a twisted torso, little horsey, little horsey, and after that sandbags slipping off the cab of the Mercedes one by one and piling up on the dirt, and after that a stretcher-bearer on all fours bent over still bodies, and after that me putting my son in my arms to take him away from there, and after that his mother without ears and hands walking toward me, and after that the dog returning to the pit where my grandfather and my father were with a partridge in her mouth and the round eye of the partridge hating them, and after that a last round from the bazooka blowing apart a baobab tree, and after that my daughter

—Enough already

slipping off to the ground, forgotten by me without letting go of the rein made of cloth that she discovered yesterday in a forgotten drawer and me abandoned in the chair of the living room continuing to raise and lower my knees without anyone with my wife staring at me silent, full of stones lighter than water, Moscow 13,000 km, Lisbon 10,000, Lisbon 10,000, Lisbon 10,000, the first dogs from the camp approaching fearful, one of them stopping next to one of the women in camouflage to smell her, the blacks from the village were conversing softly, my wife immobile in the dark next to me

—You're not asleep?

me who didn't move, didn't make noise, it wasn't clear if her eyes open or closed and yet she

rubbing my body with her hip

—You're not asleep?

I'm sure without turning to me and nevertheless

—You're not asleep?

without going on the offensive and nonetheless

—You're not asleep?

married for almost thirty years, more than thirty and her voice hadn't changed

—You're not asleep?

as if we had met for the first time a few weeks before

—Would you permit me to accompany you?

my wife after a bit of hesitation

—Maybe

then ashamed of the

—Maybe

holding her purse next to her chest as if the purse were defending her from me and in reality it did defend because I didn't consider my words, what do I do gentlemen, what do I say now, me in search of phrases without finding phrases, a question, a beginning for a conversation, a stupid joke that would make her smile, if I managed to make her smile or she gave me an answer everything easier afterward and I discovered squat gentlemen, I tried to match my step to hers and that was all, I never had a ready wit, I don't amuse anyone, I listen more than I speak, normally I don't even listen, I limit myself to agreeing

—It's exactly that

and afterward distressed with the response, the strangeness

—It's exactly what?

at least introduce me, spell my name so that I introduced myself, I spelled my name and my wife silent, her jaw against her chest and eyes on the ground, how do I treat her, I ask something, I flee from here running and if I flee from here what will she think of me, her voice finally

—I live beyond that corner

or rather a grocery store with crates out front and an old building, like those that one realizes instantly without elevator, burned-out lamps on the stairs and very high steps where one always trips, it seemed to me that my wife in a hurry to get there but without fear that a neighbor might see us, she greeted a lady with a shopping cart, waved at a man with an apron at the entrance to a butcher shop, stopped in front of a door in a casual attitude looking for her keys in her purse where the usual confusion

—It's here

and me, stopping with her, struggling not to scratch my jaw in search of some stupidity that didn't come, with a smile that I was unable to effect, with a proposal

—Tomorrow at the same time?

no matter how I tried I couldn't explain out loud, my wife a ring with a long key and a short key, choosing the long key, turning it with a sound that appeared to break things made of iron inside or to stir up loose nails in a bag, I made a move to help her that got interrupted three centimeters ahead, I met her eyes for a second and immediately disappeared from them

hope that in January if we have to take advantage of the branches at night to help us to withstand the cold, the soldier who wasn't able to stopped being ashamed thanks to a trip wire, someone had to get caught in it and no one mocked him, we were already familiar with exposed intestines, we were already familiar with livers, he still said

—Good-bye

and the machine gunner, who never talked with anyone, I don't know why crying, afterward he leaned on a mango tree and remained like that for some time

—Damn damn

while the useless private parts of the other disappeared in the explosion, the commander

—Each of these boys

and I said, little horsey, little horsey, nothing more, a guy with white hair who I swear, little horsey, I liked sometimes, I don't know why but I liked him, blue and red marks on the map of Angola on the wall, a photograph of a woman at a desk, a second photograph of an aging woman, or rather faces of people, not us, if I looked around nothing between the collar and the forehead, we don't exist, we are not, we'll die here, a girl walking toward me in a light dress that at first, until the stones become lighter than water, I didn't notice and it was her, I swear, it was her and the same path side by side, the same silence, two or three times, I didn't believe, the elbow back and forth, while walking, rubbing mine without either of us pretending to notice, two or three times, after two or three more times, after that what am I doing at work, after that what is she doing at work, after that mother sick, after that my father's work, after that a brother in Luxemburg to escape the army, after that my father angry with the brother for escaping the army, after that no longer angry with the brother, after that one of these Christmases he visits us, he has a wife, he has two children, he, even though what he says is a lie, misses us, his profile more enticing when speaking of the family and me feeling so ugly, she for pity's sake

—Ugly, ugly I don't say

adding an amusing sideways glance to assure me

—I was joking of course

and that was the first, don't stop eating pig, don't stop, time she smiled, even today, when smiling, she always seems suddenly so adolescent, one

canine exposed, I haven't seen it since the story of the stones began, the doctor, every time when she used to emerge already dressed from the screen,
squeezing in a final grip, encouraging her

—This is going slowly but it'll go

because the last thing to do is destroy the morale of the sick, when their
morale teeters it gets worse right away, we have to keep people encouraged,
confident, make them believe in a cure with a slap on the back

—Totally vigorous today

in the same way that pigs eat so you can kill them happy, another bowl
with acorns, another bucket of peelings, more scraps from our lunch,
chicken bones, skins, those things that get pulled by a fork to the side of the
plate and my wife collecting them on another, smaller plate so that I didn't
chew on them by mistake, I began to talk with her already on the way to the
office, I began already to have, still fearful, opinions, preferences, I began
to think already like a soldier

—I'm certain of not being able to

if by chance impudent things came to mind that made me blush and my
wife, still not my wife of course, just an acquaintance despite the elbows,
more and more frequent, lingering a few seconds, actually it's obvious, without noticing it it's clear, when distracted it happens without our noticing,
we almost ran into each other how embarrassing, my wife almost worried

—Is there a problem?

and me, immediately, wanting the elbow with me forever and look, it
was destiny that wanted it, me no problem for the love of God, I'm well and
good that the word *love* came from me together with the word *God* so that
she didn't take it as a lack of respect or insolence, the word *love* right away
on the second day certainly it frightens or at the least it makes the ear rise,
makes us tense, kee, I'm certain that I'll not be able to, ping watch, prudent,
on guard, love quickly one abuse too many, patience is necessary, not to
hurry or frighten people

—certainly I'll not be able to

do everything step by step, delicate, prudent, keep advancing little by
little like one who is not advancing, a touch here, a touch there, lightly,
casual, I swear, that it wasn't on purpose, it must have already happened
to her and it has to happen again, what was missing was the on purpose, in
some way she'll forgive though I'm not guilty at all, automatic movements,

unconscious attitudes, what I can't muster the courage to do happens despite me, as the body betrays us, this of the

—Little horsey little horsey

after a quarter of an hour gets tiring, my muscles hurt here, my feet hurt and my daughter who doesn't understand that

—More

children so merciless, so egotistical

completely indifferent to what we feel insisting fearless

—More

the machine gunner to me dragging the weapon on the ground

—Don't take it the wrong way but what are we doing here second lieutenant sir?

wanting to leave it behind, break it

—What are we doing here second lieutenant sir?

and you're right, what are we doing here in fact with the certainty that we are not able to, my wife suddenly stopping, suddenly looking at me, suddenly, it seems, taking me by the hand

—Why do you blame yourself so much?

this in the middle of the road with people passing, two men taking a washing machine from a truck, a couple of old women with shopping carts, each one with her dog on a leash smelling tires, concentrating, serious, one of them small, white, the other so-so, both horrible, both with unfocussed gelatin eyes and trembling noses, my wife to us

—What are we doing here?

no, my wife to me

—I happen to sympathize with you

and me, I swear, with the urge to sit her on my knees

—Little horsey little horsey

lifting her and lowering her at the expense of the feet and the belly the legs that aren't hurting now, aren't going to hurt me, me holding onto her hands

—Little horsey little horsey

for the first time holding onto her hands thinking

—I'm not going to be able to

and though thinking that I wasn't going to be able to continuing to make her jump

—Little horsey little horsey

because I managed that, her hair to one side and then to the other, her fingers squeezing mine more, her mouth an inch away from mine saying also

—Little horsey little horsey

and despite still single, with no lace nightshirt, with no shadow of a ring on her finger her palm on the back of my neck

—Love

and all the stones in the world, I swear, much lighter than water.

14

When I think that tomorrow they'll bring the pig to the cellar pushing it out of the van with rods and canes, fat, fat, falling onto the cement dirtied by mud from the ground, trying to free itself from the ropes, trying to bite us, trying to stop us from tying up its legs wounding us with its hooves, from hanging it up on the hook turning the pulley and beginning to bring the bowls near to the table and the knives while, through the open window, I saw my father's cousin leave our tomb after cleaning it, her head tied up in a cloth and above her, very high up, the mountain birds, their wings horizontal, hovering motionless over the mimosas, when I think about the pig's death I who recall almost nothing of Africa besides the shots, the rain, the lightning that burned the huts, a mango tree suddenly disappearing and my father, in camouflage, leaving for the jungle, holding his weapon at kidney height, his thighs apart, with the edges of his mouth downward and eyes suddenly minuscule, ferocious

—Watch out if you touch him

despite the inspector from the political police

—Don't take him to Portugal second lieutenant sir he witnessed what you did to his parents and sooner or later he'll seek vengeance it's a question of time

because blacks are like dogs, they don't forget, if they were like us they'd be white, they don't get cured with a whip, open a grave, put him in there, close it and you'll see that even then he'll bubble up to hate you, if he could come up here with a machete he'd waste you, I my father's toy I recall that as I recall the only chair in the sanzala, that of the dead, placed in an empty space in the center of the huts, adorned with rooster feathers, snail shells, and dried birds, where they seated the corpse decorated with ink, necklaces and bracelets on its ankles, wrapped up in rags from the Congo, with eyelids open, participating in the festival observing everything, the inspector of the political police to my father, worried

—Watch this charred stick will have to snuff you out be warned as if I'd snuff out my father someday and snuff him out why, what nonsense, the corpse with which the relatives, concerning relatives my father's cousin waved to me from the other side of the yard wall as she was passing by the house in the village, they were sharing marufo and the blood of chickens beheaded with a machete, spilling it into their mouths as they danced so that even the trees and the air red, the sun red, the river red down below with red crocodiles, heating the skin of the drums in the flames from the straw so that the ground made the feet quiver without need of moving them and raising their tattooed arms in joyful exclamations, I remember the women's tepid singing, my father's cousin vanished down the street following ours since she lived almost at the top of the highway where my poor car had to remain still, and screams of the chief hunched over the ground that the others repeated trampling the shadows of the long dead

—Aiué aiué*

the quartered goats drooling foam and saliva, the sweet smoke of hemp, the taste of marufo in the gourds, my father pointing me out to the soldiers with his chin

—Watch out if you touch him

and the soldiers silent oiling their G-3s, the homemade rifles the sanzala militias carried, filled with twisted nails, hinges, pebbles, expressing themselves in a language that I had almost completely forgotten, but if I paid attention

—Euá

I seemed to understand the inspector of the political police to my father

—Don't tell me after that I didn't warn you second lieutenant

and understandably not only the language, the customs, the ways, the flavor of the food, despite the death tomorrow the pig still eating, hopefully it'll have time to eat all my mother's stones one by one the doctor to us, without any red circle around some stain

—She's cured

not content, perplexed, looking at the screen behind which no one, my father in the house in the village no longer thin, fat, slow, no longer young

—Watch out

old, a pair of glasses on his forehead and one of his legs, with which he was angry hitting it, more difficult than the other

---

*A word that suggests agreement, affirmation, greeting.

—What Angola gave me gentlemen

half dragging it, twisted, back from the visit to the pigsty surprising me, with an echo of drumming in some part of him, eat all the stones animal, please eat all the stones, my father

—What are you thinking about?

and I was thinking, but I don't tell him, why did he worry about me covering me with his body as soon as the first Kalashnikov, dressing all of me with himself, I was thinking, aiué, about a woman her belly down, without ears and hands, among women and muanas without ears and hands and hens and dogs, and I was thinking about men with eyes open at random on the ground, in the remains of mud and straw dwellings, about the chair of the dead fallen over, about a girl trying to hold onto a goat that was not fleeing her, sobbing, an odor of hemp mixed with the odor of gunpowder, about the smell of blood from the blood, about the first wild dogs looking at us with caution their noses in the leaves, I was thinking about the man fallen a bit farther in front who lived with us and paid no attention to me, I was thinking about the empty chair of the sanzala around which the dead man, alone, continued to dance, I was thinking about my father

—Watch out if you touch him

with minuscule ferocious eyes, and a tent sheet, and combat rations from when he left the camp with his soldiers, not in front, in the middle of the line with the guide painted in white three places ahead and the second guide farther behind in case the first got cut down, I was thinking that at certain times, here in the village, my father afraid for him and for me while the drums of death continued to beat

—What is going to happen to us?

Without words of course but I heard it all the same as I hear myself

—What is going to happen to us?

while they were hanging the animal and selecting the knives, while we were looking at it pleading don't stop eating, my father observing the pig as if the pig were him, already fat, old, slow, defenseless, without hearing

—Love

from anyone, without ever having heard

—Love

from anyone especially not in Africa when warning

—Watch out

the soldiers, when I saw him kill people wanting to die, when I saw him look at my mother almost envying her the stones, when observing the doctor knowing that at times he wanted to take her place, when looking at my sister wanting to hug her, don't conceal, don't lie, wanting to hug her without courage to touch her because her face

—Don't dare come close to me

wanting him to dare to come close and sorry to tell you father with due respect you so idiotic, so dim, you almost

—Love

pleading with my mother, in the lace shirt, that she express it for herself, you

—Would you permit me to accompany you?

and nothing more, so distressed, to trample her hair, to hurt her, to get rid of her fast

—I'll be back in a moment

and sitting in the living room in the dark without courage to return, looking at the street from the window, the lamps, the trees, you poor, you without anyone, you here in the village looking at the pig, don't stop eating, pig, rotten fruit, vegetables, scraps, the stones, all from the kidney, even the small ones and those that have not yet been born, my mother worried about the buttons of her blouse

—If I continue to get better I'll gain a bit of weight

while my father was looking at the pig as if the pig were him, surprised at my face, surprised at my movements, surprised at the table of knives while the sanzala continued to dance waiting for, so many screws in the homemade rifle of our guide, so many nails, waiting for death, Her Excellency in her room, moving away from me without courage to turn the light off

—Who are you?

ready to defend herself with a pillow, her knees, her fingernails because my body painted, my cheetah skin, my zebu horns, the mechanic from the garage

—I had to bring the car here they won't steal another wheel

to the left of the café full of motorcycles outside and men, one of them with crutches, with little bottles in their hands looking at me without words, the flies landing on the faces and not noticing, my father called the guide pointing to the path

—Where does this one go?

because it wasn't a village path, too few foot tracks and the foot tracks from bare feet without boots, the insurgents must have come through the jungle as someone must have been waiting for us to pass in order to attack us from behind, they are going to brag on the radio that they killed us all, Her Excellency to me

—You're quiet your arms in the air for a while have you lost your appetite?

sometimes her eyes not mocking, almost tender, there were whole mornings when

—Wait there

and she would fix my tie before I went to work

—since you've got to be black you may as well be an attractive black

and, I swear, a pinch on the chin with her body smelling at the same time of perfume and I don't know whatever you felt like from year to year, your toes almost touching my face, not straight, bent, please scratch my chest with them, scratch my neck, order me

—deeper

chewing the pillow, in profile for me, a vein on her neck getting larger, her nipples suddenly so hard and her eyes, without looking at me, ordering

—Now

Her Excellency lifted by her elbows licking my chest, biting me

—Beat me

my father holding the guide's shoulder

—You brought us into a trap asshole

while the second guide, leaving the homemade rifle, escaped from the jungle until he fell in a few seconds, under machine-gun fire, about ten or fifteen meters from us, a shoe on one foot the other bare while his body turned, a soldier fell on him with a knife and the pig or the guide barefoot screaming that was heard in the village frightening the mountain kites, a hawk close to the treetops, my mother calling me to help her to get up in a voice that almost gave up at each word, Her Excellency's claws inside the mattress

—My God

and her teeth enormous, my mother looking for her slippers with her feet

—This is hard

a sweater on top of the lace shirt and the bones of her hands stretched out over the sweater, I remember hearing her sing, I remember my sister in her arms, already serious, already absent, always hidden from us, even at work when she said

—Bye

and she went down the corridor, far from me and not far from me, we never far from each other, what a thing, my father's platoon entering into the tall grass fanning out, the guide on his knees pleading

—No

with hands folded as my father, no, the pig, no, my father, his snout in the bucket, was eating it, a bullet from his G-3 in the belly, a G-3 bullet in the chest, Her Excellency's arm on my shoulders not for love, exhausted, my mother

—If my appetite returned a little bit

and now the stones weightless, gone from the X-ray, hunger will return madam, believe me, the insurgents started to shoot from some trees on the left that the sergeant's section got around while firing, a dog appeared and disappeared, one of Her Excellency's ankles, half asleep, scratched the other slowly, if I tried to kiss it a confused grumble

—You're still not satisfied?

When I was small and woke up in the middle of the night crying my mother picked me up and took me to their bed where the heat of their bodies calmed me down, in Africa the man who lived with us slept on a mat next to the door and didn't talk with me, he smoked Caricocos outside, when we entered into the village just a machete, not a homemade rifle or a pistol, it was my father who shot at him, I recall now standing next to him just as I recall my father looking at me, touching the man, touching me, talking with the chaplain, the chaplain a long conversation

—Promise

and my father

—I promise

looking at me in the same way that he still looks at me and I don't understand well, the doubt if

—Watch out if you touch him

or

—Watch out if I touch him

like the doubt if his silence silence or his silence

—Kill me

my sister once, she who almost didn't talk

—You two

and silent, she was born years after Africa, she knew nothing of Angola, she didn't see on our faces the joy of going to serve the Fatherland, she didn't notice my father hating himself, when my mother in the kitchen he locked up in his room with a pot of leftovers from lunch, eating, get fat second lieutenant sir, fill the bucket with your blood and pour it over me, I'm a knife in your neck, I don't know, and the dark screaming since I don't know if what lived with me screamed, so much emptiness from the internal noise of my head, my father

—Shoot at will

and a first insurgent between two tree trunks, a second, a third, a Kalashnikov emerging from the bushes and after that an insurgent on his knees in the grass, bending over on the ground with it, Her Excellency sleeping her mouth on my neck in the house in the village and light rain outside in the garden, the doctor drawing a circle on an X-ray around a white stain, intrigued

—Is this a new stone?

my father softly because of the screen where my mother was getting dressed

—Doctor didn't you say that they had all disappeared that they were lighter than water?

the doctor softly as well

—After we return from the pig killing we'll check this in the kidneys better it's always a surprise one imagines one thing and another emerges

my mother with the butterfly jacket, smiling at us

—All is fine isn't it?

and of course all is fine madam, don't worry, it's not important that life be short or long, what becomes necessary is to be happy, your family, your house, your well-being, your daughter finally attentive

—You feel better don't you mom?

her husband not tormenting himself about Africa, her son a marriage that might bring serenity to all and peace, two or three grandchildren that always keep things lively, change so much for the better in our time, we rejuvenate, return to having surprises, happiness, some worries as well but nothing serious of course, with children, thank God, almost never serious, the usual fevers, the usual infections, the usual falls, in which generally nothing gets broken, a friendly and attentive daughter-in-law, perhaps his daughter, who knows, a healthy gentleman that calms everyone, there are still men like that, eat that new stone pig, don't forget that stone, the mechanic from the garage brought the car to the town and assured us that the tire will arrive tomorrow, at least that was the response of the representative in the city, tomorrow, not later than after lunch but certainly tomorrow, besides the tire clearly a little inspection of the engine, that it's not missing anything, there is always a piece that needs a little tightening, machines are machines, and time, it's logical, wears down the metal in the same way that one doesn't stay eighteen for all one's life, the thirties appear, the forties and so forth, we don't always remain boys, it was good as it was but life has its rules sometimes merciless, cruel, that unfortunately don't depend on us, we have to accept them, do what's possible to make the best of adversities and there it's a question of ingenuity and work, of a positive mindset too, how important is a positive mindset, not to let ourselves get cut down, we always believe what the people say, and it's really true, wisdom does not lie, better days will come, for example for you they are already starting, there was an annoyance in the kidneys but with work and patience the concern got resolved and there it is, God free us of that, ready for another, this was playful forgive me, no one normal prays for unhappiness whoever he may be, I want health and peace for all and now the lady finds herself, fortunately, on the threshold of all this with years, I don't know how many but I hope many, on her face still that smile and those colors don't lie, she's not going to let herself get cut down there is no reason for such a thing and my mother listening to him silent as the nurse listened to him silent, as my father and I were listening to him silent, as the pig eating silent, we'll return to Lisbon tomorrow, I don't know if we'll return to Lisbon tomorrow, perhaps some of us, not my father not me, will return to Lisbon tomorrow, not my sister perhaps, let's suppose she's one, to occupy the empty house in the village alone, my parents' room, the other two little rooms, the living room, the garden, the loquat tree, the old smells, the mold on the walls, the odor of my grandfather, the dog, my sister

—I only wanted to see you bye

squatting on the little wall, it was not necessary to return from work, she saw me there stamping papers, Her Excellency to me

—If we left now perhaps you

her eyes filled with fear but fear of what and suddenly silent while they were bringing the buckets to the cellar, why fear of things, why fear of the blood of an animal, don't stop eating pig, getting fat like my father, don't stop staring at me like that, one of the sergeants to the communications corporal

—If you touch the child the second lieutenant will kill you

the second lieutenant, aiué, beating the jungle with his platoon, stumbling on a Kalashnikov, on a light machine gun without ammunition, on a woman in uniform with her belly upward in the grass, her legs covered with patterns, a mulatto, still alive, looking at him, searching for a pistol with his slow fingers, blind, my father putting it in his hand

—Shoot

the mulatto and he staring at each other, both with their mouths moving though no sound, my father on his knees with his face two inches away from the mulatto's face, locking the pistol in the mulatto's fist, putting his index finger on the trigger

—Shoot

aiming the G-3 toward his head

—We'll shoot at the same time when I say now you want to?

both the same age, in camouflage shirts rese

—When I say now

mbling each other, identical canvas and rubber boots, almost in ribbons, with the same exhaustion and the same indifference on their faces, the same powder stains, ash, and sand on their skin, two pigs not fat, thin, thirsty, hungry, afraid, who licked the leaves of the trees in the morning, who sucked on roots when there was no more food, who slept on tree trunks hoping for protection from the rain, a mulatto almost the same as my father, almost white, both with a watch stopped on their wrists, already without the crystal and with bent hands, the mulatto lifting his pistol slowly when my father

—One

the communications corporal spitting in my direction

—Monkey

he who wasn't in combat, he limited himself to decoding messages coming from Luanda where there was also no combat, one lived in air-conditioned hotels, spent the weekends with black girls from the island and on the other days sent others to fight, the doctor in the circle of chairs at the hospital to my father

—So much hate

and my father no hate at all friend, what hate, the joy of serving the

Fatherland only, the supreme joy of serving the Fatherland understand, my mother in the house in the village

—I think I'm fine to make dinner for you

because the stones not only light, weightless, I don't feel them anymore, I don't, my husband with me, old, with one of his legs bad and me

—Love

me old as well

—Love

my father to the mulatto

—Two

taking the safety off the trigger, putting the barrel on the other's throat

—Two

the psychologist in the circle of chairs at the hospital

—Stop

as if the G-3 aimed not at the mulatto, at him

—Stop

while the soldiers were deactivating the grenade with a trip wire, they took a pack of ammunition boxes, searched the pockets of the corpses where plans, papers, a broken compass, a photograph filled with creases of what seemed to be a black woman with a necklace, features almost all dissolved on the film, why did the idiot want that, what will he do with her, while the tire for my car finally on the way to the town, but unfortunately the pig, but unfortunately the knife, my father repeating

—Two

sniffing, grunting while audible in the distance, coming from the north almost above the trees, transforming the branches into birds, the small plane with mail and fresh food, the sergeant who distributed the tickets for the women in camouflage

—Five minutes for each one girls don't tire yourselves out on the first one

my mother to my father in the house in the village

—Are you going to let the mulatto kill you?

and why not let the mulatto kill him, why don't the two of them kill each other, at the moment my father said

—Three

the pistol a pop because already no bullet inside and I think that in all his life my father never noticed a pop so loud, my father's cousin, returning from the cemetery with a broom and some rags, passed by the little wall of the house in the village where I was reinforcing the bougainvillea with string and wire, her nose and mouth identical to those of my family, the rest different, how strange relatives, they resemble each other only in a few respects, that I remember the woman without ears and hands didn't look like me and what a lie to affirm that she didn't look like me if I hardly recall her, my father got up slowly without pulling the trigger of the G-3, in a distracted torpor, while the sergeants were rearranging the platoon for the return to the camp, my father standing observing the mulatto

—Would you permit me to accompany you?

the butt of his gun on his hip, still today, from time to time, I notice his hand looking for it, astonished upon not finding it, saying in a low voice

—How stupid

and sitting better on the sofa with me comprehending from my mother's face, for that matter unchanged, that she understood him, there were nights when she suddenly awoke certain that he was crying in their room, his mouth on the pillowcase and shaken by my mother's voice, not her arm, but her voice shaking him

—Wake up that's been over for so many years wake up

but the pistol of the mulatto lying on the ground remains like his attitude, not of fear, not of rage, not even of hate, the same question always

—Why

and the same absence of response, the same incomprehension, the same fear, the same rain on the Lisbon dock, the same military marches, the same crying, the same handkerchiefs waving endlessly, the ship's motor moving away, the same water neither gray nor blue, almost black, in which it was sinking, sinking, the second commander in the officers' hall burning match after match without managing to light the cigarette, my mother to my father but was it my father and if it was my father who was the man lying down

—You're in Lisbon again no one's dying now

despite the pig eating, despite the knife, the blood, despite the men in the rubber aprons who were approaching him, despite the lace nightshirt to calm him

—I'm here

despite her body next to him and a hand on her breast, despite the recoilless cannon that shook the world, despite his wife cured, his wife healthy, the stones in her kidney not even lighter than water, already nonexistent, despite my sister finally looking at him

—Father

and all this, it's clear, a lie in front of the coffins, the dead, the injured, the dense swirling mist, the violence of the thunderstorms, the flagpole that lightning took away, despite the

—When my grandfather finds out he'll kill himself

and a body with a hat on its head turning on a rope from a beam in the barn

—It's over don't you see it's over

and from the day my black son smiled at me for the first time, I've looked at him without thinking about him and that's how it's been, suddenly, I smiled at him, my mother

—I'm going to make the cake you like for dinner today

the psychologist of the circle of chairs at the hospital pleased

—Now finally in a good mood

he that if he saw a bazooka he'd die of fright, that if he witnessed an ambush they'd put him in the hospital in Luanda, the mulatto with the pistol still looking at my father, waiting, the mulatto dropping the pistol

—It's your turn to shoot

and my father taking his finger off the trigger, putting the finger on the trigger, taking the finger off the trigger again, my father to the mulatto

—You

a mulatto almost white stretched on his back in the dirt without taking his eyes off him, quiet, without fear, without asking for anything, just waiting waiting for what, with a fly perched on his cheek, with the first insects around him, kinds of spiders or ants, the earth trembled but it could be my father's legs, it could be some heart, it's not clear whose, a person, an animal in the grass, the leaves, even water, at times, it shakes like that, it's not visible but one feels it shaking like that, my mother to my father in an amused tone, touching his shoulder, from time to time, when walking by him she would touch his shoulder, for years she touched him on the shoulder, I think that I always envied him because of that, if we didn't pay attention, we wouldn't notice anything

—You have the cake you like for dessert today

while my father standing in front of the mulatto without hearing him, Lisbon 10,000 km, Moscow 13,000, the stripes already faded, the color of the camouflage, a piece of band-aid from the infirmary, marked in green pencil, to mend a piece of cloth on the elbow, my sister in the house in the village looking at them, we didn't even have a portrait of my grandfather, for what, he died, the partridge dog died a little bit after that, I didn't get to know her, seems to be a small, disturbed animal, now some bones scattered, if bones still remain, I don't know where, and the birds in peace, they were lifting their heads early without anyone bothering them, they were flying, they left, I threw stones at them that didn't reach them, of course, also what strength did I have, just a child, a kind of badger that I didn't see and it got away at a gallop going around a tree trunk, the communications corporal in the camp, to the sergeant

—It's a crime to leave a black alive

while my mother, with the agile body of before, crouching, getting up, opening drawers, moving objects around in the kitchen with Her Excellency helping her without looking at me, she never touched me on the shoulder, that one, she never made a cake for me, at the beginning she didn't seek out my body, most times she kept her eyes open until I slipped over to my side and she asking me

—Are you done?

while she covered herself, with a sigh, in the sheet and the blanket and pulled the pillow under her head, eyes closed as if she were sleeping, informing bored

—You took more time today

massaging one of her legs with a grimace while my mother was beating the egg whites for the cake in a bowl, my sister holding out a spoon

—Let me try it ma'am let me try it

this at a time when she still spoke and took interest in us, she liked to search my pockets looking for a pocketknife, keys, my mother to her, still beating the egg whites

—Careful with that before you hurt yourself

at a time when my sister was spinning the keys in the air opening invisible doors, disappearing into nothingness, saying bye to us

—I'm already in another place

and she wasn't because even seated on the ground I could get her, my sister to me shaking the ankle I grabbed

—Black

and me wanting to beat her, of course, if I had my little plastic car in my hand I would hit her with it, my mother grabbed my wrist before and me protesting in a fury, regarding the car urge to throw it at Her Excellency now with eyes closed, her back to me, pretending to sleep, her girlfriend from the shop caressing her hair

—He made my little girl sleepy today

and my little girl satisfied, purring

—Doll

with long fingernails, red, caressing the arm of the other while the sergeant from the first section signaled to us that we could return, some soldiers setting up a security detail inside the jungle, my father still in front of the stretched-out mulatto who had dropped his empty pistol, with a wound somewhere in his belly, close to the exposed umbilical cord, with the emblem of the party tattooed on, his skin lighter than mine, almost the color of my family's, almost the color of the pig's, his eyes also not dark, the mouth almost thin, the hair, if he were to comb it, smooth, the left hand on his chest, the right hand toward my father still standing up next to him pointing the G-3 at him, my father young, thin, tired, though on his face, intact, the joy of serving the Fatherland, the military marches while they paraded on the docks, the military marches when the ship was leaving, the rain over the gray water of the Tagus, so much rain over the gray water of the Tagus, Lisbon smaller, the dock minuscule, my father and two comrades the door closed and the cabin curtain drawn so that they didn't hear the screams of the people who were saying good-bye, more the screams of the seagulls, more the screams of the lieutenant ordering us to run during instruction

—Those arms really high those arms really high

more trees, more rain, more birds, the mulatto to my father again

—You're not going to shoot lutenan sir?

a request smiling from under him

—You're not going to shoot lutenan sir?

while the pig continued to eat, continued to eat, continued to eat, the pig asking

—You're not going to shoot lutenan sir?

with his mouth full of slop, peels, and leftovers, my father handed him the G-3 not with the barrel turned to the mulatto, the barrel up and he returned to counting

—One

while they observed each other, he returned to counting

—Two

and upon counting

—Three

at the moment he was turning to leave with the platoon on the way to the camp taking his place in line without ever turning back the shot with which the mulatto repeating

—Three

made half of the mulatto's own head disappear.

15

And when the Jaea Cessna left me in Luso, and when the Nord Atlas left me in Luanda, and when the air force van left me at the staff headquarters, and when the taxi left me in a boardinghouse in Mutamba, and when the owner of the boardinghouse left me in the room on the second floor, and when I closed the door and sat on the bed with my suitcase lying down, to open it, on the mattress and the flushing in the little cubicle to the left continued to drip, and when I took off my army jacket, and when I untied the knot on my tie, and when I took off my shirt and was naked above the waist, only the metal medallion with the number etched in and the blood type around my neck, if by chance a flamethrower burned me all up, the metal would resist, with the engraved numbers and letters, at the window sounds of Machimbombos,* cars, and the sly smile of the nurse sergeant handing me a packet

—The tubes of antivenereal cream second lieutenant hopefully you'll use all

that I put under my civilian jacket thinking of the angry face of my wife, embarrassed

—Fifteen days of leave without getting to know anyone here what am I doing?

my civilian jacket in the suitcase for so many months above the tin armoire, creased, dirty, creased dirty shirts, my pants folded, a single tie with lining on one half, coming undone, exposed, in the window jeeps, people, blacks dressed like us accompanying the trawlers on the way out to fish, my father's voice heard, very distantly

—It's a pity that this year we didn't have you in the village for the pig boy

while I tried to fix the lining of the tie pushing it with my finger, feeling

*Buses.

more lonely than the camp at the hour when the unfortunates from the huts bring their empty tins holding them out in the hope of soup, footsteps in the corridor of the boardinghouse, a man's laugh, a sulky girl's voice

—Don't treat me like that I'm not a black girl from the musseque*

and other voices on the stairs, other footsteps, the toilet for all at the end of the corridor, always with people protesting, angry, from outside the door and protests from inside amplified by the tiles, one barely enters the toilet and the voice increases right away, with a drop from the badly closed tap blowing into the sink while the palm trees on the waterfront were shaking their arms almost lifting themselves off the ground, sloppy money changers, with a small file, they were trading angolars for escudos with the troops in civilian dress and guys barefoot hawked in the corners wooden crocodiles, Luanda this and the musseques, stray dogs, misery, my father blaming me in the little room in the village

—Weren't you better off with us?

as if the fault were mine, as if I'd chosen, one day I arrived from work and a piece of paper waiting for me, not on the trunk at the entrance where one put the mail and there was a clay plate with a knob, an empty bottle of syrup and keys, in the pocket of my mother's apron that she held out to me without looking at me

—This is for you

the paper she crumpled I don't know how and it seemed wet, she delivers it as if she were angry, me thinking

—Did I do something wrong?

without remembering anything, I never had problems with anyone, I never treated anyone wrong whoever it was and my mother in a kind of rage, with the postcard or whatever was trembling there

—This is for you

my father reading the newspaper, too interested in the news to pay attention to us, I saw just his baldness that the ceiling lamp rounded and above his glasses, the fingers left over as numerous as possible, I never noticed so many edges holding the pages and one of his shoes flattening its toe into the ground, me holding the paper looking at them

—What was that?

*Slums (from Kimbundu).

I remember myself being stunned, wrinkled, looking now at one now at another without granting much importance to what she had in her hand
—What was that?
and they silent, me twenty-two years old, in March twenty-three, to my mind already a grown man at that time, it's obvious, to my mind now a kid and I was the kid who asked
—What was that?
thinking about a broken jar and that I remembered it hadn't broken at all or about a piece badly placed on the clothesline that left stains on the sheets of the neighbors down below, I was already working, I was already married, we all lived in the same tiny apartment, my parents in their room and my wife and I in what was always my room or rather a small place so that they heard all the noises, when I felt like it me to my wife, softly as possible
—Do you think that they're already sleeping?
because it was almost always me who felt like it, naturally, me the male and she accepted or not, when she didn't accept
—I still hear a cough
when she accepted a word that I didn't manage to figure out if
—Love
or if
—Careful
and, from what I know of her, more inclined to
—Careful
than
—Love
learning at my cost what I thought impossible to exist or rather that there is no part of the body that doesn't have tiptoes and that until tiptoes relations obtain that my mother's cousin, friend of considered words, called fecund, and while I was trying on my civilian clothing, in Luanda, in front of a stained mirror, my father blaming me in the village, with fewer tablecloths than now
—Weren't you better off with us than in Africa?
the civilian clothing that was hard for me to believe my own, a squeeze on the arms, discomfort in my back, the button on the collar strangling me and a guy already purple, I found it hard to figure out if it was me, pleading with myself
—Help

with distressed eyes, I ended up solving the problem loosening the knot in my tie and becoming the same as the money changers of Mutamba, an eye always alert to the possibility of police, upon leaving the so civilian boardinghouse, my God, though my hair short, though my skin like crust, though something in my movements, more cautious, slower, that people didn't notice, as if behind the things jungle, as if on the corners a recoilless cannon, as if in the lines of Machimbombos Kalashnikovs waiting, as if forty-kilo mines under the stones of the sidewalks, as if traps on the patios, waiting, me constantly in search of the G-3 that I didn't have, of little branches broken by imprudent insurgents and thus a jumper over there or a trip wire, my mother, after Africa, bending over to get the towel also

—What are you looking at under the table?

and don't worry ma'am, sometimes I'm not here, suspicions about an antipersonnel mine they are sneaky, he next to the edge of the carpet, my wife with the urge to hold me she sensed extending her arms

—My God

and in the rain from the windows the rapid footsteps of a guide or those of my son in the camp chasing a goat, outside the boardinghouse, on the way to Baixa, the smell of funge* and fried rooster, the trawlers from the bay leaving before dusk, moving slowly, lamps lit, like those of the huts on the plantations when approaching us, one afternoon the body of a man from Bailundo that the political police hanged in a mango tree for buying dried fish in the village cantina instead of the more expensive shack of the plantation, the insults of the loyal Angolan soldiers when the rope lifted him

—Son of a bitch

the palm trees from the island were born one by one together with the lamps of four or five residences while I was walking randomly outside the waterfront breathing in the thick smell of water and gasoline from the ships that were slowly moving off, my wife to me

—Don't you feel sorry for the pigs?

the impression that a fox up there, next to the cemetery, the impression that a genet, I asked the sergeant that he take care of my son while me in Luanda, no one knew of us in Portugal, no one speaks of war, one pretends that it's forgotten or it's really forgotten, me on the street of bars filled

*Traditional Angolan dish, made of manioc, that accompanies the main dish (say, muamba, a stew with chicken or other meats).

with mulatto women and men at the counter, only elbows, as clumsy as me, with the noses in their glasses like donkeys, tied up to wagons, in front of the baskets, with their snouts in the middle of the hay staring at the people while they were eating, a woman disappeared into the cigarette smoke and emerged from the smoke, next to me, with another ring

—Are you seriously an officer?

that continued to be born in the room in the boardinghouse, my mother to my father in a low voice, in Lisbon, pulling the newspaper down and making an embarrassed eye emerge

—Do you know her?

the same as thirty or forty years ago when he came with his godfather to the third floor without elevator in the old part of the city where ladies with not much clothing, in slippers, were conversing with each other in wrecked chairs without paying attention to him and a guy in crutches dozing in the corner, calling them from time to time

—Naughty girls, naughty girls

and vanished again, diluted in eyelids superimposed inside himself, one of those places from the past where there is always a dog that we thought lost and a grandmother massaging varicose veins while my father's godfather in complicated negotiations with one of the ladies, with a more benign aspect than her colleagues, who took me up to her room where a mattress rolled out, without some straw visible, fixed to the floor and on which for some moments I felt like a puppet without strength, pushed and pulled by a creature with haste, that returned me to the world a little moister than when I had arrived

—Get out boy

and my father and my godfather back home in silence, vaguely satisfied, vaguely guilty

—But for what?

the recollection of the guy in crutches accompanied my father for his whole life, now and again, including during dinner, his invisible eyelids would open

—Naughty girls, naughty girls

accompanied by straw from a mattress in ruins that smelled of many people, my father, half forgetting

—What happened to me there?

my mother to me, no recoilless cannon, no bazooka, shrugging her shoulders in tired resignation

—You're getting old never mind

because with time we don't control the, perhaps a machine gun, suddenly, between two tree trunks but he wasn't sure, anyway no shot fortunately, because with time we don't control the stains, my mother pointing at my father with the fork

—You're making more and more of a mess

gave me the idea that not with pity, avenged, but what vengeance gentlemen if he never treated her badly, I suppose that he bothered with the cat more than with her, even holding out fish for it on the tip of, the machine gun fortunately vanished, the silverware, the woman who was adding up rings in the bar in Luanda to me

—Are you really an officer?

probably used to sergeants and corporals and me with difficulty hearing her because of the conversations, the laughter, the noise of bottles and glasses and an ambush farther away, after the orchestra platform, where an insurgent sitting on the dance floor trying to hold back the blood with his palms and the reports of G-3s fading, only the cracks of the orchestra's reco-recos and the throat of a mulatto singing, the woman with the rings, impressed, as a soldier pulled a pin and threw a grenade toward the bathrooms

—Second lieutenant?

not totally believing due to my clothing needing to be starched and the button of the collar too exposed, I showed her my card with number two uniform while some tiles from the bathrooms fell around us and the waiters fussed with a client facedown on the floor, uniform number two and the visor cap that the woman with the rings, like the ladies in camouflage who visited us in the camp, examined respectfully and returned to me holding it with solemnity by a point just as my mother the paper from the army holding it out to me without looking at me

—This is for you

and then cleaning herself with her apron, on the first weekend when she saw me in uniform her cheek backed away when I tried to kiss it, looking for who I was under the hat asking

—Is it really you?

almost without moving her mouth, meaning the words were there, it was clear that

—Is it really you?

but not all of the same size nor put in order, at random, it was clear that her index finger on her head ordering the letters, making mistakes, taking a vowel from here to put it there so that the

—Is it really you?

languid, twisted, confused, a son in boots with shaved head, with a metal star on his shoulder, who didn't seem younger or older, seemed merely a stranger, I looked for an old toy in the trunk because perhaps if I recognized myself with a tin locomotive or the articulated Pinocchio that was missing its left arm, or rather had ears and the rest, it was only missing the left arm, at what attack in what group of huts was it torn off, I didn't notice any Pinocchio in Angola, there didn't exist children's things in the jungle, little cars, marbles, the teddy bear that always smiled until it lost its stuffing after it had escaped almost all of it through the back, one picked it up and the animal hanging, empty, it couldn't even sit, it leaned on things and gave up on life, a simple lack of cotton changes people, I remembered my grandmother when she took off her false teeth and she took them off almost always to yell at us better in an anger of sucking cheeks made of spit and diphthongs that before her outburst I didn't know of, my mother astonished

—The alphabet in the end is so large

so large in fact and you only four letters

—Love

if you used a few more with me for example perhaps our daughter might have been born earlier and might talk with us instead of avoiding us silent, only grimaces and contempt, the trawler lights of Luanda out in the bay, the elbows of the connecting rods in front and back like gentlemen marching in haste sweating on the riverbank staring with their chins, not their eyes, at the fishermen with their line, with patient bait, between an empty basket and a canvas bench, one of them with a pipe in a locomotive voice sending Indian smoke messages to the tribe in Almada, the woman with the rings to me

—I came from Portugal three years ago

when they began to send ladies into the ships in order to improve the levels of tenderness in the army, treated with penicillin when accompanied by itching or pain, the woman with the rings escorted me to the boarding-house across narrow streets watched over by dogs only jaws and severe eyes held on a leash by the military police, panting in a ferocious respiration ready for transformation into barking when they raise themselves on the hind legs, the troops, those ones, kill all the cabíris, all the hens, all the goats, all the people, my son standing, alone, hugged by a piece of manioc, the cracks from the tongues of fire, the flames from one side to the other along the threads of gasoline, the golden wigs, then silver, then gray of the trees, afterward falling in black pieces, afterward dust that some breeze, not wind, some breeze is bringing, afterward the political police saving two or three emaciated prisoners pushing them with gun butts toward the jeeps, their legs without strength, their arms hanging strips, one or another head looking at us not with the eyes, with the mouth, the woman with the rings bothered by the high heels

—Is it still far?

continuing taken with me

—A second lieutenant

receiving the paper from my mother

—This is for you

that she crumpled I don't know how and it seemed to me wet while my father drowned himself more and more in the news, whispering in a kind of colorless smile

—It's not going to be very difficult you'll see

he tried to balance himself, with the help of his spread-out arms turning, on the wobbly cord of his mouth, if sometime, for example, my daughter smiled, though I don't believe it, I think something of that type, holding itself for a second before disappearing into the skin, replaced then by hardened eyes

—I only wanted to see you bye

and whose weight was hard to maintain on the top of the cheeks, explain to me how you manage when you are, please don't stop eating pig, alone, after the last light is turned out and the darkness, eat the darkness too, greater inside us than in the room, surrounded by the past, as confusing as the street, someone who picks us up and forgets us, people who don't notice us, the chairs of the future occupied by people conversing with each other without noticing us, the woman with the rings, with her shoes in her hand

—After this corner you say?

bars after bars, a shot I don't know where, the military police running, falcons on the mountain of the village, so tranquil, eat the falcons pig, my wife in the middle of dinner, holding her waist

—At times I feel discomfort here and then it passes I must have strained a muscle

and it's really possible that she had strained a muscle, always straightening up and bending over, who doesn't have back pain, there are hypersensitive people who at the first pinch think instantly about the kidneys, going from doctor to doctor changing the cream insisting

—It's inside

and perhaps it's inside, a vertebra that got bent a little bit or something, I hope they take care of my fit son, pray that he not be found without ears and hands nor go to a G-3 to make it sing and discover a soldier facedown on the ground, the doctor

—Arrange every test for me

grappling with a jaw that was missing pieces or with my wife's X-rays, scribbling red circles inside a lung, speaking with the edge of his mouth

—Then you said after that corner?

no, that one the woman with the rings, barefoot, with shoes on the hook of her fingers, leaning on the wall massaging one of her feet that a stone's edge had hurt

—I have the impression that there's something here

the doctor calling a colleague, blond, with pens of various colors in his white coat and so many trees in my memory, so many rivers, that smell of Africa, that density of the earth

—What does this look like?

the colleague his palms on his knees studying an area with a different density murmuring words in Latin so that we didn't, that smell of Africa, understand, more than the smell, the living presence of the earth, the sensation that all was breathing inside and outside of us, we were not totally independent from the insects, the plants, the hidden animals, the lungs of things, my father silent, my sister not with us, of course, I don't know where, in the cemetery, on the mountain, on one of the village paths, if they greeted her I didn't see, quiet in front of a wall contemplating a stone, me to the woman with the rings

—Right after the corner

because I remembered the pink building before and the fence in front, a lace shirt

—Love

very far from me, an arm on the back of my neck but so timid, no ambush, no shot, no scream, the operations major always smoking through his cigarette holder, the little finger ring, almost all the sergeants grabbed a glass with the little finger a ring while my son seized the food with all his fingers inside, all his fingers on the plate, all his fingers in his mouth looking at me silent, the woman with the rings older than me by the creases around her mouth and her way of walking, one of her front teeth dark, broken, if the tooth like the others I bet her voice thinner, up to my shoulder in height in a friendly tone that almost moved me

—Perhaps I'll give you a discount

and she didn't because dressed like that you can't be an officer at all, you stole the card from some lieutenant, you don't walk like them, with authority, straight, forcing the world to admire you only by the way the heels strike the ground and then ordering the world around without discussions, screams

—Undress

—Lie down

—Give me

before the

—Get up

—Get dressed

—Leave

and you remain stretched out like a mackerel, without looking at me, before that seated on the edge of the bed, face hidden in your hands, repeating a

—Leave

that I, already on the stairs, still heard, that I, already on the street, still heard, that in the bed where I sleep, eat this pig, don't forget to eat this as well, I continued hearing, a

—Leave

becoming not a man, a child with fear, a

—Leave

like the

—Don't turn out the light

like the

—At least leave a lamp on in the corridor

and a boy in pajamas looking at the mattress, leaning toward the corridor, with hands spread back on the floor, afraid of the threats and dangers of the darkness, the Kalashnikovs, the grenades, the light machine guns, an officer not hearing

—Love

hearing

—Son

and when saying

—Don't speak you're distracting me

saying

—Mother

without noticing my faster pig, faster even if you choke yourself, even if you die with the food stuck, faster now without noticing the contentment of the woman with the rings

—Sleeping with an officer brings luck

this at the entrance to the boardinghouse that seemed more modest to me, smaller, even less clean than when I entered for the first time, the counter less imposing, a half-dead plant in a vase, dripping brown or green leaves from the stem and at the end black ones, a bent photograph of Luanda on the wall, with cracked glass, two old whites, in shorts and slippers con, what a desire to say

—I love you

too, I love you, I love you, versing in wicker chairs, one of them with a band-aid on the left elbow, keeping silent to appreciate the woman with the rings, when we entered, with those eyes, that were marked like rulers by the men, at each five dashes a longer black dash, at each ten dashes an even longer red dash, my father to my mother

—You must have pinched your spine don't worry

removing a piece of dirt from his jacket with his fingernail, besides older than me the woman with the rings cheaper clothing, a purplish thing on one of her ankles that I preferred not to see, if we watch people attentively defects are not lacking, the nose, the hair, etc., I almost don't look at myself except when I shave, my daughter-in-law always ready, smartass, more lively than the damned, to point out faults, not in the form of complaints, but in the form of innocent questions

—That there on your chin is it a pimple?

and the index finger checking it cautiously because

—Perhaps it's contagious

the stairs just on the right and now there's something that we don't have in the camp, steps, everything is level with the sand, I'll have to get used even to that again provided I get out of here alive, steps, handrails, doormats, these strange frills of the rich, the one with the rings, more used to wealth than me, climbing the stairs, in front of me, without a glance at the old men, with cracking heels, and me behind with my wife in my mind, not really repentant, perplexed, given that no lace shirt, no

—Love

and consequently besides perplexed curious as well, will there be arms on the back of my neck, legs on my chest, a mouth twisted by the extraction of a molar without anesthesia and a breath on my shoulder

—Ah mother

I hope softly enough that my parents didn't notice, even before my sister I heard only silence from them and now here is the reason, probably, that she doesn't speak hardly ever, squatting in a corner, serious, absent, when she lingered a bit with us, she noticed, at best, the coughing of my father, pestered by the vertebra that later on was transferred to me, in the corridor or a pipe in the kitchen, my wife without getting annoyed with anything, at times I was certain that words were even more a way of expressing silence than of canceling it, on the landing of the first floor a ceramic Venus de Milo and a broom, on the second my room the third door on the left, each of them a number on a metal plaque with holes for two screws but always only with one so that the plaque swung always when the door was opened or closed and there was the bed for one person only, a lamp with a pleated lampshade, at that time white and now gray, a rickety chair, the curtain stained by the hands of dozens of women with rings and the armoire with my suitcase on top, all that done on purpose to upset the world

—What misery

while we were moving carefully in the hope of not rubbing against anything, an old hair on the pillow, air conditioning that didn't function, the foul breath of Angola at the window that didn't fully close, the woman with the rings to me, disappointed

—I thought that officers lived in a different way than the soldiers

and through the opening in the window the music from the bars and the hot breath of the street, there appeared to me the axles of a warped wagon on one of the village slopes, the speech of the cypresses in the cemetery before I would fall asleep, pronouncing one by one the names of the dead, the squeak of the handle for my parents' water pump, a kind of desire to cry but behind the eyes, distant, this more in Lisbon than in Africa, in Africa I didn't have time to feel pity, the political police took the old chief from the sewing machine after an attack on the camp, when a soldier's head disappeared with the seamstress shooting at us from the aircraft landing strip, thinking better it was not a postcard that my mother handed to me in Lisbon, creased, moist

—This is for you

it was the woman with the rings, almost the same age as her, sitting on the bed of the boardinghouse with legs spread, hugging her purse certainly with a knife inside if I didn't pay, even when they are with us they don't stop holding onto it, cautiously, because nutcases come from the jungle and at times are not able to

—It's because of you that I'm not able to

at times they get mad

—I didn't think that you were exhausted from inspiring fear

at times they try to beat us

—You smell like a black

at times they lean against the window and yell with their backs to us

—Go away fast I don't want you here

afraid that we'll see their faces and if we turn to them at the door they are crying, the poor fellows, suddenly so small, inside the open bead of their hands and between the fingers, softly

—Help

with a child's lip trembling, I remembered the old colonel suddenly child

—Hold me in your arms

who put me on his knees, pulled a grenade from his pocket, with the fishhook of his index finger on the pin mentioning throwing it at me, holding onto it again, saying sorry

—If I were you I'd get walking

and in no time, with me already on the street, a kind of blast and the military police running, the family doctor prescribed a cream for my wife's discomforts

—A little bit of cream before going to bed and it'll be fine within a week

and it wasn't, within a week more pain, that's life, always ready for games, surprises, the woman with the rings to me, sitting on the mattress waiting, adjusting herself a little on the bed

—I came here to work if you want to talk it doesn't matter as long as you pay the same

why did I take time to grasp that most soldiers don't want service, they want attention, they want chatter, they want a pacifier but they are ashamed to ask for a pacifier, tired of wasting themselves in killing and looking to us for attention, little celebrations, fingers that tuck them in, a space of silence where they can put all the garbage of war, for example the little girl to whom they gave the barrel of the pistol to suck on and who grew calm then, quiet, it was a blessed remedy, I barely squeezed the trigger, they want a presence that helps them sleep, fingers slow in the hair, a palm on the forehead, a promise that it was over, I promise it's over, no one will scare you anymore, which rifles, which blacks, which obligation to sweep mines since the Berliets are gold, a Berliet three thousand contos, a soldier four hundred and thus men, so much cheaper, that sweep for mines, of course a little bit of gas is wasted for evacuations and a couple of compresses but the difference compensates, keep your dick there in a corner of the room and don't think about it anymore, if it's needed, I'll tell you

—Love

Seriously I'm telling you

—Love

as if it were truth and I don't charge more for that, it's so easy to say

—Love

so simple to say

—Love

especially when nothing is felt, really thinking

—Love

even more sincere when nothing is felt, it doesn't stick in your throat, it doesn't stumble, it doesn't make us ashamed, it doesn't make us think

—And now

it doesn't hurt to leave, eat love pig, eat the peels and the slops of kisses, eat that strange thing that scares us all, look at the second lieutenant, I swear, almost serene, pleased, promising me a lace shirt if my arm on his shoulder, if my palm on the nape of his neck, if the huts stop burning, if the blacks without ears and hands once again whole, living, almost people at last, not like us, it's clear, but, up to a certain point, looking better and similar, they go too, they talk almost, there are moments when they walk too, if we pay attention, giving the idea that people, at least somewhat alike, suddenly resemble each other, of course if we observe better we note differences the little hand always held out

—Lutenan sir lutenan sir

the badly finished in the features, the junk that they eat, the skinniness, the submission, the lack of understanding of language, answering

—Lutenan sir

whatever it be, if we want to sleep with their women we sleep with their women, they quiet, serious, not

—Love

it's clear, we'll have to see and perhaps they're right, that means

—Love

at last or

—My dear

or

—Don't leave me

or

—Promise that you won't leave me

or lies like that, I never saw a dog lie or a goat cheat, they keep going and that's it, they go away to die, they don't inconvenience anyone, if we don't bury them there are always other dogs or other goats or those birds of theirs, large, ferocious, that eat them, they pull off the skin, pull off the meat, pull out the intestines and devour us, the second lieutenant, without undressing, to me, in his civilian clothing

—Are you going to eat me lady?

and he didn't dare approach, fearful, he in the bar, despite being badly dressed, he seemed to me to be a serious man, alone at the counter with a bottle and a glass but drinking from the bottle and cleaning his chin then with the back of his hand, he staring at me at a slant

—You

no, him

—Will you permit me to buy you a liqueur?

more properly for the lady, sweeter, weaker, he not

—hey you

he polite, he

—I would like to be with you

he

—I would like to talk

he the invitation to the boardinghouse

—We are more at ease

he

—No one will interrupt us, right?

always looking around afraid of ambushes, attacks, a recoilless cannon, a trip wire, he

—Ma'am

he always

—Ma'am

and me, it's logical, wanting to laugh, me so much wanting to laugh, to mock that sadness, to make fun of it and still I accompanied him to the boardinghouse, and nonetheless I helped him when he tripped on a pebble, and nevertheless he said

—Dear

and nevertheless said

—Love

and nevertheless, not believing in this, for the first time me who didn't see clearly because poor, had the urge not to accept money.

16

The only thing that I heard when awaking in the house in the village was the minute hand of the kitchen clock spinning on the wall buzzing softly trying to say what I couldn't understand, I make so much effort to understand things and I can't gentlemen, my father to me

—Boy

not

—Son

he never called me

—Son

he called me

—Boy

always, Her Excellency of course insinuating

—He doesn't consider himself your father

he brought you from Africa out of loneliness or as someone claims a souvenir, an ordeal that remained there or then out of remorse

—At least this isn't the bush

but not from love, don't think even for a moment that from love for you, a kind of living trophy that he showed off

—My boy

not

—My son

because no black really knew his parents, it could be this one, it could be that one, it could be a man passing through who bought his mother a blanket or a goat or didn't pay at all, he took her while washing clothing in the river, it's clear that there was a man living in the hut before the troops arrived but other men lived there before as well, the difference is that it's this one I call

—Father

he didn't leave with the others, he brought me with him always, he argued in Luanda with the white bureaucrats, he wrote notes, handed over money, bought me clothing for whites, traveled with me by ship, slept at my side, prevented them from mocking me, when I got sick with malaria he didn't leave my bedside, the doctor to him

—You're more mother than father don't worry the boy is almost fine friend

and I don't know if I like him or not, I'm used to him, he found a way for me to eat with the officers, not with the enlisted men, in a corner of the table, on a cushion above the chair so as to reach the silverware, he corrected my movements, if the captain to him

—Aiué mamá

he would get mad, one time he hugged me with strange eyes because I said without wanting to

—Father

the last time before his wife's sickness when his eyes became strange, meaning clouded, meaning smaller, I started to forget the language, the huts, he put me in school, got mad at the teacher

—He's not intelligent how?

and changed my school, sometimes in the middle of the night he got up with screams

—To the shelters hurry

with my mother calming him in vain

—You're not there anymore you're in Lisbon lie down

he without hearing

—Did you protect the child?

in such a way that it will pain me to have to kill you tomorrow sir when the pig and the long knives arrive, I know that I have to kill you and I didn't want to kill you, I wanted to stay with you on the mountain, I wanted us, the two of us, to listen to the badgers

—Do you hear?

scurrying among the grapevines, if he happens to smile at me

—Aiué mamá

I feel something tight here and a voice he won't hear

—Aiué Calunga*

because I stuck the large knife in his neck and the whites running toward me

---

*Greeting to the beyond, eternity, that is, death.

—Asshole

incapable of understanding that we liked each other, that I had to do that and he to accept that I did that so everything finally clear and the two of us in peace, father and son without anyone separating us, me

—Father

and he

—Child

the hut intact and my mother with ears and hands, my mother

—Muana

and me the muana of both, my father's wife without touching me, under-standing, my father's daughter understanding, cut off my neck on top of his neck, fill my guts like you fill your own, cook us, eat us, offer our legs to one neighbor, our arms to another, don't put me in the cemetery with your-selves, take away what is left over here and get out of here fast forgotten by us or perhaps, Calunga, the wild dogs and the hyenas and those white birds with a curved beak arriving finally, the village as deserted as the hut from which I come, just two or three old men, with caps, that resist the shadow of a wall in the village, immobile, waiting, gypsies passing there on the top of the mountain crest and autumn arriving, gray, brown, dull, with the first slow rains, the first cold, the hand of the clock in the kitchen remained spinning on the wall, fainter and fainter, slower and slower, without saying anything yet, becoming immobile little by little and when it stopped time ceased to exist, replaced by the huge shade of the mountain or the reflec-tion of the Tagus in the clouds, at the beginning of November, when all seems to be a sad death, with an old man and a child waiting for the morn-ing partridges in a gully and the birds fluttering one by one, emerging from the grass looking around with only one mistrustful and serious eye, the last thing I heard upon awaking in the house in the village, even at the tip of the first little hill of the mountain, beside the clock hand, was my father's wife

(alright, I'll say father)

breathing her stones against death in the bed, stones the doctor lied to her about

(—I don't see any more)

while the troops, coming from the east, approached the huts in a fan shape, with one of the guides almost in front and the other farther behind, hidden in the tall grass or hunched over from bush to bush, with grenades on their belts and rifles, horizontal, at hip height while a commissioner is collecting manioc from the fields and my mother with ears and hands disappears with one of the insurgents in the thickness of the jungle, a handkerchief on her head, barefoot as always, walking on her feet that resembled cracked roots, a lookout on all fours with his cheek against the ground

—People are coming

and the unimogs were audible waiting on the paths, the second lieutenant ordering with a movement that the machine guns aim, the pins of the offensive grenades pulled out to the middle, a helicopter in reserve on the savannah, the wind against us to prevent smells, the first cabíri giving signal moaning, rolled up in his legs or rolling himself up in himself, the men stopped smoking their mutopa pipes

—Tuga tuga

the tugas I met on the ship from Portugal, thin, silent, without understanding the ocean, those I met afterward in the circle of chairs with the psychologist at the hospital, old, some crippled, most always in silence while I waited on what they had brought me out here in a little chair, the others

—Your black's grown

and his black did in fact grow, he's now a man, he works in an office, married a white who despises and mocks him

—Darky

he still doesn't understand these smells from here but he no longer remembers Angola, he barely recalls the headless goats, the disemboweled cabíris, faint screams, at the edge of silence and my father commanding that, the diesel fuel, the flames, the burned pig hides, his, mine, the pig that I'll soon look at up there, on the final day when he eats, now alone in the sty without even looking at me, my father's daughter looks at me, also silent, serious

—I only wanted to see you bye

getting smaller outside in the corridor on the way to the street, you'll remember me, you'll forget me, I don't know, you have to forget because everything gets forgotten, we even forget what we would like to remember best, perhaps Her Excellency will stick in my mind, I don't know, pushing me away with her hand stretched out on my chest, disgusted

—There are days when you smell so black that it's nauseating

preventing me from touching her, even approaching, she sniffing the sofa, the sheets, the room

—What horror

and her girlfriend not shaking my hand, moving her head away because I smell still more if I put on cologne

—The cologne doesn't make you sick?

but the money the black makes, while not much, comes in handy and besides he obeys, he's satisfied, he doesn't claim to lead, he doesn't dare to get angry, if we drive him out of the kitchen he remains out there waiting for us to let him return, always submissive, humble, decked out with wristbands and watches that shine, they like what shines, what sparkles, what has no value, the pig was not looking at me, sustained by a bowl of worm-ridden fruit, tomorrow we three dead and the house closed, the village a mirage, the cemetery only grass, the last old man without looking at anything, my sister if by chance she happens to pass by

—I think we had a house over there

not very sure

—I think over there

observing the trees, the hill

—I think over there but I'm not sure

living I don't know where or with whom, working on what, what are you thinking about sister, what did you want from life, what interested you, tell me

—I only wanted to see you bye

and if by chance I saw you from the window you nowhere, at times, from what I concluded, I wonder if you exist in fact, you didn't touch anything, you didn't look at anything, you didn't talk with anyone, the same clothing for months in a row, the same silence, the same obliviousness, the same edge of the table without calling at all, hearing voices inside that no one knew, my father and my mother, avoided I don't know why looking at you, you didn't touch anything, you almost didn't eat, if they asked you anything a movement to push the question away, you arrived without warning, you left without saying good-bye, when mother got sick no change in you, you remained a moment without looking at anyone and after the door slamming from the street without our being aware that you were leaving the house, if I went to the window I'd see you walking in the street at the same pace as always until you turned the corner, I never heard of any boyfriend, any colleague, I never saw you laugh, never saw you cry, you never said my name and nonetheless you came every year to the pig killing looking at my father, at the knives, at me as if you knew what will happen tomorrow, I think my father and my mother knew just like you did and nevertheless they didn't speak, what for, just as neither my father nor me mentioned even once the cut-off hands and ears, the huts burning, the beheaded animals, Her Excellency to me after examining us one by one in a distressed awkwardness

—When I'm with you all I don't understand anything

with fear of us, troubled and on those occasions me not black in the same way that my father not white, us weird creatures that terrorized her, at times when alone at home I suddenly sensed her fear of me, small on the sofa, defenseless, fragile, surrounded by machine guns and Uzis, almost screaming with fear, or before I had the idea that you closed your mouth with force so as not to scream with fear, I was certain if rain out there and a voice in a microphone, between military marches

—I see in your eyes the joy of going to serve the Fatherland

while the wild dogs nipped at your ankles and jumped at your throat, while the cans of diesel fuel raised the flames up to the canopies of the trees, while your girlfriend caressing you

—With me here no one will hurt you

while the second lieutenant to the soldiers

—Kill kill

while the second lieutenant, serving the Fatherland

—Leave nothing over

and she, her palm on her mouth

—No

she almost on her knees

—No

until slowly me a black again, until slowly

—I hate your smell get away

and me inoffensive on the cot, me useless, me an animal, me a weakling

—I don't understand the reason for continuing with you

raising her head to me, despising me, ordering me to set the table, ordering me to lift the table, ordering me to serve you, to bring you a glass of water from the kitchen, sitting me down in a chair separate from yours and in that moment, suddenly, in the midst of sparks and blasts that forced the cabíris, the goats, the chickens, and the people to flee in a confusion of wings and legs and bleating and screaming, in a confusion of birds that were disappearing from the trees, in a confusion of things that were falling, rolling, coming apart, the noise from the guns began to increase suddenly, exclamations, orders, the whites and the Katanga running toward us, me alone, sitting on the ground, with a goat leaning on me calling before a GE* tore it apart with a knife, if I could tell this to my sister, if I could say to her I don't have time because she turning her back to me after

—I only wanted to see you bye

she who would remain alive unlike the pig and my father and me because we have to die the three of us, because we should already have died the three of us a long time ago, the psychologist, in the circle of chairs at the hospital

—My God

whose ears and hands does a shooter have to cut off, leave him over there on the tiles of the infirmary or on the redness of the earth where finally only the witch doctor dancing after pulling off the rooster's neck with a bite drinking it down, still dancing, in the empty village, some lepers there below, the watery mud, Hoards holding out a plate of beans to me

—Eat this

with a bracelet of beads while he was heating up water for the officers' tea, while at work they pay me less than the others, I'm black, it's a wwwwwwwwindy day and I like wwwwwwwwwind, my father to me without imagining, the idiot, that he's going to die, he's going to die, we're going to die here

—Walk up to the animal boy

so that the two of us walking one next to the other on the streets almost all twisted and up top what was a chapel and now is a barn despite the cross still above, where cheap women heat chestnuts and greens in a pot, on one occasion one of them

—Kid

a gray cat with yellow eyes on her lap, women with whom guys in the village sometimes and they didn't pay with money, they paid with fruit, gizzards, a bit of sausage, all this in silence, on the remains of a blanket or a piece of coat, one of them

—Kid

and me standing still looking at her, I never saw feet so large, I never saw hands so large, empty breasts like in Africa over thin ribs, four or five women

---

*A soldier from the African special forces (Grupos Especiais) trained by and allied with the Portuguese army.

all of them gray, the lepers at the river, quiet under the shots, a sergeant to the soldiers

—Don't waste the diesel fuel on them

but they were already burning as well when at last the unimogs left the jungle, the pig alone in a pen eating a bowl of wine soup, the cousin who took care of the tomb conversing with my sister still next to the wall looking at me, not at my father, at me, my mother alone in the house

—Love

when unsaid words become so clear but

—Love

for whom, my father to me

—Have you already seen a pig of this size?

with one of the ears hanging and the other alive, alert, flies on his back, on his neck, while he was devouring his own feces mixed in with the scraps, a lizard was missing from the wall, a cricket was not missing, the woman to me

—Come here kid

and so dark inside there, clothing on the ground, rags, one time my father found one of the women hanging from an elm tree staring at him, perhaps she's still there on the north side of the mountain where my father has always refused to go for fear of a voice swaying in the tree

—Kid

and hopefully the pig that I was going to kill tomorrow has eaten her, me in my father's lap, in an army unimog, leaving the hut, fewer and fewer paths, one or another wrecked fences, a residence that was missing columns, a leopard's head, just for a second, looking from the tall grass and thus a lost antelope trotting over there, Her Excellency on a bench in the garden rubbing cream into her arms, my father helping my mother up to the sofa in the living room

—I'm not tiring you?

putting a cushion behind her back and straightening up her spine, not in a lace shirt, with a dressing gown already threadbare and old shoes with untied laces, like those polished ones from weddings, this is my mother who was not my mother with pale, thin hands, small fists, her ring on the middle finger, our indifferent eyes wandering at random in the cage of the eyelids, next to the wall the idea that a genet disappeared in a thicket not mentioning the foxes watching over buildings the small rabbits that fed themselves more on fear than on grass, the black woman who used to carry me on her back and give me her empty breast no longer fleeing the troops, motionless, and the finger of a soldier, suddenly without courage, hesitating on the trigger, there was someone behind him, I think a corporal, I think a sergeant, I think a second lieutenant, I think my father, knocking her down, pulling the knife from his belt and kneeling, now I remember the blade, I remember the blood but it could have been from a goat, from a cabíri, from a rooster, all so remote, so imprecise, so silent despite the shots, the connecting rods, the screams, of a helicopter gunship spinning, of an insurgent trying to wear the uniform of a South African fallen on a beam and running away to crush his machete into the other's chest, my wife shaking me in our house in Lisbon

—Don't cry

without me crying, instead of huts a chair with my clothing, instead of sun an unlit lamp on the ceiling, instead of trees the cars out there, me on her lap looking for her breast with milk, not empty, or what I thought was milk, me to my mother

—Get me out of Africa madam

imitating my father to the psychologist in the circle of chairs at the hospital

—Get me out of Africa sir

get me out of Africa and assure me that I was never there, never witnessed those dusks, that rain, that wind in the tall grass, those bats in the mango trees, those savannahs sown with lights at night, my father almost in a child's voice

—For what reason am I not here with you?

because I don't march slowly and at ease, because I can't escape, fall asleep without fear that they'll wake me calling out

—Second lieutenant sir

without soldiers to put the barrel of a G-3 under the neck before declaring

—Until soon second lieutenant sir

and passing the rest of the night washing pieces of bone off the zinc ceiling, my parents with a piece of paper in their hands

—This is for you

handing it to me without wanting to hand it to me or leaving it on a corner of the table waiting for me to read it

—I see on your fac

for what reason doesn't my brother, killed in a car accident, come to help
me putting his hand on my shoulder promising me

—You'll stay here with me

in your lounge chairs, in your little statues, in the pink smell of your perfume, I didn't undress in the boardinghouse room with the woman with the
rings, I stayed at her side, not in Luanda, in the house in the village, sensing
the pig eating on the next street, sensing her hand on my head

—I'm here

seeing her cross her legs like women cross them, waving to me like
women wave, putting my face in her lap like women do, stroking my cheek

—Brother

with such delicate fingers, so feminine, so sweet, my father despised him
trying not to despise him, my mother acted as if she didn't notice, my daughter kept looking at us not on a tripod far away from us, nearby, my daughter,
for the first time not indifferent

—My men

almost like us, almost from our family in fact, my father pretending that
he didn't notice and my mother embroidering more quickly, the cousin who
dealt with our tomb staring at us coming from secret conversations with the
dead, my brother to me

—You

my brother to me

—We

and after that the automobile, and after that your death, and after that
me to my wife

—Would you permit me to accompany you?

and my wife first astonished, after that serious, after that smiling

—Perhaps

my wife

—Yes

and me at her side, distressed, twisted, happy, thinking

—What do I say now?

and without saying anything, only happy, sorry to have forgotten you, only happy or then perhaps I hadn't forgotten, you came with me, my mother to my father

—At least all three get along well

and we did in fact get along well the three of us, meaning I don't know if we got along well, we got along the three of us and now my daughter and I alone while the pig eats the memory of my brother until I forget, my son is looking at me, choosing the knife, showing it to me pretending not to show it to me, my son to me

—You sir

not angry with me, not detesting me, as tense as me, as serene as me, as decided as me, explaining to me without words

—I didn't want to I didn't want to I swear that I didn't want to

just as I didn't want the woman with the rings in the boardinghouse and, nevertheless, I had her, I returned to the bar and had her, she came back to the room with me asking

—At last lieutenant?

and it wasn't that I wanted to but I wanted to, it wasn't that I felt like it but I did feel like it, when asking me

—How would you like me to call you?

I answered her

—Love

she while getting undressed

—Not that it bothers me much like that but you'll pay a bit more for love

adding

—Then you'll pay more if there'll be kisses

without me figuring out what would be more expensive, kisses or love, my mother offered me all this for free

—But I'm not your mother

and frankly I don't know if she was not in fact my mother, everything confused in me, my father in the armchair

—I'd like you to be a gentleman son

satisfied with me

—I'd like you to be tender boy

so that I touched the neck and the shoulders of the woman with the rings who was laughing at me

—So respectful this one

was explaining to me

—You can beat me if you like as long as it's not on the throat and you don't hurt me

but I didn't feel like beating anyone, I didn't feel like treating anyone badly, I didn't feel like killing anyone, I killed the mother of my son who tomorrow, when the pig arrives, mistrustful, slow, will kill me, the knife in the carotid boy, the knife in the carotid, stir my blood quickly so that it won't coagulate, won't spill, won't be left on the cement, clean it with a wet cloth so that nothing will be left over, my brother to me

—These things have to be done well brother

I kissed the woman's breast, I kissed the woman's belly, I felt a missing canine when I kissed her lips but that made no difference I swear, my tongue in her mouth like a serious gentlemen, struggling of course, nervous, not very competent, her tongue in my mouth without any enthusiasm, I looked for it with my fingers without finding it but her hand helped me

—Higher up stupid

not very much higher but higher where a ledge, some hair, the scar from an operation

—I had a son

and at the end of the scar I found it, she warned me

—Nothing rough now

so that me nothing rough, cautious, slow, moving my little finger on her soft thighs, discovering it with the thumb

—It's here

the woman with the rings almost mocking me

—Did you wish it were on my neck silly?

sorry for calling an officer

—Silly

as if I were an officer and I don't know what I was, I was shyness, I was shame, I was my wife's arm on my back, I was the lace shirt, I was a heel rubbing my belly with the leg, I was a palm guiding my hips

—Try now

remembering suddenly who I was

—Try now Mr. Lieutenant

no, a longer phrase

—Try now Mr. Lieutenant and you'll see if it works

and despite a few strange resistances

—It's still not in place

I managed or rather was sliding inside almost without noticing, one thing inside another thing and the woman with the rings applauding me

—That's it

and now that's it what do I do, move in and out, move to the side, not move, I hope only, saying

—Love

the woman with the rings

—With more spirit boy

and me speaking up

—Love

me like with my wife though it wasn't my wife

—Love

a

—Love

that didn't come out well nor badly, it came out strangely, in an oblique voice

—Love

and after that as me in and out little different from my wife

—Love

while the one with the rings helped me with friendship, involved

—That love like it should be

me, in a tone like it should be

—Love

thinking about my wife in Portugal, alone in her bed, perhaps her head on my pillow to feel less alone while my son came toward me with the knife, found my carotid, found my jugular, whispered to me

—Father

at the same time as the one with the rings was saying to me, pushing me

—For a first time it wasn't bad but now if you don't mind take it out of me because you've already died it's done.

17

Today that is the last dinner before the pig killing my daughter deigned to eat with us at the table, meaning she added a plate for herself and she sat at a corner of the tablecloth between my daughter-in-law and my wife, she accepted a napkin, accepted that we served her, hoped that I picked up the cutlery to start, her face finally resembling ours, not closed, normal, the elbows not on the tablecloth, just the forearms, her movements not angular, her features tranquil, my wife happy, my son smiling at her and her eyes didn't flee, they accepted the smile without turning away, without leaving, the black loquat against the closed window, no light outside, only us in this world, one or another small lantern in the cemetery but distant, trembling, then the quiet figure of the mountain, all my family with me and me so content gentlemen, my wife put her hand on the nape of my daughter's neck for a moment and she didn't object, meaning she had a reflex to shrink up but immediately relented, my mother took advantage to put the bones on the side of the plate with deft delicacy and she also didn't object, my father always wanted the pig killing to be festive and it will be, I won't forget the contentment with which he looked at us that day, he was sitting with a hat, tie, and watch chain crossing his vest, my grandmother, always in mourning, with the ring she kept in a box on her finger to adorn her movements, my father's buddy lifting a glass of muscatel

—Yes sir yes sir

the button on his collar closed out of respect and formality, at the end of the meal my father considered the dinner finished going to urinate in the yard, we saw him from behind his legs spread apart, with a shining bisection of the angle of his pants and after my father liberated himself of the last drop, peremptory and solemn, and tidying up the equipment that he spilled into the box of his fly, slow operation, full of shakes and lateral movements, we sat down on the bricks in the garden, between the loquat tree and the cabbage, almost invisible to each other, breathing in the darkness of a silent satisfaction, with the peace of the dead arriving from the cemetery together with the palpitations with which the hens change the direction of the dreams on their perches, we felt ourselves eternal on those nights when the air entered and left us without being from the mouth, through the skin because our bodies were suddenly permeable to everything, at a certain time I realized that my daughter, who remained with us, didn't smile at us, but at herself and so different in that way, almost pretty, satisfied by being all together and by tomorrow's celebration, with my wife distributing the meat, already free of the stones and the emaciation and the pain, emerging from the doctor's screen not fragile, not sick, at the age I met her, walking at my side toward the house, timid, embarrassed, content, without any war separating us, without the Mercedes outside the dirt roads under the enormous trees and the soldiers sweeping for mines on the way to the target, me behind the minesweeper, in the second vehicle, the one with the radio and the machine gun, the corporal and the loader there above, in a type of short tower, and the bazooka looking from one side to the other, still without my son, alone, thinking fourteen months are left, thirteen, soon, it'll be an instant, I'll return and returned, without a wound, without shrapnel, whole, and my wife on the dock amid people waiting, perhaps a little thinner, a little older, with a dress I didn't recognize and short hair, a kind of bang that almost covered her eyes when she became, for example, serious suddenly, thinking, the hair disappointed me but I didn't open my mouth about that, the ears showing, the earrings I didn't recognize, who gave them to you don't lie, tell me, I asked myself in that confusion of people, embraces, laughter, tears, if you had seen her like that when you asked her for the first time

—Would you permit me to accompany you?

her embrace rapid, without strength, my embrace rapid, without strength, behaving like strangers with each other, it wasn't like that when we used to embrace each other, it wasn't like that when we used to touch each other, it wasn't like that when we used to look at each other afterward, the rest of my family identical, me changed but I barely recognize these expressions, these movements, it's with you that I'm going to live now because the intimate you* wouldn't come out, I put my hand on your shoulder and took it off right away since your shoulder different from my memory of it, I recalled the creature with the rings

---

*Portuguese, like many other languages, distinguishes between a formal form of *you* and a familiar one used with intimates.

—I went to Portugal once and returned with the first boat because I didn't understand anyone

not my mother, not my father, not a cousin with whom I'd lived, how Angola changes people gentlemen, they become different, formal, distant, pretending to know us without knowing who we are and in a moment a mine an attack, in a moment a goat blocking our legs, rusty tins next to the camp's fence asking for food, my father to me, with a new wrinkle on his forehead while it seemed to me that an explosion in the distance, probably an antelope that stepped on a mine, probably a wire barely connected, so many embraces suddenly, so many tears, so many dead over there that the helicopters didn't pick up

—Seems that you're not thrilled to see us

my mother almost hanging from my body but is that my mother, my son stumbling rolled up in my legs, a group of girls jumping around one of my soldiers

—Fernando Fernando

who saw them terrified, certain that the general, invisible, reading from a piece of paper that didn't exist, reprising his speech from two years before

—I see on your faces the joy of going to serve the Fatherland

when the Fatherland squeezing, screams, shawls, handkerchiefs, frightened seagulls that were cawing, cawing, my wife giving me her arm but is that one my wife, this profile says nothing to me, this voice says nothing to me, this scent says nothing to me, this tongue in my mouth from the creature in Luanda or her, this breast against me from neither of them, a discreet palm and rapid in my pants without me having paid her, without me having asked anything of her at all, not

—Would you permit me to accompany you?

I asked, if I saw her pass by me and that was all, she wouldn't attract me much but just now, that's not so, and then it may be that I'd take the bait, it may be that, this without compromises, of course, without guarantees, without promises, a game though expressed seriously, a pastime, at twenty we didn't appreciate things and after, of course, we pay for it, we look at each other's hands and a ring, imagine, an apartment that we didn't recognize, women's clothing mixed with ours, those gentle fabrics, those colors that excite, hair dryers, perfume bottles, things for nail polish, smells that arouse, the bed done better, the pillows smooth, slippers our feet don't fit into, a sigh, in the middle of the night, making me ticklish on the back of my neck, my wife less different from the woman before the war, the one with the rings disintegrating little by little in my memory, I've forgotten her features already, I've forgotten her forms, I'm losing the surprise

—A second lieutenant

in a voice dimmer and dimmer, the military police passing us, mistrustful, severe, the murmuring of I don't know who inside me

—When my grandfather finds out he'll kill himself

my wife on the sofa, at midafternoon, while me looking for

—Which rifle

and, in the room's darkness, again

—Love

and lace, to return from the war at last is this, at last the dead have stopped, it's only this, my son looking at everything without understanding, he took two steps and curled himself up in himself or in the second lieutenant of the paratroops touching the antipersonnel mine with the tip of his boot, the guide examining tracks

—We are still far away

my wife to me

—When you saw me on the dock you didn't seem to recognize me

her eyes wrapped up in each other it's usual for them before crying

—You stopped remembering me

my father opening the door to the house

—Now we're here

and what a disappointment my God, to think that I went twenty-seven months dreaming about this, so beautiful in Africa and then looking at this thing, modest compartments, furniture without charm, a sunroom in the back like all the other sunrooms also with faded clothing on springs and an invalid's tricycle where Mr. Araújo's son installs Mr. Araújo, all bent, on the chair of that thing, advancing in jolts, chased by a small dog, on the way to the alley, swinging in the rain puddles and jumping on the stones, Mr. Araújo's son following him for a moment and returning to the building kicking a tin when, in reality, he was kicking his own life and then, it was obvious already, the lace shirt and the

—Love

that initially is pleasing and then tires us, what do you mean

—Love

what do you think you're saying when you say

—Love

the apartment at the same time familiar and strange, not only our home, a second lieutenant in the bed to the left and one more second lieutenant in the other bed on the right, or before the bed to our right empty because the second lieutenant on the right in Luanda recovering from a mine, shrapnel in his belly, his thigh, a piece of his intestine cut away, my wife mumbling words that don't exist in the voice of a tired child, that is words that didn't exist before her, they exist now and I don't understand them, what do I know of your childhood, what do I know about you, two or three photographs, a doll, on the bottom of the trunk, with one eye, the other a little glass sphere lost I don't know where, how strange that hens and goats don't exist here, how strange the stars don't make noise in the mango trees out there, my wife's arm over mine but the scent changed, a new jar on the dresser next to a picture of me, in uniform, on the ship to Africa, another officer, almost from the back, farther away

—I see on your faces the joy of going to serve the

my father coughing in the sunroom and my mother in the corridor, barefoot because the tips of her toes remain on the ground, bringing a glass of water to calm her throat, I feel my wife's pubic hair against my side and I get hard, I still thought to hide myself but her hands took hold of me and I grew larger at the same time as my voice, without noticing that

—Sorry

she moved away offended

—Sorry?

and I went about for a good half hour with justifications and caresses until I convinced her but the

—Love

didn't come nor the usual collaboration, she rigid contemplating the ceiling, the bulb from the lamp came to the end and a policeman's brow with a sulk below

—Did you get addicted to black girls?

I who had never seen her cry, I noticed a tissue, but her back turned, when I went to Angola, upon returning a rainbow smile, more purple than the other colors

—Two years passed in an instant

and

—I see on your faces

a transparent strip, insecure, ready to drip from the chin and it didn't drip, I had never imagined that a uniform might hurt but it hurts, I never was with a black girl, I don't really know, only after dead do they not make me afraid and besides the smell of the skin, the smell of manioc, the smell of the earth, the operations major did that with his cigarette holder lit, surrounded by smoke, muttering

—Man oh man

softly, quicker and quicker, more and more confused until suddenly silent, fortunately he never shook my hand, his cigarette holder wouldn't allow it, the commander to him, pushing him away with his sleeve

—You stink of black

despite Lisbon, the normal trees, the houses, the streets, the absence of blacks except for my son, Africa remained with me in truck exhaust, in rustling leaves, in the impression that someone watching me where I couldn't see him, hidden in some corner or in the half-light of a store, perhaps lepers on the village mountain, something in the wind where presences, whisperings, my father to me

—You're hearing what?

when I straightened up, at the table, listening, trying to grab the G-3 that I don't have, I found myself looking for my camouflage clothing in the armoire, my wife in the middle of the night

—Who were you speaking to?

and me, slowly coming to recognize her, me silent, smiling at her while finding her leaning over me, me

—It must have been a dream

the doctor who managed my wife's moods calming her

—They come back from the war a bit unhinged madam it's a question of patience it'll pass

as if he had been there, as if he had seen, as if they had lain him down in the helicopter with an IV running in his vein and the doctor

—Thank God he'll forget everything

behind the pilot and the mechanic occupied with a lever

—Faster for fuck's sake

as if he had died, despite a kind of smile and with a weak voice

—See you soon

and a soldier drying his sleeve, soon the pig dead, no groan, no sigh, to go up a ladder in order to take it off the ring and stretch it out on a sack on the ground, its eyes open, blind, with a kind of thread of mud sliding from its snout, a corporal toward the helicopter, drying his sleeve

—See you soon

and the blades of the machine shaking the tall grass, me to my wife's doctor

—Everything passes with time the doctor is right

there is nothing that doesn't get lost, that's life, there remains one or another memory but more and more tenuous, for example I am stuck with the word

—Love

that I've not heard for a while, from time to time her body but in silence, rapidly, a half glass of water afterward, her back turned to me, an

—Until tomorrow

confused, syllables melting into each other, everything passes with time, it's true, I don't remember what you wore yesterday, I don't remember talking, I remember you going to find a bottle in the pantry because the wine was finished, everything ends except the stones in the kidneys, emaciation, slower movements, bringing you a cuddle for your back, the phrase suddenly, that you cultivated lost, in a pause from the pain

—Didn't you get addicted to black girls?

my parents, in the cemetery, listening to the autumn wind, still not cool but so sad, my mother saying to me

—Good evening

before dying and me, astonished by the phrase, answering her

—Good evening

without wanting, if she happened to pass near the tomb sometimes I repeat

—Good evening

and my mother silent, some time ago I asked my cousin if when cleaning the coffins a

—Good evening

reached her ears and she staring at me astonished

—Is this one drunk?

and as for my wife a lace shirt at the bottom of a dresser drawer, I don't know your body anymore, sometimes, when you undress, I see a thin leg and the bones of your ribs, the doctor, who gave up hoping

—Two three months more it's impossible to know

and after that I don't know if I have the courage to return to this house, what for, I only ask my son that he aim at my neck well, my son looking at me for almost the entire dinner with a woman without ears and hands in his mind, with a man, who still tried to run away, two or three steps in front, facedown, my son as if he had finally discovered who he was, I should have left you in Africa, among slaughtered animals, until the wild dogs grew interested in you, they don't kill all at once, they tear off pieces, Hoards to me, rigorous in his labels

— Do you want me to refer to the kid as boy lieutenant sir?

the Thin One, if she still lived

— During the time of the war I went out with a boy who stayed in Angola but I lost his picture and don't remember him anymore

I remember, what, he was tall like so, thin, with one nostril more open than the other, when he laughed he was missing a canine in the same way as his white jacket was missing a button, by chance on his belly that was more noticeable, my daughter suddenly

— Dad

and me without believing

— What?

I swear

— Dad

imagine, now that my wife no

— Love

and her

— Dad

this is the world upside down, when on Monday if she returns from the house in the village my wife's doctor will put her in the hospital and there'll remain only a very old

— Love

floating around here without anyone noticing, so faded, so faint, perhaps someone will rent the apartment, on our wedding night my wife

— Would you permit me to accompany you?

and me trying to match my step with hers, under the sheet waiting for me, extremely distressed my God, and me even more distressed having a disagreement with my shirt, a button sticking out here and I squeezed the other without wanting to, I was ashamed to take off my socks, to take my underwear off, to put on my new pajamas that my parents gave me in the same way that the starched uniform intimidated me on the embarkation dock for Angola

—I see on your faces

and on my face pure fear of her as on her face pure fear of me, soldiers marching to the music and the rain, seagulls, in Luanda enormous, in the interior, far from the water, bats with screams constantly hitting the walls of the air, my father to me after the food, in the darkness of the garden, hitting my knee with a jovial palm

—How I liked this when I was a child

the village much bigger than now, even the priest had a house with a trellis and a housekeeper who never smiled at me

—I wish I was your age little one

a shawl even in August, hanging socks on a line, she liked to take his head and squeeze it against herself, Dona Eurídice, my father always remembered the name

—Eurídice is a pretty name

she reeked of lye and incense from the church, stories were told between bouts of laughter but stories are always told about the maids of priests who gave us their hand to kiss, much smoother that ours and the same phrase always

—You are a man

my father who had no way to stop being boyish even more so when he walked on tiptoes and thickened his voice, how slow time in childhood, from a certain time on, boom, it starts to move very quickly and there is no one stopping it, from there to legs buckling for a moment and no one talks about buckling legs in the coffin, my grandfather for example all energy

—On the double march

he complained for three days and remained, for an

—Ah Jesus

he didn't even have time, the chapel illuminated with him inside, cramped with shawls that were conversing, men drinking from a small bottle outside and nowadays almost no one, the blind man remains always calling his goddaughter

—Arminda

because he's cold, because he's hot, because he lost his hat, because he wants to go home, because urgent pee-pee, because he feels like grapes even out of season, his mouth, chewing, an empty bag with a lizard its tongue darting around inside it, if dogs pass nearby an angry question

—Who's that there?

whipping the emptiness with a cane, we silent taking his jacket and he turning back, always in the wrong direction

—Sluts

there was a blind man in the village of huts, next to the camp, who didn't need to see, he figured out everything with his sense of smell, if by chance I was close even if silent

—Muata

squatting on a slope chewing roots, the pig in the sty was no longer eating now, it stared at us from inside there, mistrustful, severe, my daughter to us

—He knows

just like my son knows that it's evident from his face and the way he doesn't look for me, he turns away from me, he stopped answering me, avoids me, when he thinks me distracted I notice him looking at me, what do you know, what do you want to do to me, a woman without ears and hands, a man bent over in the grass, his silence accusing me

—You killed them you killed them

you not the old man of now, you young, the unimogs entering the village of huts, the diesel fuel, the shots, a child running, hens without necks jumping, the odor of corpses stronger than manioc, a machine gun shooting without pause in the direction of the lepers, my son who was not my son, never was my son, never will be my son

—You killed them

you brought me to Lisbon, convinced Her Excellency

—I'll pay I'll pay

to get married to me, he meets with her without my knowing, hands her money, she convinced herself that she likes me and doesn't like me, she won't forgive herself, and that's everything or then she feels forgiven already, or then she will feel forgiven when I agree to take the knife, they'll hang me by the feet, choose the bigger blade, open my neck, put a bucket below and listen to my screams, watch me die, the psychologist to me, in the circle of chairs

—Shut up

the psychologist in the house in the village witnessing my death, it's not my wife's stones, they are mine that had turned lighter than water, my wife in the lace shirt

—Love

with me motionless on her side of the bed, with one of her legs slipping onto the ground, with one of her arms slipping onto the ground, my wife so thin, already incapable of embracing me, my daughter finally interested in me

—How is it to die father explain to me

and after that the ears cut off, the hands cut off, and after that the G-3s that don't go silent, and after that the wind taking the remains with it, and after that the lightning bolts, still in the distance, on the side of the Cambo, and after that the wild dogs sniffing not with their snouts, with their ears, that gait of theirs on springs, that horrible stench, the pig in the sty was no longer eating now, he stared at us from inside, mistrustful, my daughter to us

—He knows

just as my son knows, of course, just as I know, and the stones really so light that I can't complain, they don't cause discomfort, they don't hurt me, the doctor to me

—With the medications that exist now your wife won't have any pain

or rather all tranquil, all in peace, the house calm, each of us next to the other, serene, listening to the trees beyond the cemetery, listening to the mountain, on one occasion, many years ago, I saw a wild boar gallop next to a stream moving the knitting needles of his legs, if I asked my wife today

—Would you permit me to accompany you?

she after an embarrassed silence, without looking at me

—Maybe

and the two of us walking side by side, formal, distant, I left the headquarters in the last unimog, shooting a final shot at a chicken that remained alive, perched on the remains of a branch, with one of its feet suspended in the air in the middle of a phrase or of a gesture, I'll not return to Africa, I'll not return here, my cousin who took care of the tomb consoling me

—Despite everything there were many years

while my grandfather and my father were waiting, crouching in the bushes, the first partridge, with the dog's body getting larger little by little, the tail slowly sweeping the earth, I knew her when already old, almost incapable of walking, my grandmother mashing her food before pouring it into her bowl, my grandfather with the damaged left arm, silent in the living room because the words stopped staring at me without recognizing me

—Who is that?

my father with pity for him

—Your grandson

and he intrigued, examining my boots, my shorts, the stains, while the partridges returned to the nest afraid of a genet nearby, crouching in a box-wood, at the same time that in Angola the guide

—Lutenan sir

pointed out tracks toward the north, in the direction of Luanguinga, that disappeared in the savannah, the deepest I bet with a recoilless cannon, the lightest Kalashnikovs, the last ones of one person only who turned back I suppose to watch us, one person and then two, then three, then a group, one of the sergeants to me softly

—If we do things quickly and hide our tracks with a branch we can get them from behind

this with a section and a bazooka, the rest remaining more than fifteen minutes left before returning too but by the opposite side, my wife to me

—Tomorrow I have the dentist I can't but after tomorrow at the same time

without looking at me, polishing a nail with the thumb from her other hand, perhaps she wasn't pretty but the hair lived alone, the legs a bit strong, even with the problem in the kidneys in contrast to the rest of her body they hadn't gotten very thin

—After tomorrow at the same time here

the eyes always escaped me, it wasn't good that they stayed on the other side, she was interested only in half of me in the same way that when she said for the first time

—Love

I had the impression that only one part of her in the voice, still today I have the impression that you didn't give me all you knew, a piece of your mouth was missing, a chunk of the body was missing, the insurgents had you look for us with us already waiting, they left a small campfire barely extinguished, some empty tins, two or three tubes from combat rations, paths with masks, only on the fifth or sixth trip from her work home did we start talking, meaning me a question here another there and such faint answers that I barely heard them, I ended up discovering a mother, a father, an older sister married in the north that came for Christmas with two small children, all this reserved, hesitant, at a certain moment, suddenly, her voice troubled

—What I'm telling you is tedious isn't it?

in a tone with much more life than hitherto and me astonished looking at her, for the first time when saying good-bye she let me squeeze her fingers and her thumb a type of caress toward the right and the left in my palm, for the first time her face in front of mine, with a small scar on the corner of her mouth that moved me, she touched me lightly on the arm and right after a first insurgent, a second one, both with Kalashnikovs but without camouflage, barefoot, in shorts, with a foreigner in glasses behind, some more distant, parallel to these, my daughter looking at the pig, suddenly serious

—Father

with an expression that I didn't recognize, perhaps friendship I don't know, perhaps something else that I prefer not to know or speak about, what for, what does that serve now, how many times did I feel like putting you in my lap, how many times did I feel like having a gift from you, silly things like that, how many times above all the wish that you call me

—Father

her expression changing suddenly

—You'll die tomorrow

and a big surprise in fact, look at the news, as if I didn't know that I would die tomorrow, which of us, the animal or me, it's the pig, which of us is here looking at the sty right next to you, we began to shoot at the insurgents from both sides of the jungle, on one the bazooka, on the other the machine gun and the G-3 in volleys, the Kalashnikovs almost didn't sing, the recoilless cannon silent, a mulatto tried the trigger two or three times before crashing twirling in the middle of a flight of birds, when my grandfather finds out he'll kill himself, the second lieutenant of the paratroops waving at us while the helicopter took off, a black still on his hands and knees, then on all fours, then stretched out on the ground, then a kind of stuffed animal without filling, then silence, then nothing, sandals at random on the grass, a key shining, the little medallion on a thread around my neck, what seemed to be a pistol, still pointed at us, that relented little by little, not stiff, with soft metal, the soft butt, the barrel soft, the shadow liquid, the radio calling the company base

—Take notes from these papers

and for what reason the blood not red, dark, my blood and the blood of the pig tomorrow not red, dark, when my son goes through me with the knife and at that moment the stones, now there it is, lighter than water, a lot lighter than water, floating around my wife and she cured, the doctor

—It may be it may be

floating around me and me dead, my son's mother to my son

—Let's get out of here

and as we are going from here if the village closes over us, we can't escape, we won't give our consent to escape, all stopped even above us, until the mountain kites imprisoned in the trees, poor useless animals, the loquat stopped, only shade, the greens in the yard quiet, my wife quiet, sitting in the sunroom, look at her jacket with the metal butterfly on her lapel, make it that the doctor encourage her

—But how chic

the doctor

—if they took twenty-year-old girls they'd come up to her heels when the lady is decked out

though so weak, so pale, and the mouth hanging from a hook in the nose, she'll die within one or two months because the weight of the stones has to return, what a remedy, pushing her down, her mouth

—Love

for no one because no one is listening, she listens to herself

—Love

without being able to imagine what it would be like to be with me because me in a bucket in the cellar, without arms and legs, without guts, without neck and even so, fanfare, it's possible that she directs herself to me

—Love

wearing a lace shirt with little bows

(I always forget the little bows)

saying

—Love

saying

—Love

saying

—Love

but to whom, gentlemen, if only nurses, doctors, visitors, other patients in other beds and she, I swear

—Love

while we returned home, outside the village, on little streets where no one dwells anymore, small construction sites where no one lives, old people with caps in the square who don't pay any attention to us anymore, one or another starving mongrel that turns away in fear, a half dozen pigeons dragging their tails against the stones, my father to me

—For the year when you turned ten I had to teach you how to hunt partridges

no longer with my grandfather's dog, of course, a younger animal, more attentive, faster, the two of us on a slope, still night, waiting for the morning, leaning on each other due to the cold, despite the caps, the shirts, the sheepskin coats, a blanket covering our knees, the two witnessing the change in the sky's color, no longer black, without moon, without stars, a first pale strip on the horizon, a second pink strip, an almost purple translucence in the air, the first sun still without sun, a tiny indefinable clearing that slowly rises, expands, grows, thickens, lets us finally perceive tree trunks, the canopies, the land, the plants, the wet leaves that get drier, drier, the first shudders in the bushes and my father

—Love

pardon, my father not

—Love

my father

—Get your weapon they'll come now

both looking at the little hill to the left, some stalks, a dwarf fig tree, hearing minuscule sounds growing little by little and the dog more frenetic, more excited, her ears frontward and her legs springs while my father

—Pay attention boy

holds the shotgun propping it up on a mound of earth, with his finger on both triggers explaining to me

—This is how it's done

bent over frontward to fix the line where a kind of thistle and where what seemed to be a bird's head, my father

—It's the female who commands the others

getting up suddenly, in silence, to look around, right, quiet, prudent, beak open, on the lookout and disappearing once again to return with two or three more partridges, my father to me

—Take the safety off the trigger now

and the weapon aimed at the animals, quiet, waiting, the dog straight on its legs, the snout extended, the ears frontward, ready to run when my father touches her back

—Doll

when the rifle, that sways a bit choosing the target, becomes suddenly motionless, when his shoulders and my father

—It's now

join quickly around the neck, when the back not bent over, erect, when the barrel of the weapon transforms itself into blast and feathers, and plants, and the head of a bird falling

and my father to me

—Do you get it?

my father to me

—Do you really get it?

and the dog sprinting toward the partridge, shaking it in its teeth, bringing it, and putting it next to us, accepting the piece of sugar that my father gave her to eat while he puts his arm around my shoulders and whispers in my ear

—Son

in a tone that even tomorrow, when they dig the first knife into me, I'll not ever forget.

18

Almost at the end of the afternoon when a flock of wild geese crossed
the mountain with necks sticking out in the direction of the marsh with a
female that was leading them describing a wide curve exploiting the wind,
honking in front, no matter how high above the trees, and the smaller geese
farther behind, messy, distressed, that a fox found sometimes, fallen on the
grass, squeaking with fear, incapable of running away with a broken leg, trying to defend themselves without managing to defend themselves, I left my
father and my sister side by side in front of the pigsty, their elbows touching they who never touched each other, looking at the pig, me thinking
astonished perhaps they like being together, imagine, perhaps we like to be
together in this family and the geese alighting in the distance, with their feet
sticking out, toward the reeds, looking for small snakes and frogs, I turned to
the house where my mother with her head leaning back on the chair without
noticing me she was contemplating the wall in front with eyes more lonely
than I've encountered at any time in my life, distracted from everything except the stones that were dancing around her, wanting to say to her those
aren't stones, it's kidney cancer that has invaded your whole body, the bones,
the liver, the lungs, it's your death understand, no knife is needed they don't
shoot a military weapon making her turn in the hut tripping over herself, so
many of their bodies tripping before falling, the kidney is enough, her legs
kidney, her arms kidney, her belly kidney, her head kidney, I smoothed her
forehead with my mouth and the kiss kidney too, a taste of sickness that terrified me, me who would give I don't know what to hear her at night, waking
without waking while she fixed my sheet, to know her there in a sleep shirt
that smelled of my father without leaving from the dream, with the loquat
tree, inside and outside the room, protecting me from the unforeseen things
of the morning, it wasn't my voice because I didn't have a voice, it was my
fingers that articulated

—Aiué mamá

for her and for a woman without hands, on her knees on a mat screaming silent while I tried to stop her from escaping me until my father put me in his lap and left with me, that I recall, handing me to the driver of a truck, forbidding him to bring the pistol near

—Take care of him

as the woman without hands was talking to me about things that I didn't understand, not angry, pleading, so that my father decided to remain with the child I was, with an enormous belly button, so thin, looking at me without expecting anything, without desiring anything, without thinking about anything, the captain to him

—For what do you want that?

and my father to the captain

—Perhaps in many years he'll take vengeance and kill me

with a kind of smile that was not a smile like my mother's smile, in the house in the village, it was also not a smile, it was a harder stone heavy in my palm, what will I do with it, what will I do with you, I don't want to take up the knife tomorrow, I don't want to kill him, I don't want to feel my sister waiting, I don't want to feel my father accepting, the doctor to me

—Your mother

and a gesture that disappeared halfway through, I don't want Her Excellency leaning on the wall with palm over her mouth staring at me, I don't want people leaning on the wall palm over mouth staring at me, I don't want someone declaring on the telephone

—He passed away

I want my grandfather, whom I didn't know, to show me the rifle for partridges, my mother without looking at me

—I'm tired

and me next to her, like my father

—Would you permit me to accompany you?

the two of us walking side by side without looking at each other, without speaking, meaning the words didn't come, the precaution of not staying too close to each other, formal, with respect, if a person from the opposite direction we'd separate so that he might pass between us, we are two creatures that don't know each other and by chance are walking at the same pace, the station head sent African troops to join the blacks and the cotton plantation owner chose them

—These are exuding health?

barefoot, thin, short, silent, my mother

—I'm cold

because the stones are floating cooling off in the air, I brought her a blanket from the bed, I brought her a blanket that I took out of the trunk, her eyes on me without seeing me

—You're there aren't you?

not a black child, a black already adult, with gray hair and I was there ma'am, I was there, hardly anyone noticed me but I assure you that I was there, the woman without hands

—Muana

was there too, my sister put, I swear, her elbow on my father's shoulder and my father

—Girl

which was all that the emotion permitted, I remember her in the crib sleeping, I remember her on the lap of my grandfather, who didn't like me and referred to me as darky

—He stinks of black filth this one

trying to grab the little medallion from the thread on her neck so worn that the image was barely distinguishable, while she pointed me out to her parents

—I will not put up with this stench

my father messed up my sister's hair and my sister, who normally didn't care about her hair, offended putting it back in order, the pig tried to put its front legs on the back of a female, aborted, gave up, Her Excellency with a sideways glance to me

—As I understand you a real monster

and lay down on a burlap sack farther away studying us, from time to time she sneezed as if she prepared it, the plantation owner's blacks got sick one after the other up there, a speech, she opened her mouth for the first snore and went silent, my sister to my father

—I don't know if I'll return to Lisbon on the night bus

suddenly distressed, tense, shrinking inside herself, my mother, with eyes closed in a

—If I stay like this I'll go with you to the pig killing tomorrow

voice resembling her old voice, when we returned from Africa she forced me to eat all the time

—The boy is still thin

my father to my sister while a dog was barking in some small street

—You'd insult me like that?

with something in his voice that I couldn't decipher, not sadness, not disappointment, a different state of the soul, what do I feel for him, what do I feel for her, what do I feel for both of you my God, at times, at night, when we are lying in bed, already with the light off, I feel like it, it's not really feeling like it, I picture it, that is I hear the unimogs approaching, I hear the people in the huts, a cabíri sitting on its hind legs and beginning to howl, not exactly howling, strange barks, a silhouette preparing a homemade rifle, steps that halt, walk, halt again, what does the earth feel when they tread on it, what will I feel tomorrow

—The tugas

shadows, bright spots, motors, my mother to my father, scratching the back of my neck, satisfied

—He's already gained two kilos and lost the belly

she young, thin, with her apron stained by housework, my father taking off one shoe to scratch his shin

—Yesterday I dreamed that one of our soldiers

and growing silent afterward massaging his toes, he always complained that the canvas boots ruined his life, the unimogs breaking the line and moving away from each other, the effort of the piston rods was perceptible, a voice from time to time, the odor of burning diesel fuel, a gun breech popping, a wheel struggling with a stone, more homemade rifles, no wick in the huts, a cabíri was barking in silence, what will my sister do after the death of the pig, I never saw her with anybody, I never knew her to have a man, a neighbor of my father's, widower, left her notes in the mailbox that she put back in his, ripped up, she didn't answer greetings, she crossed by him without seeing him, my mother silent but it was clear with pity, which was noticeable in the curve of her mouth, my father I think he never knew, I remember the wife of the widower, with a defect in her leg, coming down the stairs of the building sideways with a cane on one side and the hand supported by the wall on the other, without asking for help, without complaining, my mother to nobody, or rather to my sister

—Her husband always supported her there aren't many like that

the widower's wife struggling with the steps helped by her open mouth and the wrinkles on her forehead, if we have a problem in any part of the body the rest of us sympathetic, at night, when the darkness refined the sounds, the sick leg much louder than the other, Dona Belinha, crossing the corridor trying to balance her two halves more or less, her husband's voice, in the room

—Are you managing?

and the reply a twisted difficulty without any word at all, or it was from birth or it was an accident due to multiple causes, the pig, treacherous streets, an ignored automobile, badly surfaced sidewalks, things that slip, the pig, without more food in the sty, sniffing for my father talking to him with its minuscule eyes, what did the troops come to do here in the village, one or another man left from time to time to watch the jungle after the wicks extinguished, trip wires on the paths, if the soldiers step on them a grenade will explode at knee level, the village hidden in the tall grass, in the trees, at an edge of the savannah that the troops forgot, my sister to my father, leaning over the pigsty

—Are you sure that this is the pig they are going to kill tomorrow?

wanting to tell him without wanting to tell him, just thinking and not explaining anything, I remember a blackbird over there in a flowerbed, a cousin of my father hoeing farther in the distance, the highway to the town with a saint in a niche near an intersection, the operations major watching a young girl and the captain indignant

—The girl is seven or eight years old major sir she won't heal

while the major's cigarette holder smoked, smoked, my mother to me when I went home to give her the medicine

—There's something that's not right isn't there?

motionless, without opening her eyes but it was obvious that troubled, no matter how light the stones are a vibration in us tormenting us, we heard the female calling the other geese in the marsh, we heard the wings close to the water and the grass, a dog in a distant farmhouse, one of the last birds, bogged down, trying to get out of the mud, the silken cat on the roof of the house in the village, me to my mother

—Don't worry ma'am

it's just the troops who come to kill us, it's just the war, it's just the whites, it's just my father protecting himself from the knives

—Kill kill

the psychologist at the hospital in his circle of chairs

—All of that has been over for a long time gentlemen

and it had been over for a long time for what reason does it continue, what are we doing there still, what is Africa now, debris of trucks, debris of unimogs, crippled in the villages of huts, villages of lepers whose bell no one rings, I rang an imaginary bell so that my mother a spoonful of soup, two spoonfuls of soup and my hand pushing the plate

—Don't insist son

one day she asked me to bring her the lace shirt that I ended up finding at the bottom of the drawer and she remained looking at it for some time without daring to touch it, the shirt and a small ring in a cardboard box with pansies painted on, a small stone in a silver ring because gold expensive or perhaps not silver, one lifted up the box and the past rattled inside it, an older cousin always with her and my father, sitting in front of them with a ferocious eye, if by chance a too-open smile then the cousin right away

—Respect

my sister to my father

—Look carefully at the pig sir

my father without understanding

—What?

checking the cartridges of the G-3, my mother to me

—There are times when I would like to wear it like one should

and she was not my mother, ma'am, you have hands, you have ears, a real bed, not a mat

—Help me to lie down

so light now that the stones had disappeared and nevertheless when putting her in my arms to take her to her room I got the idea that her arms without hands, her head without ears, her face with sand on its features, the empty breast exposed and thus she in fact my mother, her back on the earth with me next to her, without understanding, while everything around us was burning as my father will burn tomorrow after the knives and me finally able to call out to her

—Aiué mamá

as I call out to her here, in the house in the village, she limp with sleep in the bed

—Aiué mamá

not looking at me, looking at the room's ceiling straw that was burning, my mother to my father, looking for the key in her purse

—I live here

without looking at him just as he was not looking at her, ashamed, timid, with the unimogs waiting and the machine gunner in search of live blacks around us, my mother to my father

—Perhaps you'll bump into me one of these days

feeling like looking at him and without the courage to look at him, the psychologist to my father in the circle of chairs at the hospital

—What story are you telling me here?

and no story doctor sir, it's true, in the same way that in my case my father this one and also a man facedown on the ground, don't force me to have only one father and mother, I have four and the four will die with the pig tomorrow except my white mother speaking with a sigh to I don't know which of them

—Love

my sister leaving the pigsty

—Are we going to spend our whole life looking at this animal?

that was no longer looking at us, he was dozing in a corner, so deformed, so fat, perhaps saying

—Daughter

perhaps saying

—Love

or it was my mother who said

—Love

while the troops moved off toward the camp in the same way as the wild geese returned to the village, with the female that was leading landing on the ground, a column, a South African jeep, the G-3s watching the trees, my mother finding me in my room

—Euá

the witch doctor, his arms in a cross, bleeding from one of his eyes, my father and my mother now on the garden step surrounded by the Angolan night, unknown stars too high up, why is it that blacks are so poor, why is it that they kill everyone, my father pulling me toward the unimog

—Let's go

and me leaving my mother, without hands, in our room and sitting on the step with my sister and my father, the smell of diesel fuel from the burned skin of the pig, the fingers that were looking for a vein under the ear, my father itching his neck

—Tomorrow

my sister to him

—Since you don't have your rifle anymore which knife do you want them to kill him with?

the psychologist of the circle of chairs at the hospital to us

—Shut up

dressed as a major, small, brown-haired, balding, with a cigarette holder in his teeth while the wild geese were coming together on a rock on the mountain with the female repeating to them

—Love

and the stones around her wandering at random, when small my father, not the one who remained in Angola, the one who returned with me, pointed out the birds to me

—One day we'll fly

my mother coughed in her room and my father preparing soup for her

—You're eating five or six spoonfuls I'm not demanding more from you than that

holding out a trembling wrist, what are you afraid of, what are you afraid will happen, all so simple, so clear, Africa is over, Portugal is over, we'll remain a few hours, after tomorrow morning no woman here, Her Excellency and my sister returning to Lisbon, the house in the village, within a year, no more roof at all, one or two old people, one or two dogs, no people in the alleys and that's it, my father's cousin looking after the tomb with little pots of marigolds on the two windows or perhaps she's coming to Lisbon as well and no tomb, a few scraps of limestone, some crosses, rusted cypresses, the highway farther out where nobody passes, a wagon perhaps, a bicycle suffering on the climb, a girl with wood on her head, a donkey tied with a spike and that's it, all empty, it's done, the pig no longer dripping into the buckets without anyone holding its guts, its body swinging from the hook and then the world stood still, it's over, the psychologist of the circle of chairs at the hospital

—It's over

the aluminum tureens for the patients' lunch

—It's over

the box of cutlery

—It's over

returning from Africa like that, it's over

—I see on your faces the joy of going to serve the Fatherland

and it's over, what Fatherland, there was no war, there were no blacks who rebelled, there was no independence, there was nothing that no one recalls, my grandmother holding out a little piece of paper to my father

—It looks like it's for you

my father with the little piece of paper in his hand and what difference does the little piece of paper make if it's all over, military marches, rain, the seagulls next to each other on the roof of the dock, they are the same as then only then is over, my father to the black child who smelled like blacks and behaved like them who are not like us, they eat roots, insects, larvae, they chew leaves

—Come here

and the child together with him without touching him, silent, they don't touch anybody, they say

—Euá

or what seems like

—Euá

and that's it, there were occasions, before the sickness, when if my mother said

—Euá

it astonished me because she didn't connect the word *mother* with the word *euá*, didn't connect the word *mother* with a glass of milk brought at night to my bed or with a presence near me when I woke up in the middle of the night surrounded by screams, threats, shots, or the trot of wild dogs next to the huts and the panic that me alone incapable of protecting myself from them, without anyone who could protect me putting them to flight, from a certain time on, connecting her with a screen in a hospital office and a man in a white coat almost speaking, not speaking, replacing speech with

—We'll see we'll see

while he pressed and let go of the button on the ballpoint pen observing its beak so as not to look at us, my father, my sister, and me waiting, an uncomfortable pause instead of an explanation and the

—We'll see we'll see

more softly, slow, with the words not walking, stopped

—We'll see

alert to the sounds behind the screen, the doctor with his chin in his tie, without looking at us, mentioning stones that sometimes got bigger sometimes vanished, not mentioning the illness except for a vague phrase

—This is of the kidneys

or

—In her present state it doesn't seem to me that surgery

and, following that, a desert silence, with more eyelids than eyes, with more eyebrows than expression, diluted into fingers on my mother's shoulder

—The thing is going to

then my father believed in the panic of no longer believing, of not being able to repeat, so many years passed

—Would you permit me to accompany you?

of not returning to hear

—Love

from a lace shirt

(with bows)

no longer young poor thing yellowish, wasted, I hope I won't fail with the knife tomorrow and I swear that I don't feel hate at the moment, sir, even though you don't understand, and I understand and don't understand but I like you, you're not guilty that they had handed you a little piece of paper when returning from work

—This arrived in the mail for you

and what to do with this but obey, agree that they shave off your hair, put a uniform on, take out three teeth

—We don't want you to have problems after and at least these are solved

forcing you to waste months of humiliations and orders in uncomfortable, freezing cold barracks because civilian rain does not make a soldier wet, because the Portuguese soldier is as good as the best, because the second platoon is that platoon, because to give one's life for the Fatherland is to live not to die, because that little arm a bit higher while marching our cadet, that arm of a girl but higher up it's a man's arm, because Portugal is one and indivisible from the Minho to Timor, because protecting Christian civilization from atheist communism is a sacred battle, because don't waste all the mud while crawling on account of the fool who is coming after you, because the fanfare of the embarkation day requires elegance and morality, the straitlaced vehicles their thugs, the same that began to leave the village of huts after destroying all that shit, because I see on your faces, because proudly alone, because we won the crusades against the infidel, because

Blessed Ferdinand, because the Constable,* because our balls mademoi-
selles, especially our balls, not one ball out of place fools, because the return
to the camp with a strange taste in the mouth, because go outside over there
chaplain the conversation is not for ladies, because the dead only die if the
living don't deserve them, because a soldier to me

—Second lieutenant sir

before a G-3 shot in the mouth and the head a watermelon split, the pig
and my father staring at each other almost with pity as they will stare at each
other with pity tomorrow, because the animal's screams, because the blood
in the buckets, because my daughter softly

—Father

my daughter so softly

—Father

that I'm not certain if I had heard her, because if someone has to kill him
I prefer that it be me, despite my father facedown on the ground I prefer
that it be me, the female who commanded the remaining geese on some
point of the mountain honking, my mother arranging her blouse better
while the doctor put the matter ahead of other matters

—Here we're in a fight

or rather another form of

—We'll see we'll see

this while my mother still with strength, already extremely thin, already
with pain but capable of working at home though a little bit slower, though
stopping leaning against the dresser, her jaw twisted and eyes on us without
seeing us, they saw what seemed to her emptiness, without objects, without people, without any emotions, that contracted and widened and in the
nothingness some feeling, some desire, some fear, something that didn't
belong to her didn't concern her but in which she would soon enter, alone,
without anyone leaning over her

(but she didn't feel alone, she felt indifferent)

relaxing her

*Ferdinand of Portugal (1402–1443), eighth son of João I (1357–1433), referred
to as the Holy Child (*o infante santo*); the Constable is Nuno Álvares Pereira (1360–
1431), an important general and key figure in preserving Portuguese independence
during the crisis of 1383–1385.

(but she was relaxed)

smiling at her

(but she didn't think it sad)

my sister afraid, almost calling

—Mother

and silent, her mouth open but silent, leaning on the wall that gave way, gave way, and the doctor, frightened

—Judging by this way of walking it'll be over soon

the walls, the ceiling, the furniture, the instruments, us, the metal butterfly remains that's not worth a dime, we're not rich, fluttering around here blindly, the black remains not as he is now, of course, small, almost skeletal, leaning against a little adobe wall, hanging onto a goat that continues to bleat, frightened by the smoke from the jeeps that were tumbling about on the uneven terrain and the ashes of the huts where one or another flame still, the feet too large for his size and bones much larger than him, my father remains who two or three guys are tying up, his wrists, his ankles, his le

—I see on your faces the jo

gs, that hang upside down from the hook in the cellar above the two buckets, a small dog barking outside, hens, the knives from the table with the metal top, my grandfather explaining to my father the way to sharpen them on a stone wheel that got faster and slowed down he pressing on a pedal, earlier the aunts would come to watch, anxious, happy, with pity for the pig's suffering, getting closer saying

—I don't want to watch

getting closer

—I can't watch

with their palms covering their ears, with tears of pity and getting closer, my father two or three guys in hats tying up his arms, his wrists, his ankles, the le

—I see on your faces the jo

gs, that hang upside down from the hook in the cellar, over the two buckets, a small dog barking outside, hens, aunts armed with benches, chairs, an oilcloth in case blood drips on them, pointing me out to each other

—Did you notice that the animal has tears?

that the animal has transparent eyelashes, the joy of going to serve the Fatherland, the soldiers crying on the ship, shouts of good-bye on the dock, handkerchiefs, a military march louder still, the general coming down from the stand in conversation with two or three respectful officers, the seagulls in frenetic circles almost crashing in the water, a warship on the other bank, the sergeants pushing soldiers into the interior of the boat, no more noise, just rain, a first knife, a second knife, the edges tested on a piece of wood, a third knife wider, but short, ideal for cutting off ears, for cutting off hands, at the second blow it's done, the police drove out people along the dock

—It's over it's over

me with an oilcloth apron my sister covering her face

—My God

not with force, with care as if stones in her as well, the soldiers already far away, the trees only and below, from time to time, the river, the antelope that drank at night, one or another leopard that was not chasing them, my father with my sister piggybacking here and there in the corridor, first at a trot, then a gallop, then at a trot again, then stopping

—You're killing me

he who before ran with her all the time, my mother worried

—Watch that you don't get tired

while I tried out the movements of the knife with my wrist and he tried to follow me twisting himself in the ropes asking

—Are you the one who is going to kill me?

the man facedown on the ground who pretended not to know me and I didn't know him, when he lay down on my mother's mat the hut swung and despite the silence the goats were trotting toward the yard, frightened, I never had brothers, I had this white sister

—My God

Lisbon was no longer visible from the steamship, only the gray sea was visible, a sergeant wiping away tears, the Portuguese soldier is as good as the best, the Portuguese soldier is as good as the best, the Portuguese soldier is as good as the best, we see between two life jackets, for a moment, dolphins, then not one dolphin, just the noise of the blades, nothing but my father putting my sister on the ground

—I can't anymore

loosening the knot on his tie on the sofa, my mother tidying up the sewing basket on her side

—Do you feel like eating something?

And he didn't feel like eating anything

—I'm not capable of swallowing just anything

the captain waiting for us in the camp

—No casualties?

while the Katanga were conversing in Swahili next to the storeroom and the man from the political police entered with two uniformed militia men and disappeared with a black his hands bound behind his back who one of the militia was stabbing, Portugal one and indivisible, with a pocketknife, Portugal one and indivisible from the Minho to Timor, I switched the wide knife for a longer one thinking where is my father's carotid, next to this wrinkle, next to that tendon, I don't know if the pulsing I felt was mine or his, my father to me, putting me on his legs, in the jeep

—Boy

when we went hunting at night with the light on the hood, sometimes gray forms galloping in the distance, sometimes noth, the first platoon is not better or worse, and that platoon, usually nothing, my father to the driver

—Go farther into the jungle stupid

and if an antipersonnel, and if insurgents, and if one of their spies giving signals imitating the birds in the darkness, I passed slowly, the long way, the edge of the knife on my index finger and it seemed to me well sharpened on both sides, I asked for another lamp in order to evaluate the skin better and not the skin, of course, of a boy twenty-three years old as when I met him, who had given that age to me, the skin of a man sixty years old and I'm being generous, the skin of a man seventy years old, no longer elastic, no longer supple, with the stains and irregularities of time, a skin that will never be mine seeing that they'll kill me too, I don't know which of the other knives but they'll kill me too, perhaps the thinnest, perhaps some other one, what difference does it make to me, I only hope that they cut off my ears and hands fast, and my last night here, and my father's last night here, I noticed an owl flying and the wind in the loquat tree, the already old leaves a kind of paper noise, the light on in the living room of the house in the village and a slow shadow, or what looked like a slow shadow moving inside between the kitchen and the living room, a brief sound of dishes on dishes, a tap, what seemed to me to be shoes dragging like slippers, a drawer opened and closed, I noticed someone entering the house in the way my sister used to enter, disorganized, rapid, pushing the door not completely opening the lock and thus an ugly scraping of metal, I seemed to hear your voice without distinguishing the words, perhaps a question

—Father?

or I suppose a question

—Father?

and following that I was betting that your steps in the living room, a cough, a pause, another cough, a chair's protest, the sound of glass on glass from a pitcher pouring water into the glasses, what was doubtless my mother taking time to sit down despite not understanding her taking so much time if the stones had become lighter than water so that I put the knife for tomorrow on the knife table, I hung the rubber apron on the nail and upon entering for my turn I was with the three at the table and my mother scolding me while she distributed the soup into the bowls beginning with Her Excellency

—Because of your lateness boy I thought you weren't coming.

19

Like everybody I have a mother and father, or rather a mother dying of
kidney cancer, the doctor placed X-rays against a plate of matte glass with
lamps behind that also lit up his fingers, the cuff of his shirt with a gold button, and a pen in his hand, drawing ovals around the stains
 —Medicine is not a totally exact science there are surprises
and a father sitting at the table in front of her looking at her, surrounded
by ghosts that haunted him without pause, military vehicles swaying on the
path rattling the troops, soldiers that were shooting, trees that the defoliant dried, the commander showing journalists having come from Luanda a
blanket in a storeroom
 —How can you honestly verify there is no trace of napalm here
and under the blanket part of several pumps visible and above all that
smell, that smell, destroyed villages, burned trees, towers of corpses missing pieces, several of them burning still, besides my mother and my father I
have a black brother that my father brought back from there as a child, after
the T-6s had gone through leaving the villages of huts in terminal flames,
the doctor to us, content with the buttons of his cuff while my mother was
doing her treatment in the other room
 —Human resistance is a mystery
my brother who remembers hardly anything of Angola with his head, remembers, without knowing it, with the rest of his body, above all the parts
that were missing on the rest of the others' bodies, eyes that were not seeing
for themselves, he saw people through them, they appear blind but they're
not, they appear dead and they keep going, even now, under the earth,
speaking, there are those who smoke mutopa with bubbling water in the inside of a gourd, there are those who eat crickets that are fried on a, the doctor
to us straightening the button on his cuff
 —Perhaps we'll succeed in helping her live for a little bit more I don't
know
there are those who eat crickets that they fry on a spit, those that nibble

manioc that has not yet dried on the mats while the doctor was speaking of patience and courage, he was going away without saying good-bye, only a button on his cuff declared to us

—That's life

an ambush is life, a mine is life, some glasses for the blind, gentlemen, are life, only one more fragment of the nose, one more fragment of the jaw that's missing, one of these days the street down there, five floors don't give time to think, one feels it, at best, a rapid coolness, and then one ceases to be anything at all and it's over, one of the T-6 pilots, sitting on the landing strip, scratching the earth with his finger dejected like a child

—I can't stand this anymore I can't stand it anymore

waving away shadows with his palms and embers that were still flashing, what must have been a woman with her hair on fire, a face all teeth, no features, just teeth, not thirty-two, one hundred, two hundred, and not black, red, that were dripping, dripping, each tooth a flame and the tongue falling on it, a sort of purple worm that was turning into ash, how can they verify there is, the communists' lies never end, gentlemen, there is not a trace of napalm here, a clean war, humane, defensive, and here we have the lies of Soviet propaganda, the Portuguese soldier is as good as the best, who civilized the world if not us, and with many Hail Marys and much armament we went to them and in less than one Apostle's Creed we killed them all, my father has a small house in a poor village, of course, close to Lisbon, that his grandfather's uncle had built between the cemetery and the base of the hill over the highway embroidered with plane trees that leads to the city, how many times did I chase butterflies over there, my father never spoke about butterflies in Africa, bats yes, enormous, not an important highway, the secondary highway that led to the important highway always with so many trucks, factories from time to time, not one deserted hut, no blacks and where the family gets together on one weekend every year, since many years before us, for the pig killing, as so many people in this area used to do, gathered together in the cellar, in silence, listening to the animal's screams that are becoming more and more human, weaker, they end by transforming themselves into silence with our silence all around, not merely the silence of my mother, of my father, of my black brother, of me, the silence of the old relatives who still live here, breathing through their open mouths because living takes effort, in this place without anyone now except lost animals, ever fewer, that keep on still, drifting in the small streets, stray dogs, some goats, a crippled donkey, without owner, that the gypsies let loose for not being useful for anything, my father and my brother cut the pig apart and divide the meat up, with my brother, as he was growing, observing my father more and more closely in the same way as always, obedient, peaceful, but with something, perhaps arms without hands, perhaps heads without ears, perhaps my father, on his knees, cutting, cutting, my brother who scared me for the first time, my mother, since she became ill, almost always motionless on a chair, surrounded by stones that the doctor affirmed she had inside her body with the idea of saving her the suffering of knowing that kidney cancer, crumpling the sheet dejected like a child

—I can't stand this anymore I can't stand this anymore

and who can stand this, fever, pain, fatigue, the doctor explaining to her, drawing on a piece of paper, that the kidneys produce stones continuously spreading out inside and medicines exist that with time dissolve them liberating us from the pain and eliminating swelling in the bones since the bones, and there is no one who doesn't know this, stones too because we're made, it's clear, you just need to think a little bit, of stones and some meat, bump against your skin in bed, for example, and you realize that stone underneath, or for that matter against your knees, that are rounded stones and perhaps my mother believes that, I don't know, she always spoke so little, she always hid behind herself and the tin butterfly, even when saying

—Love

even when accepting that they accompany her almost silent, my mother who insists on cooking and busying herself with us walking supported by chair after chair, with one of her feet slower than the other because the ankle or the hip stones refusing to move ahead, my father pretends not to see occupied with Angola and attacks and rifles, stamping on the floor attentively in case of mines and stopping suddenly because a helicopter on the way, in his mind, toward us, calculating by the angle of the trees and, consequently, of the furniture, with the leaves of the dresser and of the armoire vibrating, at certain times with a meticulous cannon aiming at the tall grass of the floor, at others to take the wounded that never cried, they were waiting lying down on a tarp, asleep, pale, with many more furrows than before on their cheeks and eyelids, already so far from us, without being interested in anything while a soldier, squatting, was speaking on the radio, the second lieutenant who was in command was smoking in the unimog cursing himself, the general who was speaking on the dock proud, with riding crop and gloves

—I see on your faces the joy of going to serve the Fatherland

and in the second lieutenant's memory seagulls, the slight January rain, the Tagus almost black, the general who adjusted the microphone better

—Young men

thus I have a father and mother but I don't live with them, for as long as I can remember myself living with them I didn't live with them, I always thought myself alone, perhaps I live more with my black brother who didn't live with anybody, leaning on the veranda hoping for huts, hens, mats, alert to a distant machine gun that didn't stop singing, even after married he continued to live without anyone except goats and cabíris, he saw through his wife a witch doctor dancing, he noted the chief pointing his cane at him

—You abandoned us

dressing himself like the whites, eating like the whites, behaving like the whites, neither of us speaks much, we answer but I have the sense that we answer like photographs answer, they're there and that's it, that of my grandfather for example, with a cap and an extinguished cigarette in his mouth explaining

—I am not bringing the shotgun because I haven't seen partridges

following the pigeons and doves with contempt, sitting on a crate with the dog at his feet, where did they go to, the wicked things, no female at daybreak, not even a peep, a man with three eyebrows that curled all at the same time, two in their own places and the third, like them, between the lip and the nose, making a moustache and me incapable of pointing out which of them more severe seeing that all are curling, attentive as if something important were happening on this side of the glass where what happens is just to be far too late for whatever it may be, the pig tomorrow, the cousin of the tomb with more work and that's it, my mother's doctor

—A week perhaps

the portrait of an aunt taken months before drowning in a well now empty, with earth and grass at the bottom that shone among shadows, barefoot, after leaving the slippers on the side of the pump, aligned, placed like they should be on the edge of the bed because winter, because cold, the cousin whose features, despite the smile by chance like mine, meaning the face more serious than anything else, crossing people with rapid indiffer-

ence, appeared to drip I don't know what between old sorrows and secret
anguish, my father studying the carpet in the living room

—Careful with the traps aunt Sabina

because one foot has had it and the slipper of the other one the odd one
out while my mother excuses him with a gesture

—The misery of war

the house in the village with an empty chicken coop, with a broken perch
against the wall where only spiders can lay eggs, when small I played in the
square with the goddaughter of the owner of the store, throwing clods of
earth at the birds from the trees and looking for nests while the pigeons from
Cardal Florido were flying without rest and at a certain time, I don't know
why, I stopped talking with her in the same way that I stopped answering
anybody, my mother shorter than me and at that time extremely tall

—Is she angry?

and I wasn't angry, it wasn't that, I was in a corner and that's it, my palm
on my cheek, empty, even at school, even in the playground, even with the
other girls, what will happen after Sunday at the house in the village without anyone, perhaps a lonely shadow, from time to time, looking at it with
nostalgia I don't know for what, perhaps for my mother

—Daughter

with a glass of milk in her hand while I woke up and things became
themselves, the window became a window, the door transformed itself into
a door, the features occupied their places one by one, adjusting to the spots
where I had left them the night before, my mouth correcting itself a bit
between the cheeks, the birthmark that was missing on my jaw finally appeared there, my mother to my father, in camouflage that no longer served
him, he was thin at twenty, hidden under his clothing, what a contradiction
time making our bodies bigger while our arms and legs narrow, the back not
straight, soft, and the neck shorter, the features descending toward the collar, she'll be old there's no delay, wrapping her words in saliva, my mother's
voice distant, confused, my father's, younger than me, next to the driver of
the Mercedes

—Aim at all the holes on the road

a while ago I accompanied him to a lunch with the battalion, baldness,
white hairs, embraces, large bellies without exposed intestines or shrapnel
from the mortars, a lot of time against his which had also grown, eyes with

tears I don't know if from the war if from time, when the eyelids no longer have strength

—I can't stand this anymore I can't stand this anymore

and at times a shudder in the temple or the nose that the mouth chews before swallowing, it seemed to me that from time to time a crocodile in the restaurant, an antelope, a man facedown who I don't want to talk about, a cluster bomb exploding outside, rushing, bleating goats, the immense peace of certain nights, my mother insisting

—Now the milk?

while the pig was arriving, badly balanced on its hooves, in a wagon falling apart and my brother looking at the knives avoiding looking at my father, it's already late for the soldiers to die young, they'll end as old men now, the death of old people so simple, a little sob and the eyes open, or rather the same expression of alienation, they weren't looking for the glass of milk if my mother

—Children

sucking from time to time on her own tongue thinking about what, I remember a cousin

—Dulce

without our knowing any Dulce, there was none in the village, perhaps someone he had discovered in the army in Viseu and who he never had spoken to, he was passing with a colleague and coming across a girl we didn't know who she was some

—Dulce

and she turning back, it's clear that she had already lost her looks, meaning she was a yellow handkerchief, my cousin

—Dulce

to the handkerchief, surprised at recalling the name, the stubbornness of lost memories that return, the stubbornness of things that we forget and abide in secret watching us from a distance, my cousin still asked

—Dulce

and no response, no helicopter will take them above the trees, no nurse will accompany them with an IV bottle, my cousin on the way to the hospital with his guts darned with bullets, he ended up paralyzed in a chair, a shawl on his knees, and my mother insisting on the milk

—And what for today?

with him looking at her with contempt, angry, the fingernail of his little finger bigger for the sake of the hygiene of his earhole and concerning the fingernail how do blacks cut theirs if they don't have scissors, the pilot of the T-6, when putting two napalm bombs on the plane, staring at them furtively

—And if that shit explodes with me in the air?

and if that shit explodes with you in the air you'll become a trail of black smoke, in successive explosions, that will end in a pinwheel next to the river, making the mud and the tall grass burn, my mother while my father was trying to slip onto the bed, convinced that the mattress would protect him

—Relax you're not dying it was a tire that got pierced on the street

and my brother in one corner of the hut while the man facedown on the ground stopped moving, it wasn't my father, it was some sergeant on my father's order, who struck him on the neck with a machete or the like, if I spoke with people I wouldn't stop gentlemen, the first time I shot up I felt nothing, I swear, my mother only

—Now finally I get to see you in a good mood

only because at a certain time, halfway through the fish at dinner, I smiled at her, this at the time when the doctor to her

—A little stone of nothing

and to my father softly, behind closed doors

—We have to look more carefully at this

adding slowly

—It can be a cyst it can be another problem let's order a biopsy

as various antipersonnel mines were exploding at the same time cutting our legs off though we remained identical, my mother, returning from having dressed herself behind the screen, straightening her dress up a bit because the zipper was hurting her

—Now the milk?

no, my mother surprised

—You're all so serious

because just discomfort, perhaps a vertebra that the mattress twisted, perhaps a wrong movement while sleeping that offended a muscle, my mother staring at us, at first intrigued and then troubled

—Did they discover something that is worrying you?

and nothing annoying madam, some tests just to set us at ease, an X-ray, analyses, doctors' offices had to have toys, balloons, and candies instead of tables, desk, and mysterious instruments, solemn, set out in a kind of threatening tranquility, the cellar of the house in the village a door window there above toward the yard that prolonged the day, I remember my grandfather on a small bench witnessing the arrival of night, on one occasion while calling him to dinner he remained seated, his cap toward the back of his neck, when my grandmother touched him on the shoulder he leaned to the left, fell, and then what I recall are his enormous boots, without laces, and the copper clock whose top opened to confirm the time which is always the same in the village, why ask, Her Excellency to my brother, pulling him by the arm to call him aside

—We're leaving I don't feel like staying here tomorrow to witness an animal dying

and my brother looking at her, looking at the knives, looking at her again, alongside the aircraft landing strip two recoilless cannon shooting at us, they didn't hit us but they destroyed a part of the camp and the storeroom for dry goods, then the cannon went silent, then the platoon that caught them from behind forced them to run out of the jungle, the rain that began to fall, my father was recounting this, wiped away the tracks and we lost them, the doctor to my mother

—An insignificant cyst in the kidney an operation is done that is not complicated and that's that

my mother without changing expression as when my father

—Would you permit me to accompany you?

and he accompanied her for more than thirty years, before the war normal, after the war always attentive to the noise of the doors, the noise of the windows, an exhaust pipe on the street, he asked my mother to sit next to him on the couch, if he got home and we were not there he locked himself in his room, bothered by the noises from the floor above, with the noises from the floor below, with the voices and the footsteps on the stairs, despite having the keys I yelled to him always, in the vestibule

—It's me father

sensing that he was looking at me, mistrustful, through some keyhole, one night, at the table, he turned to my brother and said to him

—Sorry

without adding anything more, just

—Sorry

and a movement that erased the

—Sorry

thereafter, whenever I got money I shot up, my mother alarmed

—You have such shining eyes now

and it's not just the eyes, I feel almost happy, everything suddenly easy, everything right, everything pleasant, what sold to me visited me from time to time

—I think you need a boyfriend

he ate the stuff in my pantry, smoked my cigarettes, lay next to me in my bed, hurt me with the haste of his fingers and on the following day left me paper with powder, not even a dose, not even a half dose, a quarter that was not enough for a dental filling, the bathtub dirty, the towel on the ground, and then he vanished for days on end, I found him with his friends, on some nights he spoke with me, other nights he didn't see me, other nights

—I don't have time now

turning his back to me or pushing me with his elbow, my brother, mistrustful

—What's going on with you?

because my pupils sharper, my movements looser, my mother to my father, without understanding

—Sometimes she changes character

and who took money from her purse, my mother guessed because I guessed that she guessed even without talking or changing expression, one time it seemed to me, I'm not certain because she wasn't soppy, that tears, tears is exaggerated, a bit of discreet moistness as when my father suddenly interrupted, after dinner, his reading of the newspaper and opened his shirt showing her his chest

—Didn't they wound me here with a bullet a few minutes ago?

my mother brought a mirror from the bathroom to calm him down, though my father with a finger sticking in his ribs

—I feel something metallic it might be hidden

from one side to another on the carpet with the desire to call the army nurse and so that the helicopter could prevent him from dying, the nurse pretending that she took out something from the skin with tweezers and showed it to my mother

—Your husband was right madam look only the projectile

and my brother and me silent though my brother's silence

—I only wanted to see you bye

different from mine, with a sort of rage that I didn't understand appearing and disappearing in his eyes where it seemed to me that trees, animals running, a blood-colored mound on the ground but perhaps I'm mistaken, I don't see my father harming anyone no matter what, he was in Africa with other old men but what can the old men do, get up with difficulty, sit down with difficulty, walking slowly without the strength to hold each other up, none of them, it's clear, capable of putting a bazooka on his shoulder, pecking at food followed by a thimble of wine and for that if my mother

—He suffered every hardship in Africa poor thing

of course I wouldn't believe as I wouldn't believe that if he had died there, upon saying this to my brother he silent, leaning toward the sty to examine the pig, lingering in the cellar to reflect over the knives, me different because the injection

—I only wanted to see you bye

made the world more welcoming, more cheerful, because it's not just the pleasant mood, I am capable of speaking despite my father

—Watch out for the tracks

examining the floor with the tip of his feet, this not always, of course, now and again, suddenly, when the neighbor's sewing machine seemed to knit the world, an April, when small, I woke up because my mother, in their bed

—Love

and then keeping silent afraid that I'd hear, minutes after, she came into my room without turning on the light and though I couldn't see her I felt her arm that while not touching me weighed on me, a different smell on her, the palm on my shoulder, a whisper in the corridor

—Thank God we didn't wake her

and the mattress springs when they lay down again, enough to shoot up so that everything returns or I feel my father fumbling about in the armoire

—What about my G-3?

and then a long silence, and then him in an altered voice

—The foolish things that come into my head you've seen?

and the bedsprings before falling asleep, and seagulls, and people, and when they already sleeping a voice in what seemed like a microphone

—I see on your faces the joy of going to serve the Fatherland

and next nothing but the sounds from the street, a truck, an ambulance, footsteps, wind in the tipuanas but softly, whispering, my mother drinking water in the kitchen murmuring

—My God

the pianist on the third floor who arrived late from playing at the casino, dripping keys from his hands, the pig tomorrow morning and returning to Lisbon I miss the injection, my arms hurt, my intestines hurt, I feel the absence of the peace it gives me, I stop being afraid that my parents will die and leave me defenseless in this rented cubicle that they don't know where it is and despite not knowing they found me right away, me in my father's arms without my mother's smell on his neck, I heard him

—My little girl

that I heard so few times and to feel a kind of, that is not to feel anything, a bit of relief only, his hand on my back, the contact of his beard, that grew during the night, on my forehead, I swear, that there are moments when if I could say

—Love

I would say it and here between us I envy you mother, you who made me suffer when trimming my nails as a child, above all the little corners and me terrified to be left without fingers, your way of combing me that pulled at all my hair and if I complained then the order

—Stop whining girl

with me in search of a mirror to see myself bald, the shoes always too large, with cotton on the tip

—Because you are growing

unfortunately you're growing too fast, it's not slowing down you're at the minimum two heads more than me, forcing me to perch myself on a bench, those that are always shaking, to reach up to you, this so as not to break a

—I see on your faces the joy

not to break a leg and I'm here to see who is cooking and to take care of this house afterward, giant shoes

—We're not rich you know?

forcing me to skate with them like skiers when they don't glide, lifting their knees like lumps not to mention the ordeal of the braids that my mother tortured me with, the agony of earrings with the pin to slip into the tiny hole in the ear always missing the hole, chewing with the mouth closed before I dribble all over myself, it's not pretty to see oneself with food on the right and left inside there, you seem like your brother who is black poor guy, they never taught him those things, of course there's always the excuse that for a mother to teach without

—You still haven't seen tomorrow's pig?

for a mother to teach without hands is difficult, even teaching with them God knows, we really try, I wish I were a man like your father only having to worry about war, there's not a week when he doesn't wake me up shaking me

—Don't you hear the seamstress?

and trying to push me under the bed where there is only dust and a rubber boot, look look, that we thought lost centuries ago and at last there it is alone waiting for a foot that fits, now there is an advantage of machine guns, leaving us with our shoes on, the problem is that it's hard to grab them with the fingers, the sucker so distant, you have to push with the broom handle from the other side of the mattress and we become thin as possible because the other side of the bed almost flush with the wall, I still haven't seen the pig for tomorrow, it's true, but

—I see on yo

I'm not much for pigs, first they smell bad, second they're ugly, and third they seem like people in their way of being, their rapid movements, the grumbling, the obliviousness of others, what sells injections to me lowers the prices whenever I respond to his order

—Come here

and while I'm there, nose pointed at the ceiling, I try to think of something else, sometimes I succeed, others just

—When will this be over?

and if by chance he hurts my breasts or my belly I hold on until he gets up disgusted

—You seem dead

and I don't appear dead, I'm dead, I've been dead a long time and no one knows, from time to time my father

—You always spoke so little daughter

and speaking to say what sir, what is there to say still, what can be said, what do they want me to say, it's better to walk in silence so that the insurgents don't notice, my grandfather, at least, liked partridges and to take them from the dog's jaw in order to hang them from his belt, some still shaking, my father looking at the ceiling lamp referring to my mother, I think

—If I'd not gone to war perhaps we would have been happy

and what he wanted to express by happy, fewer second lieutenants of the paratroops, fewer fears, fewer dead, a desire for grandchildren that I don't understand, trotting about without a break until we are exhausted, the doctor to my mother in a triumph that appeared excessive to me

—The operation went splendidly

and she, without managing a word, agreeing to please him, to please my father, to convince herself that she was pleasing herself, she couldn't move a finger but was in a good mood, calm, and now, isn't it true, the concern about the stones becoming lighter than water is being resolved, me to my brother, in the cellar

—You appear indecisive about the knives

he without responding, only a vacant glance, he

—If I could tell you

and he couldn't tell me, he also didn't tell anything no matter what, silent in Angola, silent in Portugal, my father

—Boy

and he silent remembering what had been forgotten for so many years, hands, ears, the man who lived with them, he slept on another mat, came and went, didn't speak to them, didn't appear to worry, didn't appear interested, smoked with the others and ate chicken, trying to run away and not the G-3, my father running to him with a blade, the man fell without a sound, first on his knees, then facedown, then still, meaning his hand took a bit of earth, closed and that was it before it opened slowly, me to my brother

—Who was that?

and my brother still studying knives, the wind was making wood sounds in the leaves, a broken tile I don't know where, on the top of the chicken coop or on the roof of the house I don't know how long it will hold on still, my father sitting in the living room observing my mother with eyes closed, a dog, not the blacks' cabíri, trotting after a smell, its snout near the bushes to get a better smell, it was the density or the color of smells that guided them, a guy on the ground waiting for them to kill him, the goats trotting far away, the manioc twisting ceaselessly on the mats, lightning bolts on the savannah but it was not raining, the crocodiles of the Cambo half in the water half on the sand, some of them so long that my mother couldn't believe it, the small snakes in the mud twisting, the mountain kites watching everything, taking advantage of the wind to remain quiet and the certainty that something was going to happen in the house tomorrow, if I were able to ask my brother

—Is it you who is going to kill the pig?

and I'm not, it's not that the words are lacking, I lack the throat, something prevents the sounds, I think that I like my father, he worried about me, he didn't ask about anything, he didn't reproach me, I'm certain that he knew that I bought injections from the other guy and he kept silent, one afternoon I thought I saw him in the distance and then he disappeared bumping into people, bumping into a wall, he didn't scold me, didn't tell my mother, when I didn't see him I sensed him attentive to me, observing my fingers that trembled, he got frightened when I botched a gesture, he ate without lifting his head toward us, all inside the plate, my mother

—An insurgent?

and he silent or waving no, he was at the door to my room, leaning against the threshold, waiting for me to awaken, with the word

—Daughter

caught in his mouth, unable to get out, the word

—Daughter

that got fainter afterward in the corridor transporting itself, me to my brother, in the cellar

—You're not going

without continuing the phrase and my brother his back to me, motionless, my brother

—I like him too but I've got to do it

as my father knew that he had to do it and didn't protect himself, he accepted, all this because of a black facedown with a bullet in his back imagine, what is a black worth gentlemen, who hasn't heard them shout with napalm including the lepers in rags burning let him speak or who has not seen them flee from their huts toward the river while the machine gunner picked them off one by one, trotting or on all fours or crawling until, my father told us that the water in flames as well, the branches of the closest trees were falling one by one, the exposed bones charred but the Portuguese soldier is as good as the best, charred, black, the doctor to my mother

—With problems of the kidneys the only thing that is needed is patience

my mother for now not thin, only pale, walking with more difficulty than before, without cutting my nails for some time, without combing me, indifferent, looking within, spending double the time in the kitchen, engrossed in the tiles, if my father, for example

—Would you permit me to accompany you?

I think she didn't hear him, she continued toward her room not paying attention to him or then

—Leave me

or then

—Don't bother me now

the fish too raw or too cooked, if my father interrupting himself suddenly, not sitting, not getting up, in an attitude of alarm

—Don't you hear steps in the corridor?

my mother without patience for the footsteps

—While they enter and don't enter take advantage and eat

and regarding my brother my father with caution, it seemed clear that he imagined his intentions, he watched his movements, checked if he on the landing signaling to other blacks or if some bazooka on the street, between two cars, aimed at the window, the impression that goats and hens in the room, in the corridor, in the living room, a circle of old men smoking in silence, women who were returning from the river with tins of water on their heads, forms that were moving in the tall grass of the vestibule, huts instead of buildings on the street, antipersonnel mines in the pavement down below, a trip wire on the steps, the kites that precede the rain flying blindly over the savannah, a first flash of lightning, a second flash of lightning too distant but rumbling already from hill to hill, the exposed tombs of the chiefs with palm trees on top, one of the Mercedes waiting for repair after a mine, with its front wheels and the motor dented up, my father to my brother

—You're no longer my son

don't always follow me, don't lean on me, don't sit in my lap, don't sleep at my side in the bed of palm fronds, you ceased to know me like I ceased to know you, tell me what separated us, was it because of a man who I don't know facedown on the earth, a woman without ears and hands, a black on his knees in front of a soldier who is shooting at him, an old man squatting

—I see on your face

no, an old man on all fours

—Lutenan lutenan sir

the chief of the sewing machine sewing, sewing, the unlit cellar perhaps with the pig already hanging from the hook inside, Her Excellency to the black, to my son, to the black

—For the love of God let's get out of here fast

dragging a suitcase and me next to the loquat tree listening to them, me shooting up listening to them, each to each

—Love

far from my bed and me hearing them

—Love

or before just a woman's voice, not a man's voice

—Love

and then silence, and then the wind on the mountain, and then my brother with me, in the darkness of the garden, next to me

—Do you understand?

and me quiet, my brother again

—Do you understand?

and me indicating yes, I believe indicating yes, I'm certain indicating yes just as my father indicated yes, just as my father to him

—Yes

my father hesitating

—Son

more firmly

—Son

firmly

—Son

and so the knives waiting, he waiting, my mother waiting and morning soon, the rubber aprons, the little light on the ceiling, me covering my face with my palms, me

—Father

and the eyes of the pig, serious, calm, sharp, that liked me.

20

I was in the cellar finishing the preparations for the killing, the buckets, the ropes, the rubber aprons, the blades of the knives, the shadow of the loquat tree that I pushed with my elbow and then, without understanding the reason, I felt the body swaying to the right and to the left until I realized that I thought I was playing piggyback with the man stretched out facedown on the earth, who I didn't know, with a bullet in the head and a wound in his back, near the hut, just after the woman without hands and ears, and the man took me toward the river holding me by the ankles with his palms much larger than mine, skirting the little manioc fields, going around the hemp stalks, making the hens that remained flee and leaving behind a goat moving its bony hips, independent from each other as if they belonged to different animals, to get away from us, how strange to be made of bits nailed together at random shaking out bleats, is this leg mine, is this nose mine, who dictates what I think, napalm in the distance, on the border with Zambia, the Katanga
—Uhuru*
I discovered on the same spot on the man's neck the birthmark I had, how strange birthmarks and how strange to remember it suddenly me who I thought had forgotten everything, besides the birthmark the shape of the fingers identical, the final edge of the thumb very short, he didn't talk with my mother, he didn't sleep with us, he came in and went out, uhuru, oblivious of us, without a glance, without a question, on one or another occasion he pulled her to the mat amid the gourds, the chickens, and the brothers and they lay down for a bit, face to face, in silence, my mother without pushing away the wing of a chicken that was flapping, all claws and beak, becoming muamba and an old woman smoking in a corner, her jaw on her knees, without paying attention to them, chewing her own gums emptying herself out, what is going on inside her, the man and me stopped next to

*Freedom (in Kiswahili).

the lepers, on the way to the river, holding tins with what was left of their stumps, their teeth, because they didn't have lips, enormous, an almost nude girl chasing another girl squealing with anger, holding a flimsy stick on her elbows, the man picked me up from the ground while he was looking for fish in a net, found a small one that he kept on his belt, pushing away a cabíri that jumped around him with a kick, he returned to put me on his shoulders and we entered the jungle while a crocodile with lifeless eyelids slipped into the mud, all this without speaking with me while I decided finally in favor of one of the knives in the cellar, Her Excellency fearful, softly

—Are you certain that it's the pig they'll kill soon?

in Bundo, not in Portuguese how strange, at times, when looking at you, I didn't think you white, sorry, I thought you black, like me for love of me, imagine how idiotic I was, and I almost loved you, almost not, I loved you, I didn't mind that you mocked me, treated me badly, I didn't mind that you did little, I didn't mind your girlfriend, it was enough that you were there, you understand, it was enough to hear your footsteps, hear the objects when you touched them, your fear at times

—Didn't you hear a noise inside there?

your request while huddled on the sofa

—Go see if there is someone in the sunroom be patient

it was enough that accepting, from time to time, I wouldn't say an embrace, I say a discreet celebration, like of a friend only, on your shoulder, asking you

—Don't send me away

asking you

—Stay with me

and instead of that Her Excellency fearful, softly

—Are you certain that it's the pig they'll kill soon?

in Bundo, not in Portuguese how strange, where am I after all and in the cellar of the village the chairs already against the wall, already people waiting outside, for example my grandfather, with the partridge dog, to my father

—I've always wanted to see how you fended with the animal since I died

with a depth of irony, a depth of mockery, a depth of disbelief, he never really believed in my father of course, he never believed that he would survive the war, he never thought that the radio

—Send the chopper send the chopper

and the helicopter taking him, who an ambush, who a well-aimed bullet, in the village a breeze on the corners, a threat of rain, me piggyback on the black on the way to I don't know where, colonial residences from time to time that the tall grass had devoured, tombs of chiefs surrounded by palm trees, the man facedown resembling me even in his way of walking, Her Excellency to me

—Who is your father after all?

and me

—I don't know

as I swear that I don't know where they are taking me now or how this will end so many headless animals so many dead people and birds flying at random, and wild boar, and an old water buffalo, motionless, studying us, and my father looking for the machete on his belt, the pig that they must have put on the van by now striking its back with sticks and it twisting and protesting while it was walking, it trying to bite the people chewing the emptiness in a terrified desperation, scratching the ground with its hooves, Her Excellency to me

—Don't you feel pity?

and I don't know if I feel pity because I don't know who will die when it dies, my father, me, some other person and then the house in the village deserted, no one, some junk that the cousin who takes care of the tomb will rob, some old photographs, some clothing and finally the rain dissolving everything, not only my past here, in Africa with my father, sitting in a unimog with him on the way to some target

—Kill kill

not just women and goats trying to escape bleating, he a match and diesel fuel and ashes that the wild dogs sniff in search of a bone, a piece of meat, a piece of mango with a piece of skin that they fought over threatening each other, snorting, biting each other, who will explain to me if I'm in Africa or in Portugal gentlemen, who will explain to me where I live, if I asked my mother she

—I don't know

because the stones wouldn't let her see, so many stones around her, so many stones in her eyes, all lighter than water, all lighter than the air, the doctor to her

—I think you more lively if you didn't have a husband you would ask him then if he'd give me permission to accompany you speaking of this and the other thing what is not lacking is life, we little by little better friends, more intimate and your husband, present here, perhaps smiling at us, understanding, forgiving, going away because I have my tactics, my tricks, my way of insinuating myself with women, my wife, for example, didn't resist for much time and it's already going on thirty-two years that she tolerates me, of course we've had our problems but with a bit of patience everything gets resolved, two children, four grandchildren, a solid relationship which does not mean that at some moment, we never know, and I'm being completely frank, whether things won't change, let's increase the IV a bit, let's stir in some morphine, I want you more relaxed, more lively, interested in the death of the pig because with me only the pigs die, my patients don't, can I bring you various, let you speak with them, believe again, more than believe, be certain that it will be cured, the doctor to me

— She seems to be in a better mood already don't you think?

with the metal butterfly on her jacket, with another ring on her ring finger with a wheelchair so as not to get tired between the bedroom and the kitchen, everything appears so far away when we don't feel good, I have noticed that you, blacks, are not lacking in certain matters, you're closer to animal instinct, closer to simple perceptions of the world, you don't stuff your heads in school with useless nonsense, what matter capitals, mountains, battles that happened centuries ago, what was holding me on piggyback finally found a path

— Euá

and we began to follow it, I had the idea that something because voices, motors, time, and again a flash from the camp between the trees, people washing themselves in a pond, my sister holding my elbow forcefully, her nails hurting my bones

— I'm in pain and vomiting you don't have some stuff by chance?

with shaking movements, pale, with a thread of saliva sliding out of her mouth

— You don't have stuff by chance?

suddenly so fragile, so poor, swinging her body frontward and backward, trying a step, slipping, getting up, supporting herself on the wall, not with the movements of a person, but with the movements of an articulated doll swinging insecurely

— Stuff

cavernous eyes, strange, only the iris

—Do you think in town

at the same time as my grandfather to my father, in a little sigh

—Still

because the grass was moving near the ridge where the first partridge finally emerged, turning its head to us without seeing us, not even the dog's ears that started to swell in the same way as the tip of two exposed teeth while my sister's body vibrated, with a mouth eating itself like it ate the sweat from her nose and her forehead, me to my sister and to the loquat tree that were holding each other up, the two with so many arms, which of you will dry up more quickly, lean over, fall, if at least lightning flashes in Mussuma burning the tall grass that the electricity helps, if at least in this garden a small hemp plant that might calm bouts of colic, I don't know anyone in the town except the man from the garage, we go there and ask who, tell me, of the old people in sheepskin who don't even speak, the only response they give, while sharpening a stick with a razorblade, it's sucking the spit from cigarette papers, in a street near the chapel declaring Sunday, no one resembles autumn as much as the bells, when a person dies, even in June, October always and the light, right in the morning, with nostalgia, and then the man who carries me piggyback doesn't stop, he'll never stop to flee the army, the helicopter gunship, the G-3s

—Kill kill

my sister to me

—Let's go to Lisbon please

and me to my sister or to the loquat tree, which of the two suffered, how do we have time to go to Lisbon with the pig killing, already in the van sniffing the ground, in an hour at the most, the blood in the buckets, the body that almost bursts the ropes, the screams, you can't stand it without distressing your parents, you can't behave like a serious woman, smile at bouts of colic, be silent, don't itch yourself like that, the wild dogs around the lepers, waiting, and the man that carried me aiming at them with his homemade rifle, those sharp snouts, those teeth, my father, even with the newspaper on the sofa, always in the war, forcing the unimog to advance next to the path, my mother removing the stones that tried to prevent her from breathing

—Would you permit me to accompany you?

and she silent in the armchair, calm, without seeing us, you in that state, me black, there is not one normal person in this family, my God, capable of existing for all of us, my grandmother

—What a hand got dealt me

breathing those flowers of diabetics, with moist cloths on the leg wounds, it was the pig that existed alone for all of us, it occupied the house in the village and not the sty, it slept in our beds, hung out with our neighbors, sat on a bench to take in the afternoon without talking with anyone, the changes of light, the arrival of night when the acacia stops existing transformed into sighs and the chicken coop discreet sobs, the man facedown in the savannah with me and the strange sensation, difficult to explain, that between him and me, that between us, this a short time before the army entered the village of huts, before the ears, before the hands, the grenades together with the diesel fuel in the hay, the chief on his knees

—Sir

losing his machete, looking for it on the earth, crawling in front of the boots of a soldier

—Sir

who stamps on his fingers pushing him with the barrel of his G-3

—What do we do with this one?

lost memories that suddenly return, having arrived from what part of me or then was it the coming of the pig that brought them back to me, Her Excellency

—What is going on?

and I don't know, I swear that I don't know, what happened in Africa, that almost never was with me, to return now, I feel like eating crickets, cockscombs, ants, smoking mutopa, shaving my canines, trapping wild boar, greeting

—Aiué mamá

the dead women, suckling on an empty breast, burying the dead on a plank conversing with them, something between me and the man facedown that I didn't understand what it was, after the attack I forgot and he returned with the arrival of the pig in the cellar I already hear it outside, the sniffs, the sighs, a snort that questions and to which I don't know how to respond, my sister

—Help me

more loquat tree than sister, twisting on the wall

—I only wanted to see you bye

Her Excellency pulling me toward the street in the direction of the automobile

—Please

afraid of what tell me, wanting to run away, wanting that I accompany you, a black in my bed what horror, a black at my table, that whispering, that clock, that ridiculous bracelet, those cheap perfumes, that golden tooth in front that I didn't need and nonetheless

—Please

calling for me, looking for me, holding my arm, the

—You

as if me almost white, as if me finally white, my father in camouflage

—Boy

younger than me now and nonetheless

—Don't touch him

and nonetheless

—Boy

pulling me next to him on the seat of the unimog, farther away from the soldiers and the flames and I don't know what resisting in me since then, not accepting completely, hesitating, escaping, meaning accepting and flee-ing at the same time, forgotten the cut-off hands, forgotten the ears, for-gotten the woman on the ground who earlier used to carry me on her back, wrapped in a cloth, shooing the chicken away so that I might sleep, applaud-ing me

—Euá

when I began to walk, the man facedown didn't speak to me, he came and went and I hardly ever saw him, he didn't come near, he didn't pay attention to me, I don't recall him being interested in me as my father was interested, asking me questions, putting his palm on my shoulder, me sharp-ening the knives better on a leather strap, in the cellar, without noticing my father alone

—Which one will you kill me with?

and a little slap on my back, funny, observing me better, becoming serious

—I was joking silly

becoming still more serious

—Don't tell me that you believed what you said

in an offended expression

—As if I were capable of harming you as if I were capable of hurting you

and a face identical to that when he was annoyed with my mother because the soup too cold or a stain on the collar of a starched shirt, he who was at first all formality, bows, respect

—Would you permit me to accompany you?

and then some impatience here, another there

—You take so much time to tell a story

my father examining the cellar

—Yes sir yes sir

thinking that my grandfather would like to be here poor fellow, we still have money to kill a pig, we're not yet poor, the dogs must have begun to smell something because they were restless, trotting from one side to the other with their snouts in the air and then my sister calling my name, bent forward, vomiting in the lettuce, meaning first bent forward, then on her knees, then lying on the earth, please get up before father sees you, don't frighten him, while my mother was walking slowly trying to balance the stones, inside of her, toward the back door, what ill did we do to our body so that it will avenge itself today, Her Excellency to me

—Please don't force me to go away alone

frightened by my father, frightened by the pig, frightened by my mother, frightened by me, thinking, without understanding that I thought

—Who are they killing?

—Who are they going to kill?

—Why do they have to die?

understanding only her fear, the urge to curl up on the sofa in our living room and forget the house in the village, my family, everything, just look at the Tagus, look at the seagulls, the terns, the albatrosses, the clouds, my mother walking slowly toward the gate to the yard with all her stones around her, entering into and leaving her body, flying around her, nearing her, moving away from her, so many stones, my God, so much lighter than water, only the dead on the ground in the huts heavier, coming down onto the earth slowly and transforming themselves into grass, the doctor to my mother

—We're still here aren't we?

and we're still here in fact but where are we, in the body of an animal or in the buckets of blood, my sister upon seeing the knives

—No

in the same way that my mother to the stones

—No

looking to remove them with her fingers that still worked without getting anywhere, the man that lifted me on piggyback didn't try to protect me fleeing the war, he tried to protect me from the house in the village, with the wound from his bullet in the head and my birthmark on the neck, far from the old men who watched me in the square, far from the little buildings in ruins and from the wild geese, with the female honking in front, who was escaping too, Her Excellency to me

—The geese can't stand this you've noticed?

my mother in the yard, supporting herself on the wall now that no one

—Kill kill

that no trip wire, no napalm, no bazooka, no defoliant, no general

—I see on your faces

just the humidity of the mist, the toads, the frogs, the black woman with hands

—Aiué mamá

staring at me, the witch doctor who danced over the beheaded rooster shaking a gourd with beads, the wind, suddenly, pushing the tall grass down, the trees confused, the animals, the silence of things, the machine gunner silent, serious, tranquil and despite the sun so much night below my God, so much night, the life of insects in the darkness, conversations of the dead, Her Excellency

—I'll pack the suitcase and walk to the car

and me

—Wait

because within an hour if that much all will be over and we on our way back to Lisbon already almost forgotten having been in the village, perhaps my parents will stay there longer to leave chrysanthemums on the tomb and my father looking at the mountain before leaving, according to him he was happy there, the hens in the brush that the foxes ate, the village larger, a pharmacy, a café, if the captain to my father

—Let go of childish feelings and destroy all that for me second lieutenant sir

surely we were luckier now, Her Excellency from the kitchen door

—I have the suitcase ready now

she who since the night before, I don't know why, has treated me like a white, the same consideration, the same formality, her girlfriend jealous of me, without touching her, without smiling at her, walking around on the streets planning vengeance, suddenly older, almost the same age as my mother without the stones, watching me with hatred, my sister who was vomiting next to the loquat tree so troubled, exhausted, the man facedown on the ground, with me on his shoulders, so far away now, if I were to call him, for example

—Father

he wouldn't understand, going around one stream, another stream, we saw a herd of gnus trotting without haste, we saw deer, the army camp so far away, from time to time small thatched houses that the red ants were eating, vines in fallen columns, a lynx sitting back on a table watching, if I called

—Father

nothing changed in him, we ate roots, some berries, ants, some or another fruit that fell from the trees, fish eggs from a lake, time and again a village in the bush, women, old men, hens, naked children uninterested in us, adolescents laughing and the man kneeling in front of the chief's chair with a painted bone in his hand, guys smoking without curiosity about us, a small plantation with a white on a decrepit tractor and a dozen blacks working in the cotton, the white an old guy dragging a plough and the rods of the tractor squeaking broken down, he lived with two black women, who carried water on their heads, in a building with an old wall and the rest thatch another billy goat covering a female, the only white I saw before my father's soldiers only with shorts and barefoot, prodding the blacks' laziness from time to time with his cane, the two women, already old as well, pounding the pestle side by side, the chief remained in his chair, me who up till then had never seen one, motionless, without paying attention to anyone, a movement from time to time and a helpful guy bringing him water or manioc, the god Zumbi, in wood, at his feet in a kind of niche, minuscule chickens, cabíris, all dark, miserable, not very clean, Her Excellency now so changed, without despising me, without saying anything bad about me, dragging her suitcase toward the car

—Won't you help me?

and me, without words, of course I'll not help you, even if I wanted to I couldn't help you, remember the burning huts, remember the women without hands, the flames from the diesel fuel annihilating everything, the machine guns, the shots, my mother who will die without delay, weighing less than the stones, I assure you, walking to the cellar without looking at us, remember me next to the second lieutenant leaving from the camp, the wooden huts, empty tins of food spread out on the ground, the second lieutenant behind the tool hut raising the G-3 up to his jaw, to shoot at me, putting it down, groa

—I see on your faces the joy of going to serve the Fatherland

ning softly while he hugged me

—I'm not able to I'm not able to

and me surprised for a moment to be of the same age, meaning we weren't of the same age but we were of the same age, sometimes he was older than me and other times I was older than him, how strange when we were of the same age but it gave me, how to express it, pleasure that we were of the same age, we are of the same age still today, I'm going to kill a man of my age, they're going to kill me with his age or then he more grown up, or then I more grown up and younger, the two of us behind the tool hut without Her Excellency and my sister seeing us, no one saw us other than us, no one knew, no one ever found out, we friends right, if we weren't friends I wouldn't kill him, if we weren't friends not one of us, Africa Africa, would die, we in an embrace only that he, I see on your faces, his shoulders, so to speak, jumping while he rubbed his sleeve

—I can't stand this anymore

not just the eyes, his whole face that tried to smile because the Portuguese soldier is as good as the best and Portugal, the last bastion of Christian civilization, one and indivisible from the Minho to Timor, Her Excellency trying to kiss me us who for centuries didn't

—Please come with me

kiss, in a voice that didn't order like usual, pleading

—Please come with me

my father waving at us in the distance

—You came early

with my sister set loose from the loquat tree and the branches moving up and down a little, the white on the tractor, I now noticed, one eye more open than the other, without a pupil, blind, how long ago did he come from the garden of Europe planted at the edge of the ocean, almost as destitute as the blacks, almost as miserable while the wheels, poor things, trying hard on the grass, of course I arrived early, neither of us could miss his death isn't that right, Her Excellency a child's expression that I didn't recognize

—I don't want to be without you

as if I were important for her, as if she liked me, or pretended that she liked me, a bit of me, my father

—Good that you don't understand me black boy

ordering a sergeant to form the platoon, with me behind him and I didn't understand anything in fact just as I didn't understand the weight of the stones or the woman without ears and hands, the man lifted me again up to his shoulders and the jungle again while a cabíri sniffed his ankles before forgetting about us or afraid of the wild dogs or of a hyena with yellow pupils advancing toward us, hesitating, moving off, my sister to Her Excellency and to me, scratching herself without pause

—I'm going with you to Lisbon

and we're not going to, the second platoon isn't better or worse it's that, and we're not going, platoon, to Lisbon, if you go down to the highway no truck because no one at this hour, you'll be in the midst of the plane trees waving at you, a corporal from headquarters was distributing combat rations while a Berliet waiting to transport us up to the bridge and leave us there, the captain on a crate in silence, the last butterflies in the mist, the god Zumbi everywhere now, the second lieutenant from the Berliet waving to my father

—Even though I called for you you didn't come for me

the stray dogs from the camp smelling us, the faded camouflage after so many months, almost colorless, mended in haste by a needle, Hoards on the step of the mess scrubbing a plate with his mortar in front, vertical as always, the hospital psychologist listening to us in a circle of chairs, crossing his leg, uncrossing his leg, crossing his leg again, the space between pant and skin without any hair how time passes sir, still twenty years old now and already fifty, already sixty, fewer and fewer soldiers at the veterans' lunches because they continue to die not here, in Angola, despite not being there it's in Angola that one dies, even though it seems to be a town in the north with a beach nearby, of the kind where the seagulls land on the windowsills, the commander passed away a while ago, of course, the operations officer, friend of female prisoners, passed away as well, the house in the village, it's immediately clear, taking its leave of us, the man facedown, with a shot in his head and a wound in his back, started walking again, on one occasion or two

—Muana

and me always silent, I started to recognize some parts of the jungle, some paths and a string of ancient mango trees, traces of water buffalo that rubbed against the trunks, a still distant smell that began to resemble the smell of the hut, the sun not round, twisted, liquid, my mother crossed the yard always supported by the wall, I asked her

—Would you permit me to accompany you?

and she didn't look at me, dragging one of her legs in a long wandering that left a furrow in the earth, the back so thin, the curved neck, the doctor

—Sincerely I don't note any worsening a certain pallor and that's it these new medicines while safer are slower we have to give them some time

and Her Excellency's eyes fixed reproaching me, what changed in you, what changed in me, what changed in both of us, my mother softly, what theater all this

—Perhaps I feel the stones less

floating in her mind, now here now there, so simple, so clear, the body weak but the stones not hurting, free, meaning floating on the surface of pain, not in the depths, it was just her body that made it difficult, not them, the stones surrounding her without doing her any damage, the door to the cellar open though the animal had not yet arrived, in a moment we'll begin to hear the wagon with it, the axles of the wheels, the planks, all that coming down the slope that passed by the chapel, Her Excellency looking at me, her mouth moving in one single word that despite the silence was not silent in me

—You

without my father, who was approaching us, hearing her, as if my grandfather were there pleased, with a shotgun serving as a cane for him and the dog curled up around his feet, Africa so distant, the war over, the napalm forgotten, the crackling of the huts dissolving in the rain, the beheaded animals the earth ate, the cloister of the mission only a few arches or part of a plastic bin on the edge of the well, cells without doors, dead lime trees, me on the shoulders of the man who was always walking, a group of mandrills on a slope with one male chasing another male and a female, that I confused with Her Excellency, squealing, squealing, the first wind of the rain, the first flashes of lightning but still distant, small, a goat tried to run away until softening sideways and the male that was chasing it left the others showing off his long canines, my father brought a plush chair for my mother and put it right next to the entrance to the cellar that she filled like an empty dress, her shoes next to each other, without a body above, like when we go to bed and they remain there, solitary, empty, same as my sister's face with no features at all, the few that remained deprived of contrast, drawn on her skin, the people waiting in the cellar silent, the cousin who took care of the tomb, the daughter of the cousin, a guy I didn't know next to a little mule, my father amiable

— This boy still alive

and me next to him returning from the camp, not next to the driver, on the seat here above to fool the insurgents and without stripes on his shoulder insignia, a flock of pigeons passed close to the roof, took a turn around the eucalyptuses and vanished toward the town, they must have slept next to the church bells where the rats can't reach, with incisors that seem to be claws, curved, empty, after finishing the pig this house empty as well for a whole year, we keep the towels, we keep the curtains, we keep the dishcloths in the trunk, on the dresser there is the picture of my father's sister who passed away at three years old and my mother kissed it so that there were always traces of saliva on the glass, dry stains and a column of ants on the kitchen tiles, with painted turkeys and geese, one turkey one goose, one turkey one goose, one turkey one goose, I remember the turkeys sobbing, they showed their feathers puffing up their breast with a red double chin swinging from their neck, my father was proud of his father's accurate hand and that the pig didn't touch his arm, he cut the woman's hands off, I saw that, I'm not sure if he cut her ears off just as I'm not certain, we're friends

— Boy

if we're more than friends, relatives for example

— Son

always with one another, always together, on Sundays, near the Tagus, with my mother knitting, the joy of going to serve, he taught me to fish, how to set the bait, how to throw the line, how to estimate the paths of the fish by the stains in the water, my mother from time to time almost lau

— Would you permit me to accompany you?

almost laughing at us but while working in the house, and though they say that white women sing I never heard her sing, not because she was sad, I don't know, but I never heard her sing in the same way as she put the ros

— Shoot at will

ary on the radio however she didn't pray with the voices, why did you marry my father

— Do you get along well with him?

and she didn't answer me or answered

—So many questions kid

and nonetheless I don't know, I remember the sewing box with the buttons in a cough drops tube, needles sticking in a cork, pins in a metal tube with a bearded gentleman half faded out on the lid, two buttons with two or four holes, never one, never three, never five, Her Excellency's no hole at all, they were sewed on inside, I never noticed them and now the kidney and the stones, and now no delay, if I were able to tell her, if I managed to tell her and I don't, I can't, the dead woman is not leaving, between the two of us she understands, between the two of us, forever, I'm and I'm not your son and it's over, I say

—Mother

I don't say

—Euá mamá

I say

—Mother

and that's everything, and the

—Mother

it's difficult sometimes, I force the lips to

—Mother

and it happens that I feel shame, feel that I betray her like I betray the woman without hands and ears that if I would cry would extend her empty breast or would take goat's milk to give it to me to drink, the hollow breast in my mouth and me already without crying, ma'am, me without fear of the army and the shots and the blood and the jeeps on one side and on the other trampling us and the voices that were screaming and the cabíris trotting a few steps before falling and a second lieutenant, I don't know why, grabbing me

—That one is mine

warning the G-3s

—Watch out if you touch him

a guy once thin and now old who in the last weeks we fattened like the pig forcing him to eat, and the rubber aprons, the buckets, the knives, Her Excellency trying to keep the knives away from me

—For God's sake let's get out of here

pushing me, pulling me, hanging on me

—For God's sake let's get out of here fast

while the thin second lieutenant smiled at me pleased

—It's you who will kill me right?

the second lieutenant showing me to the people in the chairs, with his hand on my neck

—I want my boy to do this

radiant, proud, looking at the knives with me, moving one of the buckets a little with a kick, estimating its distance from the hook on the ceiling while my mother's stones, surrounding us, were turning, turning ever more quickly, the stones to my mother

—Would you permit me to accompany you?

the doctor, triumphantly

—As you see there is no reason for alarm

the man who was carrying me piggyback kneeled in the hut with a final shot and I stood there, hesitating between the yard and the cellar, with a word

—Father

fallen from my mouth, the word

—Father

the only stone that belonged to me, hesitating between the two.

21

When a voice next to me asked

—Would you permit me to accompany you?

I was about three blocks from work, coming around the corner of the café where the waiters, in shirtsleeves, started to put the tables out on the sidewalk and the umbrellas, I didn't usually respond to the men who said things to me on the street, giving me words wrapped in smiles and gestures that I didn't understand, with the cherry of a wink that seemed to have teeth on top, but as they had never asked

—Would you permit me to accompany you?

I looked sideways to the left and discovered a short guy, more or less of my age and thus, because a boy, younger, tormenting his ear to give himself courage and insisting

—Would you permit me to accompany you?

in a voice of a tap about to be turned off, with syllables dripping at longer and longer intervals

—accompany

flattening itself out with timidity in the drain, in a drop already regretting itself

—Sorry sorry

so that I consen, when small I wanted to be a butterfly, ted to let him accompany me up to the entra, until I saw a gecko swallow one in my aunts' backyard with a scrap of wing twitching in his mouth and I had a horrible fear of dying just like I'm afraid of dying now, to let him join me up to the entrance, the doctor to me

—This metal butterfly is you right?

with me understanding by his face that he didn't like it, he thought it was in bad taste or cheap and in fact it belonged to my grandmother who wasn't wealthy, she had a little store above Portalegre that sold from boots to rice and a mule that hated all of us kicking in the stable, I remember the animal's red eyes and those of my grandmother beating it on the belly with a slat from a crate, my mother said that she only softened with me

—Girl

almost with a smile but hiding the smile

—Girl

and ferocious with the others, on the only occasion when my grandfather raised an arm against her she pointed his shotgun at him

—Faggot

and it would come in handy if she could help me with the stones, taking the safeties off the weapon

—Faggot

the doctor, who never saw her, of course, rubbing his chin, in doubt

—That's capable of getting a result who knows

when my husband appeared in a uniform I went to cry in my room and if they called I responded from the pillow

—I'm coming

and the doctor

—It's all going to go well

not at that time, now, and of course it will not go well, legs weaker and weaker, a difficulty in the chest as if my breathing were stumbling I don't know where and I were left to plead with my lungs, sitting on a step, massaging my knees

—You were coming to be with me

and no one came to be with anyone inside me, things that hung, rattled, avoided each other, episodes, stones, pain, very old memories, my father to my mother

—Don't dye your hair blond again this is a serious house

and my husband, in uniform, I see on your faces, even more defenseless, accompanying me on the way to work, accompanying me on the way home, if by chance his elbow touched mine I moved away in a little jump

—Sorry

one afternoon, because of a gesture that explained I don't know what, his baby finger took hold of my fingers and stayed there, ashamed, inert, the second or third afternoon he added the ring finger then the middle and I hesitated between squeezing them a little or shrinking my hand slowly, while shrinking my hand I caressed them without wanting to, he grabbed me in

response and I couldn't get them out so that we remained like that, indecisive, sweating with shame, sensing me blush, it wasn't pleasant nor was it
unpleasant, it was strange, or rather I must confess that pleasant and at the
same time strange, it was gradually becoming less and less strange, days later
he put his palm on my neck, days later he put his arm around my shoulders,
days later I told my mother, days later, when I entered the room, my parents
were talking on the sofa, with my father asking my mother

—Really?

and they became silent when they saw me, during dinner they observed
me furtively, rapid glances, words run together being careful that I not see,
while I sank into the painting of apples and pears on the wall, I never looked
at it so much in my life, six pears and four apples, one of them with a little
leaf at its foot, we have it in the corridor now and I almost didn't notice it
but perhaps noticing comes to mind just that night, I imitate them, only
becoming aware of that afterward, one of the run-together words of my parents and the picture, in general distracted from me, then attentive, claiming

—Why not?

so I'm certain that my mother, arguing softly, while she took the plates to
the kitchen thinking that I didn't hear

—I see on your faces

what nonsense

—I see on your faces

upon the departure of my father for the war, my mother

—Why not?

and my father's response was to serve himself another drop of wine, he
who almost never touched wine, staining the clean towel that by chance was
there so that on the following dinners, without my parents noticing, a constant dialogue, full of indecision and questions, between me and the stain,
without major results because always me

—And now?

a vacillating silence, the doctor to me while he listened to the stones

—You're thinking about what?

in the office where everything was too white not to be tragic, the table,
the screen, the desk, the chairs, the tree branches on the window, the sun
out there, only the clouds dark, my husband and my son seated behind me,
the nurse replacing the sheet on the table for the next patient, they're not
going to take the illnesses from each other, the doctor's face, while he lis-

tened to me, too close to mine, the frown a fountain debiting a trickle not very convinced of hope on its limestone mouth

me wanting to press his honker of a nose like I used to do to my daughter saying

—Pópó

and a spoon of soup, in the other hand, ready to enter the garage of her lips, we a pack of losers lying to people, so infantile, so ridiculous, how it hurts to pretend that I believe the story about the stones, how it hurts to agree

—Of course

while I die, my God how the death of others frightens us, how leaving life terrifies us, we remain there not being there and the impulse to search for them under the furniture, perhaps we come across a look, a phrase and what to do with the look, with the phrase, I recall my mother in the hospital, with difficulty

—There's a little sun isn't there?

and you're right, ma'am, it's sunny, all illuminated, shining and we illuminated, shining, we the tones, the colors, the reflections, they're still noticeable from time to time, it certainly still feels like July, whenever I get better we'll go up to the river to look at the boats, the seagulls and the boats, a gentleman in a wheelchair cleaning his forehead with a handkerchief or we'll return to Portalegre even without grandmother, we're thinking, and the doctor listening, listening

—Very well

because even without grandmother she out there waiting for us, serious as always when she appeared radiant, the more radiant the less pleasant she who was never pleasant, more serious, my husband looking at the doctor in the hope that he might explain things to him with his eyes and the doctor not even a sideways glance, he expressed himself with his shoulders, a shrugged shoulder this, a soft shoulder that, the shoulders or the neck, for example the last time, last week, just the neck

—Five or six weeks at the most

like the voice on the dock with the soldiers, with my husband there below without me being able to distinguish him from the others, there were so many, poor fellows

—I see on your faces the joy of going

or rather, in fact

—Five or six weeks at the most

due to all those instruments of war, pistols, rifles, cannon, what I would like the doctor to tell me

—There is a little sun there is a little sun

and my husband taking me to the dock instead of bringing me here, a village embracing a cemetery, a mountain full of furtive animals watching each other and the pig killing more his human screams, every year we bleed one and for this there exists hardly anybody on the streets except a half dozen sexless old men, just immobility and silence, squatting on pebbles, devouring little by little what remains of the bowels, I brought the

—Would you permit me to accompany you?

my parents walking and the apples and the pears measuring him from the wall just as the doctor measures me, the apples and the pears shoulders only, the

—Would you permit me to accompany you?

on the edge of the chair, hands tied up in each other I suppose that still with my finger inside that didn't even help him, inert, as our fingers change if another person holds them, I know nothing more timid than the

—Would you permit me to accompany you?

same as the pigs in the cellar only that incapable of fighting, trying to balance himself not at the end of a sofa, on an edge of himself while the doctor called him aside when me on the other side of the screen and he whispered to him, the butterfly barely appeared on my lapel he louder, not to the

—Would you permit me to accompany you?

to me

—Here we continue the fight

with my son agreeing, or rather waving in agreement, or rather not believing because five or six weeks don't make a fight, it's waiting but for what, if I managed to feel like my mother in the hospital that there is a little sun, daughter, right, that there is a little sun instead of this dull afternoon, a little sun, what is better than the little sun while the stones are turning around me, I watch them passing without haste, almost still, now inside now outside my body, at times the

—Would you permit me to accompany you?

sits in the bed in the middle of the night although I continue to sleep

—Kill kill

and me awakened because the stones remain, when they enter me they hurt, when they leave they hurt, when they surround me they hurt, even lighter than water they hurt, even without edges they hurt, they take over all my organs and they hurt, the water I drink hurts, the soups they give me hurt, the clothing I wear hurts, the shoes I wear hurt, soon they will drive me to the cellar where they will put me, with a pillow on my back to make me comfortable, in a wicker chair, the one where they sat the father of the

—Would you permit me to accompany you?

before he died, I'm witnessing the animal's agony at the same time as I am in agony, I wonder if I have feet why don't I feel them, legs still more imprecise, my mother to the

—Would you permit me to accompany you?

increasing the seriousness of the question putting her glasses on

—Where do you work?

with the apples and pears increasing, curious, the furniture in the room suddenly solemn, more expensive, my mother leaning frontward so as to hear the response better, my father echoing himself, separating the syllables

—At an insurance company?

as if he heard the words *insurance company* for the first time, calculating with his tongue the weight of each syllable

—Insurance company

studying one each time, joining them afterward and thinking the response so-so, he wanted a doctor, that one, but in the final analysis an insurance company well then, an acceptable occupation, the employees of Portuguese insurance companies are as good as the best and a marriage bed in my room, new curtains that my mother made, a bigger armoire, me looking at the

—Would you permit me to accompany you?

with a strange

—What is he doing here?

because suddenly a person we're not used to in the house, the surprise of the first reaction

—Who's he?

the second, still a bit bizarre

—Is he the Would you permit me to accompany you?

the third, with a wrinkle of astonishment on her forehead

—He's my husband

and my husband means half the bed, half the closet, half the air, an unfamiliar breathing startling me in the darkness, an unexpected cough, immense sandals on the floor, clothing who knows whose, for that matter not in very good condition, twisted on the chair, not dresses not blouses not bras, a gigantic jacket, unfamiliar, with the lining of one of the shoulders almost loose, pants sliding onto the ground in an irritating wandering giving the impression that they were going to stop and they didn't stop, they got loose finally to be brought together in a kind of hill with the belt buckle sticking up toward the ceiling, ready to cut through my heel, a sock on the carpet with a hole on the big toe, some striped boxer shorts with an opening in front, all property, at first glance, of an unusual creature, not forgetting a bath towel hanging at random from the doorknob and a tie, in a knot, on a corner of the mirror, prepared to hang me, it would be enough to put it around my neck and hang myself from the lamp at the room's entrance, hand on my chest, looking at myself without understanding, understanding that my room irremediably occupied by the

—Would you permit me to accompany you?

having become that inexplicable creature we call spouse, always with the wrong cologne, the wrong shaving cream, and the wrong deodorant, nauseating, too sweet, those of the doctor, alright, a bit better while he removed with the back of his hand one of the stones from my kidney that was floating around it, to the right and to the left, hesitating about where to land, I undressed in the bathroom so that the

—Would you permit me to accompany you?

didn't see me without clothes on and even so I asked him to cover his eyes with his arm, not with his hand, of course, because the fingers have cracks, how many times did they say to me when small

—Cover your face I don't want you to look now

in order to hide a fellow that I had to meet afterward, fixing the pillows, and me seeing all between the edges, the eyes hidden cautiously by the arm, even in the bathroom what I did was put on my lace nightshirt above the blouse and the skirt because of things and to unbutton myself below letting everything fall about my feet, hitherto attractive, pinkish, rounded, without any vein sticking out, that changed so much with age, gentlemen, calluses, bent bones, yellow stains, a complete mess, and

—I see on your faces the joy of going to serve the Fatherland

I don't know why this phrase has stayed with me, heard from loudspeakers spread out throughout the army embarkation dock and spoken by a general, full of metal on his chest, in January, in the midst of rain and the seagulls and marches all wet and that removed everything majestic, just like the scream bursting out from time to time, during sleep, from the pillow at my side and the pleading, near the dresser, of a different creature, I don't imagine who it could have been, pleading

— Send the chopper send the chopper

in an authoritarian supplication that appears to be a contradiction, but isn't, I heard it dozens of times, every time different, throughout my life, no one is more pressing than those who ask the

— Send the chopper send the chopper

at times he appeared to carry tears inside, after I lay down and put out the light I felt myself at the bottom of a pit with an inchoate presence at my side that expanded and contracted, that turned itself into a sigh that wanted

— Good night

or into an ankle that rubbed me lightly, or into a quiet figure sighing, or into a squid's tentacle that tried to grab me, even with the blinds down the window was vaguely visible, halos of lamps, wind in the corners, ambulance sirens because, I never understood the reason, one gets sick more frequently at night, no

— Would you permit me to accompany you?

replaced, I see on your, by a sigh of lament, a caress masked as a casual touch and me a refugee on the tip of the mattress, afraid, we hear so many conversations, on one occasion a kiss on the back of the neck, another occasion a kiss on my shoulder blade that softened me a bit and made me feel a kind of shiver up my spine my father's footsteps in the corridor, when I was almost turning for the kiss, they strangled me, until July, the twenty-eighth of July, a palm on my bum that I couldn't run away from and that was spreading, enormous, throughout my body, not only my back, my belly, my breasts, my neck, finally the root of my legs, increasing the

— I see on your faces the joy of going to serve the Fatherland

that started to stretch out in me having come from the top of the rain with a few microphone whistles in the middle, my body, without, I swear, my noticing, my back on the mattress, a sigh that I don't know where it was born, the knees that began to move apart because the root of my thighs started to swell separating my legs, a mouth searching for mine that helped to find it, the smell of shaving lotion, I'm for knowing why, less awful now, then awful, then merely pleasant, I assure you, I found a head, I found a chest and contrary to what I thought, the hair didn't disgust me, I curled my index finger into one of them, I curled, because besides the rest it was charming, the ring finger on the other, I discovered, with one palm, the belly button, the pelvic points, the silky bones of the pelvic basin, a leg between mine mixed in with the joy of going to serve the Fatherland that almost pushed into my crotch, first on a slant, then more and more present, between the bones of the pelvic basin a part of the

—Would you permit me to accompany you?

growing, I tried to help it because, I'm here to learn the reason, if it stuck to my hand, a kind of cylinder with a moist end that continued to get bigger, the

—Would you permit me to accompany you?

pleading with me

—Don't leave

in a supplication that whispered in my ears, in my lips, on my throat, if he folded my tongue, became tongue also, became roof of my mouth, became teeth, became saliva, became a whisper that wasn't understood, became a plea

—Let me enter you

without making it to the door, his whole body over mine that didn't smell of lotion, it smelled of a mixture of the zoo and haste while me, helping it, only haste, a kind of necessity of becoming complete because something was missing in my body, something of

—Would you permit me to accompany you?

inside my body, kept inside, closing me off from myself, closing me off from others, closing me off from the world, the

—Would you permit me to accompany you?

in a kind of, at the same time, an order of a man and plea of a child

—Now

until I found him aimed at me, down there, lost, almost succeeding, not succeeding, almost succeeding again, getting a bit smaller, getting bigger once again, getting smaller again, expanding triumphantly when I grabbed him, stuck on my little finger, guiding him toward me while the

—Would you permit me to accompany you?

he whispered in my ear

—Damn damn

he licked my ear

—Damn damn

he ate my nose

—Damn damn

sliding into the bottom of me, taking root in my depths

—Damn damn

throwing tentacles around my thighs, my lap, my breasts, my entire body, especially my toes that I never thought capable of sticking so high up, while my eyes navigated, closed, through the entire room like those weightless seeds, hairy, that entered by the window, setting down here, setting down over there, leaving, returning, one is trembling on the curtain while the other in the tipuanas made me deaf

—Damn damn

the wind

—Damn

getting smaller and growing, my blood was vibrating in my neck, in my temples, in my belly, my huge heart, much bigger than me, much stronger than me and me fearful

—It's going to burst it's going to burst

and losing fear, me at the same time with myself and far from me and with myself again, the general's microphone announced with electric energy

—The joy of going to serve the Fatherland

so intense in my ears, damn, while me the

—Would you permit me to accompany you?

now existed now didn't exist, that is, what seemed to me to be a thigh existed, a piece of instant belly button, the face that resembled and didn't resemble him, a cheek against my cheek, my arm on his back

—Love

above my arm on his back

—Love

pinching him, twisting him, taking little parts of him, returning them while a distressed voice pleading

—Send the chopper send the chopper

and a motor sound nearer and nearer filling my ears, my immense ears, I never knew ears as large not a

—Love

so strong, so dense, so hoarse, so me and not me, who said that for me, my grandmother scratching my head

—How you've grown girl

and I grew, bigger than her of course, bigger than the apple tree, bigger than the house

the

—Would you permit me to accompany you?

so unimportant, so small, so light, my mouth no longer

—Love

silent, my body reducing itself slowly or rather my genuine body emerging from this gigantic body that was slowly dissolving, me aware of the bed, coming down from the pillow to the ground, crumpled sheets, a blanket somewhere, me aware of the room and a voice inside me, the voice of I don't know who inside of me that began to belong to me, belonged to me, was mine, almost the usual voice and then the normal voice I'd lived with for years

—What was this my God?

under the voice of my deceased grandmother on the week of my confirmation, almost making fun of me

—You took time to be a woman get up and bring the bowl with plums my sciatica won't let me be

and the room around me, the clothing of the

—Would you permit me to accompany you?

surrounding me, so many shoes, so many shirts, so much junk that little by little got reduced, the

—Would you permit me to accompany you?

stretched out at my side, his nose on the ceiling, I remember him only with clarity on the day he left and on the day he arrived with our black son, the

—Would you permit me to accompany you?

so different in uniform, more adult, older, when the ship returned wrinkles I didn't know, the skin darker, the mouth narrower, almost a scar right about the chin, more rapid movements, his weightier embrace, it seemed to me that more decided

—Kill kill

bigger, among uniformed guys, to him

—Second lieutenant sir

and handshakes, good-byes, embraces, my father-in-law crying or rather a kind of humidity on the sides of his nose, a secretion, the black glued to him, motionless, looking at us, the doctor to me with a gentle pinch on the cheek

—The big job the lady gives me

keeping X-rays and collecting devices, me on the other side of his desk, with the metal butterfly on my jacket, with a stone that didn't fly like the others hurting my spine and another at hip level that hindered my step, wanting to order for once but whom

—Bring the bowl of plums be patient the cancer is not leaving me

my daughter, Her Excellency and with shame to ask too, there were no plums, nor Portalegre, nor a store, there was the doctor staring at me astonished

—Pardon?

and the metal butterfly sorry for me

—Don't worry doctor sir at times the past comes back to mind

the

—Would you permit me to accompany you?

sitting on the mattress putting on the pajamas

—Hopefully your parents noticed nothing

with my fingernail marks on your ribs and my tooth marks where your neck starts, what really happened, what did we do, I only recall joining and separating constantly, I only recall a breeze inside me opening up my entire body, I only recall the

—Would you permit me to accompany you?

existing and not existing at the same time, what did you do to my body if I have blood down there, what did you do to my thighs that hurt without hurting, what happened to us, to the trunk that belongs to me again, I have parts I know, parts I don't know, parts that I'd forgotten, feet small again, round, my hard breasts, my knees not so sharp, a long peace in me, a kind of sleep, don't touch me now, don't kiss me, leave me, the soldiers to the

—Would you permit me to accompany you?

—We'll see each other over there second lieutenant sir

those that stayed there we'll have to see over there, Carrot, Dry Cellar, Hoards, the others, the machine gunner

—Here I'm going to Trás-os-Montes second lieutenant sir

in his always tranquil voice and the gigantic eyebrows, the doctor, amused, interrupting the recital

—Dry Cellar?

and suddenly in him so much pity for me

—We finish by taking a liking to our patients you know that?

so that he benefits by taking a liking quickly, the doctor, who no longer has much time, a few more weeks, two months, three months, and I stop answering him as I stop listening to him, I stay over there in the bed looking at the ceiling without seeing, without breath, I stay in the village graveyard, against my will, with the whole mountain above me, I hear the genets in the winter, I hear the rain and the trees or then I don't hear anything, I am not, when they lifted my grandmother some loose cartilage and scraps of fabric from the ground that broke apart in my fingers, two broken planks, what is left of her authority, what is left of her anger, the doctor took me by the hand

—What is going on there my God

afraid not for me, for himself, for none of us has a lot of time, it's like that, there are more dead under us than grains of sand on the beach and regarding the soul what is that, not the stones lighter than water that will remain here, they decay with the rest of the body, my son to me

—I'm taking her to the cellar

with his help on one side, a cane on the other and looking down to avoid stumbling I can still pass the house, the garden, I still smile at people, I still nod my head, the

—Would you permit me to accompany you?

to my daughter

—Doesn't your mother look better?

my daughter a glance that said it all and a wave that said nothing, my son next to the knives, without turning to me

—Of course you do

with a voice echoing on the cement and the grumbling of the pig nearby, it traveled by van, they are tying it up, they are going to bring it, there are times when I think that me transported in that way to the hospital, like a suit, the

—Would you permit me to accompany you?

always a blanket for my knees because me cold, so much cold in this moment though I look better, look really good, the doctor

—If I hadn't discovered the stones I wouldn't have believed it

and thus it's a question of time, a question of patience, a question of the medication cleaning, cleaning, those five or six weeks, years, I don't know if it's a good idea because he already imagined the quantity of grandchildren that he would need to tolerate, sticky hands, diarrhea, everything in different places, Portuguese grandchildren are as good as the best, still distant, upon approaching the house by taxi, my parents already waiting on the veranda and the

—Would you permit me to accompany you?

in uniform waving at them with me thinking

—You've changed

thinking

—I don't know in what way but you've changed

not happy as I imagined, strange, the size of the mouth different, no smile, a minute attention to everything, ears on the alert, his hand not holding mine, forgotten on his knee or rising suddenly in search of I don't know what on his waist when some exhaust louder, watching the other cars, watching the sidewalk, looking furtively behind the glass, suddenly awake, touching me on the knee with his knee

—You're a little bit thinner

me who unfortunately was not thinner, was two kilos fatter, which showed on my cheeks, my waist, the

—Would you permit me to accompany you?

observing me better, in a way that I am never going to forget, the

—Would you permit me to accompany you?

next to me in the taxi asking

—Would you permit me to accompany you?

in the tone with which he asked me for the first time on the street

—Would you permit me to accompany you?

hesitant, timid, a trickle from a tap that's being turned off, with the syllables farther and farther apart, flattening themselves in the drain until the last drop, already repenting themselves

—Sorry sorry

and something inside of me

—Love

without even touching me or perhaps my arm on his back

—Love

on the back of his neck

—Love

on his neck

—Love

the doctor to us, surprised

—How many years have you been together?

with the pig already in the cellar, its head lowered, sizing us up while my son slipped on the rubber apron, put on the rubber boots, looked for the nail where the gloves were hanging and despite so many stones around me, going up, going down, going away from us, coming closer again, despite my fatigue, despite my fear, the voice of the general on the embarkation dock to the people, the two, not for the army down below

—I see on your faces

the doctor in the taxi with us holding a pen with which he drew around the stains in the pocket of his white coat

—How long have you been together?

and my palm on the knee of the

—Would you permit me to accompany you?

my jaw on his shoulder, my eyes closed, the uniform of the

—Would you permit me to accompany you?

that smelled of sweat, earth, gunpowder, the brush against my lace night-shirt and my toes suddenly big, my body that he closed with his, a shoe on its side on the floor, a falling pillow, not falling, falling, a mouth weighing on mine and despite the pain, despite the weakness, despite the hesitations of my breasts, despite my hip, me to the doctor in my old voice

—Perhaps you won't believe it but we began just now doctor.

22

At the end of a half dozen months I didn't read the letters they wrote me from Portugal, what for, news from a world that had ceased to exist for me, their health and what does the health of strangers matter to me, the weather in a place I don't even know what it's like, the marriage of a cousin me who stopped having relatives, my wife perhaps no problem in the kidney an organ that they have, not me, seeing that the tests almost normal except one without importance that according to a nurse my father-in-law knows it's enough to cut down on sugar and you what are you doing in Africa boy, the newspapers assure us that all peaceful in Angola, a little problem here, another there but a bit of conversation with the native chieftains and life goes on, by the way why don't you answer us, do you remember that you have a family that despite everything worries about you, don't ignore us and in fact I ignore them, now on the step of the mess looking at the emptiness now in the jungle with the soldiers

—The left flank more to the inside of the road

what mattered to me of a country that existed only in the form of kisses before the names, my mother added greetings from my father who approved with a nod

—I sent your greetings

thinking about something else, the girl in the pharmacy who referred to him as

—Hello honey

or the bothersome hernia that stained his life, my mother with mistrustful eyebrows

—Hello honey?

and my father making excuses

—She's a polite girl

by chance with an even more polite chest, ready to explode in her white coat, I remembered the scar on her cheek that diminished the merit of her chest, perhaps it was too expensive for her salary to have the scar removed, my father calculating prices and my mother who had antennae for certain and particular subjects

—Are you thinking of paying her for it?

leaving the girl in the pharmacy to the mercy of other generous and freer men, the scar ended up vanishing and it was the left flank that paid for it

—I said holy fuck farther inside the dirt road

because one never knows what the insurgents are preparing, when you least expect a grenade, fire, what does it matter that their rifles are older, almost homemade rifles poor, from time to time they jam, I left the letters from Portugal in the wastebasket at the mess, this is the girl's scar and the marriage of a cousin, it seems that the bride epileptic poor thing, Portugal some envelopes that didn't interest me at all, my wife's kidney wonderful, why think about this, we are worrying needlessly, we make ourselves miserable for no reason, it's enough the left flank and the recoilless cannon that they admit to having already, the radio says that they brought down a Do* with a missile, sometimes in bed, in the mess tent, in the dark, I suddenly felt little in the house of my parents and it came to me, that is nothing happened but I felt a kind of obstruction in my throat, difficulty breathing just as before tears but without any tears, of course, all this inside, until I thought I heard the footsteps of my mother and then I was suddenly growing and ordering her to leave

—Let me sleep in peace

angry with her, angry with the world, angry with me, I'd like it if they brought me dozens of letters from Portugal in order to rip them all up without opening them, to rip up the robbery at the jewelry store, the neighbor's divorce, my wife's tests almost normal, all that doesn't exist anymore, all that I lost, what a thing the camp, what a thing Africa, what a thing the war, what a thing the breathing of the trees, what a thing the dense smell of the earth, he put on his boots and left to the military parade in pajamas, looking at the outlines of the Berliets, the unimogs, the twisted storehouses, sensing the lights that were moving in the tall grass, sensing the lingering bad breath of the heat, remembering my mother at the entrance of her room

—Are you sleeping?

and me silent, of course, at best

*Dornier Do-27, a very light plane used primarily for transport by the Portuguese forces in Angola.

—The left flank farther inside the road

how many

—There's no hurry there's no hurry

testing the earth with the tip of his boots before stomping on it and inside me, furious with myself

—Mother

who used to write me about the breakdowns of the water heater, about the death of the neighbor's dog in the basement on the right, the price of meat always getting higher

—At least you don't need to worry about the problems

and me happy not to have to worry about problems, I have only to command a platoon, hold out until March of the coming year and then I'll be a person again, I have only to take care of thirty men who believe in me perhaps me who doesn't believe in myself, perhaps I would believe if my father or my mother

—Son

I still hear him

—Son

even today, on the day of the pig killing, I hear him

—Son

thin, with a flimsy beard, when small I wanted to have a puppy but my parents didn't let me have one, how I hated them for that, if I had a cap gun I would be capable of killing them, how would the nights be alone and without knowing how to turn on the stove, besides my mother's footsteps in the corridor would be enough, at night, with me already lying in bed, to scare away thieves, with her present who would dare rob me putting me in a bag, even today there are times when I dream about that, when my grandmother died I saw my father cry and I was so afraid that he younger than me that I didn't shed even one tear, they didn't take me to the funeral, I stayed at home waiting to play with a train, when they returned they found the carpet twisted and no one said a thing, they sat down in their chairs calm, without speaking, while I ran them over, one by one, all of them, one of the minesweepers hit something and the soldier responsible for mines and traps, squatting, was removing the earth with a cautious hand until he lifted up a wooden box that we exploded with a shot in a dark smoke, sheltered in foxholes, a little box of wood filled with pieces of metal, nails, screws, there was no other one exploding in solidarity, merely the brush recuperating slowly, this year's pig the same as the others and at times, without my expecting to, I felt pity for it and I noticed only that I felt pity because of the way my son, suddenly, looked at me, already with his boots and rubber apron, upon our starting to walk again I sensed the dampness of the water and saw the river appearing, in Africa the water never blue, brown, with traces of footsteps in the mud, they put two tablets in the canteen before filling it so that besides tasting dust a taste of medicine too, sometimes when drinking water from a pitcher, at the table, I still felt it on my tongue, my wife

—What are those grimaces?

and only then do I understand that me not in camouflage, in shirtsleeves without taking off the tie, if I asked him

—Do you remember the mine?

he didn't even look at me or answer

—Eat

that is eat tubes, condensed milk, a cheese bun, salt tablets, my daughter outside the cellar, sitting on a crate without greeting anyone, touching a slug on the ground with a little wooden stick while she sweated, sweated, boot tracks next to the river, a dented Russian food tin, so much sweat on her face, a Kalashnikov shell, birds but fearful, still not landing, the pig already in the cellar, lying down, with its legs tied, ready to bite whoever passed, the guide to me, spotting tracks of someone barefoot

—There are insurgents in the sanzala

not one, two people barefoot, a man as well with boots began to clean the animal with a mop after having wet it with the hose, with Her Excellency, with palms flattened out on her mouth, looking at it, me in the garden for a minute, without speaking to anyone, until I had them bring an armchair from the living room so that my wife might participate while a flock of wild doves crossed the window, on the mountain genets, I think I saw one years ago but I'm not certain, those triangular ears, that way of trotting, more pillows than cats suddenly only claws when a hare nearby, if my wife dies how to take care of myself after, there is a widow, in the building after ours, who I meet from time to time in the café, with a shopping cart next to her leg so that she'll notice its absence if they try to rob her, one afternoon I knocked on her door to hand her a package that had come for me in error and I saw myself in a trembling eye, between the knocker and the wall, she took off her glasses thank God to make out the name of the sender, curious how the lenses and wrinkles of attention make us more profound, more secure, the

captain told us to bring the chief from the village of huts next to the camp
and threw him against the flagpole with a slap

—Where are the insurgents here?

the chief with an enormous hand on his cheek, dozens of wild doves next
to the river, coming together in their rags

—There are no insurgents captain sir

a second slap, a third, the man, so miserable, holding out to us a small
bowl, after dinner, in hopes of food, the captain lifting him up by the rags
on his chest

—Thug

I didn't write another letter until the end of my commission, what for,
if something annoying were to happen to me, the army would let them
know and, on the other hand, blubbering, a gallbladder operation, expensive classes, the painful separation of some cousins who I didn't know well,
my daughter who couldn't stop scratching herself

—Are you going to do something stupid?

my wife's stones, as was expected, expanding, me with the idea of asking
the doctor

—Why deceive her?

the doctor, softly

—Do you think that we have the right to remove a person's hope?

above all since he was informed that his duodenum whatever it was that
needed to be studied and he almost felt like protecting himself with a tin
butterfly on his lapel or a candle to some saint, planted in some church, the
flame leaning every time that they opened the door and what was perhaps
a sign of convalescence, it was certainly, really thinking about it, a sign of
convalescence, the chief looking at the pistol

—Don't kill me captain sir

while the pig in silence, with legs tied, struggling against the ropes without liberating itself from them, the village once a few businesses and the
drunk that rang the bell on Sundays, Saint Michael's market on the last
Saturday of every month, gypsies, goldsmiths, clay in cloth, photographs on
a cardboard background, with holes for the faces, that represented the Last
Supper and no one wanted to be Judas, they wanted to be the prized disciple
of Jesus, without a hole for a face, leaning his beard toward him, the doctor
always palpating the belly, does it hurt less, does it hurt the same amount,
does it hurt a bit more, sometimes it was forgotten for an hour or two until

the duodenum returned suddenly with its end in tow, my son, on a table, checked the resistance of the hook on the ceiling of the cellar hanging himself from it, pedaling in the emptiness, Her Excellency

—What horror

turning her back incapable of sitting down, for the first time disheveled, her clothing thrown together and some gray hairs that no one expected, that's life, soon forty, soon fifty, soon the catheter, and that's life too, what happened to my body, to my legs, to my way of walking, the chief returned at night, locked himself up with the captain in the cubicle that served as a carpenter's shop while I vacillated between two knives until I chose one finally and my son the other longer, larger, it seemed to me that he looked at me differently but I smiled at him

—Boy

putting the rope for the hind legs onto the hook and me and my son and two men that came from the town we began to pull the body until we hung it up there, fastening it with knots while the animal shrunk toward one side and toward the other for the time being without screams, just breathing with effort, vexed with us, with mouth open and nostrils open, still without understanding, incapable of freeing its legs, my daughter now at the bottom of the cellar, hardly scratching herself, staring at us, my wife without the stones around her and suddenly I perceived that from the beginning of her illness alone, if by chance me

—Would you permit me to accompany you?

the best was not to listen to me at all, she heard her own body or not the body at all, she heard only the illness, never again

—Love

of course, never again the arm on my back, never again that lace nightshirt, the apples and the pears indifferent to me, I would have liked to have had a puppy when small, the captain to the chief wrapped up in a faded rag, they were eating our remains and insects and young vermin, they remained for centuries with outstretched hands in the camp hoping for a scrap of dried fish, a bone, the almost empty tubes of the combat rations, they didn't have hens anymore, they didn't have goats anymore, they sewed grass, the captain to the chief

—I want the insurgents that you're hiding here

and the chief on his knees trying to kiss his boots

—There are none

while the soldiers searched the huts, they lifted mats, burned manioc roots that were left over still, kicked cabíris that ran away yelping, my wife, before the stones, waking me up in the middle of the night

—Don't cry

turning on the light on the bedside table

—Don't cry

holding my face

—It was a dream nothing happened it was a dream

when small I wanted to have a, it was a dream, a puppy, my mother

—A puppy

and perhaps it was a dream, I don't know, perhaps it is still a dream, none of this happened, none of this truth, the ears cut off, the napalm, the shots, things that my head invents, I was in Africa in fact, I brought my son from there but afterward we invent without noticing, which machine guns, which dead, what is wrong with me, if I asked my son

—Do you remember Angola?

he silent, how could he remember at four or five years old, a man face-down, a woman without ears, my son with his back to me examining the blade of the knife

—I don't know

the only answer I had from him and it wasn't

—Send the chopper send the chopper

it was

—I don't know

so that my mother is right, dreams only

—Calm down

me seated on the bed looking at her

—you're not black

surprised that she hands, that she alive, the psychologist in the circle of chairs at the hospital

—People always exaggerate it's understandable

just like the doctor exaggerates about the kidney stones, I never saw one floating around in this room, there is no sickness that can't be treated, there is no death that can't be avoided, what we construct, what we suppose, for example the captain slapping the chief in front of his people, fewer and fewer people because they were running away from the camp, one day not a half dozen unfortunates here, us merely chasing a path without catching sight of anyone, one afternoon a water buffalo galloping in the tall grass, one afternoon hyenas surrounding a deer pulling, pulling, another afternoon an arm on my back

—I see on your faces

no, the arm on my back

—Would you permit me to accompany you?

no, the arm on my back

—Love

my son to me, in the cellar of the house in the town

—We can begin here in five minutes

with the pig staring at me like I'm staring at you right now, trying to free its ankles from the ropes so that we had to tie it up better, I remember crying the first time I witnessed it, my father replacing a bucket filled with blood with an empty bucket, drops on my shirt, on my shorts, on my arms, the screams that deafened me little by little, the eyes with transparent eyelashes that stared at me forgetting me slowly continuing to look at me, how strange to be at the same time in another place and here, my daughter glancing at me furtively, me knowing what she was thinking without wanting to know what she was thinking and thus knowing and not knowing what she was thinking, or before I didn't want to know that I knew, I forbade myself to know that I knew, what will happen in the house in the village after tomorrow, in the cemetery where will they keep me, on the mountain, perhaps an old man will be left on a bench in the square, when a child the blacksmith's widow who lived farther from the chapel, at the end of the alley where the fields began, she always called me

—Boy

she pulled me into the workshop, locked the door with an enormous key

—Boy

that turned in successive blasts

—Boy

she held me against her body burying my head in her apron

—Boy

while she felt my belly, my back, my buttocks, suffocating me in her embraces, observed by a dog in a corner, my son is going, lying on a blanket, I bet that my son is going, the captain to the chief

—Get out of my sight

a small puppy, of course, who would play with me, my wife

—Don't cry

and it wasn't because of the war that I was crying now, the pigs tears as well when they are no longer screaming, a person turns up nearby and tears indeed though the suffering already over, they are sad to stop eating, they are sad and nonetheless, if they can, even their children accept it, the blacksmith's widow finally got rid of me

—Go away

after sitting on a tripod undressed to the waist, holding me against her breasts ordering

—Bite

and me disappearing in her, so frightened, I smelled the flesh and the dust from the workshop, immense soft folds, no bone hurting me but it was difficult to live squeezed between two mountains, each one with a kind of coin, hard, dark, at the top, she in a sigh, crushing the cartilage of my shoulders

—Suck boy so you grow faster

where a very old drop emerged from time to time, the blacksmith's widow, the back of her neck thrown against the wall behind her

—Tell me it tastes good sonny tell me

and as much as I remember it didn't taste good or bad, I held it in my mouth to spit out later, when I returned home I washed my tongue in the tap, a few years ago I asked my cousin, who looked after the tomb

—The blacksmith's widow?

and she changing the water for the flowers in their glass jars

—She died centuries ago poor thing she flung herself down a well

and every time that they fished for someone lost at sea she emerged full of silt, her bent head on her shoulders, the blue arms and swollen facial features, purple, suddenly the image of the sacristan appeared to me, still with a cassock in rags, and a very timid boy, always greeting

—Sorry

instead of

—Good day

who passed the winters quiet looking at the rain from inside the window, the drops fall from the panes and his face just behind, the captain ordered him to put the other fence of the camp around the village of huts that we started to patrol at unusual hours but we didn't discover anything except, from time to time, wild boar and some wild dogs, chasing us, those enormous ears, that gallop, already almost all the people were seated in the basement to witness the killing, my wife, my daughter, Her Excellency, the cousin of the tomb, the two men who brought the animal, forcing it to get into the van prodding it with a stick, each blow with the metallic tip a snorting little jump, it couldn't bite anyone because the snout tied up, it couldn't hit us with its legs, it couldn't attack us, it just hated us, a helicopter passed over us since an attack on the company after ours, we heard on the radio the requests for a chopper among dozens of salvos, static, other radios farther away, sounds that appeared to be from a 90 mm mortar, bursts, a distorted voice

—Quick

while the pig was swinging on the hook curving, jumping, hating us like the insurgent we captured, wounded in the groin, after a lucky ambush, trying to drag himself away in the tall grass, my wife

—You're dreaming again

and you're right, I'm dreaming again, it's clear that none of this happened, I invented it, just like the political police killing prisoners didn't happen, just like them digging their own graves and squatting inside them, waiting, not even raising their head toward us, hands in their laps, with eyes that I didn't imagine so tranquil didn't happen, my son at my side, the knife in his hand, referring to me as

—Father

explaining to me, inside the

—Father

without changing expression

—You're not my father you killed my father

a creature facedown on the earth where I barely noticed, lifting him up piggyback, without words, without paying attention to him that was his way of calling

—Son

the son of the black facedown on the earth divided between two fathers, at the same time indecisive and decided, reticent and firm, thinking that losing his white father was the only way to conserve the black and Her Excellency, silent in a corner, understanding without understanding, comprehending without comprehending, Her Excellency to my son, without thinking about the words and nevertheless saying the words

—Don't call me Her Excellency call me by my name

and thus all good, all good, when my daughter stops trembling all good, when my wife's kidney stones disappear all good, I'm not worried, I'm not sad, I'm not afraid, I'm happy that all good

—Send the chopper

all good, like the insurgent sitting in the tall grass

—All good

piling up on the grass and all good, as the second lieutenant of the paratroops without legs in the helicopter

—Don't worry about me all good

like the soldier on his back on the path instead of

—When my grandfather finds out, he'll kill himself

insisting

—All good

like the doctor removing the boot eyelets from the bodies of others and all good with the others, me in the cellar to my wife

—In a few minutes the dreams will cease and thus all good

me ready to walk by her side

—Would you permit me to accompany you?

me looking for her in the darkness because I have to look for her in the darkness, I have to find her body, find my body and

—All good

even the picture of apples and pears

—All good

even your parents listen to us from the other room

—All good

a dream that doesn't move on from that even, what the head invents, what the imagination does, the doctor to my wife

—This with the kidney in the end without any importance

and a butterfly in tin, cheap, large, escaping from the lapel and flying in the cellar, perhaps it'll land on one of the beams, perhaps it's leaving by the window, perhaps it disappears in the mountain, perhaps my father, forgetting the shotgun and the partridges

—Have you seen her?

my father

—Portugal one and indivisible from the Minho to Timor

but my father aiming the shotgun at a ridge of earth ten or twenty meters away

—The partridges

with the dog mouth open, leaning ahead, waiting, its snout growing and withdrawing, my father to me

—Don't breathe boy

and don't worry that I'm not breathing sir, I'm looking for the artery in the pig's neck, checking the cartilage, finding it in the end escaping from the jaw that sought to break me, my daughter at the back door constantly itching herself, wiping herself with a handkerchief, without the courage to enter, for what reason don't you have the courage to enter if all is good, all good, perhaps only your brother moving in a different way, attentive at the same time to me and the animal, that is more attentive to me than the animal, me looking for the artery on the pig's neck and it seemed to me that he looking for mine but I must be wrong, I may be wrong, I am certainly wrong, why the hell look for mine, because of some ears, because of some hands, because of a black on the ground, what black is worth anything for that matter, Portugal one and indivisible from the Minho to Timor, what do they want now, my son at my side not observing the animal, observing me, the psychologist in the circle of chairs at the hospital

—You're not exaggerating?

the way my son looked at me the same as the way I looked at the animal, perhaps he recalls, I don't know, the huts that were burning, perhaps he recalls the people, the hens, the goats, perhaps he recalls that time, we never spoke of Africa, nothing was ever referred to, I don't know what he remembered, how he remembered, what he felt, what I recall of myself as a child besides wanting a dog are big objects, the sofa, the table, windows that I couldn't reach, a clock on the dresser marking the hour endlessly with me thinking

—How large is time

or rather gigantic hands turning very slowly over a wheel of numbers and it was the hands and the numbers that took charge in us, my mother looking at them and scandalized by me

—Nine-thirty and you're not in bed

it was the hands that took charge of the days, they determined the time for meals

—Eight-thirty and we've not yet had dinner

they brought my father home at seven o'clock, they told him to leave at six-thirty in the morning, my mother alarmed

—It's already past six-thirty-one and you remain here still it seems that you want to lose your job

pointing out to him the numbers that regulated his life, my father with bags under his eyes

—Today from four on I couldn't get back to sleep

with me staring at the four, so powerful that it even impeded his sleep with consideration, with respect, how did the numbers function and how did I not understand, me to my son, softly

—Does Africa mean anything to you?

but everything echoed on the cement in the basement, even speaking big words quietly, mixed with the echo of footsteps, the bangs from a basin that they dragged over next to me or of the legs of a chair that they put next to the wall, on the window the pigeons of Cardal Florido circling, now white now dark as they followed the sunlight or moved away from it, suddenly they all landed in the square, calm, suddenly they rose up as one, my father's brother lived alone in Cardal Florido after his wife left with a peddler of jewelry, my uncle always with a knife on his belt

—I have to find them someday

my father gave him a piece of pork that he didn't, on the radio we heard another platoon asking for instructions from command, thank him for, he remained seated on the doorstep looking at his hands

—I have to find them someday it's a question of time

narrower than my father, smaller, rolling cigarette paper with interminable slowness

—It's a problem of time

he used to say the same phrase to me always, without even a look, totally concentrating on his tobacco

—Don't fall into the error of growing up kid

my father was sneaking around the pantry afraid that the food would disappear, he snuck around the armoire

—Do you have winter blankets?

he told my mother to sweep the house for him, to sew on buttons that were missing, to take a look at the sugar tin where he ke, civilian rain doesn't make one wet, pt the money, civilian rain doesn't make soldiers wet, and added a bill or two to the coins he found in the bottom of the tin and my uncle always sitting around with his tobacco, on one sole occasion, when we no longer went out, he suddenly got up, embraced my father, he said

—Brother

sat down again and aimed a match at the cigarette paper, on the way back my father with a drop in his nose that he dried off with a hardworking handkerchief pulled out from his pocket, without giving any answers to my questions, I said a drop in his nose, I didn't say a drop in his eyes, his eyes dry, of course, only the throat, though he was not eating anything, swallowing, swallowing, a little bit before he died, already in bed, he touched my hand, he said

—Civilian rain doesn't make soldiers wet

he said

—Boy

and swallowed again, no complaints no regrets, he just swallowed, if by chance I gave him some cigarette paper I bet that he would smoke avidly interested in the pigeons, I bet interested only in the pigeons, he's over there in the cemetery, I hope with a handkerchief because the nose sometimes, there is always something in us that plays tricks on us, it may be the kidney, it may be the nose, for me it's the left leg that fails me from time to time, I'm walking along just fine and it fails, afterward it goes back to normal fortunately, my wife's doctor to me

—We wear out

and now there is a great truth friend, everything gets lost on the way we who were capable of getting pleasure even from sad things, perhaps not pleasure really, a certain sweetness, a tender melancholy, me to my son

—Do you remember Africa?

and he didn't respond to me preoccupied with honing the knife blade with a leather belt, I understood that my daughter almost

—Father

for a moment without scratching herself, her mouth barely open, with phrases inside that she didn't let out, my daughter for the first time worried about me or interested in me, I don't recall a

—Father

from her for a thousand years, one or another

—You

and the rest of the time nothing, it's not that I miss her but she intrigues me, that I don't miss her is a lie, let's admit that I do, those little arms higher up, our cadets, those little arms higher up, perhaps I don't miss her that much, we get used to it like my wife got used to her stones and me to her deathbed, some weeks, some months, so much time since an arm on my back, so much time with no

—Love

as the doctor says people get worn out and I add that everything gets worn out, crawl up to me, at the same time as us, leave some mud for the comrade who is coming behind you cadet, don't use all of it, that face still so handsome, that face doesn't get dirty, this is not a beauty contest friend, don't worry after the end of the war you can go for an actress if you want to no one would resist you but until then submit like the others afterward they say that they want to be officers, you'll become ordinance corporals, boys, ordinance corporals, to be sincere if my daughter

—Father

I would like it, I must be turning into a pansy with age, becoming in fact an ordinance corporal lieutenant sir, at the least in my case you were right, despite Portuguese I'm not as good as the best, I've been holding on and that's it, me with the shin completely swollen from a fall and the lieutenant

—Don't get soft cadet sir don't get soft it's only pain

so that when the pig started to scream, filling the cellar with anguish and blood, I explain to it as well that it's only pain, it's only pain or then instead of the lieutenant the voice of my son who is warning me

—It's only pain

my son not yet a man, a child of four or six years old in the remains of a hut, hens without a neck, disemboweled goats, dead cabíris, a woman without ears and hands among women without ears and hands, a man facedown whose face one couldn't distinguish trampled on by soldiers who were still running, the smell of the wild dogs hidden in the tall grass beside the smell of rotten manioc, hyenas trotting about in wait, the smell of urine and shit in the cellar, the smell of the rubber aprons, the gloves, my father's voice as always before sticking the knife in

—Let's get going over here boy

while my mother locked herself in the house, horrified, covering herself with her hands

—I can't take this

the groans, the screams, the tears though the blacks not groans, not screams, not tears, from time and time at least a soft sigh

—Lutenan sir

or

—Corporal sir

or

—Sergeant sir

piling up on the ground, an old man who tried to run away pulling himself together slowly over rags burning and his clothing a flame that finally went out, he remained a small cone of dust, charcoal embers glowing, a guy standing up, then on his knees, then on all fours, then a skull disappearing in the dark manioc root, then nothing, my son remained barely looking, barefoot, minuscule, with a swollen belly and me

—Do you remember Africa?

me in front of him to the troops

—Don't touch him

and I was certain that my son remembering just as he remembered the woman whose ears and hands I cut off and the man who slept in the hut with her, amid the chickens, facedown on the earth with a burst of G-3 fire in his back, my son silent like silent now, serious like serious now, close to me like no

—It's only pain only pain

like now near me

—I remember

not my son, not the boy who I saved in Angola, who I prevented them from killing, who I brought from Africa, who I fed, who I protected, who I helped to grow up, who I gave my name to, the husband of Her Excellency, my daughter's brother

—It's only pain it's only pain

a miserable black, a darky that wasn't a person, a monkey who didn't speak until I made out of him a creature almost like us, a Portuguese belonging to a people as good as the best

—March slowly and at ease

a descendent of the conquerors of the sea, of the discoverers of the world, without young hens, without skeletal goats, without skinny cabíris, without unhappy huts, without insects and rats to eat, a despicable creature, ungrateful, a savage, my son who almost never spoke to me

—I remember

my son with the rubber apron, with the knife hanging from his hand

—I remember my mother without ears I remember my father of

the instructor to me

—Keep running cadet it's only pain it's only pain

my son in a tone in which people speak on siesta

—I remember my father facedown on the ground

my son who in front of me almost always in silence

—I remember that you killed them

only pain son, only pain

—I remember that you killed them

my son more an echo than a voice

—That you killed them

while the stones lighter than water turned around us, while my daughter covered herself with her elbows, while my wife

—Love

while I turned toward the pig and the knife entered as a blow to the neck, I saw the first jet of blood, I heard the first groan and I don't know who let it out.

23

Until the last moment I wanted to tell him

—Go away fast father

and I think he listened to me, I'm certain that he listened to me and pretended not to listen, to tell him

—Take mother and return fast to Lisbon father

and he continuing to prepare the cellar and making like he didn't notice me, at a certain point it seemed to me he answered without words

—It has to be isn't that right son?

in the same way that me without words

—It doesn't have to be don't agree I don't want you to die

me checking the knife listening to the wild doves

—Don't let me kill you

just as he didn't let them kill me in Africa putting himself between me and the soldiers, walking toward them decided, moving his weapon away suddenly toward a second lieutenant who lowered his

—Don't you dare

and he put himself in front of me, and he protected me with his body, and he drove me toward one of the unimogs at the entrance to the village

—Not this one

warning the driver

—If anything happens to him I'll kill you

the driver, afraid of him, backing the unimog onto the side of the dirt road without me understanding very well what they were talking about, I understand now, I wanted to tell him

—Don't stay here

but even though I asked him

—Don't stay here

he didn't listen to me busy protecting me, he killed my mother, he killed my father, he destroyed everything that he could and nonetheless something happened inside him that forced him to prevent them from killing me, on the road barely returned from a mission he asked right away

— The child

with a finger on the trigger, turning his rifle to the right and to the left until he found me squatting, near some shed, changing the path of the ants with a stick, without paying attention to me when I wanted to tell him, in the cellar of the house in the village

— Go away quickly father

and he acting like he didn't hear, perhaps he wanted me to kill him, perhaps it was his desire that I kill him I don't know but I swear that I didn't feel like killing him, I liked him, the doctor assures me that my mother will die soon, when the stones stop eating her and then he alone in the house with Angola visiting him at night, the wounded calling him

— Second lieutenant sir second lieutenant sir

and he leaning on a trunk without being able to do anything, he to me when me in the cellar

— Go away quickly father

answering without words

— Where do I go?

thinking about my mother's death and thus alone in the house looking at the street, the lamps at night, the waving trees, no one to make his bed, no one to cook for him, a friend from the army, from time to time, dragging a leg because a bullet in the knee dissolved his kneecap, when my father used to go away I would go to the veranda and remained there following him staggering down below, standing still relaxing against a trunk, if my mother had been there she would have called him inside and my father sitting in the living room looking at his own fingers, my mother

— You feel like tea?

and the afternoon darkness growing, the pig waiting like he waiting but waiting for what, if I fall asleep leaning on the body of your mother I'll improve

— Would you permit me to accompany you?

this if the stones forget to take her with them when I touched him he smiling at me

— Boy

pleased to see me, he killed my father, killed my mother and I don't know whether I'm capable of killing him, I don't want to kill him, I want to fall asleep next to him in a bed of palm fronds, I want his fingers on my neck

—Son

I want him to keep protecting me though I don't need his protection, this is necessary, he brought me a little glass of anise, set me on his knee, he was proud of me who no one was proud of, he had a portrait of me on the dresser

—My little one

while me in the cellar of the house in the village

—Please go away quickly father please go away

with the pigeons of Cardal Florido incessantly increasing, not a dozen, not two dozen, hundreds, thousands of pigeons circling, settling for a moment on the roof, with enormous claws, ferocious eyes, long long beaks, it wasn't like that before, so timid, so gentle, what changed in them, why do they detest me explain to me, why do they hate me, Cardal Florido once a little neighborhood and nowadays ruins since the cellulose factory went bankrupt, a half dozen walls left over, a piece of smokestack, rings traced by running guard dogs in the earth, an animal always trotting from one side to another at the edge of the camp, my son without letting go of the knife whose blade changed if I changed, always aimed at me

—Go away

and where to, explain to me, I've barely walked two steps your mother's stones prevented me, her face was preventing me, her arm on my back was preventing me, her voice almost against my mouth

—Love

preventing me, her face, at night in our room, growing, Africa a woman's body that never ends, so many arms, so many legs, so many

—Send the chopper

and then that carnivorous voice

—Love

that ties us up, holds us, crushes us slowly, the pig to me

—If you cut the ropes I'll help you and we'll flee from here

from Her Excellency, from my daughter, from burned crickets, from blacks seeking vengeance

—It's your turn to die

from a genet at the edge of the mountain following me from far away, stopping if I stop, walking if I walk, hoping that me unsuspecting in order to grab my neck, my wife

—We'll take you

she so timid at first, so ashamed and me with pity for my father, I swear, me half forgetting Africa and nonetheless remaining there, confusing episodes, inventing recollections, mixing reminiscences, old stories, faded memories, meaningless fragments, my mother now with us now far away because the stones leading her and bringing her, my grandmother to me when a child holding my arm

—The pig scares you

my grandfather indignant

—He's a pansy that one what did he inherit from me?

without clogs without rubber apron, my grandfather sticking the knife into the pig until he comes right up to it, his head leaning on its head as well, a second knife, a third

—It'll take time to die

smoking with a cigarette sticking in his teeth, smoking and his nose and the chest red with blood, my grandfather I don't know to which of the two, me or the animal

—He's dying

measuring us alternatively, my mother suddenly

—No

in a voice much louder than what she was capable of, a voice suddenly without illness, without stones and which I never heard, she always spoke softly, she moved almost without a sound, she existed quietly, I'm not afraid of the pig anymore just as I'm no longer afraid of war, I'm no longer afraid of me just as the second lieutenant of the paratroops was not afraid of himself, he was still waving from his equipment

—See you soon

and I didn't turn to look at him, his hand so pale, his mouth so white, his eyes almost closed

—See you soon

and it wasn't the helicopter that went away, it was the treetops that began to bend farther and farther away, they passed the savannah, they calmed down, minuscule, before the second savannah, the radio came to tell us

—The second lieutenant of the paratroops sends a good-bye embrace to all

in a voice shivering through the phrase though he thought that it hadn't shivered just as we thought that we hadn't shivered, I remember preparing ourselves for leaving, beginning to walk in a diamond with an embrace for everybody with us, I remember the beauty of Angola, of the sky, the colors, my wife's body receiving me, my son waiting for me in the camp and me pleased that my son waiting for me in the camp, I think that if you kill me it won't hurt, I think that even after death, I swear, you'll remain with me, my daughter sweating, waiting, my father to me

— Take her outside she's in no condition to attend this

the pigeons of Cardal Florido began to return alighting on the cellar ceiling, on the trees, on the roof of the house in the village, the mountain falcons intercepted one or two during their flight and they went lower, lower, with claws digging into their bodies, until they fell into a corner of the cemetery where the beaks ripped them in a half dozen blows with cats their snouts attentive, still on the wall, waiting, my mother in the cellar looking at me, looking at my father, looking at me again, when small she forced me to drink a glass of milk in the middle of the night

— You'll never get fat

and me afraid that I didn't have ears and hands, afraid that if I didn't move, I'd stretch out better in the sheets, I rounded the pillow, put a wandering finger on my forehead

— You can go back to sleep

and she went off on the way to her room, without smelling the blood nor the manioc nor the earth, I recall the sound of the bedsprings when she lay down, of my father saying something, of her answering

— The guards assure me that all is calm sleep

and I ask myself whether the falcons go out waiting for my father, now shorter now taller, gliding, until the last moment I wanted to tell him

— Go away quickly father

and he doesn't need to go very far, it's enough to be locked up in the house until the pig is dead, I think that I already killed it and I'm forgetting about you, I still thought about asking my mother

— Please take father away from the cellar mother

because she had to understand, because she understands, I never had to explain everything, most of the time I didn't need to speak given that she knew, I'm more than certain that she guessed point for point what happened in Angola, the machine guns, the unimogs, the grenades, the burning huts, I think, I'm not certain, that I had a sister like here in Angola, younger than me, hanging from my mother's breast, the woman with her hands cut off, of my mother but I don't recall her, I'm speaking merely of an impression, of course, not a white sister, black, a silent black sister and my mother, the woman with her hands cut off, holding out her breast to her that she sometimes refused, trying with a goat and my sister accepting, after the attack I never saw them again, I saw my father running behind a piglet, I saw a dead cabíri, I saw what appeared to be wild dogs running away with I don't know what in their teeth, a piece of meat that they each tried to steal from the other, they attacked much bigger animals, buffalo, antelope, they ripped the tendons from their legs, they forced them to fall and then bit into their skin, tearing off pieces between sharp sobs, until the bones began to appear gradually, the antelope lifted their heads, with less and less force, and then the wild dogs bit into their snouts and the animals finally still, just a leg bending and stretching out slowly, without strength, a soldier shot a volley against them, one of the wild dogs jumped but they continued to bite fighting against the dead flesh, fighting among themselves, with bloodied jaws, furious, tenacious, the females began to approach with their pups, a group of hyenas arrived without haste, birds with a naked neck waited on a root, one of the dogs jumped on the neck of one of them and it escaped because the bird a vengeful strike with the beak, my wife shaking me

—Are you dreaming or what?

and an ambulance on the street, my father shuffling without haste toward the kitchen, what a relief Lisbon, between the window blinds the lights of the street, the calm of the buildings, my wife's mother because my wife's father didn't stop opening and closing the armoires

—When will you return to bed?

and he returning to the room chewing, he bumped his knee into a dresser and she

—As long as you don't hurt seriously don't rest

my wife softly

—We would have to arrange a house just for us

my wife's father, already in bed, pulling clothing at random and taking it away from her

—As long as you don't have a cold don't rest

me not

—Would you permit me to accompany you?

me

—As if we won money for that

with a small daughter and the black son sleeping in the sunroom, I always would have saved something if I had left him behind in his village in Angola but his village ashes and then what I did to his mother, what I did to his father, there were times I swear, when we became crazy, who might assure me that while growing up he won't recall that and seek revenge, I don't know what went through my head to have him come back with me, during the pig killing the more he grew the more that came to mind, my wife thinking the same as me

—Don't be surprised

and then, when I least expected, the kidney, at the beginning we thought that a rib out of place but the doctor, suspicious

—There is something that doesn't fit we need to do more tests

and with more tests

—It seemed to me

then the kidney emerged, the doctor trying to calm us

—It may be only a cyst we'll see we'll see

but his face strange and his movements rapider, next to a diploma framed on the wall, Hoards brought me a glass of water without my father noticing, the doctor requested analyses nodding his head to say no, crumpling the paper, starting again, it seemed to me that the wings of the yellow metal butterfly on my mother's lapel trembled, with little glass stones in different colors and one of the antennae not as straight as the other, when Hoards returned with the empty glass to the cubicle that served as a kitchen a mortar blast twenty or thirty meters away from us which only I noticed, soldiers running, the captain's voice outside

—Quickly to the shelters

orders, screams, on the sides of the landing strip a seamstress singing, the doctor holding out the paper to my father

—I would like us to do this exam to remove any doubts

that he folded in two, that he folded in four, that he kept in his pocket, my mother silent looking at us, one of the second lieutenants ordering at double march

—Let's go there above the landing strip

as a second mortar shook the trees of the street and the captain

—Take shelter and open fire over there

a new seamstress singing, one of our mortars, another of our mortars

toward the landing strip and two cones of smoke and grass, assholes, assholes, the doctor to my mother, pointing to my father's pocket

—To remain calm madam

the captain ordering two sections to the huts and a platoon surrounded
the landing strip from below in order to catch the insurgents from the rear
after a wide encirclement, the new mortar fell without exploding between
the latrines and the aid station, that a group surrounded with bags of sand

—Very close not idiots very close not

unleashing an offensive and making it roll toward the mortar

—Take shelter behind the bags I don't want to see a head showing

in the doctor's office books, the portrait of a lady with a child whose
mouth the same as the doctor's, a hospital file, the grenade exploded four
or five meters from the mortar, when the result comes telephone to make
an appointment, the matter will take a week or two at most and the mortar
the same, fifteen days after we telephoned to make an appointment with my
father daring to open the envelope, the doctor received us blowing his nose
with a nasal voice

—I caught some nastiness there isn't a January that doesn't bring me a flu

sucking some therapeutic lozenge scented with violet, from time to time
he sinks a tooth into it and a pop is heard, he sat at the desk in his white coat
not as well buttoned up as usual, with the violets from the lozenge from one
side to the other and a stuffed nose, red eyes, sticking out, they were the eyes
that dripped like drains, not the nose, how strange sneezing from the eyes
but it was the truth, while we sat at the other side of the desk he hit the envelope on the seal swallowing without ceasing pointing with his finger at a
side of his throat

—It hurts here

not in an adult voice, in a child's voice, perhaps he thought he was going
to die or the like while the edge of the envelope was beating, beating, his
heart the envelope faster and faster, he finally opened it more ripping than
ungluing, silencing a tickle in his throat with his palm and my wife full of
pity for him, she had pity for the whole world, only she did not complain
about herself, she squeezed her waist with her palm, in silence, under the
disguise of a smile, if we were to ask her how she was feeling she would
always respond

—Fine

in a jovial voice that she pulled out of herself, I don't know if I like her a lot but she cared for me, my clothes, my soul, those minutiae, I also frankly don't see a big difference between the clothing and the soul, a dress for outside, another dress for inside, that's everything, I bet they have the same buttons, I never heard any other word unless

—Fine

extracted from where rusty sensations abide that don't adapt to each other and squeak and protest, look at those ladies who support themselves on canes of sighs that permit them to walk still, a bit sideways, a bit uncertain but despite all walking, or before they move a bit toward the nearest wall where they stay, with mouth open, waiting for an oxygen reinforcement, with a second grenade the mortar already destroyed finally in a vertical sneeze of steel and dust, when my grandfather finds out he'll kill himself, how I prayed, we found out through a message, he passed away in Luso, left a clay virgin and a father who months afterward dissolved himself in a pit, when they brought him up, a boot and a penknife came up or rather the fortune of a man, what more do we have finally, the doctor examined the envelope sneezing, lingering on the paper, informed from inside the typed lines

—We have here some kidney stones nothing that we can't treat

and nonetheless they see them accompanying us even now, the doctor calming my mother through a fog of bronchitis

—The gallbladder gets stones the bladder gets stones and what is not missing in the body

sometimes our bones grow, others circulate through our veins, others free themselves from people and swirl around us, for example in the cellar, even with the pig hanging from the hook, we see some circling over there, my father surprised

—Stones

the doctor studying my mother in the sunroom behind the screen, whispering while she was dressing

—We have a complicated situation here

while me confused inside me

—Would you permit me to accompany you?

so softly that everyone heard, accompanying her up to her house door and talking with myself without any response, Hoards to my father

—First that the Thin One might talk to me there were afternoons and afternoons you can't imagine the spit I wasted second lieutenant sir all this to die in Africa without returning to see her, he gave her some earrings too, he gave her a necklace too, he was at her house too talking with her parents, Her Excellency's mother pointing at me

—A black

despite my polished shoes, my new suit, my polka dot tie that was not quite silk

—A black?

without my father defending me

—He's my son

because he wasn't with me, he who always defended me, he took me to school, took me from school, argued with the teacher

—Because he's black doesn't mean he's stupider than the others inside he's white like them

and me in the cellar of the house in the village listening to him

—Because he's black doesn't mean he's stupider that the others

with difficulty with numbers, with difficulty with the letters, with difficulty putting together all that confusion, forming words, making sums, subtracting, rivers not real, some marks without crocodiles or snakes, no shots, no huts burning, no one without hands and ears, all of us alive, so it seems, except my real mother between two thatched huts, how difficult to understand people here, the whites, the way they live, what they say, what they do, my father told how the general

—I see on your faces the joy of going to serve the Fatherland

and some joy, fear, the dead in boxes, not on a plank, the captain to him

—You'll still regret having brought him with you

the captain to him

—When he's grown he'll kill him

and I didn't want to kill him, I swear that I didn't want to kill him, I put the knife down on the table in the basement, I returned to get it, I returned to put it back, I didn't want to kill him, I didn't want to see his blood, I didn't want to hear his screams, I didn't want to look at the buckets on the ground, Her Excellency's mother despising me

—A black

while my father didn't despise me, he defended me

—Watch out if you touch him

perhaps it wasn't him

(but it was him)

who cut the ears off, perhaps it wasn't him

(but it was him)

who chopped off the hands, perhaps it wasn't him

(but it was him)

who punctured my father's back and left him facedown on the ground, perhaps it wasn't him

(but it was him)

who beheaded the hens, the cabíris, the goats, who left diesel fuel in the hay, who set fire to the huts, who killed us all because I'm perhaps dead, I died when they brought me from Africa or soon, in Lisbon, a pack of wild dogs grab me from behind and break my ankles, knees, elbows, spine, the people waiting in the chairs leaning against the basement walls, my grandfather, who I didn't meet, washing his arms in a pot, rolling up his sleeves and drying himself with a rag in that same way as my father washing himself in a pot, rolling up his sleeves and drying himself with a rag, no machine gun on the landing strip, no mortar, just the murmur of the wind in the grass and in a window to the right the cemetery, the stone table where we put the dead before burying them and the people around silent, women with handkerchiefs, men with hats in their hands and everything dirty now, abandoned, there's no one left to die here except for one or another stray dog, one or another old man and us, the mountain falcons, the same from the beginning who had never diminished, flying up the hills or coming down suddenly toward a lizard or a small snake to fly up again, climbing the air step by step because nothingness, as we know, a series of steps, the pig no longer tried to get free, it waited, its eyes pink, skin color pink, belly round, Her Excellency's mother

—A black?

scandalized by me because me a black in fact, me a black, pink fingertips of blacks, pink mouth of blacks, the rest black, black, my father touching me on the shoulder

—Have you chosen the knife well boy?

trying them out on cardboard, my mother's metal butterfly on her lapel, her face so tired, one stone or another floating around her, a platoon arriving from the bush, exhausted, first the guides, then the escorts, then the second lieutenants, then the others, the captain telling them

—Is that everybody?

and though they didn't respond, they kept moving, they were all in the
midst of spirals of dense mist, in the midst of dust, it was everybody, the corporal mechanic leaning over a Berliet, accelerating and decelerating the
motor, another mechanic, a comrade to him

—It's that cylinder there the rod is not responding

and if the rod breaks in the jungle we're done for, the insurgents taking
the chance to shoot at will, a soldier who was talking, a second silent suddenly falling, the nurse on his knees fumbling around in his pocket, a corporal

—Stand guard stand guard

a half dozen men inside the tall grass and in there an antipersonnel exploding, the doctor to my father

—I don't know if it's worth operating on the sharpshooter let's try out the
medication

he spent fifteen days in the hospital with bags running into his veins, on
the bed next to his a sergeant who was always sleeping, he awoke from time
to time in a sigh

—Ah me

and he went away again, at the head of the table flowers in a small jar,
a small box of candies that no one was eating, a pair of useless splits at the
edge of the mattress, a blond boy leaning forward from the pillow looking
in silence, my mother showing me

—He's my son

without anyone answering her, it's impossible when they tell us

—Cough

to cough normally, we invent a new kind of frog in the throat that gets
indignant whenever someone listens

—Aren't you capable of better than this?

and I'm not, I'm afraid, of course you're not a hangman doctor, excuse
me for saying so, but I'm afraid to be near you, your face so close to mine,
your facial features so well defined, the inconceivable quantity of junk

—Would you permit me to accompany you?

that exists on a face, eyes, nose, cheeks, mouth, why so many features my
God, a hole and an eye suffice, the quantity of useless things that people
have you've seen already, we could be much simpler, we should be much
simpler, don't let me die, the doctor

—What rubbish you dying now

and this fever, and this pain, and this irritation in the belly that squeezes me, a jovial doctor

—Good day to all

and rain outside, lights on, the chrome breakfast cart jingling metallically, gray food, gray drinks, a gray dessert, a napkin wedged into the neck in order that total gray enters people

—Let's go let's go still a portion of patients and the spoon insisting against the closed mouth

—The time it takes to chew Holy God

the soup chewed, the purée chewed, even the custard, that is swallowed alone, chewed, Her Excellency's mother

—A black?

and Her Excellency with shame, even the Chinese make less of an impression, I won't speak about gypsies because the only thing they do is steal, the doctor finished by discharging my mother

—What you do here can be done at home

the stones already were walking around her without stopping, at first heavy and now lighter than water, they go up, go down, come closer, move away, you don't have much pain now right, the medicines are already doing their part, that's what they're good for too, to do their part, if they weren't good for anything they wouldn't be used, the quantity of people there is throughout the whole world preoccupied with this, deals for the laboratories that are rotten with the rich, Americans, English, Germans, dammit, this only in our country, the Portuguese soldier is as good as the best, we're broke incompetent, cheap food, cheap clothing, and it continues, even in war, toward the end, we possessed weapons worse than those of the insurgents despite they black and we white and, regarding blacks, why did the idea just get put in my head to find one of them who had manners like ours and didn't eat lizards and raw animals, mice for example, I already heard that mice, my mother in the house on the sofa or dragging herself from room to room to do the

—Would you permit me to accompany you?

tedious domestic chores, there were always plates to clean left over, she didn't have the strength to open the window locks and to air out the compartments, the doctor to my father

—This is slowly getting worse you have to have patience

and suddenly, in my head, the village of when I small, I thought it lost, a circle of straw huts in the middle of the jungle, the large mango tree, the small mango tree, the bats that were flying between one and the other hissing signals, the little fields, the cabíris lying in the yard, one inside the other, in saddest immobility, I never saw eyes more disappointed than those, more resigned, when they at last managed to free themselves they remained there mulling over brooding afflictions, what the unhappy will imagine, my God, even me, from time to time, I come to ponder, on Sunday for example, which is always a day much longer than the others, instead of twelve numbers on the clock it must have had, I don't know, thirty-six, Her Excellency and me on the sofa, without looking at each other, empty, waiting for I don't know what will make its way to us, that has abandoned us forever, the same buildings to the left, the same buildings to the right, the same buildings in front, the same jobs, the same faces, the same dishes on the table, the picture with the apples and pears now in this living room, on the wall over there, the closed variety store, the closed pharmacy, the same emptiness in my head, questioning

—And now

Her Excellency painting her nails to paint something, in Africa at least, in my father's time, there was always someone dying from moment to moment

—When my grandfather finds out

we always wanted to return, we always imagined ourselves returning, we always were certain that afterward and in the end only this, the house in the village, the way that it is, I don't believe it will last two winters, why fix it up, who will want to visit it, the grass will end up covering the cemetery, no one will pay attention to the gravestones or the decrepit tombs, nothing seen from the highway from Lisbon, the cousin in another place I don't know where, her daughter having emigrated, my father finally had the pig hung up and there it was, its head downward, protesting with snorts, not yet screams, the knives waiting, the buckets underneath, six or seven South African helicopters, without markings of course, passed over us two by two on the way to some operation, my mother with one hand inside the other, for the first time since she became ill I paid no mind to the stones while looking at her, so much lighter than water vanishing through the window forever, if me to them

—Would you permit me to accompany you?

I didn't find one, we are alone with each other, father, at the end of so many years we are finally alone, you

—Boy

with camouflage pants from the war that still served you though so faded, so old, with the camouflage tunic open over a worn shirt and wrinkles that you didn't have on the neck, your arms thinner than in those days, we looking at each other me who as a child didn't look at him, me who always looked only a little at him just as I looked very little at anyone at all after the cut-off hands and ears, after the man facedown, after everything burning while the soldiers

—Kill kill

while, even after the shots, the soldiers kept repeating

—Kill kill

and my sister continuing to sweat, three or four people whom I didn't know and the pig, the pig, us in a few moments red with pig's blood, with the blood of hens and goats, the blood of cabíris, my father in front of me

—No one touches him he's mine

and frankly I'm sorry to kill you sir, I don't feel like killing you but I have to

—Kill kill

do it, just a blow on the neck and you on your knees, you on all fours, you stretched out over a bucket and my mother

—Sorry

looking at us, my mother silent, my mother

—Would you permit me to accompany you?

turning away from us, Her Excellency to me

—No

moving her lips without sound, Her Excellency with her eyes

—No

Her Excellency only with her eyes

—No

with me trying to explain to her without managing to explain, trying to say that an empty breast in my mouth, that my hands on her body, that my body against her body

—Aiué mamá

that the man facedown smoking mutopa his back to me, the basement with a little lamp on the ceiling that multiplied shadows and people, so

many troops and so many blacks with us, so many animals to eat, grabbing my father, throwing him down, jumping on him, my father his arm
stretched out to me

—Boy

his face a moment before disappearing under the animals, a leg that
shrunk, stretched out and remained stretched out without a canvas boot for
walking in the jungle, barefoot, my father grabbed the knife and approached
the pig with Hoards accompanying him

—Second lieutenant sir

while the Thin One to her friends

—It's now look

or rather my father pushing the black woman against the wall and cutting
off her hands while the grenades continued to explode and the seamstress
sewing, while the chief got on his knees

—Lutenan sir

his head slipping, falling, his body still moving on the ground, his eyes
neither open nor closed, absent, Her Excellency to me, on the living room
sofa

—What are you thinking about?

and I was thinking about my father's death, about his hand slipping from
my shoulder

—Boy

about my fingers slipping from his chest until they finally left him, we
going down to the car helping my mother

—Would you permit me to accompany you?

she without answering continuing to walk, she thinking herself better

—Maybe

about the doctor to us, surprised

—The majority of patients in this terminal stage are no longer able to
walk

about the policemen who would come, not delaying, looking for me here
in the house, staring at the picture with the apples and pears, staring at me

—Let's go

while someone cut up the pig for us, how he screamed gentlemen, the
number of times that he called

—Boy

with his hand on my shoulder, he called

—Boy

as he was falling, his hand on my chest

—Boy

dropping to my leg

—Boy

holding onto my ankle and letting go of my ankle already without

—Boy

just an old soldier, the Portuguese soldier is as good as the best, warning us

—I'm fine

while the helicopter didn't arrive, though the radio breaking the code

—Urgent urgent

and the captain without protesting, silent, though the radio

—The black child killed the second lieutenant with the pig's knife

and my mother's hand on his back

—Love

stretched out next to him in bed trying to wake him up

—It's a dream don't worry it's a dream

and the stones returning one by one, how the pigs suffer my God, how they sob, how they cry, my father, hanging by his feet from the second hook, groaning, it wasn't a pig that came from the sty, tumbling on the highway, now on its knees not trying to get up, it was my father and I didn't want to do him harm, I swear, he took care of me, I liked him, I didn't want to, it wasn't my father I killed, it was the shots and the war, the diesel fuel, the fire, it was the recollection of the paratrooper next to the bridge, it was the trip wires, it was the jumping mines, it was the general on the dock

—I see on your faces the joy of going to serve the Fatherland

it was only that gentlemen, the joy of going to serve the Fatherland, it was the blacks that the political police forced to dig a ditch to blow their heads off inside it, to see them jump against walls of earth until they finally became immobile, it was the electric shocks on the testicles, it was the dentist's drill on a healthy tooth, it was the sticks under the fingernails, it was the psychologist in the circle of chairs at the hospital

—That could not have happened

and you're right doctor, it didn't happen except when I was sleeping and thus merely nightmares, nothing real, of course, nothing true, just nightmares, what my head will search for my God, how people exaggerate, what we think up, I returned from Africa I didn't return, I'm happy not happy, no swaying of the unimog hurt my spine, no problem in the stomach, my guts perfect, from time to time a dream and that's all, with the exaggerations of dreams, no

—Kill kill

no suffering, twenty-seven months of holidays, three or four scares without importance, a few little shots in the distance, at times problems with the food but we figured things out, problems because of no water but we're still here, the house in the village now a ruin, the garden is finished, the tank for washing clothes fallen over, the loquat tree dead with its roots almost all out, weighing on the bent wall that is losing bricks, some rotten loquat fruit, green, half the back gate standing though not capable of turning on its hinges, the other half on the ground, if I even managed to move it I bet that my father

—Boy

in the same way as my mother said

—I'm fine

she always said

—I'm fine

even the night before she died she put on makeup

—I'm fine

despite my father on the cement floor and me on my knees next to him, almost embracing him, until the police come, while suddenly March was beating the frames of the open window.

Born in Lisbon in 1942 and trained as a psychiatrist, ANTÓNIO LOBO ANTUNES was an army doctor in Portugal's long colonial war in Angola before he began to publish his first literary works in 1979. Lobo Antunes is now author of more than thirty books, including *The Land at the End of the World, Fado Alexandrino, The Inquisitors' Manual,* and *The Splendor of Portugal.* He has received numerous literary awards, including the Jerusalem Prize (2005) and the Camões Prize. He lives in Lisbon.

JEFF LOVE is research professor of German and Russian at Clemson University. He has published two books on Tolstoy, *The Overcoming of History in "War and Peace"* and *Tolstoy: A Guide for the Perplexed.* He is also editor of *Heidegger in Russia and Eastern Europe.* His most recent book is *The Black Circle: A Life of Alexandre Kojève.* He also lives in Lisbon.